Of DEATH & Desires

ALSO BY T.C. KRAVEN

Of Prophecies & Pomegranates

A DARK FATES NOVEL

T.C. KRAVEN

DIVERSION
BOOKS

Diversion Books
A division of Diversion Publishing Corp. www.diversionbooks.com

For more information, email info@diversionbooks.com

First Diversion Books Edition: January 2026
Trade Paperback ISBN: 9798895150597
e-ISBN: 9798895150603

Design by Neuwirth & Associates, Inc.
Cover design by T.C. Kraven
Chapter header illustrations by Artywings
Interior cover illustrations by Snow_WI

Printed in the United States of America
1 3 5 7 9 10 8 6 4 2

Diversion books are available at special discounts for bulk purchases in the US by corporations, institutions, and other organizations. For more information, please contact admin@diversionbooks.com.

"He saw beyond the flowers, the polite submission.

He dug into my bones and fed the darkness there.

He gave me the shadows, free from oppressive contrition.

And with it all the power I could share.

Tell me, Mother, what would you have given
for a love like that?"

To all my Rebel Girls, making their way in the world.
Be loud and take back what belongs to you. And for every person who messaged me at three a.m. to yell, "How could you do this to me?" after Prophecies, *this one is for you.*
I hope this brings you closure. <3

The Divine
OF THE DARK FATES

HADES

GOD OF THE UNDERWORLD
BORN OF OLYMPIAN ESSENCE

PERSEPHONE

GODDESS OF SPRING
BORN OF DEMETER + ZEUS

DEMETER

GODDESS OF THE HARVEST
BORN OF OLYMPIAN ESSENCE

HEPHAESTUS

GOD OF THE FORGE
BORN OF HERA
BONDED TO APHRODITE

APHRODITE

GODDESS OF LOVE
BORN OF OLYMPIAN ESSENCE
BONDED TO ARES + HEPHAESTUS

ARES

GOD OF WAR
BORN OF ZEUS
BONDED TO APHRODITE

HERMES

MESSENGER GOD OF THIEVES
BORN OF ZEUS + A MORTAL LOVER

ARTEMIS

GODDESS OF THE HUNT
BORN OF ZEUS + LETO

APOLLO

GOD OF MUSIC
BORN OF ZEUS + LETO

NICK

WOODLAND NYMPH

HELIOS

TITAN OF THE SUN
BORN OF
HYPERION + THEIA

ZEUS

GOD OF GODS
BORN OF OLYMPIAN ESSENCE
BONDED TO HERA

DIONYSUS

GOD OF WINE
BORN OF
ZEUS + SEMELE

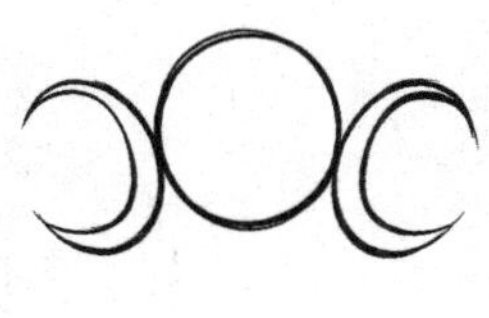

HECATE

GODDESS OF WITCHCRAFT
BORN OF
ASTERIA + PERSES

THANATOS

GOD OF DEATH
BORN OF
NYX + EREBUS

HERA

GODDESS OF MARRIAGE + BONDS
BORN OF OLYMPIAN ESSENCE
BONDED TO ZEUS

POSEIDON

GOD OF THE SEA
BORN OF OLYMPIAN ESSENCE
BONDED TO ATHENA

ATHENA

GODDESS OF WISDOM
BORN OF ZEUS
BONDED TO POSEIDON

Playlist

1. No Safe Place—Party at the Moontower
2. Where Is My Mind?—Pixies
3. Iris—Goo Goo Dolls
4. Fade into You—Mazzy Star
5. Volcano—Damien Rice
6. Rebel Girl—Bikini Kill
7. Linger—The Cranberries
8. You Do Something to Me—Paul Weller
9. Maps—Yeah Yeah Yeahs
10. Glory Box—Portishead
11. Name—Goo Goo Dolls
12. Dreams—The Cranberries
13. Pale Blue Eyes—The Velvet Underground
14. Spitting Off the Edge of the World—Yeah Yeah Yeahs
15. Lovefool—The Cardigans

16. Cornflake Girl—Tori Amos
17. Little Plastic Castle—Ani DiFranco
18. High and Dry—Radiohead
19. Exit Music (For a Film)—Radiohead

Scan the QR code
to access the Spotify playlist:

CONTENT WARNING

This novel contains a recounting of SA as told through the victim's recollection. Please protect yourself if this is a trigger for you. Other potentially distressing themes include a traumatic brain injury (and the PTSD that comes with it), slight agoraphobia, selective amnesia, murder, gore, CPTSD, homophobia (not between MCs), alcohol recovery, magical dosing, death of a parent, off-page suicide and aftermath, and more. This novel also contains explicit sexual content.

AUTHOR'S NOTE

The next eleven books in the Dark Fates will take us to all manner of places, but I would be remiss if I didn't take a moment to touch on New Orleans, where the majority of the books reside, and the importance of the representation in these pages. Louisiana is a mecca of culture, people, and languages, and you will see that reflected in the characters, in the city itself throughout the series.

I grew up in diverse circles because of my city, and because I lean so heavily on my own experience when writing, I couldn't fathom not including those voices. As they are not always my own, I have endeavored at every turn to employ an extensive and trusted group of sensitivity and inclusion readers.

To Rowe, Tatiana, Shondrell, Jeremy, Diana, Mattiew, Ashlee, and Shane, thank you for your effort, expertise, and insight for *Of Death & Desires*.

The Dark Fates explores many themes, including kink and BDSM, the complexities of trauma, a myriad of relationship dynamics, sexuality and fluidity, and the deep effects of misogyny and its permeation through society. Intersectionality, racial inequality, and class warfare are all part of the real struggles and lives in the Crescent City.

You'll find them in this series. I am extremely proud to work with the people I do, and to be blessed with their honesty, integrity, and patience. With that being said, if there is ever a moment that an own voice feels the need to raise an issue, I welcome that contact. I can only move with open intention and be ready to listen, for conversation and learning.

I know that best intentions do not negate unintentional harm.

Thank you for entering my world.

Welcome to my New Orleans.

Prologue

The Gods fell quiet.

Their names shook mountains. Once. Temples overflowed with offerings, and the world bent beneath their moods because immortality gleamed in their blood and eternity bloomed underfoot. Once.

But indifference was perhaps the cruelest god, older and colder than any Mount Olympus ever boasted, and belief is such a fragile thing. The greed of man outgrew their fear, and so a new god was born, mirrored in their image. It began with whispers, with gospel. A new name passed from tongue to cheek, soft and unfamiliar. The Olympians laughed.

At first.

They grew silent as their altars crumbled, vines curling over abandoned stone while a new Holy rhetoric overthrew them. The Death Gods were spared, to an extent, because Death came for all, but the rest? Once the prayers stopped, Olympus withered, but they did not die. Gods never truly died.

But they fell.

Not with fire or glory, but with erosion, with the weight of being forgotten. They wore mortal skins, hollow shells of their formal divine might, living as Otherworlders in foreign lands, far-flung from the roots of the lands that birthed them. Golden blood faded to red.

Zeus took to the West, to the City of Sin. Poseidon fell into the drift of the sea. Down south in the thriving city of New Orleans, Hades made his home by way of the English Isles, as many of the Death Gods did. His presence became a beacon for those who fought by his side in Demeter's Rebellion, for his realm and Queen. Life settled as time moved.

They were diminished, reduced to scraps of their former glory, yes, but they were still gods. Even stripped of thrones, even threadbare with time and shame.

It had been two thousand years since Persephone was stolen, since Hades shut the gates and left the others to their ruin. Even still, he held her memory under his skin, the sharp blade a reminder of what he lost, unaware that deep beneath the bones of the Crescent City, something had shifted.

The arrival of a reckoning.

A spring awakening.

The gods were not slain. They were forgotten. And that, in the end, was worse.

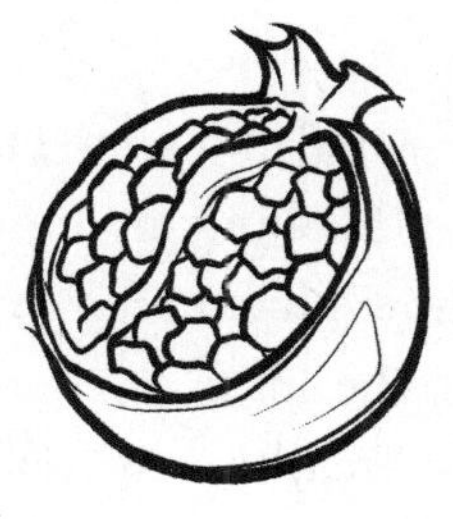

Persephone

CHAPTER 1

APRIL 21, 1996

"W*ake up. Open your eyes.*"

A persistent command struck through me, rousing my consciousness to the despair I'd been left to rot in. "*Please. Open your eyes, reach for the surface. Try.*"

The voice, my only comforting companion to the screams that berated the side of my skull, rousing me closer and closer from the depths within, until a small sliver of stale air crests under my heavy eyelids.

Darkness.

Surrounded by the ink of shadows, I struggled to adjust my sight, raging against the voice that pushed me to the torture of *experiencing*. I had only known of it and the maddening screams that tore through my mind for so long; it was impossible to remember a time before. A cacophony of dreams and lost moments overwhelmed me, ensnaring my thoughts. I had slumbered until the screams dulled to mere whispers. And then, grateful for the quiet, I had slept.

Trapped.

A soft tremble shook the world around my prison, the tiniest crack in the darkness of wood and pain. I felt the movement in my fingers first, a slight tingle calling my limbs back to life. I didn't know where I was, or how I had come to be here in the fathomless abyss, but I clung to the spark of energy seeping through my bones, sucking in a deep breath as my lungs expanded on a harsh groan. The air was stale, ripe with the overwhelming mix of dirt and moisture, the scent crawling into the crevices of my skin, lingering like a leech as I willed my body to move.

How did I get here? I couldn't remember. I needed to remember.

I cried out, the cracked skin of my lips aching in protest around the sound. The madness had taken my memories long ago, stolen them, and locked them away. I poked and prodded at the wall of stone encasing my mind, flailing in this space between spaces. If my body wouldn't respond, perhaps my mind could be coerced. I felt great crags etched there in my mind's eye, obscuring the answers I sought, but I dug deeper, using my meager reserves of strength to dig through the shadows of chaos keeping me at bay. Something stilled inside me, a small, quiet voice in my ear, urging me to turn back. *Danger there*. It echoed in my head, a warning, and without knowing why, I heeded the words and obliged as pain radiated from my skull.

I focused my attention outward again.

My torn lips let out a small breath of air, propelling my body forward. Something had changed, as the oppressive weight of chains no longer sat upon my chest. I lifted a shaking hand toward the top of my prison and pushed.

Nothing.

Solid wood. I willed for someone, *anyone*, to come save me. A pair of ice-blue eyes flashed across my mind, bringing with them a modicum of comfort, but I shook my head at the thought, unable to recall who they belonged to.

"*A little more, come now. Almost there . . . Don't stop moving . . .*"

Desperately, I pushed on my prison once more, and this time, it moved. With renewed hope, I bent my knees slightly and heaved, willing my feeble body to work for me.

It did.

I was rewarded with several pounds of loose dirt cascading into my prison as the wood gave way. Groans escaped my lips as I pushed forth, crawling from the depths until my hand broke the surface. I squeezed my shoulders through the oppressive earth with gusto, this time until my head and torso joined my hand. I gulped in several mouthfuls of air as thundering sounds of metal and yelling amped up around me. A putrid stench assaulted my nostrils, causing my stomach to roil. The air smelled . . . *sour*. The taste of metallic residue rested on my tongue, and I resisted the urge to bury my face back into the heady scent of the dirt. The ground still smelled like *home*; like musk and rainwater.

The sun was harsh against my eyes, and I pulled my hand high to shield my face. *No*, not the sun. Some sort of conjuration of light, as the world beyond it sat dark still.

"What the fuck, lady?! Are you okay?!" A crowd of men stood above me, strangely dressed as they yelled at each other in nasally accents that I had never heard. Rough hands hooked under my arms, pulling me from my would-be grave. They settled me gently down as one of the men pushed the hair from my face, cleared the residual dirt from my nose. "I gotcha sweetheart," he soothed, bringing a strange chalice to my lips offering it to me. "Who hurt you? Did someone bury you down there? What's ya name?"

His voice was smooth, kindness and concern etched in his deep brown eyes. He was older, with wrinkles around his mouth and white hair that peeked out haphazardly from under his yellow helm. I wanted to answer him, but my throat croaked when I opened my lips to push air through. The man tilted the chalice toward me, and I took it, relishing the cool liquid as it soothed my dry and aching throat. A rancid aftertaste hit, making me choke and gag on the clear liquid. *Was this poison?*

"That's it, ya safe," he repeated, breaking the loop only to ask again, "What's ya name, sweetheart?"

I glanced around at the small crowd who had gathered, saw many were yelling out orders, murmuring to each other. I looked back at the man kneeling before me, eyes wide.

"M-my name . . ." I managed to choke out, "My name is . . . My name . . ." Confusion flooded me. It was just on the tip of my tongue, dancing at the far edge of my consciousness. I reached deep, searching for the voice who had kept such close company to me, but there was no voice to answer, no comfort left in it to give. I was alone.

Tears pricked the back of my eyes. I began to panic. *My name.* What was my name? Who was I? A loud buzzing noise shook through my ears, humming high, obscuring the world around me. A tightness coiled in my chest, constricted my breath. "I don't know my name." I sobbed, clutching my chest. "I don't know . . . I don't know." I rocked back and forth, shaking and light-headed. Darkness crept up into the corners of my eyes, and I felt the sweet relief of unconsciousness take root as I collapsed backward into the disturbed earth.

"Jesus Christ. Mike, call 9-1-1!" the man with the kind eyes yelled, somewhere far in the distance.

It wasn't his eyes I saw last, those dark brown orbs etched with concern. Instead, it was a pair of blue irises with brutal rivers behind them, deep as the currents that pulled me under as I sank into nothingness.

Hades

CHAPTER 2

The sun lay low, casting a yellow tinge to the banks of the river. Persephone sprawled across me, staring up into the sky, her golden skin soaking up the last rays of the sun. Flowers grew and bloomed of their own volition, stretching toward us, toward her, despite my icy demeanor. Delicate fingers skated along my skin, bruising warmth into my ribs as she went.

"Why do you hate Olympus, Hades?" she asked in a soft voice.

Each time my eyes raked over her, I discovered something new. A freckle on her arm, a speck of gray flecked in her green eyes. Today I learned that her golden hair held subtle streaks of red as I twirled the strands casually around my finger.

Our routine was something I lived and breathed for. Sitting together or walking through the Wild Wood, we shared all manner of things. The way I ran the Underworld, what she loved about ushering in the spring. Sometimes we fell silent, just eager to be near each other, but I had a feeling that today, she was going to ask me the harder questions, her insatiable curiosity on full display. I looked down, meeting her gaze as she waited for my reply. A defeated sigh wilted from me; I could keep nothing from her, even things better off not being spoken into the cosmos.

"I chose to not be there because I rival Zeus's power. He is not prone to sharing his toys." Her pupils grew wide as shock flashed across her face, and I grinned at her reaction. "Surprised, Little Flower?" I teased, watching as her cheeks set aflame.

Persephone cast her eyes from mine, mumbling incoherently. "I just . . . never heard of anyone, God of Gods and all . . ." She looked flustered, and it was all I could do to keep my composure. My free hand slid down to cup her chin, raising it to have her eyes meet mine once more.

"No need to be embarrassed. It isn't something advertised. We were created from the same matter, after all. They would call us 'brothers' but it is in name alone. I never really shared their lust for power, never felt a sense of family or connection. When we defeated Cronus, splitting the realms seemed the easiest way to broker peace. Once he was gone, there wasn't a common enemy to unite us, and without that distraction, it was only a matter of time before we began to clash. Poseidon took the sea, and Zeus took the sky and heavens. I think it's because Zeus never really saw Poseidon as much of a threat; he was always more interested in being out in the wild than ruling."

My goddess shifted her body against mine and I sucked in a breath at the pressure resting on my torso and hips, willing any rogue reactions to keep their stay. The last thing I wanted was to make her uncomfortable or do anything that may dissuade her from wanting me to lay with her. I lifted my chin, throwing my head back to focus on the clouds floating lazily above our heads. Persephone folded her hands beneath her chin, snuggling closer, creating a deliciously torturous friction that had me swallowing hard.

"So, how did you get the Underworld?" she inquired, studying my face.

"When we fought Cronos, my full power emerged. I could draw on this . . . almost infinite spring of shades. I think it frightened Zeus, though he would never admit it. He suggested the Underworld, and I imagine in his eyes it was a banishment, a form of punishment. He's so obsessed over the worshiping thoughts of the mortals that he couldn't fathom not being in that spotlight. I have no desire to be ogled and demanded upon. The Underworld is a refuge for me. I have the darkness, the calm of the Hells. I have no reason to venture up here often and quite honestly, this is the most time I've spent topside since my coronation."

Persephone tensed, drawing my eyes back to hers. A flash of hurt spread across her face as she turned away.

"I'm sorry to have kept you." Her voice was small, and I grit my teeth against the pain laced in her words.

"Persephone, I come back because I want to. I want to know more about you."

Her eyes softened as she looked at me, fluttered shut as I stroked my thumb across her cheek. Persephone's teeth sunk into her lip and a small groan rumbled through my chest, unchecked. I wasn't quick enough to suppress it this time, the urge for her, the desperate longing that lived inside me, just beneath my skin. She sat up, hopped to her feet with her chiton a mess around her, a mischievous glint in her eye.

"Well, if you want to know more, then I should warn you that I won't make it easy. Catch me, Lord Hades, and I'm yours." With that, she took off like a shot, barreling into the woods, her laughter trailing behind her.

Without haste I rose, chasing after her. My shadows swirled around me, propelling my body forward, aching as her words caressed against the hungriest part of me. I could hear her feet rustling branches and leaves as she went, glimpse the beautiful light pink swaths of fabric as she flitted through the trees. I searched and searched until I heard . . . nothing. No laughter. No rustling.

Not even the chirp of birds or the slither of insects. The silence built around me and I faltered in the deafening vacuum. I spun, unsure of which way I should go.

"PERSEPHONE!" I bellowed, panic rising in my chest, because everything felt suddenly wrong. "PERSEPHONE!" No answer came. No rustling. Only more silence.

I tore through the trees, eyes alert and breath stripped with fear. The meadow was empty, no sign of my beautiful goddess. My world glitched, images flashing before my mind's eye and grief, all-consuming grief. Her kissing me. The creation of our Bond. Her eating the pomegranate seeds on Mount Olympus. Her body entwined with mine, the sound of her soft cries as she chased her pleasure. Panic at her being lost.

Panic . . . panic . . . panic . . . the death of Narcissus . . . the taste of ash on my tongue. Persephone was gone. Tears fell down my cheeks, fear and despair swelled before me like a tidal wave. This wasn't real. She had loved me, we were happy, and he took her. He stole her from me. I fisted my hands through my hair and let out a wail so full of anguish that the earth shook. I dropped to my knees, burying my hands into the ground, willing her to come back to me, but my fingers sunk into gray ash. A sharp pain constricted my chest as though I had been stabbed, and I cried out from the violence of it. The force flipped me backwards, pinning me to the ground. My fingers grasped at my chest, clawing the skin, begging for the relief of nothingness.

A faltering THUMP resounded from between my rib cage, stealing a strangled cry from my lips. Thump . . . thump . . . again and again. Painfully, slowly and uneven at first, but steadily it built into a rhythm as I struggled to fill my lungs with air. My heart was beating. Thump, thump, thump.

My eyes flew wide, and I was no longer in our meadow in Greece.

The cold cedar floorboards of my penthouse pressed into my back as the pain in my chest slowly subsided. The hand still clutching my ribs shook, sweat pouring from my body, slicking the wood beneath me. The nightmare had let me loose, but my mind was still stuck *there* in the pain of it all. For centuries, I'd dreamt our memories on an endless loop, but they hadn't turned against me in a very long time.

Thump, thump, thump . . .

I froze, listening. My heart pumped steadily, gathering steam as panic and excitement rose within me.

Thump, thump, thump . . .

It trilled on, beating a bruise against my rib cage. Disbelief and shock tore through my body as it carried on, as though it had always worked, as though I hadn't gone without it beating for over two thousand years. My muscles screamed in protest as I struggled to catch my breath and right myself, that deep ache in the pit of my chest roaring to life. The beat of the cursed organ could only mean one thing.

"*Persephone.*"

Persephone

CHAPTER 3

I awoke to light. Not sunlight, or firelight, but a cold, buzzing whiteness that came from nowhere and everywhere all at once. The sky above me stretched on, no beams or cracks, no soot . . . just *white*, stretching on to infinity. I managed to pry my eyes all the way open, my vision blurred and strained. There was no scent of earth, just the sharp, acrid tang of a putrid odor burning my nose.

I tried to sit up, but my limbs felt like they didn't belong to me. Heavy. *Weak*. Dead weight rested over my body as I tried to raise my hand to my face, but something tugged at my arm. Looking down, my eyes widened in horror as I saw a thin, clear serpent burrowed into my skin, attached to a metal stand beside me. A bag of liquid hung above, slowly dripping into the serpent.

Was it feeding me? Poisoning me?

The walls were too clean, too smooth. No windows. No fireplace. Just strange, humming panels set high in the corners, their purpose a mystery. I couldn't even hear birds, just the unpleasant tone, thrumming in tandem with my heart.

Where was I? A prison?

My heart thudded in my chest as that strange beeping began to tick up, faster and faster beside my ear. Sharp. Insistent. *Unnatural*. I turned my head. A black box blinked back at me with green, eerie light. Jagged lines danced across mirrored glass, like the scribbles of a madman, sigils I couldn't know or understand. Another box beneath it glowed blue, unreadable, arcane in nature.

I reached for it, the tones matching the thud in my skull, the galloping of my heart, but the moment I moved, pain lanced through my side. I gasped at the sharp tug from my chest, and when my trembling fingers pulled back the thin material covering me, I cried out. Several thinner, brightly colored serpents stuck to my skin like leeches.

Panic overtook me and I tugged at the snakes, cursing the infernal machinations, the deafening din of the world around me. I attempted to pry them from my arms, despite the excruciating pain that overtook me at their release. My skin gave way in a sickening gush of blood, and it was too hot as it splattered over me, red and vibrant from the wound, ripping a cry from my lips.

Red? That wasn't right, something was *wrong*.

Voices came from the doorway and my vision swam as several people appeared, faces contorted in horror at the deluge that gushed from my wound. I kept moving, ripping and tearing from my chest. Hands descended, strong and foreign and I fought them, thrashing backward from their grips as I struggled to free myself from the bindings that shackled me. A blonde woman hurried in with a long, sharp object held aloft in her grip. The bite was swift and brutal as it pricked at my skin, and within moments, an oppressive wave washed over me, pulling my body back pliantly.

"Why are you doing this to me?" I managed to croak out before the world went dark, and again, I was floating, twisting out of my body into gentle nothingness, fading away from the woman with what looked like apology in her eyes.

Hades

CHAPTER 4

I paced across the floor of my penthouse impatiently, wearing down the wood in my wake. I had called them hours ago, and yet they dared to keep me waiting. The thought was punctuated by a sharp crack, like the snapping of bones as the fireplace went up in blue flames. I whipped around, instinct driving me to clutch the long-faded Bond mark that rested above my heart. "*Finally*."

The Fates stood before me, sisters three, in their stoic formation. They waited, silently, studying me, until the air between us filled with tension, and I forced myself to still. As I slowed my breathing, steadying my temper, I reminded myself that I needed them. They were batty old witches and easily offended. I still commanded them, but they could give me partial truths or leave out vital information if I irked them.

Flattery had always been the best policy with the three.

"My dear Fates, you grow more lovely with each passing century. I am honored by your presence." I sank into a low bow.

"Lord Hades, we still serve thee," they trilled, each voice a distinct octave from the others. They dipped slightly in unison, and I relaxed my jaw.

"I felt my heartbeat today," I began, slowly unfurling the bait. It was always best to give them as little information as possible, in hopes they would illuminate something I may not know by accident. They took confirmation bias to an entirely new level, and I needed to know everything they could tell me.

"Indeed."

Frustration surged through me, and I gnashed my teeth together to bite back my impatience. "I would very much like to know *where* my wife is. Do you know where that is?"

The Fates stared at me with their shadeless pits of eye sockets, and I focused hard not to get trapped in the depths. They had one eye between them, and I watched in stony silence as Lachesis reached for a small drawstring bag at her side, made from the skin of traitors. She plunged her gnarled hand inside the pouch, then withdrew the Eye of Fate, clutched tightly in her fist. Lachesis plopped it unceremoniously into her vacant socket with a disgusting squelch, and I waited as it spun and settled. The iris twisted inwardly to stare into the void that was her mind, a place where nightmares and dreams alike dwelled.

She raised her hands high in front of her, head back, and hummed lightly as the power built around her. Lachesis let out a small, "*Ahh.*" before removing the eye and returning it to its home. She leveled that stare directly at me. "She is closer than you can imagine and walking the world of mortals. She will soon be led to you by the Messenger of the Gods."

I swallowed. *Hermes*?

She drawled on:

Words of caution, you must take.
Should you push her, she will break.

Chaos abounds in a room left locked.
The lives of Gods and mortals blocked.

A prophecy. *Dammit.*

I pinched the bridge of my nose between my forefinger and thumb, squeezing my eyes shut. "For this very unique time, could you please elaborate? My wife has been missing for two thousand years, Lachesis," I pleaded.

The Fates glanced between themselves, in silent, eerie conversation, but it was Clotho who answered me. "She is descended into chaos and may not return should she be fractured further. The Queen of Spring has a barrier in place to shield the madness from consuming all. She will not recall you or any of our world, and to force her to face reality may splinter her mind forever."

I worried my fingers through my hair and resumed pacing. The Fates remained passive, letting me process. When it was clear they had nothing more they planned to share, I dismissed them with a sigh. "Thank you for your service. If there is nothing more, you may go now. Please, take the crow as tribute." I gestured to the black bird sitting obediently inside the summoning circle. They bowed their heads in unison, accepting my offering. Clotho clicked her tongue, and the bird flew to her immediately, perching itself on her shoulder in a flurry of wings. They silently glided toward the fireplace, and I watched Lachesis and Clotho disappear in a plume of blue flame.

Atropos hesitated and I arched an eyebrow at her hands, flexing open and closed as though she were torn. That unsettled me more than anything; it wasn't often that I saw Fate hesitate. Whatever was weighing on her, her sisters would clearly not approve of her disclosing, so I drew closer, offering my full attention.

"Hades, the darkness that came for her is in this realm. It clings to *you* like a beacon. If she is near you, it will be able to find her. I'm sorry, old friend. I thought you would want to know." A sad smile and a plume of fire later, and then she was gone. I sank to the bed and waited, turning over every word of that prophecy, analyzing any meaning I could wring from it. They'd said Hermes would bring word and they would be right. *They were always right.*

The uncertainty, the twisting of my mind, sent me back to the early days in the Upper Realm, when the new hierarchy rotation of the Underworlds had been established. The lessening of the pagan worship meant that the rules were a little faster and loose among the Death Gods, and the shades ordered that only one of us holds a seat to keep the cogs turning. Thanatos, Morpheus, Hermes, and I had settled in the United Kingdom, and while they preferred the city, I'd fled to the country, the dark and dreary demeanor a perfect mirror of the melancholy thriving inside me, but it was the greenery that drew me.

Surrounded by the juxtaposition of harsh climate with rolling swaths of green reminded me of her. Of her eyes. I didn't even mind when the accent got too natural to shake.

It was hours later when my phone rang. I answered with shaking hands, already knowing who it was.

"Hades," his voice was urgent, excited, "Hygieia just called me. You're not going to believe who just got brought into the ER at Charity Hospital."

But I did know. It could only be *her*. He didn't wait for my reply.

"*Persephone*. I don't know the details, but I'm getting on a plane now. They found her, Hades. She's *alive*." His voice almost broke with relief, and I envied the joy he was experiencing after two thousand years of heartbreak.

"Hades, are you there? Did that heart finally stop? They bloody found her, mate!"

He kept talking, his words a blur of excitement through the thick English accent he'd acquired over his years residing in the United Kingdom, but all I could feel was a cold, bitter nothingness as I listened. I managed to get off the phone with Hermes with as few words as possible, promising to see him as soon as he landed. The phone fell to the bed, and a hollow, empty pit took up residence inside me. I could taste ash in my mouth, much the same as I had the day I'd lost control and erupted Vesuvius.

They'd found her. I had to hold on to that little comfort, or the emptiness would swallow me whole. To have her close, so fucking close, and unable to touch her or hold her or protect her flayed me alive. I had to calm, and I took several shallow breaths as the pain in my chest sharpened. Slowly, the weight lifted from my chest, and I flattened myself onto the floor with relief. She wasn't dead, and her shade wasn't shredded within the cosmos.

Small victories.

The darkness that stole her and locked her away was still a threat, and I could focus on that, instead of my inability to be with her. We'd assumed Narcissus had done the deed alone, but I'd always wondered *how.* Helios had been in no condition to question anything after that day, having lost both Persephone and Narcissus. Even through my rage, I'd seen how broken he was. Just as broken as I was, and in many ways, possibly more.

I'd wanted to hate him, to blame him, but he'd blamed himself enough for both of us, and I had wronged Narcissus in my way as well. I had to hold on to what I could control. Persephone was back. We'd get a chance to see her smile, to hear her laugh, even if I had to stay in the shadows. I made a note to call Helios once I found him. He never stayed in one place long, but he deserved to have some relief. She hadn't said *he* couldn't be near her; only me.

It clings to you like a beacon. If she is near you, it will be able to find her.

Atropos had cursed me with that last bit of information. It was my penance, I knew. I'd allowed something beautiful and delicate into my world, let the darkness corrupt her, poison her, and then break her for my own selfishness. I didn't deserve Persephone. I never had.

I knew what the implications of that prophecy meant. Wherever she was kept was just enough out of the reach of the Underworld that the chaos had overtaken her . . . *It had maimed my flower*. I tried to imagine what that pain must have been, how anyone could have possibly survived that type of torture. Bile rose in my throat as I pushed the tidal wave of despair back. I had to do something. I *had* to.

I dressed quickly and grabbed my keys off the counter, lying to myself as I went. I told myself as I exited the door from my building into the parking garage that I was only going to check on her, just make sure she was okay. I didn't have to touch her, just be near her. I just needed to see that she was alive, then I could leave her alone forever to live her life.

Liar.

The night was buzzing as I tore out of the garage and flew down Canal Street toward Tulane. I could have run there, but I needed to pace myself. If she held no memory, then convincing her that we couldn't be together was suddenly not an issue, and that realization tore a fresh, jagged wound open inside me. I shifted and skidded up to Charity Hospital, not bothering to even cut the engine as I hopped out and sprinted toward the double doors of the emergency room.

It was crowded as mortals rushed around the sick, wounded, and maimed. A few addicts huddled together around one that looked blue around the lips, just inside the waiting room. I could feel the delicate thread of his life pull taut, pulsing under the deft control of Atropos and her sisters just before the cut. His eyes fluttered shut, and even before his companions could realize, I felt that he was gone. He belonged to me now, and to the others who shared my domain. His shade pulled from him incorporeally, searching, lost, and I took pity on him. Thanatos, or one of his Reapers, would be here soon, but the boy looked so alone.

I waved a hand in his direction, dissipating him from the realm before he could get stuck in between. His shade would re-form on the banks of the Styx, and Charon would take care of him. His pain was done.

I tore through the intake doors, earning the attention and ire of several attending nurses and staff, but I cared little. My eyes swept the room, every patient, looking for my green-eyed girl. As my gaze landed on Hygieia, her eyes went wide with shock and alarm. She had come out of one of the private rooms, an empty syringe in her hand. I could feel my love in there, the tethers of our Bond flickering to life, but just barely.

"Where is my wife?" I growled.

Hygieia's gaze darted behind her briefly, telling me everything without a word. The widespread panic in her eyes gave her away as she realized Hermes had already contacted me. Rage she didn't deserve boiled within my veins, bubbled up, and broke through my chest. I stalked forward, anger pulsing from my very core, the primal reaction warring with my reason, but Hygieia, to her credit, didn't cower. She stood, head held high, defiance etched into her features.

"Hades, you can't go in there right now." It was half a warning, half a prayer. She threw her arms across the doorway, her body between me and the reason for my existence.

"Move." A command, a warning of my own. The only one she would be getting, and she knew it. Her eyes flicked to others who had begun a slow approach, cornering me, or so they thought. I cracked my neck once to the left and felt my hands flex into fists. If they thought they had a chance, that would be the last miscalculation of their lives.

"My wife is in that room. I will not repeat myself." My words were cold. I knew that whatever she had been through put Hygieia on edge, but all that managed to do was spur the intense need to see her with my own eyes once more. There had been many "almosts" since she had been taken. This was no false flag.

She raised her hands to me, pleading. "Hades, she is in shock, and there is an incredible amount of degradation in her mind. If you go in there, you could break her." Hygieia, the Goddess of Mental Health, stood before me, echoing the warning Atropos had lain at my feet. She was protecting her patient, who was also her friend.

You could break her. It reverberated through my skull, a sickening vortex of doubt and despair that played on repeat. *The darkness that came for her is in this realm. It clings to you like a beacon.*

My knees gave way as I struggled forward. When had hands been laid across me? Strong arms attempted to hold me in place, and I thrashed, renewed with anger.

A scuffle ensued. I couldn't know if I was winning or losing, but I knew that even outnumbered I was gaining ground. The door past Hygieia burst open under the weight of my shadows, and in the darkness, I could see the glint of dark golden hair. More words were exchanged, more pleas. Hygieia used any card she had in her arsenal, but none found purchase in my brain as I thrashed against my captors until she said *his* name.

". . . Hermes will be here tomorrow. Let him see her first, test her mind safely," she begged.

My bones settled. The arms around me tightened at the release of tension in my posture, taking any advantage to find a better grip. Hermes would be here. He would help her. I owed him so much, much more than anyone else. I hadn't known it at the time, but he was the one that left Olympus the day of our hearing. They were moments from wrenching the two of us apart and he had brought her the seeds of the pomegranate. Hermes had given her the choice that I never could.

Hermes.

The Messenger of the Gods. *My friend.*

The one who ran circles around the world when she went missing. The one who crossed over into the forbidden territory of the other Pantheons to search when we heard she was on another continent. The one who keeps a garden for her in whatever city we settled into. He was the only one of any of us who had the courage to let her choose to be tied to the Underworld. To me. He had strength when I couldn't, and it most likely saved her life when she was taken in Greece.

"He's coming?" My voice came out harsh, a crack in the foundations of control I usually held tight. Hygieia nodded, something like hope flashing in her eyes. Hope that she had broken through.

"He's on a plane now. Pulled every string and cashed in every favor he had to take over her care. This is going to be a long road, Hades. We only get one chance." She still hadn't moved from the doorway, but I could see past her into the room beyond. Persephone looked so small lying there, buried in covers and hooked to machines.

I felt sick.

"I just need to see her." I bargained, begged. "That's all. I just need to see for myself. I won't wake her." I was not above pleading at this juncture in my life, and that more than anything spurred the shock on Hygieia's face. To her, I was still Hades, God of the Underworld. Many hadn't seen me when we'd lost Persephone, hadn't watched me shatter to pieces under the devastation of her absence.

No, there were only a select few privy to those moments. Hygieia studied me, calculating how sincere I was in my promise. She must have decided it was the quickest way to be rid of me, because she sidestepped slightly to give me access.

"*Five* minutes, I mean it," she warned, and I let out a breath trapped too tight in my chest. The hands holding me released as I stepped across the threshold silently. Too late, I realized my hands were shaking as I approached the sleeping form on the too-small bed.

Persephone's hair fanned around her across the pillow in a messy break of blonde waves. Her lids were shut but I could see her eyes moving beneath the thin skin, fighting the drug-induced sleep she was rendered helpless under. The soft curve of her cheeks was gone, replaced by a thinner, hollow gauntness that tore at my shade. Where had she been kept? I still had no information, and there seemed to be no responsible party identified. She looked insubstantial, her muscles atrophied. I nearly choked as I took in how lithe and sickly she appeared under the thick hospital blankets.

I prayed she would eat and be restored, that her weight would return, that her pallor would glow golden once more. Hygieia's eyes bore into my back as she watched from the door, as if she knew I was considering breaking my promise not to touch her.

She was *so fucking close.*

I had to know she was real. Carefully, I swiped a hand along her chin, barely a centimeter of open air separating us. A soft little sigh left her lips, and I would swear on all that was holy that I felt her pull her face to meet me. My sweet love. *My beautiful, poisonous, Little Flower.*

"You're sure he'll be here?" I asked, flinging the question over my shoulder to Hygieia.

"Tomorrow." she answered from the door.

"Good."

With more strength than I knew I possessed, I pulled my hand back, muscles screaming in protest at the separation, but I knew if I didn't retreat, I would never leave her side. She whimpered again, but her eyes remained closed, and I bit my lip until the skin tore and blood filled my mouth. I wanted to shout and wake her, to see her eyes, to taste her lips. Every nerve in my body felt flayed as I stared at her chest, noting every rise and fall. Proof that she was *here*. She was alive. Temptation ripped through me, and I tore myself away, each step taking the effort of killing a thousand men. Hygieia closed the door behind me, tiny hands pushing me toward the back exit.

Two nurses stood sentry outside of Persephone's door, Otherworlders who knew who we were and how important our secret was. They'd known enough to try and keep me back, at Hygieia's request, but they hadn't called the authorities. Nymphs, dryads, demi-gods—they could have been anyone of our kind, but the goddess trusted them, so I would have no choice but to as well. Hygieia pushed me farther and farther through the door marked "EXIT" in glowing red letters, and I found us in a stairwell. She looked up and down the stairs to make sure we were alone.

"Tell me everything," I demanded.

Persephone
CHAPTER 5

"*Where is my wife?*" a low, deadly voice hissed.

I could feel that voice pulling me to consciousness with persistent command. I heard it again over a thrashing scuffle as I struggled to open my eyes, to obey the call, but the weight was too heavy. I drifted in and out, floating in the endless beyond. Waking meant questions I had no answers to, meant confusion and a pounding ache near my temple. It was easier to sleep, but I had to wake.

I managed to crack an eye, my vision swimming and further obscured by low light, but that *voice*. I curled toward it, seeking it out, comforted by it, both familiar and somehow slightly different. There were several bodies huddled around my door frame, struggling against one another. I could make out the blonde locks of the armed attacker who had knocked me out, but my attention pulled beyond. I struggled to look past her, something important lay just behind, my mind knew, if I could just focus. I didn't know who or what that may be, but I felt my blood calling to them, singing from my veins, soaring toward them like a bird in flight. I fought harder against the drug-induced stupor, but my eyes were so heavy, my mind thick with fog.

"You *can't*!" the blonde shouted, standing her ground. A towering figure loomed over her like dark shadows, several pairs of hands crossed over his chest and arms as they held him at bay. "Be reasonable," she pleaded, pushing her weight onto him to keep him from entering the room. Muffled words and scuffling came to a brief pause and then there was silence. The man must have relented because the rustling of clothes died down and all that could be heard besides the insistent bleating of the box next to my head was the sound of ragged breathing.

"Hygieia, *please*." His voice crumbled at the end, the pain evident. No voice that beautiful should sound so broken. I tried in vain to open my eyes again, but they refused to admit the light, to let me gaze upon the face that voice called home.

There were more words exchanged but I couldn't make my mind focus on them, couldn't make my body move to open my eyes fully. I could hear the tentative scrapes of footsteps approaching me as I evaluated other parts of my body, willing them to relent from their stillness. *Nothing*. I felt the pressure when the bed I lay trapped in dipped, felt the warmth of a body near mine. Goose bumps erupted at our nearness through the fabric, yet still, I could not move. The sea of unconsciousness swelled around me, lifting and crashing me into the shore. I needed to fight, to remain *here*. This was important. That voice was important.

"Little Flower." An exhale. Breath fanned over my cheeks. He was close, and I wanted to study the features of him, see his mouth as it formed words that produced that voice. "I'm sorry, I'm so sorry," he murmured over and over again, each apology more sorrow-stricken than the last.

Why was he sorry? I wondered. Such a pretty voice; like a warm embrace, it held me tight as it wrapped around me. The tidal wave rolled back over my mind, sucking me to the bottom of the ocean, and try as I might, I couldn't hold on to his voice enough to make out what he was saying. Instead, I let the rumbling timbre lull me to sleep, hanging on to the sounds coming from my darkness.

Somebody came for me.

I wasn't alone.

I woke over the next few days slowly, groggy and disoriented. The room I was in swam into view, and I struggled to remember where I was or how I got here. Or *who* I was. *They had asked my name, but I had none to give.* Bits and pieces of reality slammed into me like a boulder, and I began to breathe heavily as panic overtook my body, paralyzing me with fear. Something swam at the back of my consciousness, a soothing voice urging calm, but I couldn't grasp it as it taunted me from just beyond my reach. It felt important, a necessity, but all I could remember was being stabbed, and then nothingness. The bleating from the large box grew more frantic the more anxious I became, mirroring my own fear.

A soft knock pulled my attention to the front of my prison. The door cracked slightly as a tall man with strawberry blond hair peeked through. He had adorably boyish apple cheeks and a smile that extended all the way to his eyes, which glistened with promised mischief but held warmth too.

"Ah, Sleeping Beauty has awakened," he teased as a dazzling smile lit his features. "How are we feeling today?" He walked in slowly, gently closed the door, was easy on his approach. I loosened my grip on the edge of the bed a little.

"I'm Dr. Dixon," he introduced himself as he pulled the chair near my bed out and straddled the back of it. He had an easy posture and perhaps he sat to make himself look less threatening than someone looming over me. My grip lessened further.

"I've heard that you have no memory. You don't know your name?" he questioned, keeping his voice soft. There was another accent there, one different from the men from the box, different from the others I heard passing by my door.

I nodded, as he pulled his lips into a thin line.

"I understand that has to be very scary for you. Is there anything you can remember?" he prodded, again gently. Something in his voice, his demeanor, made me *want* to trust him. He had said he was a doctor.

"Is a doctor like a healer?" I inquired. Some of the language used here I just didn't understand.

His face lit up as soon as I spoke, even though my voice was rough and scratchy.

"Yes, it is. I'm a healer of the body and sometimes the mind. Your accent is unique. Do you remember where you're from? Sometimes we remember less personal details, like where we are from or how old we are," he asked, encouragingly. I frowned, pushing at the walls in my mind.

"I can't . . . I don't remember. I'm sorry," I sighed, dejected. "It's like I can feel this barrier built around my memories in my mind, but I can't bring them down. I-I can barely t-touch them." My voice felt small, so incredibly small. He bent closer across the back of the chair that rested between his legs.

"You know, I spent a lot of time on the islands in Greece. Your accent is very reminiscent of some of the people there. Perhaps we can start there as a means to unlock the mystery hiding in your mind. I can get you a list of traditional Greek names and maybe one of them will jog your memory? At any rate, maybe you can choose one so we can stop calling you 'Jane Doe' and you can have some control over what's happening. How does that sound?" He studied me, awaiting my response.

I nodded my head slowly, chewing over his words.

"That would be nice. Thank you. What does 'Jane Doe' mean?" I asked, curious.

"It's just a name we give to those who we can't yet identify," he assured me with a wave of his hand. "Now, I need to unfortunately put you through a series of tests."

My eyes widened in alarm, and he held both hands up unthreateningly.

"There's nothing you need to do besides let us take some of your blood. Not enough to hurt you in any way. Just so we can analyze. Would that be okay with you? We just want to see if we can figure out what happened to you. You *can* say no. It's important that you know that," he said, eyeing me seriously.

I trusted him. He could have hurt me, like the other had with that pricking object. Instead, he was talking to me, giving me the information to choose. My heart rate slowed, and with it the raucous noise from the box. His brilliant smile split across his face once more and he clapped, standing too abruptly, startling me. I slunk back at the movement.

"I'm not sure what has happened to you, but I can promise you that while you're here you are safe. No one will hurt you. We only want to help you."

I gave him a weak smile as he walked to the door, but a burning curiosity had me clearing my throat. He turned, waiting with a raised eyebrow. I toyed with the hem of the soft fabric of the blanket on my lap.

"Has anyone— I mean, has anyone come to find me? I c-can't, I can't remember clearly but I thought I heard a voice, when I was first here . . . ?" I asked, lip trembling. A sad, pitying look overtook his features, and I felt despair well up inside me.

"I'm sorry. You were on a lot of medication, and under heavy sedation. I'm sure you heard many voices, but . . . there haven't been any visitors since you were admitted," he replied gently. My face burned with embarrassment, and I turned to look away, running from the pity and kindness in his eyes.

"I'll get you that list of names as soon as possible," he promised, and with that and a wink, he was gone.

Persephone

CHAPTER 6

Dr. Dixon kept his word. Over the next several days, I fell into a routine with the rest of the hospital staff. The physicians were kind, mostly. They would ask me questions, run tests. When nothing conclusive came back, no malady or injuries that gave any explanation as to who I was or what I was doing in that grave, they began to move toward the unseen probabilities.

"Dissociative amnesia," he announced, after a week of analysis with no other valid diagnosis. "It's your mind's way of protecting itself. Whatever happened to you, your brain decided it was unsafe for you to know, that you may not be able to cope. Physically, you're fine. So, we should shift and focus on healing the injuries that we can't easily see with our eyes. I want to move you to a facility that specializes in that care."

My back went rigid, and a sweat broke out against my brow. "You're sending me away? Alone?" I panicked.

"No, no," he soothed, "I'll be joining you, as will Dr. Galapagia. As your primary physicians, we want to make sure you adjust well to avoid any complications."

The knot in my chest loosened as I gulped in several deep breaths.

And so I had been moved.

The new place was nice; it had a large room with huge windows that let me see the grounds beneath, painted a pale blue hue with a simple, single bed and bedside table to decorate it. I was grateful for the door, separating me from the rest of the patients and the outside world.

They had no idea how long I'd spent in captivity, but I felt completely and utterly panicked in spaces too large. I needed the safety and comfort of these four walls to keep me contained, keep the broken parts of me stitched together. At night, I struggled to adjust to the quiet, with no machines to beep and monitor me, no nurses popping their heads in to check every few hours. I dreamt, but I never recalled anything more than those same eyes that haunted my thoughts.

When the therapies started, I suddenly found myself completely off-kilter; reconciling what I knew of the world before my trauma, and all there was to know now felt daunting. I knew many things: what water was, some foods. Other things I couldn't comprehend: a toaster, indoor plumbing. The doctors still held no helpful theory as to why I couldn't recall common objects and procedures, but I did my best to take the new information in stride. Dr. Galapagia joked I was getting the chance to relearn humanity. She had come a long way from being the person who'd attacked me to someone in charge of my care. I knew now what she'd done was just in the interest of my safety, but it had taken some trust building to get us to a good place.

Everything outside of that box was loud, beeping, and urgent. I listened and learned how things worked in this new life of mine. They introduced me to the radio, a small contraption that produced music, and then to records and tapes and eventually CDs. I found I had quite a love for music. Dr. Dixon gave me a Walkman the second week I arrived at the facility, a recovery hospital they called Brookhaven.

I saw him at least three times a week, and he seemed to make it his personal mission to acclimate me to the world around us. It was exhausting and some days completely overwhelming, but not all that bad. I especially enjoyed television and the music channels that showed moving pictures of the songs I loved so much.

The pieces of information that leaked through the cracks in my brain from my old life came in small and violent bursts. I found I could speak languages. Not just one or two, but *most* of them. I could identify nearly all plants, knew their properties with perfect recall, as if they spoke their histories right into my mind. I devoured books, soaked up their knowledge hungrily, thankful for my ability to read.

My accent was slight and fading by the day, but strange to those that surrounded me. The detectives assigned to my case searched missing persons reports both here, a place I came to know as New Orleans, as well as abroad. No match was found, or so I had learned. They couldn't know for sure how old I was, but they estimated twenty-five, based on my body. Visits from the authorities came less and less, as they were just as baffled as to how I ended up buried at a construction site as me. With my memories locked away, they had no leads to go on.

Days passed into weeks, and true to his word Dr. Dixon brought me a list of Greek names to look over. I hadn't been able to bring myself to dwell on the sense of defeat that I couldn't remember the most integral part of my identity: my name.

I couldn't keep from obsessing over the possibility that I would never have a sense of normalcy at all. It felt as though all of my forward progress rested on this one scrap of information. What if I stared at this list and nothing registered? I'd be broken, and I knew it. With a sigh, I folded the paper and slipped it under my pillow.

Still, I did not know my own name. And still, no one came to claim me.

Persephone

CHAPTER 7

I stared down at the scrap of paper folded neatly in front of me for the hundredth time this week. I'd taken it out multiple times a day, tucked it safely back like a coward without unfolding it each time. It was simple and innocent, how much harm could a list of names really do, truly?

And yet, I was terrified.

I splayed my palms wide in front of me, focusing on the way the wood grain of the desk felt as it flowed under my fingers. Sweat beaded on my brow as I blew out a low breath.

Enough was enough. I was terrified that if I didn't do something soon, I would grow attached to the name Jane. It had grated on me in defiance at first, abrasive to my skin when someone spoke to me using it. Then just yesterday, I'd answered to it casually without much thought in group therapy. No, now it was time to move forward.

I had so little control of the things that happened *to* me, but this was my act of defiance, of independence. I could choose my own name. My hands shook as I reached for the folded paper, dry and soft to my touch as I unfurled it. My fingers flattened it out, smoothing the creases under my palms, and I willed myself to browse.

Dr. Dixon had written about twenty names on the paper in his messy scrawl that was, thankfully, still legible. My eyes skimmed over each name as my heart willed just one of them to jump out at me.

Aikaterini. *No.*

Elini. *No.*

Sophia, Dimitra, Kostantina. *Immediately no.*

Chloe? *No.*

Ella. *No.*

Lydia, Hermione, Adara? *No, no, no.*

Acacia, Theresa, Persephone, Anthea? *No. No. Wait.*

My eyes snapped back to the third to last name on the list and I felt a pressure build from somewhere deep inside the recesses of my mind. I ran my finger over the ink, scratching at the scar tissue within, begging for just the smallest crack to peer through.

"Persephone," I whispered. I was rewarded with a blinding pain that struck through my mind, unseating me from the desk, slamming me to the floor. I writhed, clutching my head as bile rose in my throat while I thrashed. Fragments of memory slipped through, quickly. *Too quickly.*

I couldn't control the stream and so, between the speed and the pain, my mind tornadoed around of its own volition. I dug my nails into the sides of my temple, fisting my hair, tearing at the root. I cried out, the bite of pain bringing me back from the edge, just enough to catch my breath. My mind reeled as I pushed again, my hands shaking as I cut half-moons into my skin with my nails.

The flashes came again, this time a little slower. I focused on the pain, willing it to slow the memories so I could catch one. Just one.

"Persephone," a deep voice breathed.

It wasn't mine, but I *knew* that voice. And I pushed harder, deeper, screaming my frustration as it slipped through my fingers and spirited away. Then hands were on me, shaking me, begging me to wake.

I cracked an eye as the pain abated, a low pulse still throbbing in the base of my skull. Dr. Dixon and Dr. Galapagia swam into focus as my eyes adjusted, concern etched into each of their faces. She had her hands on me, prying away the death grip I had on my head and in my hair free as she soothed salty tears from my cheeks.

My body shook uncontrollably as Dr. Galapagia fussed over me, checking my pulse, searching for other injuries, but my eyes were beyond her, searching for Dr. Dixon. He had gone pale, his usual boyish demeanor replaced with something *else* . . . Was it guilt? He looked nervous and apologetic, but I felt triumphant. I smiled at him between shaky breaths.

"It worked." My voice was ravaged, but clear. "It worked."

Relief flooded my body. *I knew my name. I had a name.*

Dr. Galapagia's head whipped around, as she leveled a look of pure fury toward him. "*What* worked, exactly?" she spat. Dr. Dixon shuffled his feet as he cast his eyes down.

"My name." I laughed, steadying my lungs and urging them to work. "I remember my name . . . I think it's Persephone. *Persephone.*"

Her eyes went wide, eyebrows arching so high they threatened to disappear into her hairline. She turned on him, still helping me stand on shaking legs as she guided me to bed. "*Hermes,*" she snapped, her voice low and deadly. *Hermes?* Something pricked at the edges of my mind, but the pain in my temples was screaming in protest too hard for me to focus.

"No, this is good. I remembered," I interjected, confused, "Isn't this what we want? If I can just get a few minutes to catch my breath I can try again. I pushed, but it worked, it came to m—"

I was interrupted by the sudden release of the vomit that had threatened to overflow earlier. I jerked toward the side of the bed opposite Dr. Galapagia and let loose over and over until there was nothing left in my stomach but curdling acid.

She glared at him. "Get an orderly. And then, you and I are going to talk." Her eyes narrowed.

Dr. Dixon nodded once and was gone in a flash, so quick that I barely registered he'd left the room. She pulled out a small light and flashed it into each of my pupils, turning my head back and forth.

"Listen, love. I know you're excited you remembered something, but you must stop forcing your mind. It's extremely dangerous to try and bring forth memories before their time. The mind is a delicate and fickle engine, and whatever it is protecting you from, it's built a labyrinth of walls to keep from you. If you start tearing those walls down without knowing which are load bearing, then you're likely to bring the whole house down, does that make sense?"

I nodded, tears stinging the back of my eyes, the muscles in my stomach cramping in protest. Dr. Galapagia stood as one of the orderlies came in with a mop and bucket.

"I'm happy that you have a name to hold on to, but promise me you won't push on those walls again forcefully? I don't want that brain of yours to scramble like a dropped egg. Who would watch the Top 20 Countdown with me then?" she joked. The ghost of a smile slid across my lips.

"It's a lovely name, *Persephone*. I'll be sure to change your paperwork." She hesitated with her hand on the doorknob and flashed me a worried look. "If you feel any residual side effects like more pain or nausea, I need you to call me."

The abrasive scent of bleach and lemons assaulted my nose from the floor cleaner, and I winced, but I managed to give her a small smile. "I'm okay, Doc. Right as rain."

The skeptical look plastered to her face told me she absolutely did not believe me. "Swear to me you won't go digging?" she pleaded, genuine worry laced through her tone.

"I swear. And, uh, Doc? Go easy on him. He was just trying to help." I lifted my head in the direction Dr. Dixon had gone off.

"I'll do my best but no promises," she offered with a shrug before closing the door.

The orderly made quick work of my humiliating throw-up situation, and I thanked him sheepishly. He offered a smile then he, too, was gone. When the door opened for him to step out, I caught a glimpse of Dr. Galapagia and Dr. Dixon as they argued, but their voices were too low for me to hear from here. She was red-faced with her hands on her hips. He had his arms crossed, nose upturned in defiance.

I lay down, guilt rocking through me. He had only tried to help, and because he had, I now had two pieces of my past unlocked. First, my name. I turned over and buried my head in the pillow, savoring the new information. And second, the voice who'd spoken it in my memory. That voice spoke my name with reverence, with *worship*. That was the voice of someone possessed by love.

I drifted off to sleep with that voice wrapped around me like a cocoon. They had assured me that it was the cocktail of trauma and sedation that had me hallucinating that first night, but that voice clung to my mind, and I'd heard it again, in that memory. Maybe it wasn't real, maybe no one had come for me, but maybe, just maybe, that voice would.

Persephone

CHAPTER 8

The common area was quiet as I passed through, and I smiled.

Morning washed over Brookhaven with a gentle calm in the winter. Well, what this place called winter. There were storms and mostly gray skies, but the temperature rarely dropped below a shiver and the air felt thick with the sea. I had learned all the states, read up on what made each of them unique.

Louisiana, famous for its Cajun and Creole cuisine, Mardi Gras celebrations, diverse cultural heritage, bayous, music, and is the birthplace of American jazz. The state also has strong French and African cultural influences.

Not that I had seen any of that. I went from one hospital to the rehab facility, and though they had tried, I hadn't been able to step foot outdoors since they'd brought me in.

Galapagia said I was also suffering from "PTSD" or what she explained as *post-traumatic stress disorder.* I had gone through a traumatic event and been buried alive for who knew how long. Too small spaces made me cringe, but wide-open spaces made me feel too exposed. Both spun me out.

I made my way to Dr. Dixon's office and tapped on the door. His lighthearted voice called from somewhere inside. "Come in."

Gently, I cracked open the heavy wooden door and peered around. Dixon was sitting behind a large mahogany desk, papers askew, and scrawling furiously on a notepad. I glanced down, but at this angle his words were little more than scribbles. He looked up, worry trekking over his features, lips flattened into a straight line as he gestured for me to sit. "What can I do for you, Persephone?" he asked, setting his pen down.

I savored hearing my name fall from his lips. Anytime anyone addressed me with it, it cemented further into my mind. I sank down in the overstuffed chair in front of him and tried not to be too pleased at how easily he accepted and acknowledged my name. Despite only ever knowing me as Jane, he spoke it as though we were old friends and he'd been calling me it for ages. I smiled nervously and wrung my hands together.

"I just wanted to thank you. I'm sorry if I got you into trouble. You don't understand . . . It's just . . . My name . . ." My voice faltered and I scolded myself for choosing now to get emotional. I looked up and around the room, studying the medical license hanging on the wall. *Dr. Hermes David Dixon, MD.* He'd graduated from a place called Johns Hopkins.

I made a mental note to look that up later.

"Persephone," his voice was soft with understanding, "it's okay. I knew there was a risk that Hygieia—*Dr. Galapagia*, would wring me out to dry if she found out. I should be apologizing to *you*."

My eyes shot up, wide with confusion. "Why would you apologize to me? I got you in trouble." I fidgeted with the hem of my top as he surveyed me.

"What I had you do was dangerous, as we saw. You could have had a seizure and hurt yourself further. I took a risk, and it was calculated, but as it turns out I'm not the best at math." He chuckled. "We shouldn't dig at the walls. With time they will come down on their own."

His voice was so soothing and confident, so self-assured. I wondered if he genuinely believed I was fixable or if it was solely for my morale.

"I want to go outside," I announced.

His eyebrows shot up in surprise. He had been with me when I had the meltdown as they transported me from the hospital to here. In the end, I had to be sedated to even make the journey. He looked so incredibly wary as he studied me.

"Are you sure? There's no need to rush—" he began, but I raised a hand to cut him off.

"Respectfully, we do. I don't know how long they are going to keep me here if, on paper, I can function on my own. We have a name but nothing else to go on, and the name isn't even complete as it is. I need to figure this out. Will you help me?" I chewed on the inside of my cheek, a nervous tic that betrayed my anxiety.

Dr. Dixon stared at me for a long while, his eyes boring into mine as though searching for some form of dishonesty. He sat back in his chair and steepled his fingers together under his chin, weighing his options. "For your sake, and my medical license, we're going to consult Dr. Galapagia . . . but I think it's an excellent idea."

I huffed a sharp breath and felt the tightness in my chest abate.

A smile cracked across my face so wide my cheeks started to smart, but just as quickly, panic took root at the base of my stomach and sat like a stone. I grimaced, steeling my nerves, ignoring the tinge of fear that trickled down my spine at the thought of being out *there*.

Dr. Dixon stood, gesturing for me to follow him out the door. I stared, alarmed; apparently, we were consulting with Dr. G now. *Breathe, just breathe*, I reminded myself, the mantra beating a bruise against my temple. My feet felt like lead as I willed myself to walk forward, hands fisted at my sides. *This is what you wanted,* I scolded myself. I wouldn't be able to start truly living until I could convince myself the outside world wasn't going to swallow me whole.

In group, we'd talked about our fears and how adjusting to the rigors of the outside world could take its toll, and at the least seem a daunting endeavor. In our private sessions, Dr. G and I went deeper. Sometimes, I felt like she asked questions that surgically cut through me just to see how much I would bleed. Other times, we hardly spoke at all. She never made me feel foolish for my fear of small spaces or the big unknown. This bubble of peace was safe, a haven from those who'd tried, and succeeded, in hurting me, but there was something completely debasing in baring my deepest fears to another when I wasn't even sure *why* I felt that way.

All I knew was that I felt alone, and so very isolated.

The people at Brookhaven were kind. Through the laughing and crying and tantrums, there was so much *good*. Healing and acceptance and growth, they sprang from the tiny cracks in the floor and twisted up the walls like ivy climbing high.

My feet shuffled into Dr. G's office, and she frowned at Dr. Dixon. For her part, she seemed not to have forgiven him so easily. He flopped down in one of the chairs in front of her desk, stretching his long arms and bringing them to rest behind his head as he propped his feet up on her desk. His shoes were something called Chuck Taylors, and I liked them a lot. The other doctors wore such mature and practical footwear, all browns and whites, neatly polished. I loved the contrasting black and white of his shoes, liked the laces and how they crisscrossed up higher on his ankle. They would be the first thing I bought when I was able to make my own money.

"Hermes, get your damn feet off—" Dr. G stopped mid-sentence as her gaze brushed past him and zeroed in on me. Her eyes narrowed to slits as she looked between us, accusatory lines etched into her fair face. She knocked his shoes off with considerable force and muttered, "What are you up to?"

He scooted out the chair next to him for me to sit. "Persephone has had an idea," he announced, and she barked a laugh as she leaned back, crossing her arms over her chest.

"*She* did, did she? Like the list of names?"

Dr. Dixon scrunched up his mouth into a frown, dipping his head once before sucking his tongue behind his teeth. "I deserved that one," he admitted, "but it doesn't change why we are here now. She came to me with an idea, and I think it could be a beneficial part of her therapy. She would like to go outside."

I blew out a small breath, wringing my hands in my lap slowly as I fought back the tension constricting my throat. I didn't *want* to go outside. I *had* to. I glanced at Dr. G, who sat back watching me curiously as though she could see into my soul if she stared hard enough.

"This was your idea, Persephone?" she asked, voice gentle. "You can tell me the truth," she coaxed.

I lifted my eyes to meet her gaze, letting out a sharp breath. "It was. I just keep thinking . . . I can't stay here forever. I'm learning so much, and I know there is so much left to figure out. But I can't live my life in this box. It'll be no better than that coffin if I don't learn to live." I exhaled deeply again, relishing in the cool relief the air brought to my throat.

Dr. G's eyes softened as she leaned forward and rested her elbows on her desk. "If you are sure, and it really was *your* idea, I could be on board with that. I don't have to express to you how delicate the walls of your mind are now, but I also understand your need for answers, need for progress. I'll sign off, on the condition that the minute you feel like you're forcing those walls, you'll back off and try again another day."

Her words were clear, her terms fair. I could be patient, I told myself. "I will," I promised.

Dr. Dixon grinned widely, then stood, bouncing on the balls of his feet, practically vibrating with energy. “Let’s light this firecracker, shall we?”

Dr. G eyed him warily and I often wondered how long the two of them had known each other. I’d spent many days watching the dynamics between the players in our little troupe here at Brookhaven. These two moved with symmetry, a complex dance that kept the place in orbit. He was a jokester, a big kid in every sense of the word, while she was practical and took his playful banter in stride. Their relationship felt more familial than collegial, but they made an excellent team, and it was clear we needed them both to keep the balance in our little world. I sighed.

One day, I would have that comfort with others, with people who knew me well, that I could feel safe with. I just needed to figure out how to feel safe in my own body, first.

Persephone

CHAPTER 9

I stood at the doorway, feet pressed just behind the threshold of Brookhaven. Air was all that separated my feet from the vast openness beyond, and I tried to pull the bile rising in my throat back down, commanding my anxiety to settle underneath my bones. I needed my body to work with me, and yet I didn't know how to convince it to *move*. My white slipper shoes refused to lift, to cross over the threshold as sweat beaded over my eyebrows, more pooling at my lower back. The air outside was thick, heavy with moisture, barely cold in the unforgiving sun despite the December date. December was meant to be winter, a tundra of sorts. Too bad no one had relayed that message to Louisiana.

Dr. Dixon and Dr. G stood just beyond the doors, speaking with each other in hushed tones. Their posture was relaxed, but they were just far enough away that I couldn't quite make out their conversation, and anxiety flared in the pit of my stomach knowing how keenly they were observing me. My chest tightened; they were trying to give me the space to work this out without putting pressure on me and I was grateful, but I felt like an experiment under their watchful eyes.

I steadied my breath and lifted my thousand-pound foot, planting it firmly beyond the threshold.

Right foot. Left foot. Right foot. Left foot. I could do this. I *was* doing this.

A squawk resounded from somewhere up above, a fluttering of wings filling my ears. I glanced up to see patches of sky peeking through the considerable trees and felt my world spin.

Outside. It was too much, *too big.* I had to get out of here, get back to the safety of the box. I was sweating profusely—hot, too hot. My chest heaved and pulled, and I wanted to be anywhere but out here, exposed. My knees buckled; great sobs wracked through me. I needed *in*, but I couldn't tell which way was up.

Was this up? Voices. Muffled, like they were coming from the depths of a sea. Hands, under my arms, pulling, *pulling*. My own fingers found purchase in the grass, the lithe blades soft to the touch.

Comfort, I thought. *Safe*. I wanted it to drag me under, to rip the earth wide and hide inside. Darkness, *the darkness.* Shadows flitted into my mind as my throat locked up, my chest constricting with tension and hurt.

Safety in shadows, I begged whoever was there to listen. The last thing I saw before blissful darkness took me was that piercing pair of blue eyes.

It took me a solid week of attempts to get to the gazebo nestled in the middle of the property. Every day, Dr. G and Dr. Dixon would accompany me out, watch me get a little farther than I had the day before, then hold out a life vest while I panicked through my trauma. They hadn't gotten there fast enough that first time, when it had swelled up like a tsunami and almost killed me. Now, every panic attack was interrupted before I could completely devolve, and I was learning how to cope, how to manage the debilitating openness.

Which brought me to today, triumphantly seated in the gazebo, overlooking the trees and grounds. I had managed to make it here, still with tightness presenting in my chest but sans the hysterics. It was a victory, and after a week of failures, I was happy to have something to be proud of and hold on to.

Metal caught my eye in the distance, a structure that peeked through the trees. *It called to me.* I stood on shaky legs.

"What's that over there?" I asked as I pointed toward the building.

Dr. Dixon shot Dr. G a wicked grin. I watched something pass between them, a silent conversation lingering. Neither of them felt inclined enough to share with me. Dr. G bit her lip as they walked toward me, closing the distance.

"That's the greenhouse, Persephone," Dr. G offered, studying me.

A greenhouse? On the Brookhaven grounds?

It felt as though a tether sat between my chest, pulling me from the gazebo, wrenching me toward the mystery structure in the distance. The pull was warm, blooming inside me, urging me onward. I barely registered when my feet descended the stairs, even less when the grass path rose to meet them. The sky loomed overhead, gray and angry with deep blue clouds that threatened rain at any moment, but I desperately needed to get to that greenhouse.

I needed to see.

Dr. G caught up to me and grabbed my elbow, gently tugging me back to her. I frowned. "Perhaps we've had enough for today? You've already done so much, we shouldn't push."

I scoffed, wrenching my arm free and continuing, determined to release this ache the tether in my chest enacted. "This is the clearest I've felt since I got here. All I did today was make it to a seat. I need this," I croaked, eyes wide. I needed to go there, I wasn't sure why.

They followed closely behind, but neither tried to deter me again. We reached the crest of the hill where the structure loomed against the stormy sky, and I felt my breath catch. The iron framing of the greenhouse was set into beautiful stained-glass windows, twice as tall as me. The double doors stood slightly ajar, and a new rush of excitement surged through me when my fingers made contact with the handles, wrenched them open. The heavy door gave way with a groan, its only protest at my intrusion. I peered in, eyes wide with wonder.

It was an absolute jungle in there. Wild vines crawled up the sides of the glass, desperately clinging to the iron framework as it reached toward the ceiling. Overgrown tangles of plants and snares sat in raised boxes along the floors, half dead and very brown. The cold and ravages of time had taken their toll on this tiny sanctuary, but I felt a kinship to it, an outward mirror that reflected the mess inside me. I looked up into the ceiling, past the glass, and into the endless stormy sky, and that barrier gave me comfort.

Safety. I could see the sky, but the glass also held protection and containment. The excitement entwined like vines with the anxiety that was constantly settled in my chest and before I knew it, I could breathe just as easily as I did inside Brookhaven.

Dr. Dixon and Dr. G followed behind me, mumbling amongst themselves. I rounded on them excitedly.

"Isn't it the most beautiful place?" I crooned as I surveyed more and more of the space before me. There were wooden worktables and hanging plants peppered amongst the sconces. The architecture was old, all delicate angles and iron swirls against the glass. Considering the state of abandonment the place was in, I was shocked all the panes were intact, and I smiled, the motion unfamiliar as it strained my cheeks.

Dr. Dixon stumbled over a planter sticking out just a hair too far in the aisle. I tried, and failed, to keep my laughter in. He cursed under his breath, running his hand hurriedly through his hair to smooth his embarrassment. “I’m not sure that’s the word I’d use, but if you like it,” he shrugged.

Dr. G was staring at me, surveying my actions like a test subject.

I suppose I was.

“How are you feeling, Persephone?” she asked. I felt pinned by that intelligent stare. There was no need to lie though, the warmth radiating from my chest was real, and I realized that maybe what I was feeling was . . . joy?

“I’ve never felt better, honestly. You know, I remember all these plants. Some of them I can tell you their properties, and some do seem new to me, but this space . . . It’s comfortable. I think I loved gardening or, at the very least plants, in my life before. Can I stay? Is it allowed?” I met her gaze, hopeful. I wanted to be here. *I needed to be here.*

Dr. G’s face softened into a small smile. “If Dr. Dixon will accompany you, I don’t see why you can’t come here. We’ll call it art therapy.”

A squeal of excitement burst from me, taking us all by surprise. I think it may have been the first time any of us heard me really laugh, loud and excited, and Dr. Dixon’s eyes went wide, but I could not bring myself to reign it in. This place . . . This moment. It felt monumental. It felt important.

Like little by little, I was becoming.

Day after day, I returned to the greenhouse, and each excursion felt a little less draining. I was still required to do group and individual therapy, and I still read in the evenings, still devoured knowledge in all forms I could consume it in. Each night, I fell asleep with one of the CDs Dr. Dixon had brought me spinning through my ears. The Meat Puppets, Spin Doctors, Soundgarden, and Pearl Jam, among others, often set the soundtrack to whatever dreams I may be having, though when I woke, I couldn't remember them.

The routine I had settled into gave me structure, something I desperately needed to keep myself together. I would wake and eat, do my required work for the day in therapy, and then, every afternoon Dr. Dixon and I would wander down to the greenhouse. The panic attacks became less and less frequent until I could get all the way there with zero spine-crushing terror, and both Dr. Dixon and I took that as a win, though he never commented on the fragility of my mental state. His stewardship of my care seemed somehow personal, the way he devoted most of his time and instruction to me.

He never complained as I spent my time pulling weeds and separating the different plants that shouldn't grow together. The earth was cool and moist, and every time I dug my hands into it, I felt a sense of grounding. I couldn't know for sure, but I suspected Dr. Dixon was the one stocking the greenhouse full of gardening supplies, and for him, I was grateful. Each day, I found it full of tools, spades and other handheld shovels, all essential to the task I'd taken on. There were also gloves and an apron, but I left the gloves untouched, much preferring the feeling of the earth beneath my fingertips.

Bags of compost and soil sat waiting for me, along with various packets of seeds. I worked until my muscles strained and the sun set low, until it grew late. Dr. Dixon would have to pull me back to Brookhaven to eat and shower and start my evening routine.

During our visits to the greenhouse, he mostly let me be. He would sit on one of the benches reading or with his own headphones on. I knew this was his way of giving me privacy while still being present in case I needed him.

Weeks passed into months, and I diligently worked, scrubbing the built-up grime off the delicate glass walls, only fighting

Dr. Dixon slightly when he wouldn't let me get on a very wobbly-looking ladder to get the ceilings. The raised planter boxes grew full of robust foliage and kaleidoscopes of colored flowers.

I cared lovingly for each bloom, each vine that stretched above me. I spoke with them, hands in the dirt, willing them to thrive when they fought me, praising them when they grew strong and tall. Dr. Dixon praised me often for my *green thumb*, and I couldn't help the contentment that settled into my bones when I worked in that room. I ate. I slept. I went to therapy, lovingly sowed the seeds in the garden.

And from the death of winter, spring bloomed.

Hades

CHAPTER 10

I sat at my desk, pouring over the pathetically small evidence files on Persephone's case. NOPD had sent over what the investigators managed to find out, and I was basically staring at nothing of note. I scoffed, flipping the page over. I knew this would be futile, but I had to know if there was *something* we'd missed. The Otherworlder Council had done their own investigation, though it had yielded even less.

Frustrated, I rose from my chair, stretching out my legs to cross through the double doors of my study. There, in the middle of the floor sat that fucking box. I had it fully excavated the day after she was discovered, and Hecate had been hard at work deciphering the spell work that lay carved in the ancient wood, but its origins proved difficult to pinpoint. It sat there, this inanimate object, the source of my rage and anger, centuries of loss. Sigils lay dead and ruined, stricken through with burns etched into the wood, some release of the spell that had allowed her to break free. By some miracle, it had preserved everything inside, including Persephone.

I stared down at it, leering into the knots of planked wood, seeing too clearly the outline her body made against it. The wood was smoother there, worn from centuries of her imprisonment, but the thing that broke me was visible along the walls, on the splinters of wood recovered from the top of the box. With trembling fingers, I pressed my hands over the claw marks etched into the grain, the wood stained a burnished gold from her bleeding fingers, then red as her divinity had faded. The tiny slivers of glass they'd found embedded in the bottom of the enclosure sparkled with the light.

The visions came to me, the distress she must have suffered. The maddening chaos as she begged for me, called my name into the depths of her despair . . . The torment would have been endless. I dug my fingertips into the deep grooves, markers of the passage of time of endless brokenness and bloodied scratching. The love of my life clawing for freedom that would never come.

I braced my hands on the edge, concentrating on steadying my breathing. I should have been the one in this box. I should have been the one with broken, bloodied nails. She had bound her body and shade to me, to the Underworld with those seeds, and whoever stole her knew just where to suspend her body, out of the Upper Realm, but out of ours too, and so the chaos had come for her.

The fall of Olympus lessened the weight of our responsibility in the Hells, but when Persephone was taken, she was afforded no such mercy. At least not at first. My mind raced, wracked with guilt at the gnawing thoughts beating against my skull. Her imprisonment meant that for some time, she was trapped in that box with nothing but the relentless torments of the screams of the dead, the specters and shades that taunted the fugitives of the Underworld. It was a testament to her power that she hadn't broken completely under the onslaught.

It clings to you like a beacon.

Atropos's words resounded in my head, over and over, like a curse. I had to get it under control. Had to focus on the things we knew now and give the looming prospect of her disappearing again as little space as possible. We could do nothing if we remained afraid.

When she spent five days at Charity with armed guards and vetted nursing staff led by Hygieia surrounding her, I told myself it was better to stay away. It took everything within me, but I did not go back. The risk was too great that I would bring danger, paint a target on her as she healed. As it was, we were unaware if whoever hurt her even knew she was gone. I went to painstaking lengths, and enough money to keep a mid-sized country afloat had exchanged hands to keep it as secret as possible. No media attention. *Nothing*.

Then, when Persephone was transferred into Hermes and Hygieia's care at Brookhaven, I told myself I could be patient. We needed a private hospital. The two of them would have to have the run of it if we had any chance of recovering her memories, or at the very least, give her any semblance of a life after such profound trauma.

So, I bought one.

It was simple to find a hospital in financial crisis and swoop in. CEOs were often neglecting their bottom line to pad their pockets, and it almost always caught up with them. Griffin, the former owner of Brookhaven, had made more money than he'd ever seen in his life when I'd made my offer, and he was too greedy not to accept.

Months had come and gone, but she only regained the memory of her name. The head-splitting migraines were a side effect of the chaos trying to break through the mental walls she had erected in her mind to keep it at bay. A small part of me was grateful for the progress, while another deep and dark part felt sorry for myself that she didn't remember us, our life together. It was pathetic and cowardly, but it was there, just below the surface simmering. More than anything, the shame of it kept me from going to her every night.

I lived for the daily reports from Hygieia and Hermes, but the urge to go to her drilled a hole in my skull.

She had no memory of us, but she recalled her love for flora, so Hermes gave her a greenhouse. She labored and she thrived, and still I was deprived of her warmth.

I drank. No, more accurately, I *drowned* in liquor. I missed her, more now than I did in the two thousand years she was gone, the torture nearly exquisite in its cruelty. She was half an hour away and my bones ached, the hooks of her embedded so far into the marrow of me that every breath she took was a command, a call to go to her, to *serve*.

This was my punishment, my penance for loving her. For promising to protect her and failing. For letting her love me at all.

A better man would have drunk himself into oblivion and passed out on his floor, leaving her in the safety of her haven.

A better man wouldn't have let a small, gnarled woman sell a pomegranate pendant to him in the middle of Jackson Square because it reminded him of *her*.

A better man wouldn't have imbued some of his power into it, so he could always find it in moments of strife.

I was not a better man.

I tumbled through the shadows, commanding them to bring me to the very edge of the property of Brookhaven. I stumbled through the glass doors of the greenhouse, this now beautiful sanctuary of growth and spring. The talisman she made for me all those years ago still hung over my sternum, so my death and decay didn't leak over her hard work. My mood alone could have razed this place to ruin. A throat clearing alerted me to another presence, a whoosh of air ruffling my hair.

"You smell like Dionysus's old wine cellar," Hermes stated, voice tight. He didn't look surprised to see me, which let me know that he hadn't expected me to be a better man *either.* He lounged against a worktable, feet crossed at the ankles and arms folded across his chest. His posture was relaxed, a sympathetic look lingering in his eyes, hair tousled, as though I had roused him from sleep.

Well, welcome to the club, fucker.

"Hades. You know you can't be here. This is as close as I can let you near her, you know that." He sounded apologetic, but I hated him for it. He got to see her, *speak with her,* every day. He could hug her and hear her laugh . . . Did she laugh anymore? Suddenly, I wanted to punch Hermes in his smug fucking mouth.

I clutched the pendant more tightly to my chest, over our Bondmark, and asked the question I hadn't had the courage to yet.

"Her . . . Her Bondmark? Is it . . ." My breath hitched as I stumbled over the words that could very well break me in two, my whiskey-addled brain misfiring knowing how *close* she was. "Is it . . ." I couldn't finish the thought, but Hermes *knew*. His lips thinned and I braced myself for what was about to come.

"It's there."

Relief cracked a chasm larger than the pits of Tartarus in my chest.

"But it's . . . changed. It's different from Heph's. Even though Aphrodite has been gone as long as she has, Hephaestus's mark is still vibrant gold. It doesn't glow like it used to, but it's there, I checked a few weeks ago, when she returned . . ." He trailed off, looking uncomfortable. That small tidbit of info piqued my curiosity.

"She's back? Is Hephaestus alright?" I asked, shaking the alcohol fog from my brain. "He didn't mention it when he dropped off some information at the penthouse last week. Does he know?"

Hermes gave a small nod. "He knows. I don't know if they've seen each other, but I hope they don't. All of them, they're horrible for each other, and that's the real Greek tragedy. Euripides could have made a killing on their story. I don't understand why he keeps putting himself through this kind of agony." Hermes tossed his hands in the air exasperatedly.

"Because he loves her, Hermes. He wants her happiness more than he could ever want anything for himself, and that includes *her*." I cast my eyes down on the floor.

"You can't compare your situations." His voice hardened at my silence. "Persephone and you were Bonded. *Married*. All of them at once. She was ripped away by a lovesick psychopath that couldn't let Helios go. This isn't the same as a scorned, meddling goddess attempting to dish out justice that can't be undone."

I knew his words were true, but I'd felt a softer kinship to Hephaestus over the years. Aphrodite had displeased Hera in some way, possibly revenge for her beauty usurping the Goddess of Marriage. For as long as anyone could remember, she, Ares, and Hephaestus were hurting each other in one way or another, unable to help it.

Worry over my friend had sobered me up, but only slightly. Hermes tucked his tongue behind his teeth, drumming his fingertips over his thigh, waiting.

My fingers dug into the soil at the base of a beautiful orchid, a shiver zipping from my fingertips to my heart, stuttering it in my chest. My eyes shuttered as I relished in this patch of dirt, this tangible piece of Persephone. Her hands had touched this earth, her power had coaxed this bloom. A sob lodged in my throat, as pain and revelation and so much gratefulness my heart nearly exploded from it bolted through my body. I retreated, my fist opening and closing as I itched to do it again. To *feel*, again.

She was alive, and I was so damn grateful.

"I know I can't be here," I said, resigned.

"I didn't say anything." He held his hands up in mock surrender.

"You don't have to. I know this is dangerous. I just wanted to give her something." I held the tiny pendant in my hand. It looked so small there, like a single seed of the pomegranate. The corners of my lips ghosted up in a smile. The little meddling seed that made itself matter. It had been insignificant before her, much like my life, my heart. They were one in the same. I walked over to a small garden bed, one that still looked undisturbed. She hadn't gotten here yet. Soon, she would till the soil, rid it of invasive weeds. She would cultivate this dirty, ugly thing, and she would give it life, make it grow.

Just as she had done to me.

Forced to stare down the barrel of eternity without her, I had humbled myself to her memory. In those dark years, I'd thought about giving myself the True Death more times than I could recall, but I was unable to follow through, because what if she came back? What if she needed me to save her?

But she didn't need me to rescue her, she'd somehow done it all by herself. I knew the others would keep her safe if I wasn't around. Persephone didn't know to miss me, to love me. The darkness could not be led to her without my presence. I had never been so close to performing the ritual, taking the mortal coil and shedding it as I was now. Only Narcissus and Demeter had ever been brave enough, or cowardly enough, to attempt it, but I could do it for her, if she didn't need me. I didn't care about the consequences the realms would suffer. I'd suffered enough to cover that debt with a clear conscience.

Even if she never regained her memories, she would have to learn about her history, her goddess-power. She wouldn't grow old and age like the mortals around her, but she could be wounded, divinity so diminished from the fall. Soon, and we weren't sure how soon, her powers would probably start to remanifest, and she'd have questions that needed answers.

I turned back to the dirt, working the pendant deep into the soil, promising myself that I would not return here. Every selfish bone in my body screamed in protest as I vowed to let her thrive, to give her the chance at life with some sense of normalcy. If she found this, if she wore it, it would be a failsafe only. In an emergency, I would find her.

I wouldn't fail her again.

Persephone
CHAPTER 11

Dr. Dixon, or *Hermes* as he had insisted I call him, sat propped on a bench, feet up, eyes glued to the thick book he was reading. The flower bed before me lay soaked with water as I dug through the rich soil. I grabbed the loose pot nearest me, flattening my palm over the top of the small bulb of green protruding there, and tilted the pot until it felt snug in my hand. I transferred the clump of dirt and budding seedling into the ground, willing it to take.

Once it found itself seated in its new home, I patted the soil around it, smashing it through my outstretched palm. Something small and shiny caught my eye in the loose dirt I had yet to repack, and my hand traveled over to it instinctively. I grabbed a handful of the dirt around the object and lifted.

It was a delicate pendant on a dark chain and my breath caught. *Mine*, my brain claimed. I turned the pendant over, brushing the dirt and grime of the greenhouse free from it, revealing a small pomegranate. The pendant sat in my dirt-stained palm, and I felt something akin to happiness take root in my chest. The jagged walls of my mind shuddered, and I closed my eyes, willing myself to *remember*. For weeks, I had this unmistakable feeling of *belonging* whenever I was here amongst the plants and dirt, but this was different. There was something about a necklace or about a pomegranate that spoke to memory locked deep inside me.

Remember, I chided myself. *Remember, remember.*

Recognition danced just at the edges of my subconscious, and I knew I shouldn't push, but curiosity got the better of me. I focused on the small pendant, on the weight of it in my palm. The shape, the color. How it felt so smooth in my hand as I turned it over.

Remember.

Slowly, like a midnight blossom unfurling in the moonlight, a small piece of the wall softened under my advances. The beginning pangs of a headache seeped into me, and I knew I would pay for this, but I pressed on, and forced myself to see.

. . . A red orb. Cracked open and glistening. Seeds in my hand, blue eyes wide with fear. A feeling of determination and then seeds on my tongue, bursting . . .

The headache cleaved me in two, and I fell forward, one hand splayed in front of me in the damp earth, pendant still gripped tightly in the other. My breathing wracked through me in desperate spurts as I struggled to regain my composure, my lungs heaving against the onslaught of panic and pain. The pounding in my temples almost became my undoing as I looked around, searching for Hermes, needing him, needing to know I wasn't alone.

My eyes locked with his and he tensed as I relaxed. He was here, I wasn't alone, I was okay. Hermes had been watching me, yet unable or unwilling to interfere. I knew he thought this was necessary, but the guilt of my initial breakdown weighed on him, I could see it etched into the frown lines on his face. He made no move to rush to me, and for that I was grateful, but he never took his eyes off mine, his chest rising and falling in a slow, steadying rhythm that my body tried to mirror off instinct. It worked.

"I think that is enough for today, Persephone." His voice was clear, in his sharp accent I'd come to learn was British, but I could sense the strain there. He was straddling the line between what was safe and what would impart results for his patient. The pounding in my ears hammered on. "What's that you have there?" he asked, as I slowly steadied myself, willing my body to stand upright. I held the necklace out to him and quickly, so quickly, he was in front of me, surveying it.

A small smile ghosted across his lips. "I think you should wear this. It's beautiful, and you found it so it's yours." His fingers traced over the fine ridges of the pomegranate seeds.

My head split further down my skull as I screwed my eyes shut, panting. "I think I should lie down," I admitted.

Hermes nodded and took my arm, gingerly helping me through the grounds and back into Brookhaven. I was too exhausted to shower, too exhausted to do anything but fall face-first into the covers, filthy hands and all, but nightmares still plagued me. I found myself making my way to the showers, eager to get the sweat from the dreams and grime from the greenhouse scrubbed clean.

Water pelted my skin with far less pressure than I wanted, but the constant rhythm helped me center myself. I watched the nightmares wash down the walls into the drain on the green tile with a sense of accomplishment.

This morning an orderly had come in and replaced my patient bracelet that read "Jane Doe" with one that said "Persephone D." It was a small gesture, but it felt so big to me.

My situation was bizarre, as made clear by the expressions on everyone's faces we had to explain it to, but they were trying to give me space to celebrate the wins, no matter how small.

In my time at Brookhaven, I'd learned so little about myself, but so much about the world. My favorite time was the quiet of the bathrooms after hours. This time was one of the few I was able to be alone, without orderlies or group or doctors. I wasn't a suicide risk, and I had no desire to harm others, so I was just in recovery.

One of the few with something so trivial — dissociative memory loss as a result of a possible traumatic brain injury they had yet to diagnose. I couldn't remember, but I didn't *want* to harm or hurt, and I could regulate how I was feeling, after I got my bearings. Some of the others here suffered so much at the mercy of their fractured minds. It helped give me perspective. I could relearn. One day, I would be released, and I wouldn't struggle to acclimate as much as some of the others certainly would.

I *hoped.*

I turned the knobs for the shower off and stepped onto the cloth floor mat. My hair hung heavy and wet, splattering against my back as I toweled off my body. I turned to study myself in the mirror, raking my eyes over the sigil resting in the middle of my shoulder blade.

The lines were faint, ink long-faded, an almost brownish hue to the sprawling lines. It looked abstract, or so one of the nurses had commented. I thought it looked like flowers, poppies maybe, and a skull if I looked at it at just the right angle. I'd noticed it the first time they let me shower unaccompanied. I had been a fall risk and a bit of a basket case in those first few days. Everything had set me off, and I'd needed the extra security to make sure I didn't hurt myself accidentally.

With an escort, I was unwilling to give myself the time to study my skin for identifying marks. Nothing about it felt familiar, as though I woke up one day in a new body with no recollection of my old. It was disconcerting and it made me feel untethered. I reached a hand back to brush my fingers across the slightly raised skin of my tattoo and felt a shudder run down my spine. Now, it gave me comfort to see the marked flesh there, proof this body was used before I woke up. Lived in. I cared enough to decorate it, and like with my knowledge of herbs and plants, I had to assume the two were connected. Plants etched into my mind, also into my skin. It was a bridge, and I clung to it. *Desperately*.

I turned around to face myself in the mirror once more and took a breath, steadying my hands on either side of the white porcelain sink. I forced myself to stare into the green eyes reflected there, to follow the planes of my face down my neck, over my collarbones. I took note of the way my nose sat neatly between my eyes and how the curve of my lip formed into a cupid's bow as it rested atop the other. I ran my hands over my face, up my neck, across my features.

"This is my body," I chanted, committing every curve to memory. "This is who I am. I am Persephone. This body belongs to me."

I repeated the motions for several minutes until my hands grew tired and my throat hoarse from repetition. The affirmations had been Galapagia's idea, to help "reintroduce" me to myself. It worked. Every time I looked in the mirror, I recognized a smaller part of me that made up the whole. When I first started the exercise, I could barely get the mantra out once before breaking down and failing uncomfortably. This was me. Persephone. It was comforting and heartbreaking at the same time. Now I had a name to add to the affirmation. It was beautiful and authentic and wholly *mine*.

I took a deep breath and turned away, drying myself with the thin towel before suiting up. I let my long hair hang loose as it felt the most natural to me that way, and when it was only barely damp, I'd braid it. That was a skill I'd retained from beyond, and like every other detail I uncovered, I was grateful for it.

Persephone

CHAPTER 12

I continued to work in the greenhouse, and eventually, they opened it for the rest of the patients to enjoy as well for a few hours each day. It made me feel good to see their faces light up as they took in the wonder of the exotic flora I'd managed to coax into bloom.

The pomegranate pendant found its home in the hollow of my throat, a near constant comfort. It had taken considerable scrubbing to loosen the particles of dirt from the many cracks and crevices that made up the seed indentations in the circle pendant, and I was disappointed, at first, that the metal wouldn't shine.

It was Hermes who had pointed out it looked like neither tarnished silver nor gold, but more an iron metal that sat somewhere in between. Polished and smooth and unnaturally cold, a balm against my anxieties that I had taken to fiddling with it whenever I felt even slightly off-kilter. A lifeline in the frigid darkness.

I tried and tried to remember, but no new memories came. I grew frustrated at the lack of momentum, but tried to trust the process, as Dr. G constantly reminded me when I voiced those concerns. But I'd heard snippets of their whispered conversations, knew that my time at Brookhaven had to eventually come to an end, but I wasn't ready.

I wasn't ready to be out *there*, yet.

There was a change in the air, as I worked today, a shift in the tension. The weather outside was an uncharacteristically bitter cold so deep into spring, the snap a death rattle for the last of the season. I couldn't help but feel it was a time of change, a season of growth. My nerves stretched taut, like I could feel my feet dangling off the edge of a wet cliff, because *something* was different about today. Unsettled, I found refuge in my garden without accompaniment, but even that was short-lived. Dr. G and Hermes found me there sometime later, elbow-deep in repotting a bundle of flowers from a smaller housing to the large flower box in front of me.

I heard them open the door and come through, but I didn't acknowledge them. Everything was about to change, I knew it in my bones, and I wasn't sure if I was ready for it. Hermes cleared his throat after several long moments, unmistakably announcing their arrival, as though I hadn't heard, but I didn't want to look at them, didn't want to hear what they were coming to tell me.

"Persephone, we need to speak with you," he whispered softly, as though I were as delicate as the petals of the peonies in my hand. *Maybe I was.* I did what I could to hide the tremble in my fingers, because I had known this was coming. My shoulders sagged as I braced myself.

Do. Not. Panic.

"We know that your memory hasn't been progressing in the manner that you wished, but you are recovering in other ways significantly," Dr. G soothed, but her voice was so far away, I could barely hear her above the ringing in my ears. I was listening to her from buried deep under the dirt, muffled, surrounded by the musky soil and weight of the ground. My heart rate spiked. I reached a dirt-covered hand up to the cool pendant around my neck, leaning on it for comfort as anxiety ripped through me. The cold bit into my skin, steeling me, and after a moment of counting breaths, my lungs drew in oxygen more freely again. Dr. G's voice rang more clearly in my ears.

". . . and we just feel that to continue your journey, you may need to remain in our care, but moved toward more of a hybrid system," she finished.

I glanced into her eyes, searching. She felt uneasy about this, I could tell. It was a sentiment we shared.

Don't panic, I reminded myself.

Hermes stood just behind her, barely close enough to touch. His eyes were fixated on me, studying.

I did my best to plaster a smile on my face, despite my anxiety. "I understand, but I don't have any money, where will I live?" My voice came out high, *too high*, the stress audible. "I know money is important. When do you want me to go? I don't have a birth certificate. Can I even get a job?" Words burst from me in panicked spurts of garbled mess as my mind reeled.

Hold on to the pendant, keep calm. I tried and failed to breathe evenly, but Hermes swam into view, eyes hard on me.

"*Breathe.* Breathe, Persephone. You do not have to leave now," he assured me, and my chest imploded. I sank onto the floor of the greenhouse as tears spilled down my cheeks. He knelt with me, holding on to my forearms in his sure grip. "There are programs here, benefactors, who assist with the transition from rehabilitation. We will get you help with a job and set you up in an apartment. You'll be required to keep coming to your appointments, but they'll be less frequent. Our administrative staff will get you records. *Just breathe.* You're not being tossed aside. You aren't being forgotten, and you are not alone."

His words were so sincere, but his last sentence cracked my chest in half. *Forgotten.* The walls of my mind quaked. Had I been forgotten? The pendant clutched in my hand squeezed a tattoo onto my palm, I gripped it so tightly. If I could hold on to it, focus on it, I could keep myself from breaking into a million pieces.

My eyes swam with tears, vision blurred to the heavens as I tried and failed to hold it all together. Hermes never let me go, but he never pulled me closer either. He was a single tether, grounding me but letting me *feel*.

"Excuse us a moment, Hygieia," he called over my shoulder.

I heard no response save for the shuffling of feet over the greenhouse floor, and the click of the double doors as they swung shut. I looked up at him, begging him to help me. I didn't want to feel this. It was despair. It was a void, dark and deep, and I was falling into it. I lived there with the darkness for so long that I hadn't known to look out for it once I was back in the world. It swelled over me, as I cried and sobbed myself into a shaking mess on the greenhouse floor.

"Is this, is it because n-no o-one came f-for me? Why didn't they come get me. H-Hermes? Why didn't I matter?" The words flooded from my lips, crashing against the silence between us and I felt it then, the great ache in my chest, the big empty swelling inside me. Months, I'd been here and months, no one came for me. I had no more answers than when I'd arrived, except for a name that I only hoped was mine.

"Look at me, Persephone," he commanded, shaking me gently until I brought my gaze up to his. Golden brown eyes pierced through me, his face set seriously, his eyebrows knitted together. "You are *not* alone, and I know it's hard, but you've been so brave, my girl. I'm so, so sorry that we couldn't protect you from what you went through; if I could have traded places with you, I would have, but you *survived*. Whatever they did to you, you survived and you're going to be extraordinary," he swore, but I shook my head, avoiding his gaze as snot clogged my airways.

"You are *not* in that box. We will *not* forget you, or let you stay buried," he promised, and maybe it was just because in the moment I needed to think there was someone who cared about me, but I believed him, believed the conviction in his voice. I shook as the weight of me sank against his chest, as Hermes's arms held me together. His voice soothed as he stroked my hair, shushing my tears, and for one moment, I let myself believe that maybe if I had a brother, he was someone like Hermes.

Persephone
CHAPTER 13

I soon found out that the benefactors for Brookhaven were extremely generous. Hermes pulled up in the flashiest vehicle I could have imagined, cherry red with bright trim and the word "Porsche" set in chrome on the back hatch. It was, as I discovered on the half-hour drive into the heart of the city, very fast. Even as Brookhaven had grown smaller and smaller in the rearview mirrors, it still didn't feel real that I was leaving.

I loosened my grip on the armrest only slightly as we jerked to a stop. This was the first car ride I'd been conscious of, and a small part of me wished I was, again, sedated. Something told me not all excursions were this dramatic and fast, but I resolutely decided to walk everywhere from now on.

The drive through what Hermes referred to as the "Quarter" was beautiful. People milled around *everywhere,* and I could nearly feel the pulse of the crowd. I reveled in the strange mixture of metal and concrete cohabitating with the sprawling oaks under the city's flashing lights.

He came to a stop outside a beautiful, narrow building painted a dark shade of lavender with olive green shutters and front door. As I studied the dwelling tentatively, the architecture of this house seemed both foreign and familiar.

Hermes hopped out and scrambled around to grab my door as I reached for my satchel in the tiny back seat. Everything I owned lay tucked away in that bag. This morning Dr. G had brought me the outfit I was wearing, assuring me that more clothes would be waiting for me at home.

My home.

I toyed with the loose string at the hem of my sundress. It was a muted shade of pink, with black flowers dotting a small pattern over the fabric. It fell on me at about mid-thigh with a modest neckline. It took me a while to get used to the open air on my skin after living in the uniform of Brookhaven for so long. The dress clung to my waist before it belled out around me, and I enjoyed the way the fabric swirled when I swished my hips or turned. My favorite part of the outfit, however, was the Doc Martens she'd given me. I was *obsessed.*

I had seen them on MTV, worn by all these powerful women as they rocked out and sang songs against "the man," and it filled me with pride to be like them. As soon as I'd put my Docs on, I grabbed the Bikini Kills CD sitting on my desk and popped it in, twirling myself around to "Rebel Girl." I worried what it would mean to leave the safety of Brookhaven behind and venture out into that big world, but for a moment, I let myself be fearless. Another part of me, one that grew louder with every mile we traveled from the grounds, yearned for freedom. For the thrill of what *could be* if I let myself believe there was a place for me.

As I looked up at the lavender house in front of me, with the lush oak that stretched its sprawling branches high over the roof in the front yard and the metal gate circling the property, I was more afraid of standing still any longer. The pomegranate pendant sat like an anchor, keeping me grounded as I took it all in.

Hermes opened my door, and I climbed out clumsily. He grabbed my bag and gestured for me to follow him through the gate.

The iron swung open with a small groan, and my steps faltered as we followed the cracked path up to the green door. It opened with a crash as we ascended the steps, banging so loudly I jumped and nearly tripped over a root. A woman stood, breathless on the threshold as she scrambled out the door with outstretched arms. My feet had barely cleared the landing when she smacked into me, wrapping me up in a tangle of limbs and wild black curls.

She was *strong*, incredibly so, as she crushed my body against hers so tight I would probably bruise. It didn't matter that she was a stranger, her sheer excitement was contagious, and I embraced her back as her lithe body vibrated with welcome excitement.

Hermes cleared his throat, placing a hand on her strong bicep, disentangling us. "Artemis, go easy, there's plenty of time." he admonished gently.

The woman, Artemis, glared back at him, her eyes a stunning sliver of silver that shone around irises darker than the night sky. She was tall with beautifully sharp features, cheekbones chiseled from stone. Everything about her, from her stance to her stare, projected fierceness and I marveled at her confidence. She wore a pair of cut-off jean shorts, a black tank top that did nothing to hide the impressive tattoo snaking up the entire left side of her body. I could see the tendrils of it peeking around her midriff and down her leg, encompassing her thigh. White lettering on her shirt contrasted the dark and read *LITTLE PLASTIC CASTLE* with a goldfish under it.

My eyes lit up. "Ani DiFranco, nice." I lifted a finger to indicate her shirt, and she broke her death stare at Hermes to give me an appreciative eyebrow.

"You a fan?" she asked, curiously.

"Oh yeah, I really got into her and Melissa Etheridge the last few months." Her eyebrows shot higher with surprise as she crossed her arms. "Hells yeah. I'm Artemis." She smiled, holding out her hand to me.

"Persephone, but you can call me Seph," I responded a little boldly, reaching for her. Hermes's eyebrow lifted at the nickname, but I shot him a look that I *hoped* was nonchalant as Artemis stared at me as though she could see straight through me. We had known each other for five seconds and yet, I felt as though I could trust her with anything. I shook the thought away as I took her hand.

Don't be an absolute psycho, I reminded myself.

Artemis dropped my hand and swung low to poach the bag from Hermes before stepping into the foyer. We followed close behind.

The living room was absolutely beautiful. The interior walls were painted a shocking midnight blue with the far wall illustrated with a floor-to-ceiling mural of the moon in full bloom. Clouds floated lazily in front and behind it, and if I looked at the art for too long it felt as though the clouds were shifting with the breeze. Constellations littered the ceiling, also a deep navy. The silver paint shimmered in the ambient light as I looked around, taking in the rest of the space. It felt so calm, so homey.

A floor-to-ceiling bookshelf lined the wall to the left, and I longed to run my fingers across the spines of the tomes, to delve deep inside and soak up the knowledge they so freely gave. A comfortable-looking oversized mustard-colored couch sat against the opposite wall facing the bookshelf, flanked by two purple puff chairs on either side. I wanted to sink into the velvet cushions. The glass-top table rested on a stunning silver stag head, while pieces of what looked to be expensive art adorned the walls, an eclectic mix of painted media and photographs.

I took my time, soaking it all in as Hermes and Artemis headed into the next room, which turned out to be the kitchen. The dark and moody theme followed suit with an emerald green coating the walls against black countertops and black glass tile backsplash. A rack of herbs, hung drying on a wooden ladder laid horizontal was suspended from the ceiling. I walked toward the rack, curiously. Bundles of wildflowers, as well as herbs, hung drying out. On a quick glance I noted lavender, verbena, sage, and rosemary. My heart swelled. I wasn't sure how they had chosen my roommate, but I was exceedingly excited to be in this space with Artemis.

I was vaguely aware the two were speaking amongst themselves but there was so much stimulation in this home that I couldn't be bothered to be embarrassed for zoning out. After the plain, light blue monotony of Brookhaven, I wanted to see all the colors, feel all the textures. When I'd had my fill, I turned my attention to the small wooden kitchen table Hermes and Artemis perched at, moving my feet to join them.

"This house is incredible; I love all the colors. Your style is rad," I gushed, studying the stained glass on the kitchen window over the copper basin sink. Artemis let out a small laugh. "I think it's fairly cool. I'm glad you like it. We can add some plants to the space to make you feel more at ease here, too, if you'd like."

I cocked an eyebrow at her. "How do you know I like plants?"

Artemis started to answer, but Hermes interjected first. "I told her. I've filled her in on your situation and the medical needs associated with it," he clarified. My face burned bright with embarrassment.

So she knew. She knew I was a freak with no memory and a claustrophobia issue on day one. *Fantastic.*

"No need for the red face, Seph," Artemis offered with a shrug. It was the first time anyone had ever used that nickname, and I adored the way she said it, so natural and unaffected.

Like it was no big deal to have friends with which to even use a nickname.

I smiled sheepishly and sat in the empty chair nearest the wall. "How did you end up in this type of arrangement? Do you work with Brookhaven?"

Artemis studied me for a beat, then relaxed back in her chair. "My landlord does." She shrugged. "I had an empty room and I'd been looking for a roommate, it turns out the right one is kinda hard to find."

My eyes swept over this beautiful home that seemed to be on the very pulse of the city. "Wait, why can't you? This place is stunning."

Artemis laughed and the sound instantly relaxed me. "I keep odd hours, and I'm in a band. We practice here and we can be pretty loud. It's not everyone's cup of tea, but that's rock and roll, baby."

My heart skipped a beat when she mentioned the word "band," and I had to know more. "You're in a band? That's so sick! What's it called? What do you play?" I asked excitedly, unable to stop the steady barrage of questions from spewing from my lips.

Hermes grinned as he and Artemis shared a glance.

"You like music, yeah? We're a punk group called the GorgonKnots. I'm on lead guitar and backing vocals. You play?" she asked.

"Oh no, but I love to listen. Would it be okay if I watched a practice or two?" I tried to keep my voice natural and calm despite the rising excitement I was feeling, but it was no use.

Artemis stood and led us into the room behind the kitchen. "This is the music room." She waved her hand lazily around as she crossed the threshold. "This is where all the magic and bad decisions happen."

Several thick rugs layered on top of each other haphazardly sprawled across the wooden floor so well that my Docs made almost no sound when I stepped through the door. The walls were a bright plum, adorned with framed flyers and music sheets and photographs of who must have been her band.

The black-and-white photos called out a deep contrast to the extreme colors on the walls. I studied each of them. My eyes landed on a close-up of a drummer, a man with long hair swinging wildly around his face as his hands held his sticks aloft. The photographer had caught him mid-play and it made him look wild and free.

"There's a guy in your band?" I asked, pointing to the photo.

Artemis walked over with a grin. "Ohhh, yeah. That's Hephaestus. He's the only man that gets a pass."

"A pass at what?" I asked, confused.

"At being a man." She laughed. Hermes scoffed, hands covering his heart in mock pain.

"You wound me," he whined, sinking dramatically onto the bean bag near the wall. They volleyed teases back and forth for a few moments, and I couldn't help but notice how easy their banter was. Hermes often seemed more informal with me and Dr. G than he did with others, but he seemed even more comfortable here.

"Do you guys know each other? I mean outside of Brookhaven . . . you seem really familiar and comfortable . . . I'm sorry. That's none of my business," I dropped my gaze to the floor awkwardly.

Hermes waved off my comment lightly. "Yes, we grew up together. Same . . . neighborhood."

That made sense.

Hermes pulled a folder from the inside of his messenger bag that lay slung across him. He placed it on the table in front of the bean bag and opened it for me to see the contents. I sat down across from him on a comfy cushion. Some of the paperwork I recognized, my signature on many of the initial lines, a name change form among them. He slid a small plastic card toward me, and I saw the photo he had taken of me a week ago.

Identification card, it read across the top. I ran my eyes over the line that read, *Vale, Persephone Electra*. Date of Birth: *April 21, 1972*. My weight, my height, even my eye color. We chose the day that I was saved as my birthday, and they used my estimated age for the year.

The name was entirely *mine*.

I'd sat with Hermes for hours, pouring over names to figure out a middle and last that felt nice. Nothing stood out, no repeat of the discovery of Persephone, but I would take the feeling of it being *mine*.

A little blue book sat next to the identification card with the same photo and information inside the cover, but also blank pages. A passport, for visiting other countries. A silver card that read my name and a series of numbers that boasted "American Capital" in embossed letters.

Hermes pointed to my identification card. "Keep this on you at all times, Persephone. It's how you're identified if you're ever in trouble, or if you want a drink of alcohol. I know you've read up on most things, and we went over it with the paperwork, but I want to be thorough." I nodded. "This," he pointed to the book, "you keep somewhere here, safe. You'll only need it if you plan on leaving the country, which you can do, but in your first year of care we would strongly advise against it without letting us know." I nodded again.

Birth certificate. Social Security card. The proof now that I existed. I was someone. *I belonged*.

I traced my fingers over the small silver card with no picture and raised numbers. "And this?" I asked, unsure.

"Ah, that is how you'll pay for things. It's a credit card. We went over this a few weeks ago, you remember?" he asked. I did. "Okay, so you will use this to buy the things you need or want."

We had gone over money, and the value and meaning of it in exchange for goods and services and experiences. I understood the value of trade.

"How much am I allowed to spend?" I asked as I reached inside my bag for my notebook that said "budget" in small letters and a pen. I had been preparing for this. They had told me I was going to get an allotted stipend as part of the program. I would need to get a job, but this would get me started.

Hermes shifted in his seat. "There's no limit."

I snapped my eyes up to him, confused. "What do you mean?"

The corners of Hermes's mouth pulled up slightly at the edges. "There is more money in that little card than you could spend in a lifetime. Buy whatever you'd like."

My jaw dropped. This was not what we had discussed with Dr. G. "But who is responsible for this, then? With credit cards, it means someone must pay it when the bill is due. Who pays?" I asked, stunned.

"A benefactor. I promise it's okay and it's been approved. This is my number at Brookhaven. If you have any trouble, find Artemis or call me and we will get it sorted. Do you understand?" Hermes's face grew serious, a line between his eyes set over a worried brow.

I looked over at Artemis, who nodded in encouragement. Hermes snapped up, his long legs unfolding beneath him with ease. He looked at me slightly apologetically. "I don't mean to drop and run, but I'm sure you're tired and overwhelmed and would like to get acquainted with your room."

Fear slowly started to creep over me. Hermes had been with me since the beginning. The thought that he might be too far away to put me back together if I fell apart did little to settle my nerves. The pendant around my neck burned cool, and I leaned into the bite, doing my best to keep it together. Hermes reached his arms out gingerly and enveloped me in a brief hug, his touch so light and quick it was almost the ghost of an embrace.

"You've got this," he promised. I nodded, my throat choking around words I wished I could speak as he waved at Artemis and retreated out of the hallway through the doors.

I watched him go in silence, and Artemis let it stay that way. It didn't feel awkward to me, only sad as I watched one of my only friends leave me behind.

"He'll be around, you know?" Artemis quipped from behind the drum set. "To see us. You'll be sick of him in a few weeks."

I choked back a small sob, lifting my head back, begging the unshed tears pricking my eyeballs to not fall. I didn't want to appear like any more of a basket case than I already was.

"Did they tell you about the job waiting for you?" she asked, and I could feel the pull of conversation building in the air. Artemis was doing something I needed right now, engaging me without babying me. Forcing me to converse, keeping these tattered parts of myself together until I figured out how to make them whole again. I was not abandoned, she reminded me with every word. She was here with me.

Not alone. Not forgotten.

I shook my head. They may have mentioned it, but nothing really came to mind.

"It's at a nursery in the Garden District. A friend of ours owns it, and they're always in need of someone to help the flowers grow." She eyed me, a small, knowing smile on her lips.

My ears perked up instantly, and I stopped chewing the inside of my lip. "A nursery? That's so exciting!" Artemis leaned forward, elbows resting on the snare. "I'll drop you off on my way to work. We should be on similar shifts," she offered lightly.

"Oh? Do you work near me? I have been studying the trolley lines and bus schedules, I don't want to be any more of a disruption to your life."

Artemis stood, making her way around the drums and to the doorway we hadn't explored yet. "Oh, it's right near it. I'm a park ranger at the National Preserve." Her voice carried behind her lazily as she disappeared, and I took that as an invitation to follow her. Scrambling, I grabbed my bag and trailed behind, following the narrow hallway that led to a bathroom at the very back of the house. On either side of that bathroom were our rooms, facing each other. She went through the door on the right. I followed her in.

The space was surprisingly bright with beautiful, natural light. The bed was large, looked clean and comfortable, next to a white dresser and armoire opposite each other. A small vanity with a mirror sat next to a closet that I could walk into.

I stopped one step in, shocked. One side of the closet was *filled* with shoes, lined up on racks in every style and color I could think of. There wasn't a single pair I hated, and I turned excitedly around to check out what else was in there. The other side of the walk-in held racks and racks of clothing. All of it fun and funky with just a splash of that dark aesthetic I was so drawn to. Bags and purses lined the shelf on the other wall. I pulled the fabric of one of the dresses nearest me through my fingers, marveling at how soft and silky it was, how it smelled slightly of . . . *winter*? Like pine, maybe? The trees in winter.

I turned to Artemis, leaned against the door frame smiling. "Thank you so much!" I exclaimed, and this time it was *me* launching into *her* arms.

She laughed, pulling back only slightly. "Sorry, Seph, I'm afraid this one wasn't me. The job was, so you can hug me for that one, but the closet wasn't. The room is a blank slate, we all figured you'd want to take your time to make your space your own. The same goes for the rest of the house. If you want to change something, do it. I don't mind. I do ask that you leave my room be. It's set up just how I want it."

All of those seemed like easy requests. I moved around her to sit on the bed, taking it all in. "Who shopped for me, if not you?" I called as she turned to head to her room, giving me privacy. A mischievous glint twinkled in her eye as she gripped the door handle, pulling it behind her. "Someone who knows what they're doing," she replied cryptically as the door closed with a final click.

I wasn't alone, and I was *home.*

Persephone

CHAPTER 14

SIX MONTHS LATER

Beep. Beep. Beep. Beep. Beep. Beep. Beep.

I groaned in frustration, smothering myself into my pillow. The shrill bleat of that cursed alarm clock reverberated off the walls, down into the bones in my skull, no matter how hard I pushed my pillow over my ears. With any luck, I'd die of an aneurysm and never have to hear it again. The edge of my mattress dipped, and I let out another groan as Artemis's entire weight dropped onto my back.

"Get off of me, you jolly green giant," I drawled, the complaint muffled by my pillow. "And turn off that fucking alarm."

Artemis crossed her arms across my back and brought her mouth close to my ear. "Wakey, wakey, sleepyhead. I made you a *smoothieeee.*" Her voice was melodic as she sang to me, and a part of me wanted to be lulled by it, to do what she wanted. The other part reminded me that it was six a.m., and Artemis had been awake and exercising already for probably two hours. While she was a morning person, I decidedly was not, and on principle, she was an enemy from the other side that could not be trusted.

I frowned, bucking my hips, attempting to unseat her. "Get off me, you giant bastard! I don't want a grass smoothie, I want coffee and donuts," I whined, kicking my feet.

"That's tough luck, bitch. I made you eggs and a smoothie. Now get up before I add something horrendous to your drink tomorrow." Artemis patted me on the top of my head, hopping off my bed, not bothering to silence the incessant alarm clock as she retreated down the hall into the kitchen. I knew there was no use fighting her. Six months of cohabitation really taught you some things about yourself and the ones you chose to live with, but it was the best six months of my life. Granted, I had spent the first five of recent memory at Brookhaven, so it wasn't a lot to go on, but I was *happy*.

I crawled out of bed begrudgingly, then began straightening my pillows and bedding. The shower flipped on, as Artemis washed off the first workout of the day. She showered in the morning, and I liked to shower at night. As such, we never got angry at each other for running out of hot water, didn't fight for who bathed first, or who would be late because one was left out. Win, win.

She ran in the mornings, blazing through the trails of City Park, leaving the other runners in the dust. She attempted, at first, to get me to go with her, and out of solidarity, I *had tried*, but it didn't take long for us both to figure out that I was possibly one of the most uncoordinated people to walk the earth. I tripped over *everything*. After a twisted ankle and a trip to the ER, we both made the decision I'd do yoga instead.

I flipped on the light of my walk-in and shuffled toward the small shelf that held work clothes. During the first week at Elysian Fields—the nursery I worked for—I'd managed to mark up every outfit I wore with grass stains or composting dirt. I loved my new clothes, so that weekend Artemis had taken me to a secondhand store where I used my credit card for the first time. I'd spent less than thirty dollars but got lots of stuff I didn't mind getting destroyed.

I pulled a pair of well-worn blue jean overalls and an orange crop top from the pile and slipped them on, the former requiring a little bit of wiggle to slide over my thighs as I hooked the bib to the straps and surveyed myself in the mirror with satisfaction. My brown steel-toed boots came next, after a good pair of mismatched socks. I ran my fingers through messy curls, hurriedly gathering the strands on either side of my face, splitting them into two French braids. I grabbed a dark orange flannel to match my shirt and tied it around my waist before venturing into the kitchen in search of coffee.

Artemis was there already with her wet hair tumbling around her in thick ringlets. Her park ranger uniform was pressed and orderly, her hat resting on the kitchen counter. The table held a plate with eggs over medium—just like I liked—bacon and toast with a puke green smoothie. I thanked her and sat down, immediately digging in. I even drank the smoothie, which was, in fact, delicious, but I *did* make a big show of plugging my nose and pretending it was rancid just to annoy her.

She rolled her eyes and took a bite of her toast. "Hurry up or we're gonna be late."

Artemis was like an older sister, or what I imagined one would be like. The day we'd gotten my work clothes, she showed me the way to the secondhand store but also to the various shops and stalls in and around the Quarter. When we made our way to the record store just down from Jackson Square, I'd lost myself in the two stories worth of vinyl records, CDs, and tapes for hours. She never once complained, had looked out for me, made sure her friends did the same. They were all so welcoming and accepted me like I'd always been there. We moved together as a unit, a chosen family that I couldn't dare have dreamt of in the months before I'd come to live with her.

I'd met them all for the first time the weekend after I'd moved in, when they showed up for band practice. I'd come in from the garden in the backyard to the thrashing sounds of punk instrumentals, and the most amazing timbre floating over the melody. The music pressed around me, and I felt my blood sing with excitement. The lyrics were anti-establishment, pro-movement, every riot girl dream come to life. I'd edged toward the doorway, just wanting to catch a peek, but Artemis spotted me and stopped practice to introduce me.

The lead singer, Medusa, had an incredible stage persona and voice. At five foot four, she was small in stature, but she towered over a room in presence. Her voice was soulful and elegant, but at a moment's notice, could scream and yell and still sound like the sweetest song while she encouraged you to Molotov cocktail your local rapist. I'd loved her immediately.

Medusa's dark skin was always adorned in beautiful, delicate gold jewelry that perfectly accented whatever she wore, and I'd rarely seen her out of shimmery and shiny materials. Dreads twisted high on her head, inlaid with spiral cuffs and tiny hair jewelry as it twined into a labyrinth on her crown. Two snakes lay tattooed around her neckline, down her collarbone on each side of her head, each with a set of ruby eyes that drew my attention every time. Everything about her screamed venom, cold and beautiful, like the snakes that decorated her skin, but she was joyful, always quick with a smile and kind word.

Hephaestus had stood next, hand outstretched with an easy smile. He was even more handsome in person, his photograph did nothing to show how much warmth radiated from him. So devastating was his beauty that it took me several meetings to notice the scar that ran jagged down the left side of his face. He kept his dirty blond hair a little longer than the photo had shown, and I surmised it was an attempt to cover it. "How ya doin'?" he had asked, clasping my hand with a shy smile.

Hecate drew my eye last, the sleek black guitar strapped across her midsection sporting a bright pink sticker that read *PUSSY*

POWER. Studded black boots, at least four inches high, and her skin-tight leather pants showed off the powerful flex of her thighs. A glittering nose ring sat on her flared nostril, as long box braids fell in thick ropes around her. Her dark skin had a gorgeous hue, like twilight sat coiled within her, but it was her silver eyes that unnerved me as she took me in. She searched for something in those small glances, and I wasn't sure if she found what she was looking for, but I wanted her to. There was a quietness to her demeanor, strong. An old soul, they'd say.

I'd listened to them practice for the rest of the afternoon, amazed at how tight and together they sounded, fascinated with the music. A few days later, Artemis found me tinkering around with the bass that hung in the music room, and before I knew it, the GorgonKnots were a five-piece instead of four, with Hecate offering to move to lead so I could learn bass. We had yet to play a show with me in the mix, but we sounded really, *really* good. Even with me fumbling through parts at the beginning, there was something so freeing and empowering about playing with reckless abandon.

Artemis snapped me out of my memory, snatching my plate up and pushing a coffee cup into my hands.

"Bag, now, woman." She shooed me out of the house, and I barely had time to grab my tote before the door swung shut behind us.

I bounded down the stone pathway and took in the morning. The sun shone brightly through the canopy of our great oak tree I had affectionately named Lila, and it was already oppressively muggy as I rounded the corner to the driveway that ran parallel to our home.

"You left the top and doors off again, now we're gonna have swamp ass." I frowned as I threw my bag into the back of Artemis's jeep and scrambled inside. True to my assessment, a thin layer of morning dew blanketed the interior and soaked the seats. I pulled my seatbelt on and buckled it as Artemis rounded the front of the silver Wrangler.

"You'll survive, Your Highness," she teased, swinging a leg up to hoist herself in the driver's seat with ease before buckling in tight. She pressed the clutch while shifting into neutral and cranked the key. The engine roared to life as "Cherry Bomb" blasted at inhuman decibels from the speaker bar above us.

"I may die from it, or at the very least, go deaf!" I yelled as she slammed the jeep in gear and tore out the drive. The wind whipped any stray hairs that dared to break rank around my head, and I propped my foot out, resting it up on the footpost just outside where the door should be.

Artemis wove in and out of traffic with ease while I laid my head back toward the sun. The summer had been brutally hot, stifling in its humidity. I thought back on how the seasons had changed, and with them, so had I. From surviving my first hurricane, and by association, my first hurricane party, to the flood that didn't quite breach the porch but stranded us in the house for a few days to drink and play music. I liked this little life we'd built, and the parts of me that had flourished and bloomed with it.

She reached for the volume controls and brought the music down to hear a little easier. "Are you excited for tonight?" Artemis asked, her voice blown wide on the wind. I nodded, doing all I could to suppress the thrill of fear that tightened my chest at the reminder.

Our first show was tonight at a bar called Styx. I had been in a few times and the crazy thing about the place was how much of a chameleon the space could be. For a punk show, it felt down-home and grimy, but we attended another show there that required a more sophisticated atmosphere, and the event staff had exceeded what I thought that room could look like.

I chewed the inside of my cheek nervously. Artemis glanced over as she shifted into neutral and steered the jeep into a parallel parking spot outside the nursery. I unbuckled and grabbed my bag before I hopped out, sighing. My ass was soaked through my flannel, overalls, and underwear. *Fantastic*.

"I'll grab you around five, yeah?"

I nodded as she turned the radio all the way down.

"It's okay to be nervous, Seph," she said gently.

"I know, I just want tonight to go well. Don't want to let all my adoring fans down, ya know?" I gave her my best fake smile and laid my hands to rest on my hips.

She snorted and threw the jeep into gear. "Invite *one* person today to the show. I dare you!" she hollered as she pulled haphazardly into traffic. I shook my head at her retreating taillights before heading inside to my second favorite place.

The day flew by as I worked to pot the baby bulbs into their new, more permanent homes. I tried to focus only on the tasks in front of me like fulfilling the invoices stacked up for tomorrow's pickups, but I couldn't keep my mind off my nerves. What would happen if I got stage fright and couldn't play? There were so many ways this could go terribly wrong, and that panic spiked through my body at the slightest provocation.

The tinkling doorbell sounded from the front of the building, and I sighed, pulling my gloves from my hands as I walked to the service area of the shop. Saturdays, I spent solo at the nursery so Jamie, the other horticulturist, could have the day off with her daughter. It was usually a fairly chill day as we were closed on Sundays and just the floral shop, Elysian Fields, in the Garden District remained open for pickups. Occasionally, we got deliveries here for products, and unloading was a bitch by myself. I must have forgotten we had something today.

I rounded the corner, smoothing back wild hair half fallen from my braid when I'd moved the heavy stacks of potting soil earlier. A man stood in front of the counter, checking out the bloom displays on the shelving there. I stopped short.

To call him a man seemed a sin. He was tall and built, but not excessively muscular. He wore a black leather jacket slung over a form-fitting shirt and dark wash ripped jeans. His biker boots protruded from the hem of his pants, contrasting against the silver wallet chain crossing the dark denim. His face was beautiful, and for a moment, I felt my eyes gloss over. It was like looking at a painting of the immortal gods of old, painted by Leonardo or Michelangelo, and I had to struggle for a moment to regain my bearings.

Blond hair fell in short waves across his face, mussed like his favorite pastime was running his fingers through the golden tresses. I wondered what it would feel like to run *my hands* through them.

The thought struck me hard in the temple and knocked me back to my senses. For the first time in a long while, I felt the pulsing barrier around my memories shake and stir. It decidedly did *not* like the idea of me touching this man. He turned to me, brown eyes lighting up, a smile over his face. I was dazzled by the beauty there, *again*.

"Can I help you?" I managed, only slightly breathless.

The stranger plunged his hands into his pockets, lifted his shoulders shyly. "I'm here to order some flowers." His voice was soft, tender, like warm honey, and I had to visibly shake the stupor from my brain to answer him.

"We don't actually take the orders here; this is the nursery. You're looking for the shop up in the District. It's called Elysian Fields, too, but we just grow them here." I smiled, a strange sensation overtaking me, like I couldn't help but be charmed. Half of me wanted to throw myself at this man's feet, and the other part of me, the part restless behind the wall, recoiled. I felt torn.

My memories had remained dormant for the most part over the last few months. There were certain smells that triggered me, and when I'd read a book on Greek mythology some tiny bit of recognition struck through. It also could have been because

I found I shared a name with the goddess of the spring, and the rest of my friends also shared god monikers. Artemis had laughed when I'd asked her about it and explained how she and the others are from the same small community that immigrated to New Orleans from Greece. Their parents had all chosen to give them names of prosperity. It was endearing in a way.

The stirring in that dormant part of my mind piqued my curiosity.

"Oh, I didn't know. I'm sorry," he muttered sheepishly. "I just passed this place on my bike a few times and thought I'd see what I could get here."

I rested my hands inside the top bib in my overalls and pursed my lips. "What are you looking for exactly? Maybe I can make an exception."

His eyebrow lifted as he leaned onto the counter toward me. "Can I be honest with you . . . ?" He trailed off, the question dying on his lips.

"Persephone," I answered, ignoring the growing pressure pelting behind my eyes.

"I have no idea what I need. It's for a friend's birthday, but it's more of a polite gesture. I don't know her well enough to know what flowers she might like, but I heard there's a certain . . . language to flowers. I don't want to send the wrong idea either." He made an apologetic face.

I let out a small laugh. "I totally get that. It would be terrible to give a Tibetan funeral flower to a girl you want to ask out."

The stranger scrunched his face, tilting it to the side slightly. "More like the other way around. She's a co-worker and she's, well, sixty-five. Wouldn't want to confuse a birthday bouquet with the beginnings of a courtship."

"Ahh, I gotcha. Well, you're right. There is a flower for every meaning and a bouquet can tell an entire story, write out a poem with its blooms. It can be difficult to navigate, but to help with confusion, how about a plant instead?" I gestured to the succulents resting in their individual pots on the second shelf.

He turned to study them, running his fingers across the shelf but careful not to touch the petals or plants themselves. He came to rest in front of a beautiful deltoid-leaved dew plant.

"That's a tough plant, it can handle some extreme conditions."

He gently lifted the pot to his face, observing the little purple-petaled flowers that peppered against the spiky green leaves. "I'll take this one, so long as its meaning isn't 'Hazel, I'm madly in love with you, will you marry me?' because I don't think I'm ready for that kind of commitment just yet."

We both laughed, and though my chest felt lighter, the pain in my head continued to build. I wrapped his succulent up and handed it to him. He pulled his wallet from the back of his jeans, but I raised a hand to stop him. "No, it's okay. We aren't set up to take sales here, and I think Hazel deserves this plant. It is her birthday after all."

He looked moments away from arguing with me before he thought better of it and pocketed his wallet. He hesitated, looking down at me. "Could I maybe . . . Maybe I could buy you a drink to make up for it? If you wanted to, I mean. It's the least I could do." He looked nervous, almost hopeful.

The tension in my brain reached an unbearable pinch and I grabbed for the pomegranate pendant at my neck, willing the cold metal to ground me.

I had never been in this position before. When we'd gone out, I was always surrounded by the others, and though men approached, they never got far before one of my friends whisked them off. I never minded it. It wasn't as though I really connected with anyone like that. I could recognize that they were good-looking, but nothing *sparked*. Even now, the handsome man in front of me, whose name I realized I hadn't gotten yet, didn't *spark*. He was beautiful and I appreciated him the way one appreciated art when it hung in a museum. The dark current in my brain settled, tension coiling around those memories at my admission that I didn't truly desire this man, but I wanted it to fight back again.

Artemis's words echoed through my head: *Invite one person to the show tonight, I dare you.*

Earnest eyes, hopeful brown orbs streaked with sunlight, awaited my answer.

"Maybe tonight? I have a thing tonight at Styx if you're interested. Starts at ten."

His face relaxed into another full, dazzling smile. "Styx? I'll be there. I'm Nick, by the way. Where should we meet up, outside?"

I shot him a coy grin. "Oh, you'll see me, don't worry."

Hades

CHAPTER 15

The months ticked on, the seasons passed and still we made no headway with discovering the identity of whoever put her in that box. The reports from Hermes were that she loved music, loved to garden, still struggled with open spaces occasionally, but his recommendation that she leave Brookhaven to try to assimilate had been a divisive one. Artemis had insisted she come home with her, and none of the others had the nerve to argue with the Goddess of the Hunt. Arrangements were made, homes purchased. I stayed away from the decorating of the house, but I did outfit some clothing for her. I knew what she liked, heard she had a penchant for shoes. I bought her one of everything.

I wanted her to have everything.

She grew in her new life, thrived like a flower in bloom, and I kept my promise to stay away.

I purchased a flower shop and nursery, kept the previous owners on as figureheads so she could work somewhere warded. She lived with Artemis, spent time with our old friends. Hephaestus, Artemis, Hecate, and Medusa played in a band with her. Cate commented on how good she was. Hygieia and Hermes met with her weekly to gauge her progress. It was the best-case scenario, as she got to live and grow with the people we loved the most, that loved her. It should have given me peace, but it didn't.

Instead, I *hated* them. I lived for their tidbits of information, desperate for the smallest morsels of crumbs they fed me about her. I was a thirst-starved man on a desert island, and her name hung over me like water I could never reach.

They told me she thrived, but she didn't remember.

Even when Artemis left out books on Greek Mythology, nothing. My heart panged. Not that she would find anything that was the epic of our love. I had made Hecate use her magic to rewrite our history. All written mythos of us were erased under Cate's power, hidden from Persephone's eyes. All but one; a vile retelling of how she came to be in the Underworld, one Demeter had endorsed during her rebellion. The "Rape of Persephone," a revolting and biased tale rooted in a twisted bastardization of the facts, but it only made sense that if she never recovered her memories, she might go looking for information. It was natural for her to want to know her origins, but the prophecy had been clear; I would cause her destruction.

Better for her to think of me as a monster.

Better for her to keep away, far away.

Better for her to hate me, to curse my name than to allow me to destroy her. *Again.*

Helios

CHAPTER 16

The setting sun hung low over the horizon, casting the ocean in molten gold as it bathed my skin in its warmth. Waves rolled gently in a rhythm as old as the cosmos, their crests catching the dying light like liquid fire. The sky above bled orange and rose, softening to violet where the stars waited their turn, and I breathed in deep the salt and brine, clearing my mind of any fears or concerns, letting only feeling and truth guide me. Out this far, there was nothing but ocean and sky to witness this offering, but I hoped, as I did every year, that wherever his shade was, he would know it was for him. That even thousands of years later, I remembered.

I would always remember.

I straddled my board, still and reverent amid the breathless hush of twilight, salt clinging to my skin and tangled hair. The last droplets of my ride out slipped from the waxed fiberglass into the vast, pulsing sea while I waited for the perfect moment to let go.

Cradled in my hands sat a wreath, delicate as *he* ever was, the white narcissus flowers woven together with slender reeds and fine seagrass, petals pale against the deepening hues of dusk. Their fragrance, faint but sweet, mingled with the air and I let my eyes flutter shut, getting lost in the memory of who he was, the smile he wore, the trust he'd always held in his eyes for me. My head bowed under the weight of my regret, his pain, our lost future, and when the wind swept over me, it was nearly his touch I felt against my shoulder, over the top of my cheek.

With careful hands and a silent prayer, I placed the wreath on the drift. It floated lazily, slowly, from the edge of my board, caught in the gentle tug of the current. Each lull of the waves brought it farther from my body, and I lifted my hand to rub across my chest, over the raised lines of the ancient tattoo of those same delicate flowers and spindles sprawled across my heart. The dying light cast hues of deep russet over the blooms, fragile and serene, spinning slowly as the tide carried them toward the horizon.

A wave lapped at the side of my board, lifting my body gently before setting me down again. In the water, I could feel the creatures moving below the surface, the sharks that circled in the distance beneath me, giving my power a wide berth. I watched the wreath until it became just a glowing speck on the golden water, until it disappeared into the shimmer of the dying sun, and only then did I let myself feel the weight of his loss.

"Happy Name Day, baby," I whispered, voice cracking.

I spoke to him then, about everything and nothing, the words spilling from my lips, from my shade. I asked the same questions I had a million times, asked him why he left me, asked if he could forgive me for what I did to us, but as it always was, only silence answered me.

The quiet was deafening.

I sat there until the sun dipped too low, until the stars rose high into the heavens and the stillness overwhelmed me. When everything of me had drained into the ocean, a weariness overtook my body, seeping bone deep. Under the release of so much, I turned toward the shore, paddling through the glowing swells, leaving behind silence, sky, and sea.

Leaving behind the sorrow and crushing weight of his absence.

My feet sank deep into the sand as I trudged out of the water, my board tucked under my arm through the dunes. I followed the familiar trek over the thicket of wild grass and paperbark from the beach, my footsteps eating up the narrow path of crushed shell and sand that led to my porch. I could still hear the surf from the back steps, a deep, rhythmic crashing that ebbed and flowed with every breath I took. My bungalow sat nestled with banksia trees and scrubby coastal palms, their leaves whispering gently with each pass against my wide shoulders as I made my way through them. The veranda was shaded darker by a sagging overhang, strung with an old fishing net, a pair of well-worn surfboards leaning lazily against the wall, their wax mottled and chipped just waiting for me to make them whole again. I sat my board down on the rack, promising myself to do it tomorrow, knowing that I probably wouldn't. I passed by the mismatched chairs surrounding my driftwood table, where the twilight pooled nearly purple across its gnarled surface and swiped up the coffee cup I'd left there this morning.

I stripped out of my board shorts, slinging them over the porch railing to air dry before stepping inside. The bungalow was modest compared to some of the other homes I'd built, but it felt the most *mine*. Timber floors warm underfoot, cotton throws faded from too many washes, windows that I kept open wide to let the breeze drift in. There was no fence, no gate, just open space between my sanctuary and the sea. I figured if the land itself had never bothered to draw a line between the two, why should I.

Dropping the mug in the sink gently, I headed to the waterfall shower and flicked the tap on, letting the heat of each droplet pelt against me, hoping it would drown out the ache in my chest. I normally didn't let myself dwell too long on shit I couldn't control, but this day, every year, I gave myself permission to mourn. To rage. To spiral but also . . . to be thankful for the time I got to hold him. Sitting in that despair for too long was a dangerous blade's edge for me, but I let myself get lost in it anyway, as I scrubbed the salt and sand from my skin, my beard and hair. I needed to shave, needed to make myself presentable to drive into town and find company among community.

On any other night, I might have. Might have had a few drinks with the locals, maybe even let one of them catch my eye, but not tonight. This day was for *him*.

I had taken lovers over the years. Some, I had truly cared for, but never like it was with him. Narcissus had been a lightning strike, the kind of love that rewrote me down to the essence that created me. I hoped to feel it again, one day, but I would carry him with me until the True Death took me from this world. With a sigh, I turned off the tap and dried off before wrapping the towel around my waist. I made my way around the house, straightening up, when a knock at the door caught my attention.

"Post!" a voice rang through, then the thud of retreating footsteps over the worn wood. I pulled the door open in time to see a driver hopping back onto his bike and roaring away. A brown box sat on my front mat, and I leaned down to pick it up. Inside, I found the replacement battery I'd ordered for my phone, but when I opened it up and slipped it into the device, it only fired to life for less than a minute.

A litany of messages and missed calls flashed across the screen. Some from Ares, some from Hades, but it was Hermes's last message that had my brows creasing in concern.

Where are you? You need to get back to New Orleans ASAP.

It was dated months ago, right after my phone had taken a dunk in the surf and I just hadn't bothered to get it fixed. I pressed his contact to call, but the screen fizzed out, a burning smell emanating from the hot phone in my hands. Apparently, the salt water had done more damage than I'd thought. Unease curled in my gut as I grabbed a shoulder bag and started packing. I didn't necessarily *want* to leave Australia, I'd found home here in Yamba, New South Wales, but the cryptic message and the number of missed calls had me worried.

Dressing quickly, my mind raced as I locked up the bungalow, mounted my bike, and set off for the airport. There was a shift in the air that I *could* attribute to me just being keyed up over the date, but I had a nagging feeling this was something bigger. *Deeper*.

That everything was about to change.

Persephone
CHAPTER 17

"Oowee mami, you look hot, hot, hot!" Hecate praised, looking me up and down as she came through the front door, clad head to toe in skin-tight leather. I blew her a kiss over my shoulder and popped my boot. Medusa followed behind her in a solid, emerald green snakeskin bodysuit and a pair of high-waisted black shorts that cinched in. "Go on, girl!"

Heph was already packing up the gear with Artemis in the music room, and I turned back to the mirror to finish up my lipstick. I stepped back to better see the completed look in the glass, giving myself an appreciative nod. I *did* feel good in this hybrid homemade outfit. The dress came from one of the many thrift store runs we'd made. It was a light pink that flowed into deep fuchsia at the bottom of the hem that fell just past my mid-thigh. The soft tulle fabric clung to my chest intimately and puffed out around my thighs. The thing I adored about it most was the slightly puffed princess sleeves that rucked up around my elbows, just large enough to be extra but short enough to not interfere with playing. A perfect balance. I had layered the dress with a black underbust that pushed my cleavage practically into my chin, but it was adorned with large, three-dimensional flora. I loved the way they made me look like a poisoned flower. Fishnets and a pair of pink pumps completed the look.

As I dressed, I felt a little more of the nerves subsiding, as though I were donning battle armor. I let my hair hang in loose ringlets and grabbed a pair of oversized pink heart-shaped sunglasses the same color as my lipstick and perched them in my hair. I was ready to go.

Artemis came down the hall carrying a few cases, her slip of shiny silver triangle fabric balancing precariously over her chest. Her wide-bottomed black trip pants on top of the heavy cases left little room to maneuver in the small corridor, so I popped up to help her. She handed my bass to me, and we headed out the door to load up Hephaestus's Bronco parked by the curve.

The heavy stuff like our amps and the drum set had been loaded before we started getting ready, everything packed tight.

"This is gonna be excellent. And you look amazing, by the way. Is that the dress I found?" Artemis loaded our cases and nudged me toward the Jeep as the others spilled out of the house behind us. She bounded up the stairs to lock up while we scrambled into the vehicles.

Hephaestus had a few tiny braids threaded through his blond mane, with a pair of ripped jeans and a faded tee that read *COLLEGE EDUCATED FEMINIST SLUT.* He hopped in the driver seat of the Bronco as Medusa settled in next to him.

Hecate joined Artemis and me in the Wrangler, and we were off to Styx, bobbing through traffic behind Hephaestus. That Bronco was clean, well-maintained, and so loud you could hear it down the block. He was a mechanic in his everyday life and poured everything he had into rebuilding her a few years back, or so I had been told.

"Think she's gonna be here tonight?" Cate asked, shouting slightly over the din of rushing wind that assaulted us in the open air as we gunned it down the street.

"I hope not. He's just barely gotten over the last time and he doesn't need that in his life right now." Artemis thinned her lips in a grimace.

"Who?" I asked, completely lost.

"Aphrodite," Hecate answered.

I shrugged in confusion. "And that is . . . Heph's ex? He's never mentioned her to me before."

Artemis's eyes darted to Hecate's in the rearview, a warning. Whatever happened between Heph and this Aphrodite was touchy.

"Not exactly an ex. They're . . . *married*. It's complicated," Hecate offered, reluctantly. My jaw dropped. He never spoke about a girlfriend, much less a wife. Then again, he was always so gentle and easy and kind, but he rarely spoke about himself unless it was in regard to music.

"Let's table this 'til after the show?" Artemis quipped, ripping a hard right and pulling into the back alley of a large, dark building behind the Bronco. I nodded as she killed the engine and we all disembarked, grabbing our equipment. Moments later, we were pushing through the crowd to load in, back staging our equipment behind the opening act playing a thrashing set onstage.

A thin curtain blocked both the opener and the rest of the venue from our view. We finished setting up, then Medusa dragged us to the bar for a pre-show shot. I glanced around, taking in the ceilings vaulted high with intricate white beams pressed against the roof. From this angle, it almost looked like a rib cage holding the place up.

Styx was packed and loud, bodies pushing and pulling together as the band on stage, Muses on Parade, belted out a tempo-busting tune. Medusa bent over the bar talking to a beautiful bartender with blue-black spiked hair, and when she turned around, a tray, full of glasses of a swirling golden liquid, sat nimbly in her hands.

A large hand came down on Heph's back and he turned to embrace the owner with a bone-breaking hug. The man lifted Heph from his feet with ease, and that alone was a feat of strength. The stranger had skin so tan I was sure he must spend all his time at the beach or in the direct sun somehow. And he was *warm*. Even from the distance between us, I could feel it.

His eyes fell on me, growing wide as he paled. He pushed past Hermes, who reached out and grabbed his arm. "Helios," he warned, voice low. I squirmed uncomfortably under his gaze. It pierced right through me, pinning me in place. The man looked on the verge of tears, and suddenly, everyone grew tense.

"I'm sorry, hi? Do I know you?" I asked, a feeble attempt at breaking the tension. For the second time today, the corroded memories behind the protective wall surrounding my mind balked. I could feel the low thrum of a headache coming on. After the interaction with Nick earlier today, I'd slept for a few hours to shake off the migraine that had overtaken me, but I couldn't survive two in less than a day. Hermes murmured something I couldn't quite make out in the stranger's ear.

"No, my mistake." The man, Helios, broke our stare and looked back over his shoulder at Hermes, who dipped his head almost imperceptibly. He turned back to me and smiled, but it didn't quite reach his eyes as he looked me over, almost wistfully. I couldn't help but wonder *why* he looked so haunted. Artemis tugged at my arm, and I let her steer me away, leaving the others to catch up with the golden stranger with the sad eyes.

"Did I do something wrong?" I asked, nervously. My hand slid up to my pendant and I squeezed, centering myself as I fought against the low thrum of pain threatening to rear up in my temple. Something flashed in her eyes, almost like pity, but it was gone as soon as it had appeared. She turned to face me with her full attention, her tone low and serious.

"Absolutely not. Helios has just been gone a long time, and you do very much resemble a friend of ours . . . I'm sorry. We should have told you, I thought Hermes had warned him. He was in Australia, and I know the phone service there is shitty . . . But you did nothing wrong." I felt a pang of sympathy for Helios. He had looked so . . . stricken.

"What happened to her?" I asked, unable to help myself.

Artemis took a deep breath, studied me as though figuring out how much she *should* tell me, then tucked her tongue behind her pearly white teeth, glancing around. "He thought she died. She disappeared and there was no news for a long time." She glanced over her shoulder again, but I could tell there was more in her hesitation.

"He loved her," I concluded. There had been such a deep longing in his gaze, a deep well of haunted pain.

Artemis's eyes snapped back to mine, and she pushed a piece of stray hair past my shoulders. "Yes—but it's very complicated. Now come on, put that out of your mind. We've got a show to do." Artemis instructed, pulling me through the side door that led backstage, just as the Muses were crooning out their last song. The rest of the band found their way to us on their own time as I strapped my bass over my shoulder and plugged in my cable. The ground below us started to shake, and I braced myself against my amp for the turn. Medusa had warned me that this stage revolved so more than one band could be set up and flip sets at the drop of a hat. It was new technology that set Styx apart from other clubs in the area. They were always pushing the envelope, according to the rest of the band.

The room slowly came into view as the lights facing the stage grew brighter and brighter. I slid my heart-shaped sunglasses down and glanced back at Heph. He was twirling his sticks between his fingers at breakneck speed, and I could see him bobbing up and down with anxious energy. He nodded at me once and we started together, him striking a steady tempo beat and me letting my fingers pluck up and down as my bassline fell into the pocket with him.

"We're the GorgonKnots, and we want you to make some noise, MOTHERFUCKERSSS!" Medusa shouted into the microphone. The crowd went wild as she started thrashing around, swinging her dreads wildly. She reached up and unclasped the stretchy cord keeping them tethered, letting them fly free. I stood in awe as they flung around her, almost like suspended snakes floating on the air in slow motion.

Artemis and Hecate were backed against each other, thrumming out the rhythm and leads as they danced and jumped around. I focused on my fingers, willing them to be precise in their picking, but the muscle memory in them made it almost too easy. I turned to walk back toward Heph, who was losing his mind on the set, a flurry of arms and hair, somehow already drenched in sweat.

The crowd loved us. They jumped around, swinging their heads, punching the air as they sang along. The energy in the room was infectious, and I found my head lolling harder and harder as I played, letting myself get lost deeper in the music.

Medusa's every word commanded attention, working the crowd into a frenzied fervor. She stomped over to me and put her small body against mine, pressing her back to my arm as she sang.

Yeah, yeah, yeah, punch your local rapist.
He don't deserve no peace.
NO! NO! NO!
Yeah, yeah, punch your local rapist.
Sock it to him nice and hard,
Just like he said she wanted, yeah.

In a whirlwind she was gone, and emboldened, I walked out a little farther toward the front of the stage, catching the rhythm that had my body moving. I danced, swinging the neck of my bass around as I twirled, my dress lifting and sailing as I let loose. I glanced down and caught sight of Nick, that shy boy staring right at me from just next to the stage. His hands were back in his pockets as he bobbed his head intently to the music, his eyes bouncing from me to the back of the crowded room. I stepped toward the very edge of the stage, dropping my sunglasses just a fraction to send him a wink, feeling just a little loose, a little more electric. The crowd roared as he laughed good-naturedly when a few hands came down on his back, hyping him up.

The pendant around my neck felt like ice, cold singeing my sweat-soaked skin, knocking the wind out of me for a second. I straightened and retreated toward the back of the stage, working overtime to catch my breath. Hephaestus finished the song with a flourish, and I looked around, head spinning. I could hardly hear anything over the cacophony of cheers washing over us, until Heph clapped his sticks together in a countdown, and once again, we were off.

Forty-five minutes later, my fingers were exhausted and sore, my hair plastered to my neck and chest with sweat, but that was the most exhilarating thing I'd done since I'd woken up in that coffin. Medusa belted out the last note while we trailed off in a myriad of excessive runs and trills. I'd lost track of Nick somewhere around the second song, and I'd hoped he'd found good company to spend the night with, because now that the adrenaline was gone, I could admit that I was decidedly *not* looking for that drink he'd offered to buy.

"We have been the GorgonKnots. Tip your bartenders! Thank you and good night!" Medusa swept forward in a low bow, sending her dreads high in the air, then back down to kiss the space just above her ankles.

The stage started to spin again, and I had just started unplugging everything, when a cold gust of air washed over me, sending chills down my spine. I raised my eyes toward an impossibly dark balcony just above us, and though I couldn't know for sure, I *felt* eyes on my body. The last thing I saw before the stage pulled me around completely was the slightest hint of blue glowing in the shadows.

Helios

CHAPTER 18

Hermes stood with his hand on my arm and another on my chest.

She was here, alive.

"We sent word to you—I did and so did Hades. We couldn't get in contact with you. That's what happens when you fuck off to Australia to bury yourself on the beach and the sea." His grip on my arm loosened the farther Persephone retreated away from us.

She was here. She didn't know me.

"Why didn't she know me?" I blurted.

Hecate leaned in, her long braids swiping over me. "She's suffering from memory loss. She doesn't remember any of us. We've just ingrained ourselves in her life now. She doesn't even know who she is yet. I promise to explain it all tonight, but for now, we need to play this show, so keep it together?" She gave me a soft peck on the cheek then bounded off backstage with Medusa in tow, after shooting Hermes a tense look. The God of Thieves' eyes stared after the goddess for a beat too long.

"Something there I should know about?" I asked, smirking. His eyes narrowed dangerously, his grip turning bruising on my shoulder as he steered me to a booth, filling me in on the insane story of Persephone's arrival. I listened in a daze. There were still parts Hermes wasn't telling me, but that was just the nature of who he was, so I tried not to be bitter at being left out of the loop.

"And Hades?" I asked, guilt ripping through me. I couldn't imagine the agony he was in, being so close, knowing she was alive, and not being able to touch her for fear their memories would break her mind. To hug her. If the tables were turned, I would have had to be restrained.

"About as well as you'd suspect. Self-flagellation, martyrdom for the cause. Typical Hades shite."

The first band wrapped up, and an alarm went off on Hermes's wrist. He glanced around the dark club while the GorgonKnots took their place on the spinning stage. I tapped his hand and took a swig of the beer he'd set in front of me.

"Waiting on someone?" I inquired and he nodded, still scanning the room. A small smirk lifted the corner of Hermes's lips as he gestured to the balcony. A swirly mass of deep, dark shadow pierced a black hole in the opera box.

"Hades. Right on time," he smirked.

I frowned. "I thought he had to keep his distance?"

Hermes nodded. "He does, but I knew he wouldn't. I worry he may do something drastic to keep himself away from her . . ." His voice trailed off as he scanned the room again." Stay close, Helios. We may need you in a little while." He didn't feel the need to elaborate more, but tension rolled through my shoulders, a protective aura that pulsed from me. I carried the weight of what happened to her with me with nearly as much guilt as I'd felt for Narcissus.

"Stay calm. You're pushing out your power like a beacon. Go find someone to shake off that tension with. Smirking, he slipped from the booth to most likely go find a "distraction" for himself.

I grabbed another shot of nectar from the bar and slammed it back. The super-sweet golden liquid slid down my throat, the burn settling in my chest. I swept my gaze across the room, scanning for danger, but caught on a pair of brown eyes, the color of warm honey, staring back at me instead.

My heart stopped.

For the second time tonight, I was seeing a ghost, frozen in place as I let my eyes wander unabashedly over the man those eyes belonged to. He was beautiful, delicate, but pain lanced through me when I realized that I hadn't gotten lucky enough to have two return from the dead. His frame was slight but strong, and that leather jacket hugged him expertly, but the nose was different, his shoulders a little narrower than they would have had to be.

The music began and he bobbed his head, but his eyes stayed on mine.

Pressure in my chest coiled tighter, nearly binding the longer I watched him, pain and regret mixing with the lust dancing inside my belly. Those eyes lit something in me, called to a door I'd shuttered two thousand years ago. I hadn't fucked a mortal, or otherwise, with brown eyes since. None of them were quite right, and I'd only see *him*. My greatest failure. The one I'd let down the most.

I had let him down and he had been deceived into betraying us, became nothing more than collateral damage in the name of the Olympians. Two thousand years, and I still burned for him, deep down. No amount of drink or sex or denial ever soothed the ache . . .

And yet.

The Otherworlder by the stage gave me a small smile before turning back to the band, and my eyes followed his to the Goddess of Spring. She looked the same but different, somehow younger than I'd remembered. If she truly had no memory, then I supposed the person she had grown into had been her own, shaped without the fingerprints of an overbearing mother, a manipulative father. Persephone looked adorable in her bubble-goth outfit and heart-shaped sunglasses, but when she tilted her head down and leveled a wink at the brown-eyed stranger, I felt my chest swell with possession, with curdling jealousy that sat hot and thick.

Not for her. No, it was for *him*. The way that wink earned a smile, at the catcalls and whistles and back pats of encouragement. How embarrassment at the praise painted his cheeks ever so softly in a blushing pink. I wanted to be the one to pull those reactions from his bones. *Mine*.

The thought shook me hard, and I returned to my senses, reeling. The nectar shooting straight to my cock. Maybe I just needed release, needed to find a safer outlet that wouldn't flay me alive with guilt or longing in the morning after the thrill and drink had worn off. To fuck was one thing, but not someone who looked so close to him. It felt like being unfaithful.

As if on command, a gorgeous woodland nymph glided into my view, all blonde hair and long legs barely clad in a slip of a dress. She bit her lip as she circled me, pressing her chest into the hard planes of my torso, fingers skating under the hem of my tee as she looked up at me. Otherworlders had a sense about one another, could feel when the vibes were right, and it was clear by the heat in her eyes she had been hunting me before I'd even seen her. I let myself get lost in her eyes, blue eyes. *Safe eyes*. Her hands drifted up, curling around my neck as she leaned up to kiss near my ear.

Yes, this was *exactly* what I needed. She needed it, too, judging by the heat coming from her core as I slid my hands down her sides, her body supple and incredible.

"Let's get off the dance floor," she encouraged, taking my mouth onto hers, sucking my bottom lip. My dick lengthened in my jeans as her scent enveloped me, a rumble of satisfaction bubbling up from my chest. I palmed the globes of her ass, pressing her farther into me, and bent my chin in to kiss and nip the soft flesh of the crook of her neck.

A pair of brown eyes leered at me, hot with desire, from across the club, all thoughts of the stage abandoned as he watched us retreat. The nymph in front of me walked me backward into a hallway in the darkness and I allowed it, but my eyes, traitorous as they may be, stayed on him until the crowd grew too dense to see past. Retuning my attention to the beautiful nymph in front of me, I pressed kisses into her neck, down her breasts, back up to her lips. She felt good under my hands, obedient as she let me take full control. Her fingers traced back down the muscles of my abdomen until her hand disappeared completely into the waistband of my jeans. Pleasure curled my toes as she grasped my cock hungrily, pulling a groan from my lips.

"I've never fucked a titan before," she mused, stroking me from root to tip.

"Wrap those pretty lips around it and get a little taste first," I commanded. The nymph smirked up at me devilishly as she unzipped my jeans, and I leaned my head back against the wall, closing my eyes, fists in her blonde tresses, guiding her to kneel. The view of her on her knees, the underside of my shaft resting against her cheek was precisely the distraction I needed. She took the tip of me into her mouth, swirling her tongue expertly as she sucked me deeper, faster. I pulled her closer, applying just the tiniest bit of pressure, but otherwise, let her set the pace. This was a marathon, not a race, and I didn't want her too sore to take me until I came.

She did her work, sucking me into hollowed out cheeks, pretty blue eyes lust drunk as she gagged so beautifully. "How does that cock taste, hmm? Don't be afraid to make a mess, baby," I encouraged, brushing stray pieces of her curls past her face. She moaned, nodding her answer and the vibrations sent me to the moon. I let my eyes fall shut, getting lost in the moment, just feeling, but a tingling jolt tore through me, nearly causing me to come on the spot. I hissed as a second pair of hands made their way up my body, soft and delicate, sending sparks of electricity over my skin in their wake.

I opened my eyes as the nymph bottomed me out in her throat and saw golden brown irises, hooded with lust, staring up at me from behind her. His fingers curled over mine in her hair, guiding her movements, and she suctioned around my cock, reaching a hand back to grab his jean clad leg in permission. I let out a pant as she took me deeper, harder, as he bent his beautiful face toward mine, swallowed the noise with his mouth, his lips soft and hungry against mine. He was hot. *So hot*. Supernova fire that shot straight to my balls, and I had to ease back before I ended this party before it could even get started.

The kiss was electric wildfire, but I needed *more*, wanted his hands on me everywhere as she sucked me off. All thoughts of caution, of how against my carefully crafted rules regarding someone that looked the way he did, silenced. He pushed away from me, and I dropped my hold on the nymph, desperate to pull him back, fucking needy to feel him again.

He bent low, wrapped his fist in her hair, gently tugging her head back until she let loose my cock with a wet pop. He grinned, his face inches from hers. "That's enough of that, love. That isn't for you." Soft, deadly words sent a chill of anticipation through me. She whined, mouth seeking my shaft, but he just kissed her deeply, sending more liquid lust burning through my body as he whispered, "don't worry, I'll take care of you. I'll make it feel so fucking good," he promised. She smiled as he closed in with another kiss, melting for him as I stood over them both, panting. His voice was comforting as he explored her mouth between whispers, hot and deep. I wanted to kiss him until I devoured all the little sounds that mouth could make.

Watching the way he dominated her made my throbbing cock ache, but the cool air of the nightclub reminded me we weren't somewhere exactly private. As though reading my thoughts, he lifted the nymph to her feet, then grabbed my hand, leading us deeper into the darkness the alcove provided, all thoughts of potential threats silenced. Suddenly, the nymph's legs were wrapped around his waist as he pinned her to the wall, long, deft fingers digging into the thick expanse of her thighs. His leather jacket hung haphazardly off his frame as he plunged those fingers inside her cunt and she cried out, clawing against his back while he worked her over.

Her eyes glazed as he rolled his hips, teasing, the wet sounds of his ministrations filling the very small space as he focused all his attention on her pleasure. I couldn't bear to be on the sidelines for one more damn second, and desperation propelled me forward, had me grabbing for them both. I brought my chest to his back, felt him quiver slightly at the touch as a satisfied groan ripped through my chest. The nymph was falling apart around the two fingers he had plunged deep, and I watched over his shoulder as he swirled over her clit, demanded her pleasure, ground his hips into her spread thighs. The poor girl's eyes were almost to the whites with how far back in her head they rolled, a thing of beauty to witness. Her body shook as I reached around him to the nipples peaked in her dress, squeezing through the thin silk fabric with gentle pressure, as she chased her pleasure.

"See, so fucking good, isn't it?" he asked, smirking as he placed gentle kisses to the side of her mouth, over her brow.

"Oh Fates, this is, oh my *gods*," she whined, lips trembling as she dug scratches into his neck. She came with a shake, desire flooding from her core, soaking his hands and jeans.

"Exquisite," he rasped, voice catching like he was close just from being between us. I pulled his jacket down nimbly, let it drop to the floor and the smell of him, so light and airy drew me closer. His fitted tee was soaked and so off that went too, as I placed a kiss in the center of his back. My lips tingled at the contact with every drag down his spine, and he moaned, rotating his hips to grind back into me. I reached around to fumble with his pants button and zipper, needing to feel him in my hands. He was still talking to the nymph, coaxing her body down from the orgasm he just ripped from her, but an uncontrollable wave of need washed over me, and I *had* to be inside him. I *needed* to claim him, own his moans.

I tugged his pants down to expose his smooth, toned ass, biting back a low growl. It was *perfect*. It swelled just slightly at the drop, and I ached to taste him, to devour, to mark that beautiful skin. He kissed her again, body pressed against hers as I knelt down and spread him apart and, like the obedient nymph he was, he adjusted his stance, opening for me. From my knees, I could see his cock pressed between them, covered in her slick. I spat into my hand and gripped him between his legs, stroking the soft skin of his seam, my fist tight on his shaft. He was warm in my palm, against my fingers, and the way they both whimpered when I smeared his cock head against her drenched lips set off a feral need inside me. I shifted, peeking around the side of his hip to get an unobstructed view as I lined his cock up with her entrance.

"Go on, then. Give the lady what you promised her," I instructed as his hips punched up, weight shifting as she cried out in pleasure from the stretch. He was careful with her, as he slid her slowly over his cock, thrusting deep. He pinned his hips against hers as she whimpered against him, her legs shaking. Unable to resist, I shifted back around and split open his cheeks, my fingertip ghosting over the pretty little hole winking at me as he clenched and released. I gathered some spit on my tongue and pressed it against his knot, savoring the way he bucked hard, forcing a moan from them both. I traced my tongue around his ring, tempting and teasing to open him up, before pressing a thick finger inside, pushing and pulling the crook to spread him.

He pulsed around my knuckle as he rocked his hips into her, still talking. "That's it, sweet girl, take it deep. I want to feel you from the inside when you come again. Do you like that?" He thrust harder, faster as he grabbed her chin and forced her to look at him. "So pretty when you're drunk on my cock, aren't you?" he teased. Lost in a daze of lust, she nodded her head.

I licked him deep, down to the seam of his balls, and he whipped his head around to stare down at me. I had never felt less in control than I did at that moment, but I didn't care. If this little vixen wanted control, I was going to give it to him—for now.

"Need. You. Inside. *Now*," he bit out between each thrust.

Without hesitation I stood, reaching a hand into my pocket to grab a small packet of lube. I hadn't expected the night to end like this, but I wasn't the kind to leave it to chance considering my size. I ripped it open with my teeth, coating my cock one handed, stroking harshly. Around us, there was no music, no club or people, only the sound of her moans and his erratic breathing. The tip of my cock, swollen and red, desperate for attention as I dragged back the skin over my shaft, ached to be buried deep inside the tight hole in front of me. I slid the fat head along his crease until the tip was lined up with him, my heart thundering in my chest in anticipation. It startled me, how different this felt, how instant the need had struck, the kismet that he'd come to find us. His body tensed as I pushed into the first ring of resistance, savoring the muffled whimper that fell from his lips as his hips stilled. I could feel his arm moving, sliding his fingers around her clit while he adjusted to my cock.

I grabbed his hip, steady between my fingers, inching in slowly, mixing some more spit in with the lube as I fucked him. The last thing I wanted to do was hurt him. He let out a stream of pants as he sucked me deeper inside his body, and I closed my eyes to the stars that were building there. My own body shuddered as he rolled his hips back with a smack, taking a little more control as I struggled being so deep. His back pressed flush against my chest, until there was nothing between us but trickles of sweat and the fabric of my shirt.

I slid my hand up under his arm, wrapped my fingers around his throat, and Fates, he *melted*, so pliant, so good for me. He had been sexy as hell commanding the nymph, but it was different now. That possessive fire welled up in my chest as I squeezed the sides of his neck firmly, pistoning my hips into him, deeper and harder with each thrust. He moved too, every jolt pushing his cock farther into her.

I had fucked a lot in my extensive lifetime. Men, women, individuals who fit neither or both categories . . . but I hadn't felt this type of connection in so long.

Two thousand years to be exact.

My hips faltered, jerking erratically at the thought, at the catch in my chest. Now was not the time to think of *him*. I growled into this stranger's ear, picked up the pace, using his body the same way he used mine. I was going too hard, almost punishingly so, but he never wavered, only took and gave, moving between us like a conduit.

I was nearing my pleasure, and he was, too, I could feel it in the way his tight hole gripped and fluttered around my cock, but he was talking to her again, praising her for how good she was doing. It wasn't possible but somehow my erection got *harder.*

"You wanna come? Take it like a good girl. That's it, look at him. Open your mouth for me, love." His fingers came up as he pressed the pads of three of them deep into her mouth, sliding over her tongue. I tightened my hold on him as I drilled deeper, giving him every fucking inch.

He turned his eyes to me, arching his neck, wearing my hand like a necklace. "Can I come, sir?" He panted, breathless, desperate. His fair golden hair lay plastered to his forehead, slicked with sweat, his eyes shining with unbridled lust.

I pushed harder, bottoming out completely to the base, watched as those beautiful pupils blew wide with pleasure. He whimpered, matching my pace with his own thrusts, throwing himself back until he swallowed me completely.

"Name?" I demanded.

"Nick," he answered, rocking between the nymph and me with abandon.

I groaned, pulling his head back impossibly far. A blissed-out smile lit his face as I took him roughly, balls slapping against his backside with satisfying thumps.

I flicked my eyes to the nymph barely holding on as he fucked into her. "Senna," she choked, biting her lip. The pressure in my balls built past the point of return, and I stretched the hand on his hip out to knock his hold from around her throat away, replacing it with my own. I could feel their pulses under my fingers, and my cock swelled at the rush it gave me.

I looked the nymph in the eyes. "Senna, come."

I watched the switch flip, the reflection of me fucking him, fucking her in her gaze the hottest thing I'd ever seen. He looked like an angel in his rapture, as she clamped down on Nick's cock. Flowers bloomed across her skin, tiny hues of blue as they burst forth from her hair and arms. He let out a string of curses as she writhed on top of him, running from the fingers he held on her clit.

"Nick," I breathed, and I felt him tighten into a vice as I pushed in. "I know you enjoyed working Senna up, but you don't need to be in control anymore. I've got you. Give it to me." I bent lower, just below his ear, took his lobe between my teeth before dragging my lips to his neck.

"Daddy's home, Nick. *Come*," I demanded, sinking my teeth deep into his tender flesh.

The words were a command, and they tore through him with the force of a hurricane. The power of his orgasm released into a still-coming-down Senna, and I watched in amazement as white blooms burst across his own chest, petals falling around us as more appeared on his shoulders.

Lightning shot down my spine, and I spilled into him with one last thrust. My fingers dug into Nick's flesh in a bruising grip as I filled him up, nearly blacking out from the force of it all, growling like a wild animal against his skin.

They slumped against each other, then back into me, the three of us panting in stuttering rhythms. I planted a soft kiss on his shoulder, soothing the reddened bite before pulling out of him gently. My half-hard cock smacked against my leg with a wet thud, and I reached to grab my pants and pull them up. I tucked my cock inside and fastened the button as Nick pulled out of Senna, who straightened her tube dress and gave us both a parting kiss before skittering off, glowing and freshly fucked.

Persephone

CHAPTER 19

The breakdown took considerably less time than setup did, but I attributed that to the adrenaline wearing down now that I was offstage and the exhaustion of the day settled in. We stood huddled together, breathing hard. Artemis insisted this was a ritual Hecate made them do, but I could feel that she needed it too. It was a way to share the energy of the show, to make sure everyone came down safely.

"That was fucking insane," Medusa panted, her head resting heavily on Hephaestus's shoulder. I nodded in agreement.

"Is it always such a rush?" I asked, and they all nodded.

"You did so well! I can't believe how natural you are," Hecate praised, reaching to hug me.

"Got our own lil' prodigy riot girl here." Heph chuckled, mussing up my hair.

I squirmed away from him and landed a punch on his shoulder. "I did okay. You guys were so good. Medusa could have probably ordered them to give her their firstborns, and they would have done so happily." She smiled. This was *good*. Amazing. The best day of my life. We broke apart to finish clearing up, eager to load out. Heph was breaking down his kit when I heard him cuss, feeling around his pockets, tossing cases around.

"What's up, dude?" I asked, walking over. My breakdown had taken all of twenty minutes.

"I lost my drum key." He was annoyed, eyes frantically searching, "I'd rather not try to pry it off by hand. I think I have an extra in the Bronco. I'll be right back." He turned, but I stopped him.

"Let me get it. I'm dropping these off anyway, and I can look while I'm out there," I offered, and he nodded his thanks. I grabbed my case and cable bag as I made my way to the Bronco, popping the hatch and settling my stuff inside, then opened the door to the backseat, grabbing his satchel. I rooted around inside until my fingers closed around the T-shaped key. My skin prickled as I closed the bag and backed up to shut the door, the air suddenly degrees colder than the humidity should have allowed.

A muffled cry sounded from somewhere behind me. I froze, the hair on the back of my neck standing up. I whipped my head back and forth, sweeping the dark alley. *Nothing*. I shut the door, and then I heard it again, only this time I was certain. A cry. My heart rate sped up, adrenaline flooding through my system as I whipped around, searching again for the source.

The "*Help*" was muffled, but it was there.

I wrenched the door back open and grabbed the tire iron Heph kept on the floorboard, then took off toward the sounds that were building up, permeating through the thick night air. My pumps hit the ground in hurried wet smacks with every step I took. I followed the noise out the alley, down across the street into another side road. A single streetlight illuminated the pavement as I raised the tire iron protectively across me, searching for the person in distress. A shuffling noise caught my ear. I whipped around.

A man walked from the darkness toward me, other shadows emerging slowly behind him. I glanced around, assessing routes to freedom, but there were none. I was trapped. I should have gone for help first, but I couldn't think about that now with adrenaline flooding through my system. My grip on the tire iron tightened as I willed myself not to panic. The shadows were other men, and a few women. They looked normal at first glance, but there was something not right about their movements, something off with the slow but jerky tics of their limbs as they pinned me in closer to the back of the alley.

I raised the tire iron. "Don't do this, whatever this is," I warned, with more confidence in my voice than I felt. Fear shook through me, urging me to run. *But where?* Where could I run? I was boxed in. A red glimmer flashed in their eyes as the one closest to me opened his mouth to speak. But it wasn't just him. Their lips parted in unison, eyes glowing a bright red, and spoke as legion.

"Stupid flower *whore*. You should have stayed below the ground. But no matter, I can drain the life from you now. Go ahead and scream. There is no one coming."

I shook my head once, backing away steadily. Slowly. These monsters, whoever they were, were right. No one was coming for me. I wasn't even near the club at this point. The others wouldn't know where to even look for me. Fear licked down my spine, the metal of the tire iron grew hot in my sweat-soaked grip.

The crowd drew closer, until the first was only a few feet from me. I raised the tire iron and swiped it in front of my body, clearing the space in warning. I wouldn't scream, wouldn't give these sick fucks the satisfaction. The leader was too close now, and I swung again wildly, determined not to end up a statistic. With a sickening crunch, the iron sank into the man's skull. Blood burst around us in a warm spray.

He didn't so much as flinch.

He reached forward calmly, grappling the tire iron from my hands with incredible strength. I used the proximity to try and rush past him, but that only earned me a heavy fist to the temple. I skidded to the ground, gravel tearing at the exposed flesh beneath my fishnets, my head banging heavily against the asphalt. My brain rattled in my skull from the impact. The pain blurred my vision as he continued his slow advance, mumbling something I couldn't quite hear. I gripped my pendant tightly, so tightly, hoping the pain would ground me so I could get up.

Get up. You can't die here. Unfortunately for me, the thought bitter on my tongue, I just might.

I had cheated death once before and maybe one was all you got in this world. *At least I was going to die in a bitchin' outfit.* A laugh choked its way out of me, and still, I squeezed the pendant. I was lightheaded, everything around me blurred and buzzed in the moonlight. Before he could reach me, a commotion sounded behind him and a set of strong legs landed in front of me, clad in leather.

Hecate stood, a fierce warrior protectively blocking me from the monster that would have killed me. I didn't even see her move to get in between us, but as she raised a curved blade—*a kukri,* my mind reminded me, though I had no idea how I knew that—I saw a glimpse of the power rolling from her. The cropped black tank top clung to her, highlighting the strong muscles of her back and arms as she flexed, daring any of these men to try her. Her black pants shimmered in the moonlight; thigh-high combat boots buckled up her legs. Hecate's long braids swayed as she readied herself for a fight.

"Stay down, Seph. They won't touch you," she shouted over her shoulder, and I could hear the urgency in her tone. I believed her. I'd never seen Hecate look so angry, and flashes of something else inched into my vision. *Three of her, clad in black silk, knives at the ready.*

The first crazed creature lunged for me, and true to her word, Cate's justice was swift. She intercepted him with an upward swing of her blade that left him separated from his arm. It hit the grimy alleyway street with a sickening crunch. I bit back a scream.

Somehow losing an arm didn't seem to affect the creature as he backed up, searching for an opening. Red eyes flicked back and forth endlessly, and though my fear was palpable in the air, all I could feel coming off of Hecate was a quiet, deadly darkness.

The creature lunged again, and she ducked, coming up from below its waist, slicing through his torso. Her blade was impossibly sharp, the cut looked like it barely took any effort on her part.

She turned back to me as the corpse collapsed to the ground, wiping the red slick from her blade as she surveyed my body. "Are you hurt, Seph?" Her tone was soft, but I could hear the hard edge there, see it in the determined set of her lips under her dark makeup. Thick red rivers pooled from the body around her feet. She looked every bit the avenging goddess, and I could do little more than stare in awe at her.

She *killed* a man. *She killed him.*

I shook my head, and she dipped her chin once. With the immediate threat gone, I was able to see what was happening behind us, and my head throbbed in confusion at *what* I was seeing. The other red-eyed people were locked in battle with . . . Well, with the rest of the GorgonKnots, and a few others from the club.

Hephaestus had a long-handled maul and was engaging two of the creatures at once. *Where the fuck did he get a maul?* Artemis had a silver bow and knife, and she alternated stabbing and shooting at her leisure. The arrows looked like pure moonlight as they pierced flesh. Medusa had an athame in each hand, dreads moving independently around her, lashing forward as she lunged, like snakes striking. Helios had a sword, and that shit was *definitely* ablaze. I blinked tears from my eyes, sitting up against the brick. Cate had moved toward . . . Holy shit, was that *Hermes*?

What in the actual fuck was happening here?

It was him, my eyes confirmed that shit-eating grin even in the dim light of the alley. He moved impossibly fast, but I couldn't see a weapon in his hands. Hermes was just plain old beating the shit out of them with his fists. There were so many red eyes flooding the alley at this point that as soon as one of ours dropped one, two more appeared from the shadows. There must have been ten bodies already felled, including the one in front of me.

My mind struggled against the wall holding back the dam and the headache intensified.

Not now, I pleaded.

I needed to get up. I *needed* to help them. I crawled through the pain, wincing at the gravel and glass now slicing into my exposed flesh, and grabbed the discarded tire iron. I used the wall to help me stand and turned, pleading with my mind to just keep the splitting headache at bay. Something warm dripped slowly down my temple, but I ignored it to move forward. My vision blurred, my head reeling from the blow and battery and the valley of pain digging through the middle of my skull.

A creature appeared in front of me, menacing, snapping its teeth.

Eyes as red as a rose and twice as deadly as its thorns. I planted my weight on my back foot and brandished the tire iron in front of me. Woozy, my world tilted on its axis as I tried hard to maintain control, but that failure had me sliding back down the wall in a heap of tulle and muck. A black vortex of shadows appeared to my right at the edge of the alleyway, and the creature registered the disturbance in temperature too. A man stepped from the shadows, let them lick and slide from his skin. A man? No, not a man. Death. *Death had finally come to reap me*. The reaper closed the distance between us, his shadows winding and twinning around the creature's body, pulling it to heel in front of me, restraining it.

"She will never be safe, and you will never know peace. I will find a way to take her, and this time it will mean the True Death," it spat at him through gritted teeth.

"You can certainly fucking *try*," he growled, his voice low and deadly. Every nerve in my body reacted as that voice broke through a piece of the wall inside my mind. Something deep and forbidden leaked out like the blood that flowed in a river down the side of my temple.

The smile Death gave the creature was unnerving, and with a close of his fist, the shadows sank into the woman's flesh. Blood and ichor splattered across me, but I couldn't have cared less. My brain was fixated on the reaper towering above me, and how he had suddenly taken my chin in his long fingers, examining the source of the blood leaking down my face. He was beautiful, the most devastatingly handsome man I'd ever seen, and the night moved around him as though it were at his mercy.

My skin ignited where his fingertips pressed into my face. I shivered at the coolness pooling from his touch, the comfort that leaked from them over my skin. A broken shard of memory sliced through my mind, and his eyes, those crystal blue eyes, bored into mine as he pulled me closer, gathering me into his arms. He smelled of winter, of cold and pine, like the closet had when I moved in. A memory carved through my bones, sank into the marrow, wound its way up my throat.

My head swam as darkness clouded my vision, the memory on the tip of my tongue. Death ran his thumb across my bottom lip, and it fell from me, a question, a prayer.

"Are you mine?" I whispered, blinking slowly.

"I am, Little Flower."

The words floated me into bliss.

Helios

CHAPTER 20

The aftermath of the scuffle in the alleyway was nothing compared to the shitshow that waited for us at Hades's penthouse. The God of the Dead demanded our presence, but I couldn't leave yet. I needed to check on Nick, to ensure he was safe so soon after our rendezvous. My mind raced as I made my way back inside Styx, but it wasn't just Hades and Persephone that had me reeling. Since the moment Hecate had found Nick and me in that alcove, had rushed me away from him while I was still administering after care, I'd felt off and wrong, rerunning that last interaction through my mind on a loop, desperate to understand it.

Nick leaned against the vacant wall, catching his breath. His jeans pooled around his knees, and I could see myself leaking out of him. A smirk of satisfaction crossed my face. I leaned against him and felt him chuckle.

"I'll need a moment before another round, Daddy," he said, and I froze.

I had no idea why I had said that to him during sex. I hadn't ever gotten off on the term before, but hearing it fall from his lips made me want to strip my pants and fill him up again right there. Instead, I ran my hands up the inside of his thighs, gathering the cum leaking out and pushed it back inside with my fingers. He groaned at the intrusion. Fates, he was perfection.

I shifted to pull his pants back up and turned him around to face me. "I want you to walk around with me inside you for the rest of the night," I ordered, and he nodded, biting his lip, though I had no authority to make him do anything. The moment had passed, but I still felt locked in, protective of him. I brought my fingers up to his mouth and he opened obediently, sucking them clean of the mess we'd made. My gaze catching on small dark bruises peppered over his skin from my hands and bites. I ran my fingers over them, soothing the hurt with light touches, kissing the wounds better.

Nick groaned and pulled my body against his again, his pillow-soft lips molding against mine. I felt my half-hard cock lengthen again, but before we could go any further, Hecate ran into the alcove. I shifted, protecting Nick's body from being exposed.

She skidded to a stop, her braids swinging wildly as she took in the scene before her. It stunned her for just a moment, but as she shook her head slightly she was once more all business. "Persephone. There's trouble."

Ice washed over me as panic coursed through my veins. I gave her a quick nod and turned back to Nick in my arms. He looked . . . almost sad, withdrawn, the early signs of a sub drop. I needed to take care of him after what we had just done, especially if the drop was hitting him hard. Leaving him that way would be cruel and irresponsible.

I lifted his chin with two fingers, connecting his gaze. "Stay here. Sit at the bar. Drink a glass of water. I will return for you, I promise." I didn't know why I was promising this stranger anything, but the way he perked up made me not even care. I kissed him on the lips, then tore out after Hecate.

I'd left Nick alone, and since that moment everything inside me pulled and tugged and demanded I go back for him. Fear licked up my spine as I thought of the implications of what that could mean, but another part of me, the part that had been destroyed long ago, perked up.

God couplings were rare, especially in this new age. A connection that deep could be wonderful like Hades's and Persephone's had been, or extremely volatile and dangerous like Hera's and Zeus's. I didn't know if what I felt was the beginning of a Bond, but I needed to find out because I had neglected connection like that once before, and I would never do it again, to hells with the consequences.

The sex had been mind-blowing, and I definitely wanted more than just a taste, and though Senna had been lovely, I didn't particularly want to share him again. My thoughts raced with the memory of how beautifully he'd bloomed as he'd come. I marveled over the way the white and yellow wildflowers had blossomed on his delicate skin. I wanted to see it over and over again, but first, I needed to see if he was even still there.

Please, Fates, let him still be there.

When I reached Styx, I searched the room with hurried glances. The remaining patrons were milling around, looking for someone to go home with, the last call in all senses of the word. I saw him at the end of the bar, a tall glass of water in his hands, perched on a stool in his boots, jeans, and jacket but no shirt. A smile broke across my face, and a sense of rightness took up residence under my ribs because he listened. *He'd stayed.*

A minor god, Celtic by the look of him, leaned over, attempting to engage. Nick sat back, creating distance between them and I smiled wider at his rejection—he was waiting for me. The big Celt leaned in closer and Nick put a hand up, pushing against the muscle. My boy was tall, but thin, and I knew he wouldn't have much advantage in a fight against a rambunctious demi-god. A primal urge to claim and covet filled me, my body humming, reacting to the thought that the little nymph may be in any sort of danger.

I made right for him. Nick's eyes lit up, so dreamy and clear in the neon glow of the club. Unable to resist the pull, I gathered him in my arms, placing a kiss on Nick's soft lips, swallowing his satisfied sigh as he melted into my touch, completely ignoring the dickhead who wouldn't take no for an answer in front of us. It didn't take long for the demi-god to catch the hint, and I watched as he scampered off to find a different Otherworlder to stick his cock in.

I tilted Nick's head up to face me. "I have to leave again. I don't want to, but it's an obligation I can't ignore," I explained, watching the disappointment settle over him once more. Nick bit his lip, and I let out a small groan. He was going to kill me with those bright eyes. "I don't *want* to leave you, and I promise it will only be for a few hours." I brought his face to mine and pressed a dozen tender kisses to his lips. "I'm going to take you to my house, get you settled, and then I will go. You'll sleep and then I'll return, and we can talk." My voice, soft but dominant as I tried to hold back the caveman like possessiveness that had overtaken me. It would need to be his choice if he came home with me. Fates, I wanted him to want to.

"Can you feel it?" he asked, eyes soft. Panic tried to claw its way up my throat, but I silenced it before I could open my lips and again ruin a gift from the cosmos.

"I feel it. Please, give me time to take care of this, and I promise I'll come back. I'm not ready for this night to end." Nick lifted his head, staring at me for a long beat. I steadied myself for the rejection I knew was probably coming, something to show me I'd misread all the signs, and this was just a quick fuck to him. That I was being crazy, so fueled on the miracle that was Persephone's return that I was looking for second chances I didn't deserve. Perhaps part of me hoped he'd walk away. The memory of another set of eyes, so like his, washed over me, threatening to break me in two. But then, Nick spoke, and it was like the dawn of a new morning.

"Yes." I grinned, kissed him softly once more, our tongues a tangle of languid desire. Pulling him from the bar, I decided to take him to the home I'd built off Decatur. I didn't have time to do all that I wanted to care for him, but I settled for washing his body clean, rubbing his muscles as he relaxed in the bath. After toweling him off and tucking him in bed with aspirin and water, I asked him not to leave until I returned, then waited. The soft sounds of his breathing floated through the room as he drifted into sleep.

Satisfied, I changed my bloodied clothes and headed to Hades's, closing the door behind me.

Something shifted in my universe the moment his eyes met mine, an instant tether I'd only ever felt once before. The warning bells in my head, the ones that cautioned too much too fast, I shoved them aside. If this became nothing more than a good time, I'd be alright, because if there was a chance of something more? I would hold on to it with both hands.

I'd made the grave error of making choices for the ones I loved out of protection, out of fear, and it had cost me everything.

I'd never make that mistake again. He was *mine.*

Persephone

CHAPTER 21

My head pounded. A relentless pressure pulled me—no, *dragged* me—closer to consciousness as I scraped and clawed for the blanket of darkness. All I wanted was to disappear underneath it, but voices, louder than loud, exploded in my ears, ricocheting inside my skull. I wanted it to stop, but it didn't, and I reluctantly peeled back my eyelids then froze.

This wasn't my room.

This space was dark, elegant. Not a single thing stood out of place, so pristine it was almost surgical. The walls, a dark slate, impossibly blue-black in the dim light with modern, practical fixtures. I was tucked in a bed that did not belong to me, surrounded by sheets so soft the air appeared scratchy in comparison. They smelled divine, like the first breath of winter through the trees, but I didn't feel cold. The pendant at my throat sat dormant, comfortable beneath the oversized black T-shirt that covered me. It blanketed my body in that same intoxicating scent lingering on the soft threads of the sheets, and I inhaled deeply, committing it to whatever was left of my memory.

I pushed myself to sit, groaning at the strain in my muscles as I brushed my hair back from my face. Something snagged my fingers, and I felt around the outlines of a bandage, tucked right against my hairline over my brow. *I'd hit my head? When?* Oh, yes, the memory resurged. The alleyway. I was being mugged by a gang, and my band came for me. My band and my new friend and . . . the Grim Reaper? Death, it was Death that came for me. I shook my head aggressively, causing the world to spin on its axis, but the fog wouldn't shake. I swallowed, my throat cracked and dry. Water. I needed water.

Muffled voices floated through the door again, this time aggressive, nearly thundering in the quiet of this room. It was a curious voice, and I wanted to follow it, to see who it belonged to. The accent was . . . peculiar. Irish, maybe? Scottish? Soothing in its fury, and though I should have felt scared at the harsh tone, I only felt a pull to hear more of it. To go to it, to wrap up in it tightly, to calm it down as it drowned me. No voice that beautiful should hold that much rage.

My feet dangled off the edge of the bed, not reaching the floor by several inches. I'd need to jump, but I was unsure if my balance would hold, so I slid on my back until I felt the cool hardwood on the pads of my feet. On unsteady legs I wobbled across the wood flooring, softly and, thankfully, quietly as I pulled the bedroom door open enough for light to squeeze through.

The voices became louder.

"It's time to tell her, be damned about the consequences." Artemis. I could hear the anger in her tone.

"It's too dangerous. She could have a complete collapse." *Dr. Galapagia*?

"She was attacked, Hygieia. Be reasonable. She can't be left out like bait. This is seriously dark power at play here." Hephaestus.

"I'm sorry, *none* of you spent the first *six months* of her life since she woke up picking her off the ground after even the slightest wrong move sent her into a seizure or migraine!" Dr. G was pissed, I could tell she was pissed.

"I was actually right there. And I think it should be her choice to know," Hermes quipped, voice low.

"Says the asshole who almost cracked her head like an egg over her name," Dr. G sniped back.

"Hecate, do we know what influence those abominations were under?" The voice, that velvet timbre surrounded me, and my mind tingled as the sound sank into my consciousness. I had to get closer.

The pain of a migraine hadn't relented, the deep throb growing more painful as I pushed my way across the threshold. The image that met my eyes was not what I had expected, but it triggered something from long ago, a small sliver of memory that crept through the cracks as the pain amped up. I grasped for it, clutching it between my fingers before it could rot away, forcing my mind to look, my eyes to *see*.

Before me, a large stone table sat, my friends around it in elegant high-backed seats, still wearing their show clothes. The new friend, Helios, was there, too, as well as Dr. G and a man I didn't recognize. My brain seared, my blood racing in my ears. I brought a hand to my temple. Something shifted in my vision as it blurred, and I blinked several times to clear it, but it was a shard of a memory, sharp and visceral clouding my mind's eye.

The same table, the same people, but they were dressed differently, clothed in long flowing chitons, sweeping strips of luxurious fabric. The room was different, ceiling vaulted and high with a blue glow emanating from the window outside. We looked to be underground, and the man with the voice looked at me, face breaking into a stunning smile as his deep blue eyes met mine. My heart felt full, bursting, as the others argued about food shortages and famines.

I could only see him.

He looked like the images of gods I'd seen in Artemis's book. The thought shook me to reality. Maybe I had a concussion from the head wound and was confused about the stories I'd read? I looked at the man in front of me now, in the impeccable, impossibly black suit, hands on the table as he stood. His long fingers splayed across stone, his gaze boring into mine, blue glaciers that screamed danger.

I wanted to run from this man. He was a predator, dangerous. *Deadly*. I let out a gasp as recognition swept through me, every nerve and my body shaking from it. *He* was Death. My Death. He had called me "Little Flower."

They all turned to look at me, falling silent, but he stood as still as a statue, waiting. Then, they were all talking as they scrambled toward me, but I kept my eyes fixed on him as they scraped their chairs back to close the distance.

"*SIT. DOWN.*" Death's voice commanded, shaking through the space. Everyone stopped moving, stopped breathing. He took up all the available air in the room, as if by sheer will of force, he could make them obey. Power rolled off him in thick currents, invisible to the eye but I could feel it. The authority. Chairs were re-pulled without hesitation; he was obviously in command.

I glanced around and his eyes flickered for a second to the seat next to Artemis at the opposite end of the table from his own. A knee-buckling urge to obey him, to listen, had me padding forward cautiously, unsteadily, still fighting the tremors of my migraine.

Helios was out of his seat in an instant, pulling out mine with a gentle smile. Death glared at him but otherwise made no comment as the massive man returned to his seat once I was settled. Still no one spoke as the edge of my vision swam, my mind working overtime to adjust.

Death sat. "Hermes," he said, that intense stare still holding mine. "Probability it shatters her mind?"

"Forty-two-point seven percent, give or take a percent either way," Hermes answered with lighting speed, as though he'd expected the question.

Death templed his fingers in front of him, still staring. Calculating. "Persephone," he spoke my name differently, reverently, with a softness that was absent from his tone when addressing the others. His lips enunciated every syllable with stunning clarity, sent a shiver down my spine.

"We have something distressing to impart to you. It will not be pleasant and may in fact break you and destroy your mind. It will, undoubtedly, destroy the life you have built because this knowledge cannot be unknown. You will know it, eventually, whether we like it or not, but you may *choose*. Do you want to know now, or would you like to wait until the burden of knowledge is demanded? It is an inevitability. But you may choose ignorance and safety at this junction," he said gently, sliding back in his chair.

A heavy silence hung in the room. Dr. G looked furious, murderous even, but she held her tongue. I looked at Artemis and the fear and sorrow in her eyes sent a bolt of panic through my body, but Hermes looked hopeful, encouraging with his small smile.

I dragged my gaze back to Death as I chewed the inside of my cheek, considering his words. "You all know something about my past, of how I came to be, don't you? You being in my life isn't a coincidence, is it?" I asked the room at large, but he knew it was directed at him.

"We do. And it isn't a coincidence. The furthest from it." His voice wasn't comforting now. It was brutal and succinct, as though, through his iron will, he could impart more distance between us. He gave little context, minimal information. Death was going to make me choose, loudly, without any chance of misinterpretation.

"Then I need to know what the hell it is. I know you know, and not knowing will eat me alive. So, obviously, whatever it is, I'd rather just rip off the Band-Aid. Who are you, and what do you know about me?" I asked, forcing calm that I didn't feel into my tone. I steadied my hands under the table as I tried to show a brave face, but between the pain in my head and the hammer of the heart in my chest, I was quickly losing grip. I was as terrified as I was curious about what they knew.

Cold eyes surveyed me for a beat more before folding his hands and resting his elbows on the arms of his chair. Artemis looked at him, a silent conversation passing between the two and he nodded at her once, curtly.

She took a breath before turning back to me. "I am Artemis, Goddess of the Hunt, Daughter of Zeus. You are Persephone, Goddess of the Spring and Qu—" A sharp warning noise cut her off, but she regrouped. ". . . Goddess of the Spring. We are deities of the Greek Pantheon." She looked terrified, like I was a delicate vase moments from shattering.

I shifted my eyes to each of their faces waiting for the punch line of the joke. The silence stretched on.

Hermes scoffed, standing, as he looked around the table. "She's not going to believe us by just *telling* her." He dropped me a wink, and in a flash, he was gone, a blur of movements that couldn't be real. Less than a blink later, he was right next to me. I screamed in shock, scrambling back, knocking the chair askew in my wake as I tumbled to the floor.

My mind splintered a fraction, and I reached inside, desperate for the offering it gave, crying out at the intense pressure.

It was Hermes, but not Hermes. He wore a golden circlet, held a tall staff with two snakes entwined. He was standing next to me in a room of yelling people, his hand on my shoulder, the other outstretched toward me.

Dr. G was on me in an instant, but I shook her off. "I'm fine," I said weakly, clutching at the side of my temple. My hands shook, the tremors noticeable from outer space, but I couldn't reconcile what I had just seen.

Hermes bent low, scooping me up under the arm. He guided me back to my seat before I could realize it was his hands on me. My head spun, gravity a cruel and debilitating thing. I waited for the fear to set in, to sink low. I waited for my mind to tell me this was impossible, that it was a cruel prank, but Hermes was there, and then he was here. Too fast. So fast. I had seen it with my own eyes, hadn't I?

I looked at Artemis, silvery gray eyes swimming on the verge of tears and it shocked me. I hadn't ever seen her so vulnerable. "And you? Show me."

Artemis set her jaw and gave me a small nod. She stood gracefully, then walked to the edge of the room. Her hand went behind her back, and suddenly, she was pulling a beautiful silver bow, the same bow from the alleyway from thin air and notching an arrow of pure silver light. She turned and let it fly, striking a pomegranate balancing precariously on a fruit bowl in the middle of the table.

I winced, wiping away the stray tear that slipped down my cheek hastily.

One by one they introduced their names and titles and showed me a talent. Medusa had snakes for hair, and I thought her power was the coolest, though everyone declined to be the subject of her Gaze. Suddenly the dark, tinted glasses she wore all the time made more sense, and I wondered if the reason I'd never asked her about them was because deep down, some part of me had always *known*.

A phone rang, and Death disappeared to answer. Hermes followed, but never returned when Death reappeared and retook his seat. He looked unbothered, unaffected even, with not a hair out of place while I was a disheveled mess over all of these revelations.

I turned to Helios, who held the light of a small sun in his hands, a nagging question burning behind my lips.

"If I'm like you, then why don't I have any powers? I'm goddess of what, spring, right? I've read about myself before, in Artemis's book. But I don't have any powers, I can't do any of these things." Disappointment washed over me, insecurity eating me up.

"You bring the spring, Seph. You make things bloom, help them thrive," Artemis explained gently.

I frowned deeper. "What a useless fucking power," I blurted, surprising them but myself as well. Unfamiliar anger swelled inside me. I didn't quite know where it was coming from, but I was going to let myself feel it, because this was too much to just accept. Maybe it was the anger of being lied to boiling up, threatening to overrun, but I couldn't help it. I lashed out, my voice rising higher with each word. "The rest of you get super-speed, or fucking snakes for hair and a stare that can turn a man to stone, and I get what, advanced gardening skills? This is trash! I was almost killed! What am I supposed to do, throw a fucking Ficus at them the next time I'm cornered?" I laughed hysterically. "Yeah, that'll show them. Death by potted plant."

I stood, pacing, as rage built and roiled inside me, clouded my senses, boiled in my blood. The air shifted, my anger more potent, more tangible. This fucking house was dark, *so dark*. Death must have had the lights on a dimming timer because it was almost pitch-black now, and I smacked my hip into a chair during my last turn. "Who turned off the damn lights?" I demanded, exasperated as I grabbed the part of my hip that felt like I'd been shot, wincing in pain.

Helios held his hands aloft, golden light pouring from them. "*You*, Persephone . . ." I looked around, shocked. Most of my body was covered in thick coils of shadows, moving and winding around me. They licked out, hesitatingly testing the reach of the light in Helios's hand, but something told me that they wouldn't hesitate to engulf him if I asked.

They felt right. *Home*.

A surge of power ripped up my spine and I locked gazes with the man I called Death at the other end of the table. His crystalline gaze picked me apart, dissected me down to bone daggers, his dark hair inky in the depths of shadows. Something whispered near my ear, something lovely and delicious, and I *felt* that my shadows wanted to go to him, searched and longed to close the distance between us. His eyes raked up and down my body as the shadows covered me, winding over my bare legs in a caress. It felt intimate, this moment, and I knew that the others couldn't see through the blanket of darkness surrounding me, but he could. And I? *I wanted him to look.*

A strange sensation pulsed through my body from my chest to my core, sending a thrill back up to my nipples. My eyes blew wide with shock, and the tension snapped as the shadows dissipated, leaving me breathless. Of everyone at the table, Death had yet to reveal himself to me and I needed to hear more of his voice, keep his attention right where it was for as long as I could.

"Who are you?" I asked, my gaze never faltering. His full lips thinned, the silence swelling between us as he sucked in a small, nearly reluctant breath.

"Hades, God of the Underworld."

There was no more air left in my lungs when the pressure in my head became unbearable. It built, it *throbbed*, and I ached. I wanted it to end, needed sweet relief but found nothing but more agony as I crashed to the floor cradling my head. The tremors shook through the foundations of my mind, rattling my carefully constructed barrier, smashing the bones of my skull into dust beneath the crushing onslaught.

A sunlit day. Helios coming down in a chariot, screaming my name, screaming for me. Me, begging Hades to stop. Blackness.

I tried to hold on to the images as they flickered past, but they were skips on a vinyl, half-truths . . .The earth cracking apart as Helios fought to get to me, swallowing us whole . . .The smell of winter on my skin, cool hands on my body. "She has been stolen! He has kidnapped her!"

I pressed my face to the floor, aware of hands on me, rolling in agony. I writhed away from them, the touch too much, too hot. I clutched for my pendant, let it ground me. With silent sobs I begged the cool metal to bring me back to earth, to the shaking mess of a body melted into the floor, surrounded by strangers who knew this vessel most ardently, most intimately. A new memory quaked across my mind, a story from the pages of a book on Greek mythology I'd read during a thunderstorm.

"*The Rape of Persephone*," I gasped, my lungs fighting to draw in air.

The God of the Underworld had taken a maiden, a Spring Goddess. Swallowed her up into the earth, took her hostage, wouldn't let her leave. He took her. *The Rape of Persephone.* I was Persephone. *He* was Hades. My body shook harder as I struggled to regain my bearings. Everyone huddled around me, concerned, hovering. Everyone except *him*.

Hades sat where he was, calm and relaxed, while I bled out my brains on the floor. Enraged, I pushed myself up, palms flat, staring him in the eyes. He didn't flinch, didn't betray any emotion. I winced as I tried to stand and something flashed, a flicker of *feeling*, maybe, in the pierce of his gaze. But then, Dr. G was in front of me, checking my eyes with a light. She and Artemis helped me into my chair, but I could only see him as acid churned in my gut.

I had questions. They demanded answers. I'd chosen this, and now, I had to see it through, no matter how badly I wanted to run away and pretend to know nothing of the monsters and gods that lived amongst us. That time had come and gone. I looked Hades straight in his eyes. The others may as well have not even been in the room.

"You stole me." It wasn't a question, but a statement. He answered it anyway.

"Yes." It was cold, biting.

"Took me from my home and held me hostage in the Underworld."

"Yes." Still measured.

"Why?" My voice wavered, only a little, but it was enough. The tension building in the room came from everyone, everywhere, all at once. His next words ignited a bomb.

"Because I wanted to. Because you were there, with the flowers, and I coveted beautiful things." The tether holding the room together sprang taut, pushed to its limit. He had stolen me, but in this new world, he had abandoned me, left me to rot away. Fury and hurt swelled inside my chest as I swallowed down the lump in my throat, obstructed the words I knew would come next, as though my body already understood the answer before I could breathe the question into existence.

Hades tilted his chin down, still pinning me in place. "Ask it," he demanded. The others looked between us, unsure of what he meant but I knew. I could see it in his eyes, in the tension of his shoulders.

I took a breath, straightening my own, and lifted my chin in a sign of measured strength. "Did you rape me?"

The silence in the room stretched on for so long that I thought we all must have died. No one moved. No one breathed. Medusa paled, a generous feat for someone of her dark complexion. Hades's eyes never left mine. I watched him shutter behind them, showing only endless depths of cold, secluded pits of nothingness. A reptile with no feeling or compassion. Just as he made me say it, I was going to make him.

"Yes," he admitted, stiffly.

The table erupted around us. Helios leapt to his feet, Hephaestus and Artemis shouted, while Medusa looked ill. The noise reached a level that made it indecipherable for me to make out quite what anyone was saying, but it all felt so far away anyway, like I was listening from under the water, the tide rushing in my ears.

Hades stood and brought his massive hands down on the table. A thunderous crack split the tabletop in two as he loomed, a great earthquake, as self-proclaimed gods cowered under his power. Except me. He had nothing left to scare me with, this monster in angelic form.

"*ENOUGH!*" he roared. *Roared*. He flattened his palms from the fists that were balled, settling them on the table.

Hephaestus and Hecate were holding back Helios who looked purple in the face, but I had gone numb.

He had stolen me, but how had I ended up in that box? Was it a punishment? Did I try to escape and he hurt me instead?

"Artemis, you and Medusa will take Persephone home. Hygieia, you will go with them and ensure any after-effects of her tremors are treated. The rest of you are with me on another urgent matter," he instructed, his tone a final decree the others bent to. No one spoke as they began to move slowly, tempered, but my nostrils flared, my body rebelling against his command. Hades's cool demeanor was carefully back in place, giving away nothing of his outburst, but I was being flayed alive under that gaze, and I snapped.

Crossing my arms, I leaned back, chin lifted. "What makes you think I'll do *anything* you fucking tell me to do?"

Hades looked between Hephaestus and a freshly returned Hermes, then back to me. His lips lifted in a sneer. "Because you are my wife, and you will do as I say." His tone arctic. Menacing.

Self-preservation fled my body as I took in his words, then snorted. "Listen, I don't know what you think gives you the right, but since none of you have explained what happened to me that *actually* put me in that box, I don't owe you fucking anything, especially any sort of cooperation. I will not abide taking orders from a man who openly admitted to assaulting me moments ago. Just because I can't remember it doesn't make it any less fucked up. And the rest of you, you knew this was my husband? What he did to me? You pretended to be my friends, my family, and then delivered me to my abuser? You can all, but especially *you*, get fucked," I finished, pointing at the glowering god, throwing my chair back before heading to the door. Adrenaline surged through me, drowning the sound of my heart breaking at the sheer amount of unimaginable betrayal.

"Everyone out. *Now*." His words were a low, deadly calm. They gave me pause when I should have run, but I couldn't help but turn to look at him, at the audacity he had. There was no trace of the piercing blue irises, only blown black against the milky whites.

No one moved at his command, but hesitant eyes bounced between us. A sharp burst of power pulsed through him, shadows whipping everywhere. They snatched everyone up, flung them out the double doors that led to hell knew where. The doors shut them out with a sickening snap. Behind them, I could hear the thumps as the others beat against the barriers, demanding to be let in.

It was only Hades and me now. Fear licked down my spine and I watched as he drew himself up to his full, considerable height. It was imposing, but I straightened my back, refusing to be intimidated. Whatever was about to befall me would not find me cowering. I was *done* letting shit happen to me.

Hades started to move, eyes stormy, every step calculated, deciding how many steps would close the distance between us. How long it may take for the others to break down the door and find a way inside.

I retreated, matching his agonizing pace as we circled the table. Whatever lesson in obedience he thought he was about to teach me would find him sorely disappointed. I was not the Persephone he had taken. I didn't even know that woman.

I saw his jaw tic the moment before he lunged, and I was ready for him. I sprinted around the table, circling as fast as I could in bare feet on the slippery floor. I stretched my arms, inches from the door, when long fingers wrapped around my throat and yanked me, almost gently, back into a hard chest.

"Is this what you want? You want something to hold on to, to make your hate tangible?" His lips were so close to mine, his big body bent in half to achieve the angle. His breath fanned over my earlobe as he spoke, and I hated the way my blood sang beneath my skin, surging toward him even as my heart threatened to beat out of my chest.

Long fingers tangled in my hair, his other arm wrapped around my waist, weight pressing on my sternum as his fingers circled my throat, nearly tenderly. I tried to ignore the flush I felt, to focus on anything but the way the echo of his voice in my ear made me want to relax, be soft and pliant in his hands. I could not be pliant. He was a predator, and he had hurt me, no matter whatever fucked up reaction my body was having to him.

The thumb on the hand shackled around my throat darted softly over my lips and I shivered, my body a confusing jumble of vibrations and overworked nerves. Hades arched my head back farther with his grip on the crown of my hair, my curls a golden contrast to his pale skin as he marched us back to the table.

"You want me to bend you over here? Shove your legs apart and fuck you? I know how to make you come, Little Flower. I can make you see things you've never seen before as you chase that high. Should I tell you about the thousands of times I've had you? How you'd cry so beautifully for me? Or will you do as you're told?"

A whimper broke past my lips as my defiance vanished, replaced by the most primal shake of fear. I was terrified, could feel it flooding through my veins, overtaking my systems as the unexplainable lust my body felt gave way to genuine panic. Gone was the bravado I'd felt earlier. How could I have been so wrong about my memories, that voice? The eyes I'd dreamt of, over and over again?

How many times had I cried myself to sleep because no one had come for me, when I should have been grateful? That the eyes I'd held on to so long belonged to a monster?

"*Please . . . Please*, don't hurt me," I choked, hot tears spilling down my cheeks at the shame, at the embarrassment of it all. Hades dropped me as though I had electrocuted him, immediately backing away from the table, hands fisted in his hair. I felt the pressure of his body go as I collapsed on the table, sobbing through the deluge of tears.

The double doors crashed open, shadows relenting as bodies spilled into the now-wrecked dining room. There were hands on me, hands on my face, and suddenly, I was gone from this room, gone from *him*. The last thing I heard before we rounded the landing was the sickening crunching of bone on bone as Helios's fist cracked across Hades's jaw, the heated yells in the throes of rage.

Good. I hope Helios kills him.

Hades

CHAPTER 22

I had her, held her in my hands the way she always liked, the way I'd dreamt of for so long, but instead of pulling her closer, I'd destroyed us. *Scare her*, I'd reminded myself as her body opened and bloomed under my touch, having the exact opposite reaction needed to keep her away. It was all an act, a show. *Be rough, but don't hurt her*. I knew her limits, I'd pushed her to them in bed more times than I could count.

She didn't flinch when she'd asked if I raped her.

"Yes," I'd answered. *Lie. Lie. Lie.*

Helios had almost lost his mind, not understanding what I was playing at, why I was pushing so hard to make her hate me. He hadn't heard the prophecy. No, he couldn't understand yet, but he would. Of anyone, Helios would respect my motives, if not the methods. She had to fear me, *hate* me, could never be allowed to uncover those sacred depths of us. I wasn't strong enough to tell her no, if she asked. I never had been good at denying Persephone anything, and look what it had cost her.

Defiant as ever, she'd stood me down, so I pushed her farther, too far. Something in her voice changed, the tremble as her body shook. I felt the shift when she crossed the threshold in her mind, in mine. There would be no turning back.

"Please, don't hurt me," she whimpered.

The darkest parts of my shade, the ones hoping she'd remember me despite it all, shattered.

She believed me. She believed I'd raped her. Stolen her. Kept her hostage in the Underworld. The pain was sudden and visceral, and when I dropped her, I'd had no rational thought left. I had to get her away from me before I ruined it all. Before I did something foolish like fall at her feet and take it all back, drag our friends in, and make them tell her it was all lies.

If they ever spoke to me again.

Persephone buckled, breathing hard, shaking as tears streamed down her cheeks. I flicked my hand to the door and released the hold there. Hephaestus and Hermes had arms around Helios as he struggled like a wounded bear to break free. Artemis shot me a look of pure anger as she, Medusa, and Hygieia surrounded the crumpled goddess, wilted like a spring bloom in winter on my floor. They picked her up, wiped her face.

Hecate passed near me, and I could feel her digging and prying at my mind. "*Let me in*," she whispered, but I blocked her intrusion with a small shake of my head.

My fists tightened by my sides, the only traitors to the stoic and cruel demeanor I projected. I was barely keeping it together, the storm inside me mirroring the rage Helios let loose in front of us.

She believed me.

A part of me never expected her to believe. I expected anger, defiance. I even expected fear. But the true belief I felt as her body trembled beneath mine? It *broke* me. I was many things, but a rapist wasn't one, despite what I had told her. A twisted, irrational, decrepit part of my shade thought she would see through the lie. *See me.* That our love would have been too strong for her to fear me.

I felt the moment she was taken from the room. Her presence wrenched away and with it the air from my lungs.

Helios thrashed, out for blood after the way I'd hurt her, and I welcomed it. I needed the pain, deserved it. So much of this was unfair to him. And because of the part he played in it, so much was his burden to bear.

I locked eyes with Hermes and nodded. He and Hephaestus dropped their hold on Helios, and he surged toward me, murder in his eyes. I made no move to defend myself as his giant fist connected with my eye socket. The crunch was loud, ghastly. I didn't care. I wanted more.

"Come on, fucker, surely you can do better than that?" I spat, ignoring my throbbing face. I provoked him, pushing, desperate for the release of pain. He lunged again, this time a combo to the stomach that radiated through my entire being as a grunt escaped my lips.

More, my mind demanded. Blow after blow landed and still I let them fall.

More pain. *More.*

She believed me. *Crunch.*

She hated me for what I did. *Crack.*

Blood everywhere. My blood, dark and slick on the ground. On Helios's knuckles. He faltered.

"Tired already, Sun King?" I meant for it to come out more of a sneer, but my swollen, busted lip and bitten tongue distorted my tone.

Helios backed up, surveying me. "You motherfucker." His voice low, angry. Not angry enough. I needed it fueled with rage. I needed him to hit me again.

I spat a mouthful of blood at his feet. "What's wrong, Helios? I only recounted our story as *you* told it." My laugh cold, cruel. I pushed, needing those fists bruising me again, tearing into my flesh, ripping me apart. The ache was unbearable, the further away from me she went. "Too sensitive to hear about how I fucked her? How I'd just made her think I could do it again, whether she wanted it or not?" I snarled, hating myself, hating every drop of venom that slipped across my tongue.

Helios blinked at me, shock etched into the planes of his blood-spattered face. "*Who are you?*" He asked, but made no move to strike me again, no tensed muscles ready to attack. It enraged me, his surrender, and I lost it. My shadows wailed, engulfing the room, pressing into every corner as they screamed at me to let them go to her, to make it all right.

"Hit me!" I pleaded, but none of them moved. "*HIT ME!*" I roared, and Helios flinched, partially obscured as the room filled with darkness. My shadows circled us, and yet, Helios did not strike me.

Helios

CHAPTER 23

Hades screamed, roaring at me to hurt him. Realization crashed over me, a cold tidal wave of horror that shot down my spine. None of this made any sense. The distance Hades was going to great lengths to solidify between him and Persephone, the outrageous lies he'd told her, that everyone else had just went along with. The rage that bolted through me as I'd watched her shatter under the weight of his words.

When the doors had opened, she had been a shaking mess, and I'd lost all semblance of control. And then, Hades had *let* me attack him. *Provoked* me. He was practically begging me for it now.

What the fuck was happening here?

"Hades." I kept my tone soft, forcing the adrenaline to still inside me. "What has happened? She's here, *she's home*. And yet you're treating her like she's nothing, you're killing her. I can't believe this is because she doesn't remember you. Your ego just isn't that fragile." I crossed the room toward him, arms aloft and palms out. *I'm not a threat.*

Hades looked wild, a wounded animal. The room held so little light now that the slightest provocation could shut it out completely.

"*Tell him*," Hephaestus pleaded.

I continued to close the distance until I stood near enough to touch him. Now that we were so close, I could see the tremble in his hands, the sharp heave of his chest. He was cracking apart at the seams. I hadn't seen him like this in a very, very long time.

When she was first taken, there was rage. Then sadness, then nothingness. He'd begun to waste away, broken and aimless without her, and that was the same haunted look I saw now. Whatever knowledge he possessed was breaking him apart, piece by piece, and shattering Persephone in the process.

I remembered those days with stunning clarity, how hard his fists had been when they'd hit me, beating me until my eye dangled just outside of the socket over what had happened with Narcissus. He hadn't been ready to hear of the drugged wine I'd found, had needed the villain to be the villain. I was so fucked up and broken that when he'd manifested his bident, I'd dropped to my knees, begging him to do it. To ease the pain, make it stop. I remembered not flinching as the steep points sailed right toward me before the sharp bite against the side of my neck, matching the scars Narcissus had worn. The bident had taken retribution. The God of the Underworld had demanded blood, and it provided.

I let him take his pound of flesh from me then, not because he was angry, but because *I* needed to feel the punishment. I looked at the god in front of me now, the most divine of us all, ragged and broken. He *wanted* me to hurt him.

I reached my hand down and clasped it round his shaking forearm. He tensed but didn't kill me, which I took as a good sign, before pulling him gently but firmly in my arms. Without much force, Hades crumbled into my chest. His shoulders shook, knees weak, and I saw Hermes and Hephaestus avert their eyes.

It was unholy to see him this way, the God of the Underworld. We all knew it. Though he shook in my arms, he did not cry. No tears broke rank.

"You went too far, Hades." Hermes's voice tight as he picked at his lip. "She'll never be able to forgive this, or you." His tone was soft, a stark contrast to the words that sliced Hades to the bone. His grip on my arm tightened.

"I know," he croaked, stepping back from me. His blue eyes rimmed in a dark red, hauntingly and stoically beautiful in his sorrow. "It was the only way. She can't have . . . She can't have hope."

"You mean, *you* can't have hope," Hephaestus corrected. "You broke her." A look of anguish washed over Hades.

I turned to Hermes. "What am I not being told? Enough of this secrecy shit," I snapped.

"The Fates came to him the night she returned. Atropos all but directly said it was Hades's darkness that attracted the psychopath that took Persephone. That they had followed them to this realm, and that if they were together, they would keep coming for her until she's dead." Hermes stared at Hades, a mix of pity and anger in his eyes.

I tried to wrap my mind around this information. The Fates were cryptic at best and misleading at worst.

"Did you make her clarify? That sounds like we have to figure out who fucking did this and scatter them across the cosmos. Not that you fucking tell her you raped her like you're this horrible monster, Hades. That's fucked up." I looked at him, begging for him to hear me. He was making himself a martyr and all we had to do was find this asshole.

Hades looked at me like I'd slapped him, his face twisted in agony. "Oh, is that all *we* have to do, Helios? Well, let's just do that! Do you know where to start? Have any idea who could possibly be at work here? No? How many years was she fucking *lost*, Helios? How many times did *you* scour the world looking for any inkling of a whisper and you came up with what? Jack shit, that's what. She's been topside for a year with no attacks or threats or issues because I stayed away. I broke my own rule *once* and suddenly she's being accosted in a parking lot by possessed mortals." Hades's voice rose to a thundering pitch, his pale skin flushed with exasperation.

Hermes whipped his head around to stare at him. "What did you just say?"

Hades deflated. "I just wanted to see her play. I stayed away from her, I didn't even materialize fully," he admitted, guilt pouring from his voice. "If I was unsure before, we know now. It follows me when she and I are together."

Hermes studied him. "But you came to the greenhouse, which was close to her. Nothing happened to her then. How close did you get? Your shadows?" Hermes started pacing, his calculating mind racing as he considered.

"She . . . There was a moment. She winked at a guy in the front row, and admittedly, I may have gotten a little . . . *jealous*. My shadows *may* have decided to put a little distance between the two of them." He looked ashamed.

I bit back a snort. "The guy with the jacket? His name's Nick, and, uh . . . I don't think he was interested in her the way you're thinking," I mumbled, cheeks growing hot. Hephaestus quirked an eyebrow at me approvingly.

"He's a nymph," I offered with a shrug.

"How do you know?" Heph asked, confused. I gave him a look that said *trust me*. There were certain things that couldn't be hidden in the throes of passion between Otherworlders, even if it was a quick threesome in a dark alcove.

On the other side of the room, Hermes stilled, and the lack of movement caught all our attention.

"Your shadows touched her?" he asked Hades, who nodded. Hermes continued on, following the trail of thought leading him around. "You've dropped by the flower shop, too, but never interacted. Never touched her." Another nod from Hades. "You didn't touch her at Brookhaven either and she remained safe."

Hermes paced, a determined look on his face. "I think that they can only find her when you're with her. Or at least, that *was* the case. After what happened at Styx, I think all bets are off. The puppet had spoken with someone else's voice, and it had said it had given warning—it was coming to kill her. It isn't as simple as just keeping away at this point. Your touching her has enraged it somehow, broken some sort of set of rules only it knows. I need to go find Hecate."

He turned, leveling a look at me and Hephaestus. "Do *not* let this arsehole do something idiotic like off himself to keep her safe. I don't think it'll help either way." He clasped a hand on Hades's shoulder, and with a smooth gust of air he was gone.

I turned back to Hades, taking in his wretched demeanor, the anguish etched into every line of his face. I pitied the pain he was feeling, but there was another part of me, one that erred just on this side of frustration, that had me exasperated by the choices he was making.

"Can we have the room?" I asked, cutting my eyes to Hephaestus.

"Yeah, man. Whatever you need. I'm gonna head to Seph and Artemis's place, make sure she's okay," he replied, shooting me a weary look before heading out behind Hermes, leaving Hades and I alone. Neither of us spoke while my truth searched on words to ride, as his head hung low between his hands.

"Hades," I called gently. He shook his head, waving me off.

"Not now, please." That pissed me off.

"Hades!" I snapped, a little more firmly. "You need to look at me and hear me." Red-rimmed eyes found mine, and I saw a god, perhaps the strongest of us all, crushed under the immeasurable weight of helplessness. "You can't keep this from her. It's too cruel. She deserves to know what she means to you, what you mean to each other. The lengths you've both gone through to be together."

"You think that isn't what I want?!" He shouted, face contorted with agony, voice full of torment. "Look at what happened tonight. How many came for her, just from my shadows touching her. *Fates*!" he swore, swiping up a glass from the table and sending it sailing into the wall. Sprays of shattered crystal shards rained down as the Lord of the Underworld came undone.

"Have you learned nothing from my mistakes? This is madness. I can understand caution, but Hephaestus was right; you went too far." I chastised, my own voice rising.

"There is no such thing as too far if it means keeping her fucking heart beating, Helios. Do not lecture me on the weight of responsibility, and do not fucking compare our situations. Persephone never chose what happened to her," he snarled, hackles rising as his rage overcame his sorrow.

"He didn't *choose* either. I told you this. The henbane—" I began, but one look at his stricken, vengeful face, and I fell silent. He wasn't ready to hear it now, just as he hadn't been ready then, and it wasn't worth the extra fistfight that would inevitably come. I pinched my fingers over the bridge of my nose and sucked in a centering breath, letting my thoughts roam to the nymph asleep in my bed, the need curled in my chest to get back to him.

"You're right. It's different, but the truth remains the same. Feed it to her in small pieces, give it to her like a puzzle to put together, but Hades, if I ever see you hurt her that way again, I will find a way to fucking kill you," I swore. He swallowed, casting an ashamed look at the ground, the anger deflated from him once more. I reached out a hand to help him gain his bearings, and he took it, sinking into the hug I dragged him into.

"You need some good liquor, and then, we need to get a plan together. You can feel sorry for yourself later. Right now, we need to act."

Hades swallowed, then pulled himself together. We had work to do.

Persephone

CHAPTER 24

I couldn't recall the journey home, or how I had come to be in my own bed. Salty tear stains covered my pillowcase, my eyes dried out, burning with irritation. Artemis had lit some of my candles and put on some music. The light peeked through my window and the birds stirred, but still I did not move. The outside world felt too big, too scary. How many more life-altering revelations could I be expected to endure?

Gods were real. *Okay*, I could see that. I read about the religions of the world during my recovery. All of them believed in some sort of powerful deity, so the fact that the Greeks had gotten it right wasn't that surprising. The fact that my "friends" were the human embodiment of these gods was a little more disconcerting, but the proof had been irrefutable. Still nothing bit into my skin more than the thought that they had lied to me. Betrayed me.

I felt embarrassed, but Artemis's betrayal stung the worst. We lived together, I'd trusted her. They'd all lied to me, but she had crossed a line that I didn't know if we could ever recover from. Then there was the tiny detail that I, too, was one of them. That was a little harder to believe, or at least, it had been, until I'd felt those shadows come to my aid. They belonged to me, and I couldn't explain how I knew that, but I did. They felt like extensions of myself, an extra set of limbs to command.

Worse still was the way they curled toward *him*.

My kidnapper. My assailant. *My husband*.

A shiver ran down my spine and I tightened my hold on my legs, curling deeper in on myself under the covers. He was cold and cruel, everything the myths I had read confirmed. The memory shards that cracked and fell at my feet were of the moment he took me, I'd surmised. Me begging him not to, the dirt cracking wide to swallow us whole, but something . . . hadn't sat right as he'd looked me in the eye and told me the things he did to me. How would Artemis have let him live? Helios had looked murderous, and I swore I heard him shout something, but there was so much noise and so many overlapping voices, I couldn't be sure. Or was this just my mind, in some sort of desperate attempt to mitigate the trauma, searching for a perfectly reasonable explanation in a batshit situation?

Those eyes. I had dreamt about them every night since I woke up in that box. Heard my name in that voice the first time I recalled it was mine. The way he came to my aid and defended me in that alley—all of those things didn't seem like they matched the personality of the man who'd held me by my throat and threatened to hurt me again just because he *could*.

A feeling, warm and hot, blossomed in my chest as my mind raced back to the way my skin had ignited when he'd touched me. Shame followed, and I pressed my face deeper into the pillow to muffle the sobs. Just because I couldn't remember what he'd done didn't mean it hadn't happened. *He'd admitted it*.

To tie up the rest of the revelations in a bow, I'd learned something, or someone, was out to kill me. I hadn't really let that occupy too much of my thoughts because there had simply been no time. Here in my room, surrounded by nothing but the sounds of Pearl Jam and the faltering of my heart, I had nothing *but* time.

I slept.

I cried.

I seethed.

Infuriatingly, each time I closed my eyes, I still saw those blue eyes, cruelly tinted, slicing through my dreams. I still heard his name, and my heart inexplicably *ached* to have him near me once more. The others hadn't tried to come in here yet, but I could hear them speaking softly from the other rooms, could feel the tension building the longer I stayed locked away. Anger welled up like a relentless tide, and I tried to compartmentalize, but I just couldn't.

The constant migraine and pressure from these revelations was a ruthless truth that they had in fact, done the right thing in keeping these memories from me as long as they had. The painful recollections of Hades had almost split me in two. I took a swig of the water Artemis had left for me on the bedside table and swung my legs over the bed, breathing deep to sate the nausea swirling inside me. I was still exhausted, in spite of the many naps I'd fallen into, but I was determined to know more. Maybe that was the only way.

I'd read a lot when I first woke up about the mind and the ways it stored information. None of the theories I read seemed right to me, save for the Method of Loci. It was invented by a Roman, Simonides of Ceos, and it showed how the mind could catalog information and memories by compartmentalizing things in a three-dimensional space—like a store or village or room. Every time I pushed my mind to let me *see*, I could feel the wall of stone surrounding my memories, could feel it pulse and breathe, could even touch it, metaphysically.

I settled on my hands and knees, sliding my body flush as I pressed my face against the floorboards. The setting sun winked at me as the darkness climbed into the sky through my window. According to my alarm clock, I'd been in here almost a full day.

I closed my eyes, willing my mind to open to me, imagining a large cavern lined with the makings of a library. I conjured great floor-to-ceiling bookshelves, oak and proud as they stretched to a large, glass dome overhead. I borrowed inspiration from the nightclub, Styx, and outfitted my mind palace with the bone-colored arches that gave the illusion of a rib cage. Row after row of these shelves filled with books. Leather-bound tomes that allied themselves with all the information I had ever known and could recall.

I walked along the rows as they circled this giant cavern, running my fingers down their spines. The case marked "Music and Lyrics" caught my attention. These books were a chromatic rainbow separated by genre, then alphabetically, from yellow to purple, and all the shades in between. I plucked a bright yellow tome, sliding it open. "Songs About Happiness" the title page read. I flicked playfully to a page at random and smoothed it flat. The lyrics to "Walking on Sunshine" danced over the page and I smiled in triumphant wonder.

This could be the way I got back to good.

I turned my attention to the elephant in the room—the giant mess of memories cordoned off. It took up the middle of the space in its entirety and seemed to stretch on forever. I could see the wall of scar tissue, but it didn't look solid. The wall wasn't cragged and black obsidian in its defiance. Instead, it was flushed an angry red, pulsing and swollen—an open wound.

Fragments of memories lay strewn around the gaping hole I had breached when I'd grenade-blasted through earlier. I gathered them up, ignoring the pinch of pain that made a home under my temples, held them close to me, running my fingers over torn edges.

Show me, I pleaded, and softly, kindly, it opened to me.

I could taste the char from the damage, and something I could only describe as pure chaos, as I patiently waited for it to help me understand. The pinch of pain lessened by a fraction, and I let out a breath.

This damage was a part of me, just as much as the memories it hoarded. I had been trying so long to overcome it, to rip it away. I didn't realize it was the same tissue. A scab my body formed to protect me. It wasn't ready to fall off completely, but perhaps with some first aid, I could soften some of the harsher spots.

The memory latched onto me, and I was leaning, falling. I landed somewhere familiar, but I could not place when I had been there.

I was running along a path, sandals slapping wildly at the bottoms of my feet as I tore through the trees. Exhilaration blew through me, and I knew at once this was my favorite game. A laugh tinkled from somewhere close behind me, and I knew without seeing that it would be Artemis. That she would be chasing me, bow poised to let loose a harmless arrow that would wrap moonlight around me, claiming her prize. I knew that I would soon complain that she had not given me enough of a head start, and that being the Goddess of the Hunt meant she should count to at least a million before starting her chase.

The memory floated around me almost playfully before settling into my mind, filed in a neat, midnight blue book whose cover said "Artemis" in silver letters.

I looked down at the other fragments held tightly in my hand and took a determined breath. *I could do this. One at a time, book by book.*

I set to work, diligently and meticulously courting each fragment into showing me the treasure it held inside before placing it within its book and shelving it.

A fragment of a time with Hephaestus as he forged great boats and a bridge of steel for the Underworld during something called Demeter's Rebellion.

Hecate hugging me with glistening tears in her eyes, telling me how happy she was for me as I stood with her and Artemis, flowers in my hair.

Hermes handing me pomegranate seeds in a giant room filled with screaming and chaos.

Hades lying in a meadow of wildflowers, his eyes closed as the sun danced over his pale skin, a small smile on his face as he asked what I was looking at.

Me in a field, willing the spring to come forth to me, to break out of the clutches of frozen ground and reach toward the sun.

Helios tucking me under his arm as we walked, and he laughed, down a forest path.

Hades running a thumb over my lip, bowed before me, gathering my dress up around my hips as he brought his lips to my core on a throne of skulls. The sounds of ecstasy falling delicately from my lips as he brought me to release.

Confusion swathed over me as I watched and rewatched the memory. Everything in my mind screamed that this was *wrong*. He had told me what he'd done and yet . . . And yet. The way his hands ran along the soft skin of my thighs as he gripped me and brought my body toward him, how he commanded the shadows to stay pliant but firm on my skin to make sure I didn't bruise. The look of pure adoration in his eyes as he coaxed me through my climax again and again and again. The way his name fell from my lips reverently, like a prayer. He was . . . worshipping me in that memory.

It was as though the memory was a different version of Hades, but that didn't make sense. Had he forced me to fall in love with him? Had I been the victim of some sort of Stockholm syndrome situation? And if he took me, kept me, raped me—why didn't any of the others come for me? They left me with a predator? Had I not tried to escape?

I walked around the perimeter of the corrupted memories, searching for any soft spots of loose threads I could pull. I needed more answers, but the fragments had gone too quickly and there were no more to be found.

Exhausted, I retreated from my mind and found my muscles sore from the hardwood floor. I glanced at the glaring, bright red neon in the darkness. I had been under for three hours. A groan pushed past my lips as I forced myself to stand and stretch, still wearing the shirt I had come home in. *His* shirt. I sighed at the disappointment that the smell of him no longer lingered there, then chastised myself again for letting the fact that he was hot and I couldn't remember his crimes allow him any space in my mind.

I needed a cold shower. And therapy. Lots of fucking therapy.

My purple bathrobe hung on the back of my door, and I reached for it. I needed some distance between myself and everything Hades. The underwear dropped from me along with the bra I hadn't bothered to take off before as I shimmied it from under the shirt. I grabbed a set of sweats, and my wool socks then slipped out the door.

The voices from the living room stopped immediately when the door creaked open, but I didn't stick around long enough for any of them to make their way to me, except for maybe Hermes the God of Being Obnoxiously Fast. Thankfully, he either wasn't here or wasn't bothered enough to waste the energy. I rushed to the bathroom and locked myself in.

The water was brutally hot when I turned on the shower and I stood just outside, letting the steam collect on the walls. The floor-length gilded mirror mocked me as I surveyed the damage done to my body.

Dried blood caked around my scalp in my hair. It was obvious someone had cleaned up my face when they changed me out of my filthy show clothes, and I cringed at what must have become of my dress. I loved it, and now it and my corset were probably ruined. Scratches and cuts littered my palms, arms, and legs from crawling on the harsh gravel, but they looked to be healing quickly.

God-powers, I guessed.

I stepped into the tub gingerly and winced. The hot water stung as it washed over me, taking with it the grime and sweat and memory of Hades's hands on my body. I had to figure out how I was going to handle the next few hours. There would be a confrontation with the people I had grown to love. They had to be told what they did to me wasn't okay, and that I was hurt, but I also understood *why* they did what they did.

I lathered shampoo and then conditioner in my hair and washed my body with the pink loofah hanging on the wall. Right now, I'd focus on the shower, then after, the drying and putting on clothes. One thing at a time. I couldn't make my mind move forward much more than that. So, I did those things. Finished my shower. Toweled off. Got dressed. I steeled myself as I opened the door, hair wrapped in a turban, my sweats hanging off of my body. I felt frail and scared. *Exposed.*

They knew everything about me, and I knew barely anything about them. How much of who they were in my eyes was an act? What of them could I trust? The voices were low again as I approached the threshold of the living room. I leaned against the doorway, arms crossed.

Hecate and Medusa were on the velvet couch and Artemis was shooting a silver-light arrow at a target on the wall. It left no trace, but she hit the middle mark every time. Hermes sat perched on the window seat, a book in his hands. Hephaestus and Helios were both on the floor, facing each other and talking low.

I didn't make a move to announce my presence, no throat clearing or words. All eyes turned to me anyway and the tension swelled in the room, displacing all the air. My chest ached at the looks in their eyes. *Pity. Regret.*

Artemis approached me first, suddenly looking very small. She had always seemed unshakeable to me, resolute and strong. Now, she looked meek and ashamed. I didn't like it or how unnatural it felt. Her hands trembled as I watched her tighten them on the bow. She cast her eyes down awkwardly.

"Okay, we have to talk about this," I managed to choke out. We had a lot pressing in on us and an awkward standoff wasn't going to make it any less dangerous. "I've just found out I'm a goddess, that all of my friends are supernatural, and that I'm married to a monster. Someone is trying to kill me. I can control plant growth and shadows, and my brain is about one overload away from imploding. Is that everything?" I asked, trying to piston things forward.

Rip off the Band-Aid, I reminded myself. I could do this.

Artemis eyed me worriedly. "You're very calm about all of this. Are you in shock?" She turned to Hermes and gestured toward me, "Is she in shock?" she asked him, for clarity. He shook his head.

"I don't think it's shock but it's *something*. Tell me what's going on in your mind, love." It was Helios who answered her, and my eyes flicked to him. Helios who looked at me with a fresh wave of despair and regret.

Hecate's words flitted through my mind. *"He loved her." "Yes, but it's very complicated."*

The brawling I saw between him and Hades must be an old debt. It felt old. Had Hades stolen me from Helios? Didn't he even try to find me?

I rounded on him, balling my fists at my sides to control the slight shaking that was threatening to turn into tremors. My adrenaline spiked at the waves of anxiety coursing through me. "You let him take me? That day by the banks when the earth ripped apart? I remember you riding your chariot down for me," I questioned, studying him.

Helios looked at me sadly, kindly. There it was again, *pity*. I straightened, puffing out my chest. I did not need his pity.

"It isn't like that, Persephone," he answered, pleading. "I can't tell you much more. Hygieia said if we told you any more it could kill you. You must work through it on your own." His words sounded rehearsed, and I wondered if that was the party line they would all use.

Something shook loose in my head as I squared up to him, a memory. I felt it break rank from the crack in the wall and float lithely to the ground. I'd have to go back to examine and file it later.

"You all just stood around and let him r—" I began, but a strangled noise cut me off.

Medusa stood, her small body void of the confidence and bravado she usually wore, as she approached. She pushed past Helios, who reached for her. She flinched, almost imperceptibly at the action, but I caught it. She held her small hand out to me, palm out. Her dreads—*snakes*—twisted and twitched atop her crown, mingling and mixing with her hair. Now that I could see them, it was a marvel I hadn't noticed before.

"We need to speak, just the two of us." She motioned toward the music room, and I took her hand, following. The others looked moments from protesting, but she turned back to look at them, face stern. "I know the rules. I won't break them."

She led me out of the room, closing the door tight behind us. We walked to the small sofa and sat together. Medusa folded herself into the couch with her legs tucked beneath her. She took my hands back into hers, her dark melanin a beautiful contrast to my slightly golden skin.

Medusa's glasses reflected my eyes as she took a deep, steadying breath. "I can't tell you what you want to know without risking harm, but I want to tell you a story about me, during which I think you will come to understand that not everything is as it seems. Artemis told me you read a few books on Greek Mythos. Did you read anything about me?" she asked. I nodded slowly, cheeks flushing.

The stories I'd read painted Medusa as a seductress, cursed by Athena until her death by Perseus. They were just myths, though. Medusa was obviously alive, so it was probable they had gotten more wrong.

"Yes, you were cursed by Athena in them." I didn't elaborate further, but the stiffening in her posture let me know she understood what was left unsaid.

Medusa wiped her hand over her bottom lip before continuing. "I was a Priestess of Athena at her temple near the sea. I grew up there, running through the great temple and learning all the ways to worship and serve the goddess. You see, I was merely a mortal—there was nothing particularly special about me, and I didn't aspire to be anything more than a priestess. I was devout in my love for Athena, and I took a vow of chastity, not because she asked for it, but because it was a matter of controlled autonomy that would allow me to focus more on the collection of wisdom and knowledge. I wore my skin adorned with gold grease paints, the better to prove my piety. One day . . ." Medusa paused, tilted her head back, and took another heavy breath.

"One day, as I walked along the sea wall, a man appeared. He came up from the spray. While I didn't know who he was at first, one look into those eyes and I knew it must have been the God of the Sea, Poseidon. He was the consort to Athena, and as such, was much revered. He was . . . beautiful." Medusa swallowed as though even thinking the thought brought her pain. She continued, "He was tall and handsome. I was struck by him. Embarrassingly so. He began talking to me, innocently at first. He was kind. He said how much he loved my hair, and I'm ashamed to say that part of me glowed at his praise, but he was a god, divinity incarnate. He came to see me every day. Sometimes, he would bring me things—a seashell or a rare pearl."

I listened, enraptured. A small nagging hit the back of my skull as my mind tried to recall some sort of recollection of this story that wasn't one I'd read in that book. I squeezed her hand encouragingly. Whatever she was coming to was costing her greatly to share, and I wanted to show support. This was my friend, and at the end of the day, she was trying to do this to help me.

"As I walked down by the ocean, a storm blew through and spit him out of the waves when it crashed into the wall. His eyes were dark, almost black. Something akin to rage rolled off him, but when he saw me, his face was serene again, and I told myself to calm down, that he was safe. *Kind*. He beckoned me to come closer as he stood, swaying. I kept a distance, but I *did* approach. It wasn't until I was too close that I realized he smelled like booze. The alcohol reeked off him and I took several steps back, but he grabbed me, and his grip was . . . crushing. I just remember panicking, stumbling, begging him to let me go. He smiled at me, but it was cruel, all signs of the god I had known gone. Then his lips were on me, painfully, and I panicked more. I managed to get my knee into him, and he doubled over just long enough for me to run. It was raining. I remember the way the water stung as it pelted me. I could hear my feet slapping against the rough stone and his ragged breath filled with rage billowing behind me. I prayed to Athena . . . I begged her to hear me and help me." Another deep breath. Another hand squeeze. My stomach twisted as I saw this all unfold in my mind.

"He caught me on the steps to the temple. He . . . She didn't come to save me. I found out later that she was on Olympus in a quiet chamber and our prayers were blocked . . . but she never came. He pushed me onto the steps, the granite bit into my skin and tore my flesh. I used to wear my hair loose in braids around me. He grabbed it, yanked my head back, and whispered how much he loved my hair, how beautiful I was to him. I can't tell you how long he violated my body. He was not gentle. He rode me so hard he tore things inside me . . . My maidenhood lay splattered on the steps beneath and around us as he brutalized me. I begged and fought, but he didn't stop. In the end, I just laid there against the steps, focusing on the feel of them biting into my cheek and breasts and knees as his hands pinned me down. I told myself I was somewhere else, *anywhere* else. When Poseidon finally relented, I felt the hot shame spilling out as it mixed with the blood and the rain and the seawater beneath me. He kissed the salty tears from my cheeks, and I just remember being cold, Persephone. I was so damn cold. He left me there in the rain, broken and bloody." Medusa's voice was far away.

My chest seized. I tried to bite back the tears threatening to fall. This wasn't my pain, but I was furious for her. How dare those fucking assholes spin her history this way? Where the fuck was Athena when they were telling these lies? I squeezed both of her hands.

She shook her head slightly and pressed on. "I laid there for a very long time. Now, we would call it shock. I couldn't move, and I was bleeding out from his size and how hard he'd taken me. I begged for Death. I prayed to him in a way I was never able to pray to Athena. If I could have made my body move, I would have rolled into the sea, but I also couldn't stand to have any part of him inside me any longer. So yeah . . . I prayed to Death, but Thanatos didn't come. Hades did." She looked at me, willing me to understand something.

"He took me to the Underworld, had his female shades clean me up. Hades . . . He came to me, and he told me the seed had taken root, he could feel the new life's spark. God sperm is apparently fucking super-semen. He asked me if I wanted to bear it, or if I wanted him to take care of it. I told him I wanted it gone, and I asked him to kill me too. He took care of the poison inside me, and then, he stayed to watch over me to make sure I didn't run off to kill myself in one of the many ways mortals can die simply by being in the Underworld." She sucked in a deep breath.

"One night, I woke up to thunderous yelling. He had summoned Athena and filled her in on what Poseidon had done. He blamed her for not protecting me, and it was terrifying. Told her if she didn't find a way to keep me protected, he would kill Poseidon himself. So she made me into this. I felt like a dirty, unclean thing. Unworthy of the kindness of divinity. She took me from the Underworld and brought me to Artemis to heal with the other women in the Wild Hunt. This gift, it's a curse too, but to me, it was freedom. I could protect myself in a way I never could before. I learned later that it was Hades's idea, to make me Gorgon. Most can control their power, but I never could keep it at bay, so I wear my glasses to keep the Stare from hurting anyone unintentionally.

"After some centuries, Perseus found me and ended me. The Shield of Athena was given to him by Poseidon, who never forgave me for the rift his actions caused with Athena. She couldn't break their Bond, but she never touched him again. When Perseus took my head, Hades met me at the River Styx and reanimated me. I lived there peacefully until I fully recovered. Over the years, I've done a lot of work on myself, healing from my trauma, helping other survivors down at the shelter. Hades has always been a staunch ally . . ."

"Do you think I could kill the God of the Sea with a Ficus? Because I totally will." I sniffed, swallowing down the lump in my throat.

"Don't worry, Seph. He's going to get his one day, and I'll be right there to see him fall."

Tears fell from both of us. Medusa leaned into my embrace, and I held her close, pouring all of my love into her. She had torn open her chest to expose her deepest wound so that I may see and understand that a man who acted that way over someone he didn't know wouldn't take a woman against her wishes. Which meant that he was lying. *But why?* Why cop to something so vile? I didn't want to make this moment about me, but I couldn't help but ask.

"Why lie?"

Her beautiful dark lips twisted into a sad smile, and she pushed a rogue curl of mine back. "You'll have to ask him, love."

I would.

Helios

CHAPTER 25

The door clicked shut behind me, soft and unnoticed over the low thrum of music drifting from the kitchen. I set my keys down on the entryway table, my coat over the nearest chair, already smiling before I turned the corner. The scent hit first, garlic, roasted and warm, and then the sound. A voice sang loudly, filling the walls of this house, half right, half playful, thick with joy. His voice.

And then him.

Nick stood barefoot, dancing a little as he stirred something on the stove, slim hips swaying in time with the music. He had a dishtowel tossed over one shoulder, sleeves pushed up over his forearms as he worked, hair a little wild just like I'd left it this morning. I liked the thought that he'd kept the mess I'd made with my fingers, my fists, as we'd kissed our goodbyes in the early morning light. He didn't notice me in the doorway, too lost in the rhythm, too comfortable in my space.

And *Fates*, wasn't that the thing? He looked *at home in my home.* After the events at Styx a few weeks ago, hardly a day had passed when we weren't together in some way.

The light caught him just right, golden and soft, and for a moment it was too much. The kitchen, our kitchen for tonight, felt suddenly too small for the feeling building in my chest. A swelling, aching kind of pressure built and built a little more each day, every time I woke up with Nick in my bed, tucked against my chest.

It had only been a few weeks, but I wanted him with the slow, consuming hunger of something I could never name out loud. I wanted mornings and evenings and everything in between, every breath and pant that fell from his soft fucking lips, every sleepy smile that quirked his mouth when he drifted off with my sweat on his skin.

I could almost see it, evenings like this, quiet dinners, slow dances in the setting sun. I saw Nick, laughing and unguarded, opening the wounds inside me, digging them out, planting fresh flowers inside the pain. I wanted to give him anything, all the things. A life. *Babies*. Any happiness he never thought he deserved.

Because he did, hells, he deserved it all.

But he refused to move in, not that I'd exactly pressed the issue. It was almost like he was skittish, like there were two parts of him at constant war with each other. One where he craved my touch, sought it out, and the other, where he kept me at arm's length, like he was terrified of being trapped or wounded. There wasn't a scrap of clothing that belonged to him other than what he wore on his back at this house, but his touch was everywhere: in the clippings set in small vases on the windowsill, in the tidiness of the kitchen, in the candle that burned in the living room.

I leaned in the doorway, just watching. The sounds of a blade on my wooden cutting board tapped methodically as he worked to slice up more garlic, adding it to the fragrant pan on the stove. Nick turned then, catching me staring. He grinned. "Hey, Daddy."

I didn't answer right away, just crossed the room, slipping my arms around him from behind, pressing my face into the curve of his neck. I inhaled him deep, catching the essence of his cologne, his natural Otherworlder scent, trapping it in my lungs.

"*Stay*," I whispered on an exhale, not even meaning tonight. "*Just . . . stay.*"

Nick's hands moved the sweating vegetable pan off the flames, and turned off the gas, then he leaned back, relaxing against my chest. His head turned slightly to look up at me as I crowded over him, his eyes glassy.

"Hard up for a private chef?" he teased, trapping his bottom lip between perfect teeth. A chuckle rumbled up from my chest, shaking through him.

"I don't actually need to eat, baby boy," I reminded him. Nymphs were Otherworlders, but I was a titan.

"Maybe not, but you love food. Or have I been slaving away in here for nothing?" he challenged. I sank a tender bite against the column of his throat, and he moaned, sighing contentedly.

"I love when you do that. Mark me as yours." He hummed. "I do need to pull the chicken out of the oven though, will you set the table?" he asked, and I nodded, pressing kisses to the side of his cheek, making him squirm and laugh from the tickle of my beard against his smooth jaw.

"I suppossseeee," I sighed, reluctantly letting him go for a second before snatching him back by the fabric of his shirt, kissing him deep, plundering his mouth with my tongue, swallowing his moan. As quickly as I'd been on him, I let him loose, and he stumbled forward, breathless and flushed, back to the stove as I worked around him, setting the table. It was so domesticated, the way we moved as a unit, but he hadn't answered me, and that gnawed at my insides.

We sat together, the candlelight between us, plates nearly licked clean. The chicken parm he'd made from scratch had tasted divine, and I took a swig of my beer as he sipped his tea. It struck me that I'd never seen him even take a sip of alcohol. He twirled his pasta daintily over the tines of his fork as I sat back, studying him.

"Can I ask you something, baby?"

His eyes cast up to mine, the tips of his lips lifting up, as he took a bite, swallowed, and replied, "Yeah, of course."

I considered carefully, wanting to make sure I handled this as delicately as possibly. Sobriety could be a touchy subject, but if it was a part of him, I wanted to know so I could respect it. Help him with it, if he wanted. Give him whatever he needed.

"I noticed that you don't partake in . . ." I tapped the label of the bottle in my hands with my fingertips a few times. The work of his jaw slowed, the muscles in his throat overcompensating as he swallowed a too big bite. Setting his fork on his plate, he reached for his glass, washing it all down. I waited, cataloging every action, every reaction.

He sighed.

"I'm not . . . sober, if that's what you mean. I was introduced to alcohol in a very dark time in my life, and the people around me took advantage of that. I, uh, I just choose not to partake, anymore. I don't need it, and the taste of wine, even the smell of it . . . It's rancid to me." His voice trailed off, shaken as anger and rage welled up in my chest.

"Did someone hurt you? Give me a name," I growled, low, primal. The glass bottle in my hand shattered, spilling what was left of the hoppy brew over the table. Glass bit into my skin, digging deep, mixing my blood with it. With a startled cry, Nick jumped up, rushing around the table to cradle my hand in his. He fussed over the glass embedded in my palm, but the rapid rise and fall of my chest was over him.

"Fuck, this is deep," he noted, bending low to assess the damage.

"Who fucking hurt you?" I repeated.

"We need to get this glass out of here before the skin regrows around it—"

"I don't give a damn about my hand, Nick. Who. Fucking. Hurt. You." I didn't miss the tremors in his fingers, the tension in his body. The trauma went deep. I fought to keep control, unable to stop myself from drawing the parallel to Narcissus, of how Zeus had manipulated him, drugged him.

Fates only knew what else.

"It doesn't matter. It was a long time ago, and I'm not that person anymore. I just want to live my life in a way that's for me. I want to put it all behind me. Can we do that?" he asked, pulling free the last sharp shard and tossing it onto a napkin with the others.

"I want to protect you. I need to." I didn't expect the desperation in my voice to be so loud, so raw. Nick's fingers were covered in my blood, but the wounds were already healing unobstructed thanks to his careful action and care. "Please. Let me take care of you."

Nick looked torn, eyes laden with longing and sadness I couldn't figure out.

"Why? You don't even know me, Helios. I'm not . . . I don't deserve this. I shouldn't even be here," he stammered, pulling back from my touch, closing himself off in that way of his. Frustration and desolation ate at me, twisted me up. He'd done this a few times, and I'd just thought he had commitment issues. I could understand, given the reputations of the titans and gods, but I thought I'd been patient.

"Are you afraid of me? Because of who I am? I would never hurt you, Nick. *Ever*. You keep pulling back and I'm here, I'm *right* here and I'm just trying to be honest with you. I have to, after—"

I snapped my jaw shut tight.

"After what?" he pressed. I held my breath as his eyes searched mine.

"Nothing. Let me clean this up. I shouldn't have pushed," I swallowed, standing. I towered above him, our chests nearly touching as his chin tipped up. The urge to kiss him, to pin him to the table and fuck the submission into him warred hard with my better judgment. His eyes begged me to do it, but my heart, and maybe his, didn't need that.

His hand slipped down to cup my length through my jeans, and I reacted to him, of course I did, how could I not? He smirked as I grew harder under his touch, leaning forward he pressed hot kisses against my chest, his breath seeping through the fabric of my shirt. Lust clouded over me, but another part, a nagging voice that wouldn't shut the fuck up, the voice of Hygieia and her years of therapy had my hands stilling his, had me stepping back to put some air between us.

Hurt bloomed over his features.

"You don't want to?" His eyebrows creased in confusion.

"Of course I do, baby, obviously. But we can't avoid hard conversations with sex, Nick, and I can't function with the right head if you're touching me." I sighed, hating the words even as I said them. "Come on," I urged, picking up the remnants of my bottle, and plate, clearing the glass-littered napkin. I dumped them in the trash, put the dishes in the sink, then reached for a trailing Nick to pull him under the heated faucet. I lathered up his hands, taking care to get the blood that had seeped under his cuticles clean, and when the water ran clear once more, I dried off my hands and went to finish cleaning the spilled beer with a fresh towel.

The mood was tense as the night wore on, as we stumbled around the elephant in the room with tripping feet. I wanted to make him talk to me, but I wasn't going to push him to *want* to be with me. We sat on opposite ends of the couch in the evening, him curled up with a book, me writing in my journal. I closed it quietly, then made my way from the couch to the bedroom.

Neither of us spoke. He didn't follow me when I went.

The disappointment stung as I showered, alone, and threw on a pair of sweats before climbing into bed. The living room was quiet, void of music but I could feel him there still, the presence of him, somewhere just beyond. I settled under the covers, turned on my bedside lamp, and pulled out my journal again, pouring out all the things I wanted to say to him between the pages.

I heard feet shuffle near the threshold of the open door, and I tried to suppress my smile that he was still here. I'd half expected him to go home to his place. Dreaded it, even.

"Helios?" he called. I closed my journal, set it to the side as I looked up at him. His weight shifted from foot to foot, hands rubbing over one another nervously.

"Yeah, baby boy?" I answered.

"Can . . . Can I stay the night? No funny business, I promise."

A smile tugged up my lips. I shifted back, opening the covers to him. "Of course, baby. You can always stay with me."

Relief bloomed over his precious face as he raced across the room, nearly jumping into bed. He snuggled close as I tucked the blanket over him, the possessive monster in my chest purring as he nuzzled his nose into my neck. I reached over to turn off the lamp, drenching us in blue twilight. His hands moved, tracing along the lines of my torso, ghosting over my tattooed chest, but it wasn't sexual.

He was self-soothing.

I pressed a kiss to the crown of his hair.

"I want to stay. I want to let myself get lost in this so badly, but I'm not a good person, Helios. I try to be, now, but I've done things, terrible, terrible things and I can't undo them. I don't deserve this, with you, but I can't make myself stay away either and I don't know why you want so badly to care about me," he confessed against my skin, opening himself. He was terrified, I could feel it in the shake of him, hear it in the unsteady warble of his voice. This was real. Open. Honest.

Finally.

I squeezed him closer, speaking into the darkness.

"A long time ago, I loved someone so much, but I never let them know because I thought it wasn't safe for them. And when it mattered, when they needed me, I wasn't there. It cost me everything, and I vowed that I would never do that again."

He stilled in my arms, then glanced up at me through his long, blond eyelashes, expression unreadable.

"What happened to them?"

I paused. It welled up inside me, the memory, the pain of it. It crawled up from the deepest pits of regret inside my body, clawed up my throat, battered against my lips like a ram. My grip tightened around Nick as I spoke it then, all of it. The words flowed like a raging river, drowning me, choking me, but Nick was a lifeline. I shared everything, even the parts I'd omitted from Hygieia in therapy, even the parts I hated to admit to myself.

I showed him the deepest shame I'd forever carry, a wound that would never stop bleeding because I hadn't been strong enough then, but I was now. He listened intently, every emotion on full display over his handsome face. He asked questions, thoughtful and deep, and the significance of his body on mine, the importance of it, kept me tethered in the reality of now.

Free to gaze into the long lens of the past without the fear of getting trapped there.

And when I spoke of the morning I'd hung up the sun and turned from Olympus, my chest was wet with tears. Not mine, but from the deep springs of emotion behind Nick's brown eyes.

"You did all that to protect him, and lost him anyway?" His lip trembled. I kissed it, tenderly. Nodded. "And he never knew? That it was an arrangement, or that Persephone never pursued you?" I kissed over the tears slipping from the corner of his eyes, admiring his empathy and compassion. His fingernails dug into the muscles of my abdomen, anchoring himself to me.

"I wished I would have gotten to tell him how much he meant to me. He died never knowing how deeply he was buried in my heart, and I swore I'd never let that happen again. You know what a Bond is, don't you?" He swallowed. Dipped his chin. I carded my fingers through his tresses, scraping my nails over his scalp.

"I'm not afraid of what I feel. Just afraid you don't feel it back."

A sob rattled from his chest, heavy and harsh and breaking. I cupped his head, brought him back against me, let him soak me with tears. "I don't care who you were then, Nick. I just want who you are now."

Persephone

CHAPTER 26

I spent my days under constant supervision, in one form or another. As much as I enjoyed the snippets of information they provided, or getting to have honest conversations with the others about memories of ancient Greece that bled through, Hades hadn't so much as checked in on me, and that disappointment sank like a stone in my chest. He either really didn't care about me, or he had been dragged back to the Underworld.

Maybe both.

Either way, it made me feel foolish and confused about my feelings. His words warred constantly with the pieces of memories that snuck through, which elicited an embarrassingly inappropriate number of dreams that left me panting and soaked when I awoke. He was the one subject that was never on the table with any of the others, but I needled them anyway, hoping they'd crack and give me something, anything to hold on to. Only Medusa had offered me insight, but even she remained tight-lipped in the following days over him, as though she had only told her story to give me the perspective that he most likely, probably, didn't *actually* assault me. He'd just . . . told me he had over some misguided attempt to push me away or something? Which was objectively still pretty fucking bad, in my opinion.

My mind palace was a bustling library, as I recovered new memories daily, breathing and panting through the painful jolts and migraines that accompanied every fragment. Still, I was going batshit under a constant state of house arrest, and I wanted *out*. I tried to get each of them to take me on any kind of field trip, but they were all so fucking loyal to Hades that they wouldn't even consider letting me out without his expressed permission. He may not have actually abducted me long ago, but he may as well have now.

Helios sat across from me at the kitchen table as I reread the same page for the fourth time. This book on Greek mythology was new, and ever since the night at Styx, I had devoured as many as I could get my grubby little hands on. I'd pumped the others for information, which they would give, as long as it didn't have to do with *him*.

I hated him. And his stupid fucking hot face. And their loyalty to him. And how he seemed to make all the rules.

I peered over at Helios, who was trying and failing to not show how much he desperately wanted his shift to be over. He had a date tonight with Nick, the guy I'd invited to Styx. As it turned out Nick, too, was a part of our world, not a god, but a nymph. Whatever that meant. Apparently, they'd met the night we were attacked, and though Helios was a little squirrely on the details, we'd all deduced they hooked up. It had only been a few weeks, but it was obviously going well.

Helios was the weakest link of the others, the soft spot he had for me seemingly familial, like a protective older sibling. It looked like I had a lot of those, with the way they all guarded me, but Helios seemed especially susceptible to my moods and emotions. It may be a dick move, but I had a feeling if I pushed the right buttons, I could get him to jailbreak me out of this fucking house.

"How are you and Nick?" I asked, and instantly, Helios lit up, the warm glow of his skin nearly too bright in the fading dusk. He smiled wide, genuine, and it filled me with a sense of happiness for him.

"So good. I think. He can be a little hard to read sometimes, but I think we're taking it slow, building a foundation," he replied, rubbing his hands over the tops of his thighs.

"Taking it slow? Aren't you living together?" I raised a skeptical eyebrow, teasing. He gave me a sheepish look, cocking his head with an adorably crooked smile.

"He's still *technically* got a place, it's just in Metairie and it's more convenient if he's . . ." he gestured his hand in the air vaguely.

"In your bed every night?" I finished with a laugh.

"*Exactly*, you get it, besides," he shrugged, relaxing back, "our kind move fast, it's not in our nature to resist impulses and wants. When you know, you just know, right?" A heavy sadness, tinged with a pang of longing swelled up in my chest, lodged itself in my throat.

"I uh, well, not really," I lied, twisting my hands together. I *wanted* to know that feeling, wanted to let myself experience it instead of a one-sided attraction that left me pining, but the Fates, as I'd learned, had other plans. A pained look flashed across Helios's face, his lips flattening into a thin line. "Seph, listen. Fuck, I'm— It's complicated, you know?" he offered. My face burned hot, undoubtedly turning red, I could feel it blooming across my cheeks, bright and impossible to hide.

"It's fine. I'm fine," I lied, and the tears that stung the corners of my eyes were real, and unexpected under the weight of his understanding gaze. He turned his body, large and imposing, the muscles rippling under his shirt to give me his full attention. Brown eyes bore into mine, full of concern and care that I didn't yet fully comprehend.

"You're not, are you? Okay. Of course you aren't, with everything. You can talk to me. I promise you can," he nudged earnestly. My lip quivered, the spasm involuntary. *Traitorous*.

"I mean, it's just hard with finding out about the whole divinity thing, the murder plot psycho situation and then on top of that, moping over a man who would rather make himself a predator in my eyes than spend time with me or be married to me . . . Fuck, man. It's . . . not great."

I couldn't bear the pity in his eyes. In my chest, my heart stuttered, then picked up, thudding in a way that made me feel hollow, so I looked down, over at the photographs on the wall, anywhere but back at the Titan of the Sun. My hands fidgeted, thumb rubbing over thumbnails, fingers curling into my palm as the silence settled between us. Too fast. Too obvious.

Fates, why did I say that out loud?

Why was he looking at me like that?

"Who told you?" he whispered gently, as I picked at the edge of my cuticle. Fuck. I hadn't meant to let that slip out, what Medusa had told me in confidence, but there it was, and I couldn't put the genie back in the bottle.

"Medusa," I sniffled miserably, swiping away at the tear tracking down my cheek, "but she didn't tell me directly. Just how he had handled her . . . *situation*." I finished cryptically. I didn't know exactly what anyone else knew of what she'd gone through, and it wasn't my business to share. I wouldn't betray her trust. Helios nodded solemnly as though he understood my meaning, his fingertips twitching on his thigh as he dug them into the fabric of his jeans.

"He has reasons. I wish I could explain them, but I can't. What you figure out on your own is painful enough, and he has it on good authority that pushing will hurt you more. No one wants to see you go through any more pain, Persephone. Do you understand what I'm telling you?" He soothed. I nodded, then cried harder, silently, hating every warm spill that slid down my cheeks, my neck.

I did understand. He was trying to protect me, they all were. But it was suffocating. I was suffocating.

"I just want to be normal. I want to go to work, and play music. I—" my voice cracked, and Helios looked so stricken, "I want to live. I was in that box for so long. Thousands of years. Don't I deserve to experience? This isn't living, being trapped here. I want to know what I'm missing, with him. Why do I dream of him, have this agonizing ache for him if he's not supposed to be important to me?"

"Persephone, can I touch you? I would very much like to hug you now, but only if it would comfort you," Helios asked gently, and I nodded through the deluge of tears, through the sobs that shook my chest as strong arms came around me. I cried into his shirt as he shushed and soothed me, promising me it was going to be okay.

I wanted so badly to believe him.

It was a long time before I pulled away from the comfort of his embrace, long after I'd cried the last tear, sighed my last sob. He brushed away the errant wetness from my flushed cheeks with the pad of his thumb, eyes flicking back and forth between mine.

"I'll talk to him," Helios promised, but I just shook my head with a sad smile.

"I don't think it matters. If he wanted to be here with me, he would. I have to let go, if that's what he wants me to do. To protect myself, Helios. I can't keep hurting this way. It's cruel."

"Tell me what to do to help you, Persephone. Tell me what you need, and we can try to make it happen," the plea in his voice, the need to stop my pain was as endearing as it was curious.

"Who was I to you, Helios? I have snippets of memory, but . . . why do you care so much about me?" I asked, throat raw, voice ravaged. His hands fell from my shoulders, and he sat back again, eyes flicking to the ceiling as the muscle in his jaw tightened.

"That's complicated, too, and I don't think I should tell you outright, because it's wrapped up in delicate threads I'm terrified of pulling before they're ready . . ." He trailed off, glancing up at the clock. I deflated, but he continued on. "What I will say, is that I loved you very much. I tried to protect you in the wrong ways, and it caused a lot of unnecessary strife and pain, but I learned, Persephone. I learned the importance of telling people what they mean to you, suffered the cost of that negligence firsthand."

His hand rubbed over his chest, and from the V of his neckline I could see faint traces of ink, a tattoo of some sort and the loss in his voice, the pain . . . It rattled the walls of my mind palace. I winced, as something small fell through the cracks, floated lazily to the floor of my mind. Despite the dull thud, I reached for it.

A throne room, the face of an absolutely stunning man, slender and lithe with white-blond hair, pushing against a raging Helios, decked out in golden armor . . .

"Does it get easier? The moving on?" I asked. Helios let out a wounded gruff from the back of his throat.

"Not *easier*. But there is a lesson in every pain, Persephone, if you can look past the wound to see the root cause. It's taught me how to be a better partner, to look at the uglier parts of my own shortcomings and confront them so that shit doesn't happen again."

I considered his words, the look of hurts long buried, carved into his features mingling with renewed hope.

"Does Nick know about whoever it was?" Curiosity burned through me, but Helios only smiled, speaking softly into the dim light. The sun was nearly set, but neither of us made a move to turn on a lamp, each of us whispering truths into the comfort of looming darkness.

"He knows. We've talked about him a lot, about my failures, about all the things that went right and wrong. I don't want history to repeat itself. I know you think we've moved fast, and maybe we have. But we're honest with one another, and there's a . . . connection between us, specific to our kind. It can be instantaneous if you're ready to receive it. A Fates' blessing—he's my second chance, Seph. I'm not going to drop the ball on this one."

"I'm glad I invited him to the show that day." I smiled.

Helios grinned back, dipping his chin. "Me too. To be honest, he'd been looking to ask you on a date, but then we met instead so . . . sorry about that?" he shrugged, good-naturedly.

"I don't mind. I get the feeling we aren't really each other's type," I replied wistfully, my thoughts rushing back to a tall, broody, off-limits deity with blue eyes.

"Maybe he could come visit with you, on one of your babysitting shifts?" I asked, hopefully, knowing it was a fruitless tree. Hades had forbidden anyone other than his approved list to come to the house. I knew he'd never allow a visitor, much less an Otherworlder, to come here with all the wards they'd installed.

Helios frowned, echoing my thoughts. "You know I can't bring him here, Seph. Until we find the source, it's not safe to give up your location." He looked apologetic, but it didn't ease the sting. I knew he hated disappointing me, and Hells help me, I was about to use that against him. I cast my eyes low, fiddling with the corners of the pages of the upturned book beside me. I let my shoulders droop, and in a defeated voice added, "I know. I just . . . It's been weeks with no news. How long can I go on like this? I haven't even been out of the yard. It feels like I may as well be back in that box."

Hermes arrived then, drawing our attention to the front door. He took one look at us huddled on the couch in the darkness, then crossed to tower over the couch. Long fingers lifted my head to face him, tipping my chin until he was staring in my eyes. "What's wrong? Why are you crying?" he asked, worriedly, voice sharp.

I explained it all again to him, pulling back on the theatrics. Hermes listened intently, unreadable until the very last words left my lips. He considered, then, a wicked, mischievous smile lit his face. Hermes, turned, addressing Helios. "I won't tell if you don't," he offered.

They spoke silently with their eyes, and I held my breath until the corner of Helios's lips curved into a small smile. "Go get dressed," he shot at me.

I squealed with excitement and disbelief at my luck, launching myself between them in a hug. I fumbled my way out of the living room so quickly I almost tripped and broke my neck in the fading light.

Hades

CHAPTER 27

Weeks. It had been *weeks* since I'd seen Persephone, and though the last big stint was two thousand years, I had grown accustomed to being able to glimpse her, even from afar. Her silhouette from across the street, the sound of her laughter in a crowd that made me freeze like she'd struck me through the ribs as I listened like a voyeur through the shadows. She hated me now and I knew it was for the best, but the Tartarus-sized pit inside my chest ached with her absence. She had to stay in that house until we had a better lead. It was protected there and if I entered, we had no idea if it would compromise the warding Hecate had put up, but every second without her felt like being unraveled from the inside out.

Hermes kept me updated on her progress, how she was doing and coping with the waves of memories that burst like a dam in her mind nearly daily, the agony it put her in. Hephaestus told me about the mind palace she was working on, the coping mechanisms she was learning, but I stomped down the spark of hope that bloomed in my chest even as he'd spoken the words. Even if she *did* remember, it changed nothing. I missed her in the small hours the worst, when the world was too quiet to lie to myself. When the distractions faded, when there was nothing left to do but think about her voice, her touch, the way she used to find my eyes in a room, her scent. It all lived in my head like a fever.

I lay awake with a clenched jaw, achy fingers curled into the sheets hoping they might keep me in place, but there was no anchor, no talisman substantial enough to keep thoughts of her at bay. Just the cataclysmic weight of everything unsaid crushing my bones to fine dust with every second we were apart. Persephone was the silence between my thoughts, and I was fucking *drowning* in her.

She didn't know how much I wanted to call just to hear her voice, listen to her breathe as she fell sleep. How many times my hand hovered over the phone, her name lit up in my contacts like a festering wound. I'd written letters, so many godsdamned letters, only to crumble them up.

Ten versions.

Twenty. Each one too honest, too selfish, too dangerous in my raw truths. They littered the floor of my study, overflowing the wastebasket, pots and pots of wasted ink, of broken words, of hollow promises I knew I couldn't keep. No, it was better for both of us if she couldn't recall our life together. My self-control was hanging by the thread of the Fates, and if it pulled any further taut, I would snap and break and ruin us all, because I couldn't trust myself to be around her. Not when every part of my being screamed to cross that line, just once. Just for a moment. Just to hear her say my name like it used to mean everything to her, like one day it could again if she could just fucking remember without chaos consuming her.

Helios's quiet judgment clung to me, a burr under my skin, all small and sharp and impossible to ignore. He thought he knew better, and there was a part of me that argued maybe he did, but it was the same part that strained toward her absence, calling to close the distance between us. It couldn't be trusted either.

So, I stayed away. Not because I didn't love her, but because I *did.*

And loving Persephone meant keeping a distance that felt like dying by degrees, if it kept her alive.

My phone buzzed in my pocket, the shrill tones taking me off guard. I slid my hand into my suit and grasped the demanding device, flipped it open to see *Hermes* flashing across the screen at me. I sighed as I pressed the green button. "What?" I demanded before he could get a word out.

"Field trip," he answered. The world around me stilled, the back of my neck hot with anger.

"*Absolutely not,*" I growled.

"Tough shite. It's not my fault that your prisoner is absolutely loveable and has won over the guards." He teased, but I had no time for it.

"It's too dangerous," I ground out, teeth clenched. Hermes let out a small sigh, like he did every time he was about to give me a harsh dose of reality. I turned and gripped the counter behind me.

"Hades, she needs this. If she doesn't get even a *taste* of freedom willingly, she's going to bloody *take* it. And as much as I'd like to think she isn't capable of escaping on her own, her shadows are starting to return to her and you know when they do, she can portal out anywhere she wants." He retorted, tone clipped. I hated to admit it, but he was probably right. Persephone had never been good at being forced into anything, and when she was given the tools to break out, she'd be a nightmare to contain. Still, a small part of me glowed with twisted pride that she was gaining more control over her shadows, inching closer to stepping into her power. They could protect her if she let them.

"Listen, I'm not calling to ask your permission. This is happening." Hermes levelled, and I stiffened. "I'm calling to let you know a certain flower will probably, most definitely, be at Electric

Delphi later tonight. Probably around eight. I'll be with her, as will Nick and Helios."

"I'll make the arrangements," I conceded, sighing in defeat. I could practically see the smug smile on Hermes's face. "And . . . Helios?" I asked, knowing Hermes would understand. Our differences of opinion on how I was handling Persephone had strained our friendship, but I still cared about him, wanted to know he was okay, with this new love.

"Happy. Nauseatingly so," he answered.

"Good," I replied. Snapping the phone shut, I ended the call, bending over to clutch at the stitch that had formed in my side from the anxiety of having her exposed and open in the world again. *Damn it to the Hells.* Pulling my shit together, I flipped back open my phone and dialed the number for Electric Delphi. He answered on the second ring.

"Dionysus," I clipped, all business, "Persephone is going to be at Electric Delphi tonight. I need her protected." I was met with a weighted silence, then Dio cleared his throat on the other end and when he spoke, his voice was full of joy and barely restrained excitement.

"Nothing will harm her here. You have my word," he promised. There was a thrum of power under his words, a current of uncharacteristic somberness in the revelry. He would take no chances when it came to her safety and that was a reason, I knew, that Hermes had chosen his club even above Styx.

Word had gotten around quickly about the return of the Goddess of the Underworld. Her abduction was legendary amongst our people, and I knew it was only a matter of time before the other Greeks came to call upon her, one bastard in particular, but Zeus was a problem for another day. As long as he stayed in his territory of Las Vegas with the Roman deities, we wouldn't have a problem.

In New Orleans, the Otherworlders had kept their space, except for Nick whom she'd met by chance. Weary of everyone by nature, I'd checked his story as soon as she'd told Helios about how they met at the nursery. He was a nymph, who worked in a temp office in Uptown, but freelanced as a model on the side. It appeared by all accounts that he was who he claimed to be, so for the moment, he was safe. I would keep an eye on him, and not just because of Persephone. Helios was involved with him, too, and I was fiercely protective of the titan, who had become a brother to me over the long years. After everything, I would not see him hurt.

Having done my part, I poured myself a few fingers of whiskey and passed the next few hours in agonizing anxiety. Pacing, I oscillated between telling myself how irresponsible it would be to show up there after what had happened at Styx, then rationalizing that Electric Delphi was neutral ground, and *because* of what had happened the last time she went out in public, I needed to be on guard. I could keep to the shadows, keep my distance. I volleyed back and forth, pretending that I hadn't already decided to go, deluding myself with flimsy justifications about extra precautions, but I knew, as I dressed in a new suit, that the only person she needed protection from was *me*.

I swallowed the thought and opened a portal of shadows, stepping through to the back alley behind the historic building just east of the heart of the Quarter.

Dionysus, God of Wine, leaned against the door frame smoking a joint as I approached. He tapped his golden watch and shot me a grin as he blew out a purple plume of too sweet-smelling smoke. "I'm impressed. I expected you twenty minutes ago," he said, stepping forward. I scowled but returned the quick embrace, annoyed at how rapidly I was becoming predictable.

"I shouldn't be here at all," I admitted. Dio took another long draw from his weed, holding the rich smoke in his lungs before blowing it slowly out the side of his lips as he studied me.

"Maybe. But the minute she decided this was where she was going to be, there wasn't a chance you wouldn't follow. You've got that look about you," he mused, and I swallowed, fisting my hands at my sides as he steered me toward the back door.

"What look is that?" I asked through gritted teeth, knowing that Dio always saw too much, that desires made themselves known to him as was his rite of divine power.

"That you're a man longing for something he knows he can't have but is about to reach for it anyway. There's no shame in hunger, Hades. Come on, now. Let's get you into a private balcony, brother." I let him escort me into his club, flayed raw by his easy dissection.

Persephone

CHAPTER 28

Anticipation made my heart beat faster than usual, and we hadn't even left the house. The stereo was low, and I swayed my hips to the Cranberries as I lined my lips in the mirror with a deep mauve color, stolen from Artemis. Just bold enough to make me feel a little rebellious.

I tried on four outfits before settling on this one, a shiny dress made of a beautiful deep purple silk that hit mid-thigh. The fabric was so dark it looked like oil when it caught the light in glimmering hues of purples and blues. I slipped it on, forgoing a bra, which was risky considering how big my chest was. They could do some damage when left unbridled, but the mortals hadn't invented a bra yet that would go undetected in this dress and I was feeling empowered, maybe even a little reckless.

The silk clung to me, cinching in at the waist, slicking down my thighs. The material wasn't skintight, but my tummy and thighs gave it a more fitted feel than if Hecate or Artemis were to wear it. I grabbed some black fishnets and finished the look with a pair of black Jimmy Choo platforms, loving the way the heels made my legs look impossibly longer. Straightening, I twirled once, just to watch the fabric move.

Nervous laughter bubbled in my chest as I touched up my dark mascara, trying my best to keep a steady hand without Medusa's aid.

The smell of hairspray lingered in the air, my curls soft, tumbling naturally over my shoulders. I packed my small clutch with lip gloss in case of a touch-up, my ID, and a little roller of perfume that Hecate had gotten me from a shop on the North Shore, after sliding it over my wrists and pulse point of my neck, just like she'd instructed.

I looked myself over in the mirror, satisfied with the ensemble, cheeks flushed with the natural blush of my excitement. The look worked together, and I felt *good*, though my body was curvier than most, soft and supple. My hourglass shape tapered in at the waist but supported my larger chest and the deep sweep of hips. My stomach had a pooch, but I didn't hate my body, no matter how much magazines tried to make me. I wasn't thin, and that was okay with me. I thought the models were gorgeous, too, despite the crushing body standards coming off runways, but there was more than one way to be beautiful. This was mine. This body had survived centuries of torment, and woke up for me every day. Was it perfect? By some standards, no, but for me? It was mine, and I was grateful for it.

I contemplated my reflection before the weight of my hair grew hot across my neck. Reconsidering the heat, I pulled my hair back in two identical high ponytails. A set of hair chopsticks were used to twist the strands to create a cool design, and the pomegranate pendant hung around my neck, nestled in the hollow of my throat where it belonged. I didn't let my eyes linger any longer on my reflection, didn't want to second-guess anything else.

Hermes let out a low whistle when I walked into the living room and Helios choked on his water as they took me in. *Good sign.* I shot them a grin and gave a little twirl before reaching for the door as they scrambled after me. We folded into Hermes's Porsche, a feat of Olympus in the tiny space with a titan in tow. Helios's legs were in his chest, and I had to stretch across the back seat just to fit. I wasn't extremely tall by any means, but the seat didn't seem to be tailored for anyone over four feet.

"Couldn't you have gotten a sensible car?" Helios grunted, but Hermes just laughed as he shifted effortlessly, guiding us through traffic.

"Absolutely not," he answered, slipping in front of a too-slow van as he zoomed on. "The lovers *adore* the Porsche. And me. If I wanted to attract six-foot-two linebacker-built sun titans, I'd have a Bronco like Heph. But for now," he patted the steering wheel, "this is my baby. Show some respect."

Helios grumbled away as I savored the view out of Hermes's back window. The flashing lights of the New Orleans skyline shone above us as we raced down Canal. The buildings rose up high against the dark, swirling sky while beneath us, the blacktop shimmered under the glow of streetlamps, the light slick on the rainy pavement. The air was thick, hot and sweet with magnolia, sharp with something just this side of sour, spiced almost, and I hummed in satisfaction, low in my throat. Jazz curled through the cracks of half-open windows and smoky doorways, seeping through the seams of the Porche, horns crying out from street corners while the city sang to itself in the falling night. Greece may have been my beginning, but the N.O. had become *home*.

I watched as a trolley rambled down the middle of the street, splitting traffic, as hosts of tourists milled around the opening of Bourbon. Hermes maneuvered us into a parallel parking spot just off South Rampart.

"Fucking Fates, finally," Helios huffed as we untangled our limbs and climbed out of the restrictive space. Hermes locked the Porsche with a quick beep, then held an arm out to me, which I gratefully took. He steered us down the block with Helios following close behind, flanking me. They may have been willing to disobey Hades's order to keep me locked up but putting me at risk of an attack wasn't something they'd do. We were just a turn or two off the main drag, but it was far enough that the hustling noise fell away. The night deepened with each step, the twilight feeling somehow sacred, like we were intruding on something ancient, though we were all far older than this city.

The magic here, the way it breathed around us, all slow and sultry, felt personal, nearly intimate. This land was home to old power, built on roots and blood and pain, but also hope and joy, resistance and rebirth. It was impossible to acknowledge one without the other, so entwined in the veins of history as they were.

Hermes steered us into a beautiful, gold-trimmed glass door, halting my thoughts. We stepped into a grand atrium, one that rose to the heavens above us, decadence lovingly laid into every detail of the space from the marble flooring to the hand-painted wallpaper.

The plaque nearest told the story of a hotel of beautiful elegance, a staple in New Orleans history. Hermes escorted us confidently through the lobby, past those checking in, through another set of double doors. The smells of delicious culinary concoctions reached my nostrils, and I let out a soft moan as my mouth watered. My cheeks flamed with excitement. In all my time in New Orleans, I hadn't been to a place this fancy, preferring to stick to the mom-and-pop spots and corner stores, but my stomach rumbled at the smells wafting around me.

We walked around the corner to the main dining room where Nick sat at a small table, drumming his fingers against the white tablecloth. Several eyes were turned on him, but he ignored them all, his gaze only for Helios. Nick was . . . beautiful. Ethereal, even. I wondered if all wood nymphs were like that, wondered more if it would be rude to ask. Everything about him seemed gentle, in delicate balance: the way he straddled the line of masculine and feminine presence, the hard lines of his jaw and soft curve of his full lips. He had forgone the leather jacket and faded jeans and opted for fitted black slacks and navy button-down. His top seemed almost painted on with the way it rested on the lean planes of his shoulders and arms, but tasteful. You could see the muscle definition pressing into the fabric when he moved, but it only made him look more regal.

Helios sped up to walk around us, smiling broadly. I realized the boys looked slightly underdressed compared to Nick and me, but I hadn't given Helios much time to change. He still looked handsome in his flannel and jeans, but I worried that we'd crashed their date night and guilt burned through me. Hermes was also in jeans but suddenly had a sports jacket in his hand I hadn't noticed before.

God of Outfit Changes.

Nick's gaze fell to Helios, his face lit up with happiness that spread over the entire area. It was such a pure moment that I struggled to calm the storm raging in my chest. Hades's eyes flashed before me again and I tensed, reeling from anxiety and a million other twisted feelings. The last thing I needed was to let him seep into this too, to taint it with the reminder of rejection.

Helios reached Nick and lifted him swiftly up out of his chair before running kisses over his face, his jaw, the side of his temple before capturing his lips. Their hands tangled together like the hours they'd spent apart were far too long, and a few of the mortals shot a side eye, clearly caught off guard by the beautiful men and their public displays of affection. One woman huffed, pointedly turning her back on them, but Helios only ignored her as he whispered against the shell of Nick's ear.

I felt hollow, swallowing down my jealousy, but I was happy for my friend. Helios pulled back with a chuckle and Nick pouted, but he bent low to whisper in his ear again. Whatever he said had Nick's eyes shooting to us. His expression tightened, a wariness in his gaze that had me self-conscious that we were in fact intruding. But it passed just as quickly, his posture relaxing as he pulled out of Helios's embrace to shake Hermes's hand, smiling. Then he turned to me and that smile faltered just a bit again before holding his hands aloft tentatively. I leaned in to return the embrace, and there was something in his touch, a familiarity that my body understood but I couldn't place.

I didn't try to break contact when Nick pulled back but kept us connected, his brown eyes sparkling into mine. I could see uncertainty there, a shy nervousness and it occurred to me that this was the first time I'd seen him since Styx, and maybe he was feeling a little weird about having originally shown up to see me, but going home with Helios.

I gave him a squeeze and a huge smile, the most genuine joy I could muster. "I'm so, so, happy for you," I said, pushing all the sincerity I possessed into my words.

His brow furrowed in confusion, as though he were torn.

I pulled his body close once more for a second hug, held him there. Nick felt so light and delicate under my hands. "I don't remember ever seeing my friend so happy. You've done that, and I will be forever grateful. Thank you, Nick." We hugged for a long moment, until Hermes cleared his throat. People were watching us, tears in both of our eyes as we broke apart, laughing softly, but I didn't care. Maybe Nick needed that hug as much as I did. *Maybe we both just needed friends*. Helios had mentioned that he kept to himself, didn't have anyone else really, no family to speak of. Maybe I could be his friend.

We sat together, the four of us, eating some of the most delicious food I'd ever tasted. We drank, we laughed, and we visited, eating our weight in pasta and fresh caught Gulf of Mexico shrimp and oysters. I could almost pretend that we were just a normal group of friends, meeting to catch up in between our busy lives, not immortal beings, out of place and time.

Helios held Nick's hand on the table, ignoring any stares leveled at their embrace, but anger threatened to burst from inside me, the injustice of bigotry gnawing at my control. I could feel their stares like tangible admonishments, and it pissed me off to no end to witness. Sexuality was such a fluid thing and had been since the dawn of time. It made me sad that mortals had reverted to some restricted and hateful mindsets in this supposedly new and enlightened day and age. They would have been clutching their pearls to see how normalized homosexuality and just plain old minding your own fucking business was in ancient Greece. I didn't remember much, but that I certainly recalled with confident clarity.

But a lot had changed when Christianity hit its rise, the others had explained. A propaganda parade by a group of men who coveted power. It had succeeded and toppled the ancient hierarchy of the gods, leaving us to live amongst mortals with a mere fraction of our original power, their worship dwindled to nearly nothing. Learning all of this had floored me, and a small part of me was thankful I didn't have to live through that time of turmoil. Not that being locked in a torment box had been great, but I could see the silver lining to my imprisonment by skipping the Crusades, the burning of women for being nothing more than independent, the oppression of women to a barbaric level, the hate crimes levied against Black and Brown communities . . .

The behavior of outright disdain for others merely because of who they loved sent rage through me. Both Nick and Helios liked men and women alike. They just happened to love each other.

The woman who'd huffed earlier was openly leering. My hand gripped my wineglass dangerously as she sat near a dark corner with an elderly man, clearly more interested in his food than her. One of the shadows slinked toward me and I grinned. I had some practice bending them to my will lately, but it typically left me exhausted and panting on the living room floor.

This felt different. Instead of me summoning the darkness, this little shadow sought *me* out. I let my mind go to it, and like a skittish kitten I coaxed it to me. It slid slowly, moving across the intricate patterns on the carpeted floor, dodging the footsteps of the waiters that could do it no harm as it slithered. I felt it curl tentatively up the leg of my chair until it settled over my thighs, and I swore I could hear a soft hum of contentment come from the inky darkness. It slipped under my dress, tickling my skin playfully until it zoomed down my shoulder and settled into my palm. It felt cool and comforting and like *home*. Whatever that meant.

The boys were laughing when Nick reached up to brush the hair from Helios's face. The grumpy old hag in the corner huffed again in protest, loud enough to draw my attention, loud enough that Nick's face fell. The grip on my glass tightened again, as a somberness settled over our table.

Fury bubbled low in my stomach, tingled down my limbs and before I knew it, the little shadow slid down without provocation, making its way back over to the homophobic asshole's table. I watched it slip between the shadows until it coiled around the base of a bottle of red resting in front of the woman. It sat poised like a cat, staring at me and, I swear, I saw its incorporeal form *wink* before it jerked the bottle abruptly, knocking it upside down, drenching her pastel suit in deep crimson. The liquid bloomed over the soft fabric, and I laughed as her face contorted with rage while she searched for a napkin and someone to blame. The waiters rushed to her as she yelled, then stood abruptly, storming off in a huff. The boys attempted polite indifference as they worked to hold in their laughter, but I held no such compunction.

"Fastest case of karma I've ever seen," I said loud enough for her to hear as she passed. She paused briefly, as if to say something and Fates, I wished she fucking would. Something on my face must have given her pause, because moments later she was out the door, the uninterested man trailing her miserably.

"Was that you?" Nick asked, leaning forward, eyes wide.

I gave him a coy smile. "I wish I could take the credit, but I don't remember actually *deciding* to tip the bottle. The shadows did." I shrugged and plopped another bite of stuffed ravioli in my mouth, savoring the taste.

"That's a real improvement, Persephone. I'm proud of you." Helios glowed. I smiled at him as he brought the hand holding Nick's to his mouth, pressing his lips gently to the back of the nymph's knuckles.

"I think one shadow-tormented homophobe is enough for one evening. Shall we adjourn to someplace a little more . . . vibrant?" Hermes asked, tossing his napkin onto his plate.

"Wait, we're going out? Like, again?" The excitement lit my voice and when Nick nodded his head, I beamed. Hermes disappeared to pay the bill, and moments later, he was throwing on his sport coat and pulling out my chair for me. We walked down Canal, all the way back to Bourbon. I was so excited. We never really went to Bourbon, it was always so crowded and such a tourist trap that we stayed on Frenchman, or up by Royal.

But a secret part of me had always wanted to grab a Hand Grenade, and as silly as it sounded, I wanted a Lucky Dog. I'd had them in other parts of the city, but I wanted one off the street of *sin*. I just thought it might taste better.

"Where are we going?" I asked, confused when Nick and Helios walked straight past all the bars and festivities. Helios had his hand in Nick's back pocket, pulling him toward his side possessively. A pang resonated again.

Nope. Nope. Nope, not tonight, not right now.

"Electric Delphi," Nick answered, turning back to look at me.

"Like the oracle?" I asked, confused, but he just laughed.

"Sort of. It's a bar, and if you're very nice to the bartender, he might just tell you what you desire," Hermes answered, pointing ahead of us to an older brick building past the other bars.

"Fucking excellent," I murmured, picking up the pace so even Hermes had to rush to keep up. I wanted to dance, to *experience*. The knowledge that someone was trying to kill me scared me, but mostly it motivated me to see as much of this world as I could—to live and eat and *fuck*—until I had my fill.

"Does everyone get to go to Electric Delphi? Or is it just a club for our kind?" I asked, slowing to walk with Nick and Helios. I looped my arm with Nick's as we made our way up to the doorman, who stood so tall his head went past the frame.

Nick nodded. "It's a kind of neutral territory. It's gay-positive, straight-positive, sex-positive, mortals and Otherworlders alike. Just be careful, little Persephone. They're like sharks and they'd love the chance to sink their teeth into you," he teased. My cheeks flamed, but he wasn't wrong in his teasing. I had to get over these obsessive thoughts of Hades. I could find someone *tonight* and let him rail me. I could do that. Hell, maybe even a she? Maybe I liked a little bit of everything? Maybe I just needed to give myself permission to take some chances, to feel that burn of desire I'd felt in his presence with someone, *anyone* else. I wanted so badly to feel it now, to prove to myself that it was even possible.

I set my shoulders and threw a smirk at Nick, who was eyeing me with a knowing grin.

"Go for it," he whispered, with an encouraging wink.

Persephone

CHAPTER 29

Electric Delphi was *incredible.*

I froze for half a second, half a breath maybe, as my eyes adjusted to the dark. The air was thick, humid with sweat and perfume, and I could nearly taste the glitter in the air, see it shimmering in the beams of light that danced overhead. The atmosphere pulsed with music that boomed from the walls, the floor, from inside my own damn chest as my heart raced a beat in time with the bass, syncing to the rhythm like my body knew I *belonged* here.

Colored lights cut through the haze in arcing sweeps of deep violets, reds, electric blues, darting and slicing into the endless depths of the ceiling above, bursting in unreal magic across the beams. A mirrored disco ball spun high above us, scattering fragments of light across faces, and sequins and drinks and bare skin that glowed and ran with sweat. It was like stepping into a fever dream, a fantasy, and it called to me, to my pulse racing in time with it, pulling me into blissful chaos.

I went willingly, Nick's hand in mine, Hermes at my back, close but not overbearing.

The crowd swallowed us without even looking, but I didn't feel invisible as bodies moved all around, dancing their joy. A boy with silver glitter across his cheekbones spun past us with his arms in the air, head thrown back as he sang "Beautiful Life" from the top of his lungs. Two women kissed against a pillar, framed in pink light, the beams of the strobes refracting a rainbow over dark skin that shimmered with scales. A drag queen glided by in heels taller than anything I could ever dare to wear, her eyeliner sharp, her makeup fucking majestic and sparkling like a fairy godmother seeing it all unfolding by her design with approval.

Nick's hand tightened in mine as my hips swayed, sashaying through the crowd and relentless house music, the remix fast and free. It lifted my arms, pulled me forward even as my nerves clung tight, but I was *here*, and I was *alive*, and this was *good*. I looked out across the swirling bodies, over the sea of shimmer and sweat and alcohol, not just observing this small universe that pulsed in time with itself but being possessed by it. Something inside me cracked open, clawed free from the hole in my chest, and spilled onto the dance floor.

Freedom.

For once, no one was looking at me like they were waiting for me to fall apart, explode like too heated glass. I wasn't someone to coddle, or be pitied. I didn't have to explain away a pained expression, there were no stares, no questions. Just movement. Color.

Joy.

A laugh caught in my throat, the relief unspoken but so refreshing and so I smiled, wide and stunned until my cheeks burned from the stretch of it. Hermes tightened his grip on my arm just enough to steady me as Nick led us to a small, round booth near the dance floor. A man in a wine-colored suit sat with his feet on the table, wild red curls quaffed up artfully on his head. His deep crimson blazer lay open across his bare chest, where several golden chains acted as a shirt of sorts while he puffed on a cigarette, exhaling purple smoke in a smooth stream as we approached. He was lithe and tall as he unfurled from the booth and stood to his full height. I blinked a few times as my vision blurred in the bursts of light, catching on the corded muscle of his shoulders.

Visions blurred and danced of this same man with a wreath of vine and ivy across his crown, standing next to Hades, the endless night behind them overlooking fields of pale wheat.

I pinched myself as *his* face ripped through my mind, ensnaring my thoughts. I was not to give Hades any space in my mind tonight. And when I did, I'd pinch myself. Associate him with pain, full-on Pavlov training. I blinked again as the stranger dropped his sweet-smelling cigarette and ground it out with the heel of a golden, snakeskin boot. His nearly violet eyes landed on me in full force, coaxing and tugging until I felt a rush of recognition and kinship well up in my chest. *I knew this man.*

No one moved as I studied him, and he only smiled back shyly, giving me time to process. My mind palace rumbled as I reached inside the cracked wall of memories, slowly and gently. I didn't rush it, just simply held out my hand to *ask*. A memory fluttered to me, and gratefully I pulled it close to my chest, sank into it, right in the middle of this crowded club.

Me, on a ferryboat coming to a glowing island. A small child clutched against me. He was crying for his momma, praying to me. I cooed and soothed him, did the same for the others that huddled around me as a dark figure, Charon, paddled us through the deep cut of the Styx. Another stood on the banks, a jovial smile on his face as he welcomed the barge into the dock. Behind him sat a large table full of glowing foods, sweets, and jugs of nectar. He opened his arms, and the children rushed over, climbing over his body to reach the table hungrily. Dionysus stood, a child still dangling from his neck, ghastly pale against his wine tunic. "Is this the last of them, then?" he asked, setting down the child before shooing him toward the treats.

I nodded and stepped off the barge to place my hand in the crook of his offered arm. "Thank you for housing them, Dionysus," I whispered, watching them graze. Never again would they be hungry. This was a land of happiness and play.

"Thank you for being the Queen they deserve, Persephone. Perhaps when this war is over we can sit and break bread together. That is unless your husband locks you away in that spire to ravage you over and over again." He winked. I laughed, biting down on my lip.

"More like if I let him out, you mean. And now that you've brought the subject up, I'll have to see if I can sneak back and seduce him away from the barge building with Hephaestus." I sighed wistfully, as he guided me back onto the platform.

"It's hot as Hells to watch him sweat, isn't it?" Dionysus winked, shoving the barge from his shores with a sharp grunt.

"You have no idea the torture. I just want his hands on me constantly. It's becoming a problem." I frowned, crossing my arms in a pout, but Dionysus laughed as several children accosted him from behind, taking him to the ground. They would be safe here, in this land with him.

The world refocused as I came to and locked my gaze on the God of Wine. Dionysus made no move, but I could sense his want, his *need* to hug me. Patience and restraint shown from a god who rarely denied himself anything.

"Dionysus," I whispered, his name ancient and nearly unrecognizable as my lips formed around it. It flowed naturally, as though it were the most normal thing, to speak in the ancient tongue. Shakily, I brought my hand to his jaw caressing the soft beard he kept trimmed now. At my touch, Dionysus's sparkling eyes fluttered shut as I cupped his face and placed a chaste kiss on his cheek.

"'Sephone," he whispered, sweeping me into a crushing hug. "You remember me?" he asked, voice cracking on a sob, laughing from deep within his chest as he sat me down. I nodded, because I *had*. I had remembered his name, his kindness and goodness. He was different now, less glassy-eyed, more alert and . . . healthy. "Oh, he's gonna *hate* this," he mumbled to Hermes, who smirked, watching me with a pleased expression. Dionysus's eyes flickered quickly up to one of the balcony rooms shrouded in darkness, and I had a feeling, deep in my bones, that I was again being watched. My spine pricked much like it had that night on stage, my body attuned to the power of the God of the Underworld.

Hades.

I swallowed, palms sweaty as I turned back to the group in time to see a criminally pretty man, bare-chested in very tiny gold shorts and rainbow suspenders, set down a round of bubbling, smoking drinks. The tall cylinder closest to me was alive with swirling blue liquid. A glowing green martini sat next to it, tiny bubbles rising to the surface with roiling pops. A short glass held something thick and golden, its rim on fire. Nick picked up the shot glass full of sparkling red liquid, and the rest followed suit, claiming the drinks from the tray. I glanced at the two remaining libations, the martini and another swirling with various shades of pinks and reds. Something like crushed candy sat on the rim and I reached for it as Nick smiled encouragingly. I brought it to my chest, nursing it there, working myself up to taking a drink.

"To a night to forget with those we wish to always remember. *Yamas!*" Dionysus boomed, grabbing a glass and tipping just the tiniest bit out onto the floor, but the liquid was clear, free of bubbles or smoke or the other bells and whistles all the other drinks seemed to have. It struck me then that he might be sober.

"*Yamas!*" the others cheered, following suit.

The sound of soft droplets splashing on the ground drew my attention back as I, too, tipped my glass before bringing it back up to my lips. The concoction washed over my tongue, coating my taste buds in a sweet and delicious combination of berries and spice. I felt the flavor hit the back of my throat as I swallowed it down. A deep, succulent heat washed over me in a wave, settling low in my belly. The flushed warmth spread out, stretching up and flowing toward my fingertips. I felt warm, so very warm, my skin tingling from the bass that reverberated through the room. The pulse from the music kickstarted a second heartbeat at the apex of my thighs, and I squirmed at the new build, the pressure it begged for. It was hot in Electric Delphi suddenly, oppressively so. My eyes drifted back over to that balcony, and I wondered if he could see me, why he had even come if he had no intention of even speaking with me.

I downed the last of my drink in an annoyed rush, setting the empty glass on the table with a little more force than I intended. Nick's eyes blew wide with surprise as he glanced from the empty glass to me. "Persephone, don't drink all of it!" he exclaimed, reaching, but I barely heard him. His voice was far, far away, a muffled sound wave passing through water in the distance because I felt floaty. Lighter than air, even.

Hermes leaned in, examining my face, but he seemed amused by whatever he found there. I began to sway with the music, let it build up and swell around me. "Well, that was an interesting twist." He shrugged, leaning away, careful not to touch me. The others eyed me with worry, but I couldn't imagine why. The warm buzz clouded over my mind, but all it did was silence the constant worry and anxiety I'd been feeling. I suddenly didn't care that Hades was here, but not with us.

"Dio, is she high?" Helios asked worriedly, straightening in his seat.

Dionysus nodded his head and my eyes went wide, the short, succinct nickname pleasing as I repeated it, over and over.

"A little. Persephone," Dionysus, *Dio* answered, voice firm. It was such a nice voice, so rich and pleasant. "You just drank a pretty powerful aphrodisiac. Don't worry, it won't make you black out or cause you to do anything you don't *want* to do, but uhm, just for the safety of my patrons—and us as well—don't actually *touch* anyone. Do you understand?" He asked. I didn't. I nodded anyway.

The moment began to slip from me, the room a blur of beautiful fractals and bright colors. I barely recalled what I drank, but I *did* know the music felt too good as the vibrations danced over my skin in its own symphony.

Helios let out a groan tipping his drink back. "This is going to get us all killed," he grumbled.

I frowned at him, unhappy with his tone. If there was something in those drinks, then this was the desired effect. I had come here with a purpose tonight anyway. Get over *him* by getting under someone else, but I had been afraid I wouldn't be able to feel it for anyone else. Looking around this room, I certainly felt *something* now.

I turned to face Helios, swaying just slightly as I tried to gain my bearings. I grabbed his arm to try and steady myself, and an incredible sensation flitted up my hands where my skin brushed his. I shivered and more heat pooled between my thighs. It felt wrong, too wrong, and I flinched my hand back like he'd burnt me because Helios was Nick's, not mine. *Not mine.*

"I don't need a babysitter. I'm not going to get anyone killed. I may, in fact, have some fun tonight." I hiccupped a small pink bubble, and watched with a giggle as it rose out of me unexpectedly. I swallowed and pushed on, wagging my finger in his face so he knew I meant business, "I'm an adult, and if I want to go dance with someone I can. If I want to fuck someone, I can."

My proclamation was met with an uneasy silence.

Hades hadn't wanted me, anyway. In fact, he'd gone out of his way to make sure I'd never endeavor to get too close to him. I was the unwanted wife. The unwilling plaything. I didn't have to be that anymore and tonight I could make my own choices. This was my life, and I could do as I pleased. I deserved that little bit of happiness, didn't I?

I felt safe here, with my friends, my family. I turned on my heel and sauntered off to the dance floor, and though I could feel their gazes burning into my back, I held my head high. I didn't let my insecurities eat at me, didn't even pause before I crossed onto the dancefloor, flinging myself into the melee of bodies moving and pumping. A supernatural fog crept low, cloaking me in confidence.

On the stage, the DJ booth was a glowing shrine elevated at the far end, where a figure in a crop top and headphones ruled like a demigod, blending beats that turned time liquid and my body languid. The music was liberation, and people danced like they knew this was religion, or protest, or maybe even a little bit of therapy. Shirtless boys in mesh tops spun in place, arms thrown wide, couples pressed close in corners, lit only by the flare of cigarette tips and strobes as I threw my hands up, swaying against the dancers around me, brushing arms and hands and hips, transferred glitter sliding from their skin to mine with the barest touches.

The haunting trill of Portishead washed over me in slow, magnetic sweeps as I made my way into an empty space, the melody lulling, pulling the blood in my veins to flush the surface of my skin. Every twirl of my hips felt defiant, felt bold and magnetic.

Every touch felt amazing as I ran my fingertips along my exposed skin, tiny sparks of energy dancing across sweat and flesh, lighting me on fire. I let the music take me over, let it guide my hips and head and feet as I moved and twirled, lost in the melody pumping through the speakers. The temperature dropped ever so slightly, but I leaned toward the reprieve from the heat burning inside me. The subtle caress sent a thrill down my spine because as I ran my hands across my torso, down, down my thighs, I knew that *he* was watching me.

Out the corner of my eye, I saw bodies inching forward, circling around in a decaying orbit. They were sharks, like Nick had warned, surrounding me, out for blood. *My blood*. Little did they know that I was the predator, setting a trap for them. If Hades wouldn't touch me, I'd make him watch as someone else did. I lifted an eyebrow, appraising the Otherworlders as I danced, as they closed in, the anticipation more intoxicating than even the drink had been. Every brush of my fingertips set my nerves alight with sensation and desire and I wanted to *feel*.

I knew this body had been intimate before. It had sex and I could assume many other things in the millennia it existed. But me, *this* version of myself, had never been with anyone, had never even properly been kissed and I wanted to feel that rush, *Fates*, I wanted to know what I had been missing.

The closest figure to me was still too far away to touch as he stalked around. He was too tall, too lean, not quite right. His abs disappeared down with a V cut into the leather pants slung low on his hips, his lack of shirt inviting me forward. I wondered if his skin would be soft if I touched it? Would he want me to touch it? I bit my lip, inching closer a tiny step, my body at war with my mind. Heat flushed my neck, under my breasts as warring sensations overwhelmed me. I wanted him to touch me, and in the same breath, I wanted Hades to intervene before he could.

He shot me a wicked smile with his very white, very sharp teeth peeking out through full lips. I slid my hand back down my thigh to the hem of my dress, daring myself to close the distance, to take the leap. Sinfully, slowly, I ran my hand back up my thigh, lifting the thin fabric as I cut a path to where I needed to be touched the most. Close, so very close to where I wanted them to be.

The temperature dropped another few degrees, the cool icy air settling over my too-flushed skin in warning. Alarm bells blared in the back of my mind, goose bumps rising where the cold caressed my arms and neck but the needy pressure building between my thighs rose ever higher. *Hades*. My gaze shot past the man approaching me, sliced into the darkness swirling in the balcony above us. I could see the impossibly black abyss obscuring him from my view and I cursed those shadows for robbing me of my spoils. It wasn't enough to know he could *witness*. I wanted to see the look on his fucking face when he realized he no longer had control, that I didn't need his permission or the scraps of attention he was so stingy with.

The control was *mine*.

Out of the corner of my eye, I saw Helios lead Nick on the dance floor near me. They moved seamlessly together, Nick with his back pressed into Helios's chest, hands roaming slowly and lovingly over each other as they circled the dance floor. Their steps were so graceful they could have been floating. Nick wasn't a small man by any means, but Helios wrapped his huge frame around the nymph like a shield. There was something beautiful in the way Nick submitted to the titan, trusting Helios completely to protect him. They were in a room full of gods and monsters and yet the moment between them felt somehow intimate, sacred. I averted my gaze, my hand roaming to my necklace for comfort. I toyed with it as I turned my attention back to the man inches from me, but the bolster was gone. Even through the haze of the drink, seeing that love, *real love*, had been sobering.

The shark was closer now, close enough that I could see the dark, black eyes staring at me through his hooded gaze, but there was no flooding desire coursing through me, like I'd expected. This man *was* handsome, sure. Dark hair tipped with bursts of blue, sharp jaw, and very full lips. I willed my body to react as it had during the times Hades had been near me, how it had felt and responded in my dreams of him, of the few memories of our married life that left me needy and empty. This man didn't even come close to making me respond how I craved. I took a breath, ready to move forward anyway, telling myself I needed to adjust my expectations. That I could do this either way.

Suddenly, there was a hand around my shoulders, pulling me back. Nick and Helios had somehow moved behind me. Nick's touch barely registered, but when he moved his hand from my neck, my necklace rested in his palm. I turned to look at him, frowning.

"I saw it sliding down and didn't want you to lose it. It looks like the clasp is broken. Want me to hang on to it for tonight? Doesn't look like that dress has pockets," he offered.

I nodded gratefully, but unease pricked at me from the loss of the weight, the comfort and safety that necklace brought me. That pendant had found me, calmed me when I needed. I would have fallen apart if it were lost. "Thank you, yeah. Please be careful with it. It's important to me." With a nod, he pocketed the chain and pendant.

Helios pulled Nick back into him possessively, a hungry look on his face and then they were gone, lost to the edge of the dance floor, Nick's back to Helios's front, grinding into the titan with a slow wind of his slim hips.

The cold wrapped around my body again, sending a shiver down my spine, perking my nipples against the silken fabric of my dress. I looked to the balcony, searching, and this time, through the slightest break in the darkness, those blue eyes were trained on me. The rest of his face was obscured in shadow, but I could feel the tension rolling off him. He tilted his head, studying me, daring me, unlocking a memory pulled from the depths of my mind palace.

"I do not share, Little Flower. If you want this, be sure. I do not share."

Hades

CHAPTER 30

She remembered Dionysus. I was trying to not be too bitter about that as I sat perched in the darkness, eavesdropping like a coward while my reason for existing sat below me, thinking me no better than a monster. I was tense, too tense, my careful control slipping. Persephone breathing the same air as me made me lose my head, and I was completely intoxicated by her presence alone. Since the moment we'd met all those years ago, wanting her had become second nature, only more painful now that she moved like a siren through a room of Otherworlders who would do almost anything to taste how fucking divine she is.

A delicate pink flushed her cheeks, as she danced, lost to the music and energy over the electric beat, and I forced myself to calm when she found a spot just for herself, in the middle of the floor.

Sweet mercies.

Then, the dance floor changed, the music slowed. Movements softened as bodies pressed closer and another integral thread of my control stretched to the limit. She moved, hypnotizing, a beacon of beauty and serenity while they all watched, while *I* watched her hips sway, arms above her head, eyes half-lidded in the soft, blue lights that made her glow. She was the vision of all my desires, half-lit by glimmers and dreams, her hair stuck slightly to the gentle curve of her neck, damp from dancing. Persephone's head fell back, and she smiled, just faintly, just to herself, but that look on my goddess was undoing me.

I watched from the balcony, hands clenched on the iron railing. Wanting her wasn't just hunger, it was starvation, desiccation, and every fucking second without her body against mine scraped me raw. She was surrounded now, soon to be dead Otherworlders drawn to her, and my fingers tightened, bending the steel beneath my grip as they hovered, the three of them, offering hands, leaning too close to *my* wife, trying to match her rhythm and be the one she turned to.

But she didn't. Not yet.

My jaw was tight, locked against the raw, rising instinct to move. *To kill*. Persephone deserved more than what I could give. That thought had anchored me before, had kept me from risking it all when it mattered. But watching her now, unguarded, radiant, full of life after so long in the chaos, I wasn't sure how much longer I could pretend that staying away was the noble choice.

My shadows closed in around me, creating a barrier to shield me from the outside world as anger and fear and lust filled my head. My mind wandered to the inevitable outcomes that tonight could bring, and jealousy swelled hot and thick in my chest. *I* couldn't touch her, but I didn't know that I would have the strength to watch someone else do it either.

I exhaled, ragged.

She didn't know I was here, watching, creeping from the shadows, but I couldn't fucking stop looking at her.

I felt the rush of air being displaced, and forced my gaze away from Persephone. Hermes leaned against the wall of my private balcony, two snifters and a bottle in his hand. He raised the glasses, clinking them twice and I nodded miserably, slumping back into the leather chair I hadn't bothered sitting in since she'd arrived. He made himself comfortable in true Hermes fashion, kicking his feet up on the balcony ledge. He lifted an eyebrow at the gnarled railing but made no comment as he handed me over a fresh pour.

"You're going to need this, I'm afraid," he said softly, bringing his own to his lips, taking a sip. I sighed, knowing he was right, and lifted the glass to him before downing it in its entirety. The mead washed over my tongue with a spicy bite I wasn't used to, but it tasted divine. An expensive bottle, stolen from Dio's private stock, no doubt.

I unstoppered the cork and poured myself another. "He sent you up with this?" I asked, taking another too-large gulp. Seductive music washed over the dance floor and the whole "fuck me" vibe of the place set my teeth on edge. I groaned when my gaze landed back on Persephone, on the entrancing way she danced to the music. Sitting back, I loosened my tie, unbuttoning the top button of my shirt with one hand. "This just might kill me," I sighed, taking another drink. Hermes studied me closely. I didn't like it.

"What?" I barked, eyes still on Persephone. A few water sprites that had caught sight of her moved closer, homing in, and I felt my muscles coil like a cobra, ready to strike if they got any fucking closer.

"I have a theory about something, but I need you to tell me where you got that necklace you left for Persephone," he asked, leaning forward.

"A theory about what?" I asked, only half paying attention.

"*The necklace*, Hades. The pomegranate." He insisted. I shrugged.

"I bought it from a lady selling trinkets in Jackson Square. It reminded me of her. *Why*?" I asked, still not taking my eyes from Persephone's hands as they trailed soft touches across her skin. I bit my lip until I tasted the coppery tang of blood.

"Just curiosity. You know how nosy I can be," he replied, sipping again. His tone turned soft. "She's ready to fuck someone. *Tonight*. You could do that for her. She wants you, too, you know."
I flinched. She didn't want me. She thought I'd hurt her.

"You know I can't," I growled, snatching the bottle up, drinking straight from the neck. The biting mead settled low in my belly, a slight euphoria tickling the base of my spine. If I was going to watch her do this, I needed to be drunk for it. I should've just picked a fight with Hermes and hoped he could knock me out.

"You *could*. I think. I have a theory, and I need to test it. How long has it been for you, Hades? You could use the release yourself, couldn't you? When was the last time?" I leveled him a hard look and his eyes went wide. "You haven't? All these centuries and not *once*?" He balked. Every glance was a pinprick, subtle jabs that left me raw by increasing degrees. I knew *exactly* how long it'd been since I'd touched her, touched anyone in that way.

"There has never been another since I laid my eyes on Persephone." I growled, offended at his implication. I shrugged off my suit jacket, rolled up my sleeves. It was getting warmer, my body running on rage and barely restrained violence and whatever Dio had bottled. My eyes stayed fixed on Persephone as Nick reached out to her, his hands fiddling with the clasp of her necklace. She hadn't noticed him yet, and a deadly rumble tore through me. I stood, anger coursing through my bones. *He'd touched her.*

Hermes had an arm on me in an instant and let out a chuckle. "Two thousand years, huh? I'll admit it does make me feel less bad about what I had to do." Nonchalant words, but I caught the nerves in his voice. I tore my gaze from Persephone as Hermes downed his own glass. He looked apologetic, shooting me a "what could you do" look as my eyes widened. A heady pulse of desire ripped through my body, tearing straight down to my cock.

He'd drugged me.

"You motherfucker!" I hissed, grabbing for him but he was too fast and halfway out the door before I could even turn to go after him.

"Try to last until the end of the song—Helios and I have a bet. Remember, it won't make you do anything you don't want to do!" That rat fucker was gone before the consequences of what he'd done could settle between us.

I grabbed the bottle and brought it up to my nose. The scent was there, buried under the sweetness of the mead. Hermes had spiked the bottle with *Amortiani*, a lust potion Dio was famous for. I pressed against the balcony, hissing at the friction, at the pressure on my hardening cock, the desire that ripped through my bones nearly unbearable.

My eyes tracked Persephone's movements through the blanket of darkness. I swallowed, breathing in heavy puffs, the need a hollow, gnawing ache, like hunger, like grief. The water sprite was close, too close and every cell in my body screamed at me to rip him to shreds, to fling his ashes into the Gulf for Poseidon to find. I gripped the railing, grunting like an animal but it was years, centuries, eons of pent-up obsession that released into my bloodstream all at once. I was hot, too hot, and my shade bent toward her, pulled by a gravity no being in the cosmos could resist. My Persephone, my Little Flower, my wife.

I was going to fucking kill Hermes.

My shadows shifted apart, revealing my position to the rest of the club, startling me. *She* had to have done that because I certainly fucking hadn't. Persephone's green eyes pierced me through those long lashes and my mind flashed in bright bursts of images, throwing me off-kilter. Memories of her looking at me like that while she had those pretty lips wrapped around my cock clouded every thought, hearing her moans, licking up the succulent tears she cried so beautifully for me. Fates, to see her on her knees, gagging and choking as she worked to take all of me, stuffing my cock past those full lips . . . My body remembered every moment in stunning clarity, even as my mind tried not to recall the way she looked, begging me for more.

Fuck.

The sprite closed the distance, but her eyes were still on mine. I cocked my head to the side slightly, warning her to disengage, that very last thread uncoiling in a slow decay. Those moss-colored orbs stared back at me defiantly as his hands reached for her neck, inches from her skin. Centimeters. A bare breath.

The thread snapped.

My shadows enveloped my body, hurtling me through the air before depositing me feet from where she stood. Hermes flashed in front of me, grabbing the water sprite around the shoulders and spiriting him away in an instant.

He was lucky the Messenger God had gotten to him before I could. Had he touched her, I would have ripped the flesh from his fucking bones and fed it to him.

The room was silent save for the music, unmoving as I stalked closer. Persephone's eyes went wide, but she kept moving, swaying and touching her delicious curves, all brat as she dared me to do something. All of these eyes could see her, and rage ripped through me again, the need insatiable, unyielding. My shadows enveloped us both, obfuscating her body from the crowd's prying eyes as I reached her without slowing, stopping with barely any air between us. She bit her lip. Squeezed those perfect thighs together and I could smell her, feel her, fucking *taste* her on the air.

Suffocating.

"Go home," I demanded through clenched teeth.

Her wide eyes narrowed in a challenge. "*No*. You ruined my dance," she said, still swaying. My chest heaved with the effort it took to keep my distance. Her hand traveled slowly, teasing under the hem of her dress again, exposing some of the soft flesh as she lifted it higher and my breath stalled, drool pooling over my tongue at the sight of her.

I fisted my hands at my sides, eyes still locked on hers. The tension between us swelled, our combined power licking against my skin, against hers as I suppressed a shudder. She didn't, and my cock throbbed, leaking for her. "Impossible. *They* aren't allowed to touch you," I replied, my voice dangerously raw.

Persephone turned, raising her arms above her head as she shot me a seductive look over her shoulder. The way that dress clung to her hips almost killed me. Two thousand years and she still owned every part of me, was buried under my rib cage, unyielding, unbearable. One touch and it could bring the wolves back to the door. One touch and it could take her away forever.

Hermes said she would be safe. His words needled into my brain, played on a loop in the back of my mind as I found myself pulling toward her energy. I was a speeding train bound for damnation, helpless to her pull.

"But he was," she teased, casting her eyes over her shoulder demurely. "He was going to put his hands on me. I would have let him slide up my thighs, like this." The dress hiked slowly higher, higher and I saw the pink cheeky panties she was wearing peek out from the swell of her hips. I clenched my fist so tightly I nearly cracked bone.

There was a tangible tether between us that Persephone controlled me with, one she kept wrapped around her little finger as she moved and swayed.

"I would have let him slip his fingers deep inside me." She turned to face me, less than an inch of air separating us, and a guttural sound ripped from somewhere deep within my chest. She was pushing me, and I was rising to the bait, too far gone, I couldn't help it, the pull and heat of her wrapped around my hips, beckoned me forward. My shadows, the very blood in my veins screamed for me to claim what was *mine*.

Persephone ran a hand up her torso, palmed her breast through the thin fabric. Her nipples pebbled, her breasts heavy and full and with a grunt, the rest of my self-control blew like an atom bomb. My hand struck forward as quick as lightning, gripping her by the neck, pulling her hard against my chest.

Persephone's soft curves melted against me, molding to my body in such perfect harmony I could practically hear the cosmos singing. Her pulse fluttered under my fingertips, and I counted every fucking beat of her heart as it pounded in her chest. She felt so real in my arms, the weight of our love and history stitching us together.

I leaned down, burying my face into the crook of her neck, inhaling deeply. "You should *run*, Little Flower," I whispered, lips brushing her ear. "They aren't allowed to touch you. They aren't allowed to fuck you." I snarled. She lit up, stretching on her tiptoes, arching against me.

"I don't need your permission," she panted, swallowing against the pads of my fingers.

"Yes, you fucking do." I moved my hand up to her chin, slowly and deliberately smearing her lipstick over her mouth with my thumb. "Yes," I breathed, bringing her face close enough to mine that my breath fanned over the bridge of her nose, the tops of her cheeks. "If you want to know what it feels like, then use your own fingers. I'll let you fuck yourself," I conceded.

She stared daggers at me, but it was hard to take her seriously when she was wrapped around me like this.

"Fuck me yourself, you coward," she demanded with a breathy little moan, and my grip on her chin tightened. Persephone smiled as another moan crept up from her throat. "I know you lied about the myth," she whispered, eyes hooded. "I know you didn't hurt me or take me without my consent." Persephone lifted a hand to my face, cupping my cheek. It was so warm and real, and it sent pleasure shooting down my neck and chest. I leaned into her touch, unable to stop myself.

"I wanna feel good," she whined, softly. "Make me feel *good*, Hades," she begged.

Her words were a war cry against my resolve, and that was all the fight I had left in me. Time stood still as I rushed right over the cliffs of my sanity, taking her with me while I crushed her lips to mine. Stars burst from behind my eyelids as she moaned hard, pressing her entire body into mine in desperate and lustful fervor. The tension in the air exploded and with less than a thought, our shadows portaled us home.

Hades

CHAPTER 31

Persephone's legs wrapped around my waist as I hoisted her up into my arms and I lost myself in the feel of her, in the sheer relief in hearing her heartbeat through her chest with mine. I kissed down the column of her throat as her teeth sank into my jaw, nipping at the flesh of my neck and shoulders, marking and tasting in the shadows. My fingertips dug into her muscles, holding her closer, thriving in the darkness that bound and deposited us in my room. I walked to the giant bed, laid her down gently, nearly unable to stand any distance between us, needing her skin against mine for eternity. I was an addict who'd been sober for two thousand years, but just one hit and she had me hooked again.

She leaned back on her elbows as I stood above her, my heart hammering and raging beneath my ribs. I had no more fight left in me, no grandiose ideals of who I was, how controlled I could remain. I reached for her ankle and relished in the sparks that danced between us as I unstrapped the platforms she wore, trailing soft touches over her skin. Her breath caught as I settled between her legs, spreading her wide until I was lying on the bed, cradled in the nirvana of her thighs. With shaking hands she grabbed the hem of her dress and pulled up for me, exposing those see-through lace panties.

I placed tender kisses up the inside of soft flesh, opening her legs enough to give me a clear view of the feast before me, my Queen, the love of this life and any other. I slid a finger up over her panties and she whimpered, sending heat shooting down my spine. I paused, letting the warmth from my breath tease her through the flimsy fabric.

"Please," she whined, so desperate, so perfect, and I nodded, unable to deny her anything when she begged so fucking beautifully. I was already bound for the pits of Tartarus, I may as well make it worth the trip. With my finger hooked under the seam of her panties, I tugged, slipping them softly to the side, rubbing over her lips, exposing the mess between her thighs.

I groaned, low in the back of my throat, seeing her glistening and shaking. "What a dream, Little Flower. Soaked like this. Are you sure this is all for me?" I asked, a little unsteady, a lot undone, needing to hear that she wanted this as much as I, terrified it was just the drink. She dropped a hand down to cup my cheek.

"You're all I've dreamt about, Hades. *Just you*. It's all for you," she promised. I sucked in a shaky breath, turned my head to press a kiss to her palm, and looked up into her green eyes, so full of open honesty.

"Then lie back, Little Flower. Let me taste you, give you what your body craves." My tongue split, the ends slipping independently over my wet lips. Shadows snaked around her wrists, maybe hers, maybe mine, spreading her apart as they bound her body to the headboard. Unable to resist, I plunged my head between her thighs, flattening my tongue as I feasted on her heady arousal. Persephone bucked her hips as her taste exploded on my tongue, her delicate moans spurring me on. I sucked up to her clit, taking the hard bundle between my lips, applying pressure that sent her writhing. She cried out in exquisite torture, arching back as I flicked my forked tongue over and around it, teasing and tempting, drinking my fill.

I groaned against the heat of her, by Fates, she was so fucking soft, and I moaned into the taste, grinding my hips against the bed as I fucked her with my tongue. I lifted one of her legs over my shoulder to give me better access as I wet a finger and pressed it slowly inside, stretching her tight cunt with steady pressure. Persephone sank farther into the comforter, running from the intensity of the pleasure taking her over. I grinned against her skin, lapping at her, sucking and savoring my Queen. Shadows tightened as she thrashed, throwing her head back and forth as she tried to steady her breathing.

"Fuck, Hades. *Fuck*. That's good, that's so good," she cried, vocal in her pleasure. This modern version of my girl had such a dirty fucking mouth, and I loved it. I rocked my hips slightly, savoring the friction on my cock as I delved between her folds with my mouth, pushed my fingers into her up to the knuckle, rubbing against her fluttering walls. I growled as she gushed around me, her body an inferno of death and desires that sent me spiraling into oblivion. There was only Persephone, her taste and moans, and her grip around my fucking shade.

It was like playing my favorite instrument after a long time away, reacquainting and recalibrating my every motion to her gratification. I'd do it again, over and over, destroy my honor for her whims. I savored the way she responded to me, begged me with her sounds and cries. I would drown in her, live and breathe and die for her as she writhed above me, restrained by my shadows while I drove her higher. I sank a second finger inside and she cried out, spasming around my hand and mouth as I sucked her clit harder, almost painfully, to compound the sharp edge of pleasure. Her euphoria seeped into every inch of my skin as I growled against her flesh, sending vibrations through her core.

Distraught and wanton, Persephone came apart, teeth chattering from the tremors that rolled through her body, tears streaming down her face as she cried out my name into the darkness.

My fucking name.

I kept stroking her slowly, lithely as she rode down her high, her cries a constant symphony in my ears, placing bites and kisses interchangeably against her swollen lips, her clit, the tender flesh of her lower belly.

It was so beautiful, this breaking of my dark queen, and the weight of her long absence crashed over me. I needed to hear her fall apart again, needed her cries and moans tattooed into the very marrow of my fucking bones so I would never again forget how sweet they sounded to my ears. Persephone lost in her ecstasy was my personal rapture, and I nearly wept as I worshiped my goddess from the altar of her body.

"*Again*," I demanded, descending.

Her wide eyes shot to mine. "*I don't . . . I don't think I can.*" Her words faltered, nearly imperceivable, but I redoubled my efforts, sliding into her soaked cunt with more force, stretching her deliciously as I devoured, lavishing my tongue against her. Persephone cried out my name, that forbidden sound almost undoing two thousand years of the tormented wasteland that was my mind. Her essence ran down my fingers, my wrists, coated my chin but I demanded more. *More* of this, *more of her.* My palm flattened over her lower belly, pressing her down, pinning her beneath my fingers and tongue, but I needed to make her remember that every inch of her was *mine*, and every atom in my body served at her beck and call.

"Again." I insisted, the fervor overtaking my better senses as she bucked and pushed, squirming away from the intensity that had her eyes rolling. "I'm not through with this pretty little cunt, Persephone. Be a good fucking girl for me if you want this cock."

She didn't remember how good it had felt before, but I would remind her. This was my chance to steal more of her firsts, all over again, and I was a greedy bastard for her moans, her sweet, sweet nectar as it dripped straight from the source. My eyes rolled back as she drenched my face, slipping and sliding against her. I circled my thumb slowly, curling my fingers inside her, searching for her pleasure, *demanding* it. Persephone's thighs bloomed an incredible shade of crimson as she flushed, body shaking as she tightened her leg over my shoulder, bringing me closer. She was desperate and overstimulated as I was, but I couldn't stop, I just couldn't fucking stop.

I glanced up to take in her face just in time to see small tears streaming down her cheeks. She threw her head back again, eyes screwed shut in rapture and it was scripture, poetry of the highest order to watch her float outside her body. My fingers curled deep, and I felt her flutter before she locked up, face contorting on the scream that tore from her chest. The sound of her climax sent shock waves through me, and I came hard, just as she did. The sticky wet mess slid down my cock and I cursed, but kept my fingers moving, more gently, as Persephone threw her head back into my pillow, muffling her cries. I pressed a small kiss to her clit, and she gasped at the barely-there sensation, drawing ragged breaths through broken sobs.

"So good for me," I praised, as the shadows recoiled, releasing Persephone's arms. They slid down to the bed slowly, exhaustion clear on her face as I withdrew my fingers, circling the pad of my thumb over her clit one more time before sliding her panties back over her dripping lips. She stared down at me, still breathless, eyes fixated on my mouth as I licked my fingers clean.

"T-that is what I've been missing?!" she panted between heaving breaths, her lungs struggling to fill with enough oxygen. I smirked, pleased with myself, but it wasn't enough. I needed more.

So did she.

"No, Little Flower. That's what *I* missed, every day, for two thousand years, seven months, one hundred and forty-two days, and eleven hours."

"That can't be right," she gasped, tears welling up in her eyes, but she never looked away. She was vulnerable, like this, spread out, exposed, but she didn't shy away as she lifted her hand out to me. I knelt on the bed, the top of my thighs pressed against the back of hers, leaning in to take her hand in mine.

It felt so damn good just to hold her hand.

"Look in my eyes, Persephone. You know it is."

She did. She stared right through me, flayed me wide open, and I would have done anything to capture that look, that decision to believe me as it clouded her features. She guided my hand back down to her thigh, nodding gently, encouraging me to keep going. There was no going back once I was inside her, and we both knew it. My hands trembled as I dropped them to my belt and slowly began to undo the clasp.

A sharp ring resounded from the front of my penthouse, and I froze. The doorbell trilled again loudly, splashing cold water over the lust-filled bubble Persephone and I had created for ourselves.

Another impatient ring had my head snapping away from her, and Persephone scrambling to push herself up. "Don't get it," she begged, reaching for my wrist as I made to stand. The doorbell chimed twice more, persistent. "If you open that door, we may never get this moment back, Hades. *Please.*" Her green eyes pleaded with mine and I knew she was right, but the distraction had helped screw my head back on straight and I jerked back, putting more space between us.

The lust-filled haze had settled enough, sated slightly from what we'd just done. Enough that I recognized how fucking reckless I'd been. I wanted to listen to her, to crawl up her body and fuck her through whatever apocalypse was happening outside those doors, but the persistent ringing grounded me down to reality.

"Stay here," I commanded before tearing from the room. My shadows slammed the door shut behind me and swirled over the door frame in a protective barrier, as the doorbell continued to chime frantically. I moved hastily to the entryway, pushing down my unease. What had those moments cost? I reached for the handle and wrenched it open to find Heph leaning against the frame, bloody and busted and breathing hard.

"Where's Persephone?" he asked, weakly. Blood trickled down his face, flowing freely from a cut above his temple, soaking and matting his blond hair. Another dark spot pooled on his abdomen, which he was clutching.

I pulled him inside and shut the door, panic licking up my spine. Heph groaned and allowed himself to lean into me, settling his weight on my shoulder as I threw his arm over my neck. "She's here, she's safe. How bad is it?" I demanded, chest tight.

"More abominations," he breathed, wincing as he sat. Droplets of crimson leaked around him, and I moved to grab the first aid kit. None of the wounds looked deadly, and as a god, he would heal. It would just take time. Even still, guilt tore through me as I popped the top of a bottle of alcohol and lifted his shirt. A nasty gash that looked like claw marks seeped and oozed just above his belly button.

"Fuck. Was anyone else injured? I *told* Hermes this was dangerous," I replied, angrily. Looking over the gash on his side, I frowned as my fingertips applied light pressure on the skin around it. Infections made the healing harder for our kind just as much as for mortals and could stunt the recovery process. I dumped a liberal amount of alcohol over his abs, flooding the floor with light red stains.

He hissed, his muscles straining and contracting as they ran from my touch. "They showed up at all the places she knew. The flower shop is burning to the ground. They overran the house looking for her. Never showed at Electric Delphi, but Styx got attacked too. It's like they knew you were together, but had no idea *where* to go to find you. Hermes is calling this a breakthrough." He winced as I started to apply gauze to catch the excess blood leaking from the God of the Forge.

"How can we think this is a win? Was anyone else hurt?" I asked, tone bitter as I pulled the needle and thread from the first aid kit. If I stitched it properly, it would heal faster and, in a day or two, the skin would look brand new. I couldn't undo what had happened to him, but I could hasten his recovery.

"Dozen or so Otherworlders are pretty wrecked. Cate was severely injured, but she's with Hermes. He had her out of there before Hygieia could even get to her." His words were pointed, and I caught his tone even through the pain.

"Half of New Orleans is on fire. Three of you are hurt. How can Hermes think this was a win?" I asked again, ignoring the implications of Hermes and Hecate. I sank the needle into Heph's flesh and drew the thread through, closing the wound with sure strokes. He threw his head back, staring at the ceiling as he worked to control his breathing and foster his healing. I worked quickly, not wanting to draw out his discomfort.

"Because they couldn't find you, Hades," he choked out between breaths. "I can practically smell it on you. You gave in." His words weren't judgmental, but they were a blade slipped between my ribs, quiet, precise. I'd faltered the course. He knew it, and I knew it. Soon, everyone would and to what end?

Shame bloomed in my chest at the knowledge that I had put them all at risk because I couldn't control myself. I could try to blame Hermes for drugging me, but deep down I knew that was a thin excuse. I shouldn't have been at Electric Delphi to begin with; I should have stayed the fuck away.

"No one is upset or even surprised. Helios made twenty bucks off Hermes when you jumped that railing. We understand." His voice was soft and calm and gentle, but I hated him for his grace.

I had fucked this up and put them at risk, *put her at risk*. I had failed to protect them. As I cordoned off the thread in a knot and snipped the excess close to the stitch, I had to focus to keep my hands steady. Satisfied, I threw the scissors onto the kit on the table and leaned in to study his head wound. "I'm sorry, Hephaestus. It won't happen again. It was irresponsible, and let's just say I won't be accepting a drink from Hermes for a long time." I ran some gauze soaked in alcohol over the cut on his head and he let out a sharp breath.

"Actually, that was my idea, and Nick may have threatened Hermes if he didn't go ahead and do it," he said.

My hand froze and I flicked my eyes down to stare at him. I sat back in my chair, letting my hands drop to my thighs as I took him in.

Heph tightened his lips into a thin line, embarrassed. "He wanted to try, and I knew you wouldn't. She was going to sleep with *someone*, Hades. It was inevitable the moment that liquid touched her lips. This isn't fair to either of you. It's fucked up what you're having to do, but we needed to know. Hermes was convinced something was tethering you to her and allowing the darkness to know when you were near. Helios noticed she's always wearing that pendant. It was a shot we had to take." His words came out rushed, almost pleading, like he needed me to understand, but if he wasn't sitting before me a bloody mess, I may have beaten him myself for his recklessness.

"*Any* of you could have been killed, and if Hermes had been wrong, it could have been Persephone." I spat, rubbing at the spot over his head wound a little more vigorously than necessary.

"But it wasn't. She's safe, and you're together. The wards of this place held."

I leaned forward to tend to his wounds again, tight-lipped and angry. "It doesn't change anything. She and I can't be together," I said firmly.

"Why not?" A soft voice floated from behind me, and I stiffened. We both turned to see Persephone standing in the doorway in just my T-shirt, shuffling her feet nervously. Her arms wrapped around her torso, looking unsure as her wild curls coiled around her face. My chest tightened at the look of hurt that shone in her eyes, of the coin-shaped blueish bruises I could see peaking under the hem of my shirt over her thighs.

"I should go," Hephaestus said, shuffling to move, but I put a hand on his chest and pushed him back down.

"You need to be tended to," I told him before turning back to Persephone. She looked small, breakable with my bruises on her skin, and I wanted to shield her from this world and all the bullshit that came with it, but I couldn't. Her vulnerability poured from her and my bones ached to protect what was mine.

I knew what we had just done would give Persephone expectations that I couldn't afford to let her have, and I should have thanked Heph for interrupting when he did. Had I made love to her, I wouldn't be able to do what needed to be done to keep her safe.

"Persephone, please go back to bed. I promise I will come see you after I care for Hephaestus. We can talk then." I begged and pleaded with my eyes for her not to argue, and to my surprise, she didn't. We watched as she turned on her heel after giving Heph a worried look. He nodded and smiled reassuringly, but then she was gone, back in the bedroom, closing the door with a soft click. My traitorous fucking shadows once again enveloped the door, and I scowled at them for answering her command.

"Suck-ups," I mumbled, and they whinnied as I turned back to Hephaestus, busying myself with his head wound. The worst of the bleeding had stopped, the skin already showed signs of healing; with any luck, it wouldn't scar. He was silent as he let me work, and though it did anger me that it had been his idea to drug me, I tried to be gentle with his stitches. He'd always had my best interests at heart.

It wasn't his fault that this one was possibly going to kill me first.

"You can be with her, you know?" He stared at me as I wiped my hands clean with the disinfectant. I didn't answer him, instead I focused on repacking the first aid kit.

The chair scraped harder than I meant it to as I wrenched it back to stand. I disappeared into the bathroom, replacing the kit, and washed my hands more thoroughly in the sink. The smell of alcohol wafted under my nose. I splashed water on my face, hating how it chased away the scent of Persephone arousal. I sighed, toweling off before heading back out to the dining room.

I reclaimed my seat and looked at Hephaestus again. "I can't. She's still in danger with me until we find who's responsible. She can stay the night, but she has to go in the morning. To a safe house with one of you. I can set it up. She can't stay."

I can't take it if she does.

The words were unspoken, but he understood. Hephaestus seemed to be the only one to understand I wasn't martyring myself out of only guilt—it was obligation. I *chose* to protect her the day I Bonded to her, in whatever form that protection needed to take. He was the only one of the others to be Bonded as well, and as much as my situation was Hells, his was probably worse. He knew a thing or two about giving up his own happiness for his partner. Heph did it all the time. I turned back to find him gingerly working his bloodstained shirt over his head again, wincing at the movement.

"Well, the thing about that is, she has to. Hecate and Hermes are going to be out for a while. Nick also got hurt and Helios isn't leaving him, not even for Persephone. Dionysus is watching over Electric Delphi and Styx, and Artemis, Medusa, and I are off to track down a lead. No one else can be trusted with this, Hades. Since you weren't attacked, we can only assume the wards are holding. So, here she has to stay, whether you let yourself be happy or not." He shrugged.

I scowled at him.

Hephaestus's words weren't biting or mocking, but they may as well have been lashings against me, logical and final. He reached the door and hesitated, his hand on the knob. "I think you could let her in, but I know you won't budge on this. I just hope you're kind to her. She doesn't deserve the anger you're feeling, and she won't understand why you're throwing yourself out to the cold. Be nice, Hades—or I'll kick your ass," he threatened.

I knew that over Persephone, he would do it too.

I ran my fingers through my hair, my seizing lungs sucking in strained breaths as I made my way over to the bedroom door. Pain welled up in my chest as the shadows parted, welcoming me back to her. I could feel their contentment at having her near, the same joy and love they'd missed all those years. It was the same feeling I wanted to let myself get lost in, but I couldn't reconcile it with the pain and terror that losing her again would mean. There was also the matter of her memories. Triggering them could be painful, deadly, if Hygieia was correct. I would need to be strong.

The room was dimly lit with the soft blue glow of my bedside table lamp that she turned on. Persephone sat cross-legged in the middle of the comforter, T-shirt bunched up in her lap. She eyed me warily as I approached, and I swallowed down the lump in my throat as I searched for the right words to say, to let us both down gently. The room smelled of sex, and my nostrils flared, every moment of what we'd done playing in technicolor in my mind. I sent a shadow to crack a window and pushed the temperature down just a tiny bit, needing a clear head to do what I was about to do.

My knees hit the end of the bed, but I allowed myself to go no farther. Persephone bit the inside of her cheek, and I could feel a mixture of anger and sadness tinged with arousal as it perfumed the air around her. I stalled, folding my hands together to keep myself from reaching for her.

"Are you alright? Is Hephaestus?" she asked, worry peppering her tone.

I nodded and dragged my fingers through my hair. She waited for me to speak, and I tried, again and again, to put into words the very things I needed to say and hated to let her hear. The excuses got stuck in my throat so I swallowed them back, my throat working a knot around them. The truth, then; it was my only hope.

"Everyone is okay. Hecate, Nick, and Hephaestus were injured, but they're all going to recover just fine." All I wanted to do was comfort Persephone, the few feet between us already a great chasm as it separated my body from hers, but I stamped down the urge to touch. To covet. My hand flexed.

"What did you mean earlier, that we couldn't be together? I thought, maybe after what happened . . .? I don't understand any of this. I can *feel* that we're supposed to be together, Hades. Do you . . . Do you not want me? Am I just too different from the Persephone you remember?" Her voice was so damn small and the insecurity of it, that fear that this was somehow *her* fault—Persephone's hand shot up to her temple and she let out a low hiss of pain, screwing her eyes shut.

Abandoning the safety of the distance between us, I clambered over the bed to take her head in my hands, needing to know she was okay. Persephone let out a soft moan, pressed her cheek into my palm and the weight of it, the warmth of her felt so good against my skin. "That feels nice. Your hands are so cool and comforting." She looked up at me through those long eyelashes. I saw my entire world in her eyes.

"What's wrong, Little Flower? Is it your head?" I asked, and she nodded gently.

"I need you to explain to me what's happening. I don't understand what I'm feeling, and I can't understand why you'd want so badly to push me away. If you don't love me anymore, I can't blame you. Helios said I was in that box for two thousand years. If you . . . If you moved on or . . ." Her face twisted in pain, but she took a steadying breath and looked up at me again, gripping my wrists in her gentle fists. "If there's someone else, I'm not going to hold you to our marriage. I'm pretty sure abandonment is grounds for divorce." She was trying so hard to be brave, but could do little to hide the hurt and longing.

Keeping her in the dark wasn't going to work anymore. Not if either of us were to survive the forced proximity of this house until the others could retrieve her. I smoothed the pad of my thumb over her soft lips. She shuddered, turning pliant under my touch, boneless. I pulled back a fraction, studying her face.

Hells, she was beautiful.

I retracted my hands, and she let out a hushed whimper. "I am going to tell you everything that I can. I will give you honesty and I will answer your questions to the best of my ability, as long as your mind doesn't cause you pain. But in return, you must promise to do what I say. You must swear that you will abide by my wishes." She looked at me, the wheels of her mind calculating my terms. Her face fell, torn between needing to know what I had to say and the thought of what I could ask of her. Reluctantly, she nodded.

"Say it," I commanded.

Persephone's green eyes bored into mine. "I promise," she whispered.

"I didn't steal you away. You were right about that. We met by chance, by a river and I loved you from the very moment I met you."

A small smile crept over her lips. She pulled the covers up around her, snuggling in as I prepared to crack my chest in two and spill out my deepest pain.

"I knew it. And did I love you too? From the moment we met?" Her smile widened, and I couldn't help but return it with a small smirk of my own.

"My hubris would say, yes, of course. But in all honesty, I'm not sure when it was you fell in love with me. We met every day for a long while. We talked and sat in silence. You showed me how to walk amongst the flora without killing it, and I . . . I was just lucky to be near you."

Persephone's eyebrows knit together in a frown, reaching out for her head again.

I grimaced. "Are you hurting?" I asked, but she shook her head once. A lie.

"Persephone," I warned.

"It's more uncomfortable than painful, now. I think I've gotten to a place of truce with the chaos wall. I can reach through at the soft spots and ask for a memory. When you speak, sometimes they force their way out, though. Sometimes it's as easy as opening up a book. Did . . . we used to meet in a meadow? With olive trees?" she asked, studying me. My pulse quickened.

She was remembering.

I nodded slowly. "Your mother betrothed you to Helios. And you decided you didn't want that, so you came to me and asked for my hand in marriage. It was very forward-thinking of you, for the time. Caught me completely off guard." I chuckled as she blushed, smirking as she peered at me from behind her hands.

Her eyes fluttered shut momentarily and she let out a long, steady breath. "You didn't want me. I remember we fought. I was angry. You didn't want me." Her voice hollowed. I couldn't risk touching her unnecessarily. It was too cruel. For both of us. I shook my head instead.

"I wasn't *good* for you. I tried to convince you that it was dangerous for a goddess like yourself in the Underworld. Helios would have made you a good husband. He could have kept you thriving in the light." Bile rose in my throat at the memory.

"But I didn't love him."

I smiled.

"You didn't. Instead, you threatened to have him fuck you in front of me, if I was too much of a coward to do it myself."

"No the hells I didn't!" she groaned, biting down on her lower lip. I chuckled, dipping my chin.

"Oh, I assure you that you *did*. But it didn't matter, I was a goner for you, and deep down, you knew I'd never call your bluff, but I should have denied you then, lived my life in anguish without you. It would have kept you safe and whole. Your mother, Demeter, she . . . wasn't well. She wanted you returned, convinced Helios and most of the Upper Realm that I had stolen you, and despite your protestations, Zeus was inclined to indulge her." I studied her face at the mention of Demeter. I knew that wound would open soon, but I wished to push it off for as long as possible.

Persephone stayed very still, pain ghosting across her face.

"I don't remember her," she admitted.

"That may be a blessing, Little Flower. She stopped growing crops, started a famine. It decimated Greece. She wouldn't listen, wouldn't see reason. Over time, our friends came to witness your life in the Underworld. We were being overrun by the dead, but they tried to tell her what they experienced when they returned. They saw you guiding shades, ruling, thriving. Those same friends all surround you now." I inhaled deeply and pressed on.

"When you were taken, it was by a former lover of Helios's who had been scorned by Helios's love for you, or what he had perceived as love. He conspired with a mortal king to steal you away. It went . . . horribly wrong. Or at least, for us. I suppose for Narcissus, it went according to plan. But after so much searching, it came to a head, and we lost you. It nearly destroyed me. It *did* destroy me." My voice wavered at the swells of pain pooling in my chest.

Persephone's eyes shone. "But I'm here, now. I'm back. Do you still love me? Why would you tell me you hurt me, Hades? Why are there no myths or stories about us other than *that* one? Everyone seems so angry at you, and I thought it was because you were cruel. But they're angry you're keeping me away from you, aren't they?" she demanded. Persephone rocked forward onto her knees, invading my space. Her wild hair floating around her. Tears, rife with pain shone in her eyes as her shoulders shook.

"You lied to me. You abandoned me, Hades, you let me think I was alone when I woke up! You didn't come for me," she cried, and I shook my head, wracking my brain to find words to make her understand the weight of it all, what was at stake.

My goddess.

"What I want doesn't matter. You aren't safe with me or near me. The Fates came to see me when you returned. The darkness that took you follows me, and when we are together it follows me to *you*. I needed you to hate me because I can't stand that look in your eyes that I'm seeing right now. You're so fucking strong, so defiant. Would you have listened to me if I asked you to stay away?" I stroked her cheek, unable to help myself. She shuddered at my caress, sparks erupted from our touch, sending electric pulses radiating from wherever our skin met.

"We're safe now," she reasoned, running her hands up and over my neck, pressing into me. "I want you in ways I don't understand. It's like you're calling to the depths of me." She placed a small kiss to the hollow of my throat. My entire body lit on fire. I needed to be strong for both of us, but I was weak. Too weak in her capable hands. My fingers trailed down to her shoulders, and I gripped her biceps lightly, pushing her away as gently as I could. Hurt bloomed in her eyes, reddening her cheeks, and the tears fell then, fat and salty and heartbreaking.

"We're *not* safe. We may be locked inside here but that darkness is wreaking havoc out there. Half the city is being torn apart as it looks for you. Three of our friends are injured. I told you I would tell you everything, and I am. I've given the others a month to find out who's responsible. Keeping you cooped up in here isn't living and it's unsafe to let you go while I'm around. If they don't find the culprit by then, you're leaving with them, and I won't be able to know where or be able to find you. Hecate is working on a reverse incantation using the markings you were buried with. If I can't find you, then the darkness can't either. You'll be safe, and so will the others."

A myriad of emotions crossed over her face before it settled on anger as I told her the plan I'd come up with, that the others had protested, that caused Helios to stop speaking to me altogether. She clenched her tiny fists in her lap and narrowed those shrewd, green eyes. "And I suppose, I have no say in the matter of what happens to me?" she spat, venom lacing her tone.

My lips tipped upward in a small, sad smile. "You promised. You promised you'd heed my words if I told you what I knew and answered your questions," I reminded her.

Her nostrils flared as she crossed her arms over her chest. "So, to be clear, you *do* love me?" she asked, voice tight.

"*Persephone*." I sighed, looking up to the ceiling, "There are no words or gospels or scriptures ever written that could describe what I feel for you. Every inch of who you are is branded into my shade, and the only thing that kept me out of crawling into a grave all of these years is the far away thought that someday I'd hear your voice. So love? That word isn't big enough. But if you're asking specifically, then yes. I do." She stared at me, eyes shining.

"And if we weren't under immediate threat of certain death, you would want me?"

I pinched my brow together, and nodded.

"Fine," she said coolly, relaxing back into the headboard. Her anger masked by a shrewd complacency. I stood, brushing off my pants, grateful for their dark color. The wet stain from where I'd come just from tasting her on my tongue was barely noticeable on this side of the fabric. It was a sticky explosion on the inside.

I walked to the head of the bed and lifted Persephone's chin to face me with two fingers. "Be good," I pleaded softly. "You promised." Fates, just having her here, seeing her in my bed, in my shirt . . . I wanted to kiss her. Just one more time.

I couldn't.

I pulled away and turned for the door, unable to stand the temptation any longer. I had to get out of here before I lost all control.

Again.

Persephone

CHAPTER 32

The door shut with finality, and I whimpered as the heavy emotions battered against my shredded heart. I hadn't realized I'd been holding my breath, but the moment Hades had touched me again, an earthquake of desire had torn through my body. He had told me everything that he could, been as honest as he could be, but it still wasn't enough.

I had a month until they came to take me away. I could work with that. He had stolen moans and screams from me, coaxed me to orgasm twice, and yet I still hadn't felt him fall apart at my feet, and that was unacceptable. I wavered, the need to please him, to be good somehow hardwired into my brain while the other part of me wanted to say fuck this and barge right out that door.

I made the choice subconsciously before the rest of me could keep up. I had promised, sure, but maybe I was a liar. I was learning all kinds of new things about myself lately. The covers flew back, and I dropped to the floor, stepping across the hardwood. I cracked the door just a bit, peeking through the swirling shadows.

The shower clicked on from the hallway bathroom that remained visible from my door. He had left the bathroom door wide open, probably secure in the knowledge that I would behave. That his shadows could keep me in. I smirked. They'd obeyed me before when I left the bedroom to find him and Hephaestus earlier, surely they would do the same now.

I focused on the swirling glimmers of darkness in front of me and placed a hand to their incorporeal wall of resistance. "Let me pass," I commanded and pushed, attempting to break through, but the shadows didn't budge this time. I hissed, annoyed. Maybe he had locked them somehow.

I focused my eyes through the gap of darkness to the bathroom, illuminated with soft white light. I could see the front half of the frosted sliding glass doors, and just barely, the silhouette of Hades behind it.

He was a monster of a god. His large frame stood taller than Helios but just as wide at the shoulders, more narrow at the hips. Hades was slightly bent over, resting his forearm against the tile of the wall. I watched in rapt fascination as his silhouette shook, thrusting forward. A blush spread across my cheeks as I realized he was . . . "*Persephone*," he groaned, the moans reverberating off the tile. Pride mixed with liquid lust within me, and in that moment, I wished my god-power included X-ray vision. He stroked, long and hard and I wanted to watch, wanted to see, needed to know what his face looked like when he let himself get lost in the thick of it. I longed to see the way his muscles tensed as he rocked himself harder. The echo of his sharp pants bounced to me, and I locked my thighs together, squeezing in search of a pressure release. Hades threw his head back and I imagined the water droplets and the way they'd cling to his pale skin, how it would plaster his dark hair to his face. His moans were hushed, muffled as he hid his face in his bicep. He stroked harder, faster, and I cursed the glass separating us.

Slowly, a tickle started in my mind palace, and I retreated inside. The memory protruded from the crevice in the wall, like a secret. I clutched it to my chest hungrily, willing it to show me more.

A cloudy day, broken up only by the peeking sun as it broke through. A river, flowing bright blue and glowing. A man, naked in the water. Pale lines cut into his flesh, marking up his skin. Muscles corded tightly around his frame, a V cut down to the massive erection he held clasped in his hands as he stroked harder and faster. Hades, his head thrown back as the sun washed over him. His hands worked, erratic as he chased his pleasure . . .

The memory released me as I heard Hades come in the shower, his sharp pants punctuated by small moans. His Welsh lilt sent sparks down my spine as I imagined him splashing cum over the walls, down the tile. That accent did things to me that I couldn't justify, but it made me want to hear my name fall from his lips over and over again. He was so good at going down on me, and I wanted to know if I was just as good, if sex would be as electric.

It was a selfish thing, to cry over my estranged husband not fucking me while outside the city burned, but I let myself have this one. I'd spent all that time buried away from them, desiccating in a wooden box. The shower shut off moments later and I panicked, backing into the room and shutting the door as softly as I could before climbing into bed.

I told myself to sleep, but the denial was unbearable. I felt sore and somehow still hungry for him.

I settled back into the bed, his bed, burying my nose in the scent of his pillow as my fingers danced over the swells of my breasts, pulling and rubbing my nipples as I made my way down my tummy. Goose bumps erupted over my thighs at the first push against my sensitive clit, and I whimpered, muffling the sound by pushing my face in deeper. I was slick in the aftermath of what we had done, each tender brush bringing me a little closer, but I still needed more.

I needed him.

The light in the room dimmed lower as I circled and pulled, working my clit harder with each pass, rocking my hips against my palm, but no matter how hard I tried I couldn't replicate the sensations he'd caused. The light became *almost* completely obfuscated by shadows as they approached me, slithering up in long tendrils, their caresses on my skin sending jolts through my body. They felt like Hades, and I knew they were only listening to my needs, but I welcomed them, the little pieces of him that I could hold on to. I flung his shirt off, fisting it in my grip as shadows kissed over my flushed skin, writhing down, covering my body, restraining my legs.

I was commanding them, just as I'd done before, more passive want than active decision, but it was hot, the way they worked me over, sucking and nipping at the soft flesh under my breasts, twisting and tweaking my nipples as I rode my fingers. Each touch was heavy, nearly there, nearly his, drowning me in his power. I whimpered when a lone tendril burrowed between my legs, possessive and patient, working me open. My eyes fluttered shut and I thought of Hades, of his body, his kiss, the way his teeth and fingers had sunk into my skin. I gasped at the intrusion, at the stretch, nearly cried out, needing Hades to feel it, to feel me. I wanted him to hold my face and grip my throat and fuck me hard. For him to take his pleasure, push me past the point of pain, and then do it all over again. I needed it like I needed air.

I called upon the memory harder, willing the shadows to *be* Hades. They obeyed, forming a solid being over me. I sank into my mind to find him, conjure him. With a sigh I threw my head back and cried out into the shirt fisted in my hands as the shadows pumped in and out of me, filling my senses with nothing but his cold, wintry scent, and from the shadows I heard my name, spoken on a desperate moan from his lips.

Hades

CHAPTER 33

The shower had been a poor substitute for the goddess in the next room, but it sated the hunger burning within me, if only just so. My shadows swirled, agitated and sulking at the distance between us. They'd missed Persephone as much as I had and I could feel my control over them slipping. The darkness belonged to her just as much as it did to me, and it was taking considerable will to stop them from giving in to her whims and breaking down the doors that separated us.

"Quit whining," I barked at the rustling darkness.

Despite the fact I'd come twice tonight, it did little to relieve my sour mood. I had gone from holding my ground to spilling my guts to her, knowing full well she would fight me for what she wanted the entire time. I knew that look that burned through her gaze. She'd get her way, but I'd hold out as long as I could. Or at least that's what I'd told myself. Part of me, and not a small part, was relieved just to be unburdened by it. She knew.

The darkness of my shadows swirled lower over the bed, and I stiffened at their scent. They moved slowly, deliberately, and they no longer only smelled like the bitter bite of the Underworld.

No, they smelled like *flowers*. I tensed, eyes sweeping the room in the silent stillness. Satisfied she hadn't portaled in, I settled back again. They were just missing her, and she was close, in the room down the hall. The shadows crept closer, that overwhelming spring clinging to them. I raised a hand to dismiss them completely when I heard it, coming through the darkness.

A whimper. A moan.

My heart stammered. I knew those sounds. I'd drawn them from Persephone's lips myself a million times. The shadows caressed my skin, pulling the towel from my waist, lifting my cock in the inky darkness. They were soft, silken as they handled me. They were *her.* I wondered if she even knew what she was doing, but the thought was ripped from my mind at the sure stroke that trailed over my ridges. I cried out, body bowing at their touch. *So long*. It had been so long since she had touched me like this.

"*Hades, yes, right there*," she moaned, echoing through the shadows.

My cock pulsed and throbbed with each stroke, wrenching the breath from my lungs. I sat up, watching them bob up and down on my length as though Persephone were taking me into her sweet, filthy mouth. I should stop them. Should stop this. She had no way to know what this was, what it meant, and that kind of consent was dubious at best. We were linked together, she and I, both through our Bond and through the Underworld. They would bend to her will as much as mine, and now she seemed to be finding her power and *Fates* . . . Another stroke sent my toes curling, my eyes rolling back.

Maybe if I give her this, it will sate her for a while?

The thought was a rationalization, an outright absurdity. I knew her appetite and it rivaled mine. She wouldn't be satisfied until she was wrapped around my cock, being a brat so I'd punish her. My body shook at the memory of being buried deep inside her, giving her my power until she was drunk on it, until it dripped from her lips and ass and cunt.

The shadows slid off me, forming at the end of the bed into a swirling mass that reached for me, begging for my touch. My eyes widened as I recognized that body, the curve of her hips as she rolled them, and the delicate arch of her neck as she threw her head back in ecstasy.

It was her.

The shadow version of Persephone cried out to me, my name falling from lips through breathy moans. I moved down the bed, studying her hungrily. She seemed so solid, so corporeal that I faltered. I could hear her taking her pleasure. Another set of shadows pulled me forward by the hand and she reached up, fingers splayed apart, legs spread wide as her chest heaved.

I let them pull me on top of her soft form, and wished I could see the color of her eyes, see how her skin bloomed with soft pink as she heated. My cock was already hard, needy and weeping just to be near her in any form, shadow or otherwise. I crawled up her body, kissing her darkness, feeling her mold beneath me. Our hands still clasped together as I lined up and sank into her to the first ring circling my cock.

The shadow beneath me whimpered at the intrusion, but I waited for her to adjust before rocking deeper, up to my third ring. She was panting hard as I leaned down to her, resting my forehead against hers. Her cunt was hot as it had ever been, silken and hungry as it sucked me deeper. I knew this wasn't real, but her voracious appetite bent the darkness and me to her will, to a pleasure I hadn't let myself indulge in since she was taken. There had only ever been her, since her, for me.

My neck strained at the force of the orgasm threatening to rip from my body. It was too early, but I hadn't had her in so long that I was losing all sense of reason. I pulled out and Persephone whimpered again, such a delectable sound. I pushed my fingers across her lips, pressed at the seam between them until the pads rested on that devilish tongue. I wanted to tell her to suck, but I was afraid it would break the spell between us.

Hells, it fucking *felt* real. I snapped my hips into her as she clamped down around my cock and my fingers, ruining me, trapping me in her orbit. My free hand slipped between us to circle that sweet clit, and she fluttered tight as I pushed lower, prodding gently at the negative space around my length. I bit back the moan threatening to tear through me at the pressure when the tip of my finger slipped in, the fit impossibly tight.

I thrust harder, past the fourth ring to the base of my cock, until it disappeared into the darkness completely. I leaned in closer, taking Persephone's nipple in my mouth and rolling it between my teeth, finger still crooking and cock still thrusting. I pulled my hand from her mouth and ran it down her neck, over the planes of her chest and her other breast. Her nipples tensed, peaked, so fucking responsive as I latched on, biting, teasing. She cried out again, echoing through the abyss, coming hard around my cock.

The grip she had on me would have killed a lesser man. Shit, it could have killed a god. She pulsed, milking me until I, too, came. I watched in wonder as thick ropes pushed through the shadows and landed unceremoniously on the bed sheets below.

My chest thrummed with relief. At least it wouldn't be inside her. There was no telling what my cum may do to her or the way she would manipulate that power. If it was anything like it had been in our time together before, it could break her.

Shadow Persephone reached a shaky hand toward my face, and I leaned into it.

"Did he enjoy it too?" she asked, voice spent and sleepy through the darkness. My chest rose and fell rapidly as I lay locked inside her, still hard and pulsing. I nodded frantically into her palm, and she smiled. "Thank you."

I grabbed her hand, pressed a kiss to the inside of her wrist before slowly, gently, pulling myself out of her. Persephone's eyes rolled shut, and exhausted, her breathing settled. And when I crept in to check on her, I found her tangled in the sheets, freshly fucked and content as she slept, and I knew, Hells I knew, I'd give her anything she wanted. I tucked her under the covers, brushing back her hair from her face, memorizing the way it fanned across the sheets. Carefully, I pressed my lips to her forehead, lingering far too long against her skin.

Persephone

CHAPTER 34

The escapade with the shadows had cost me dearly, and now I sat feet from Hades reading the same page for the eighth time. He knew I had jumped him, and while it caught him off guard once, he wasn't taking any chances now.

Artemis dropped off a bag for me before she, Medusa, and Hephaestus took off on Hecate's orders. It had clothes and some basic essentials, but luckily for me, she had thrown in some very provocative lingerie that didn't belong to me. It made me smile to know they, too, were all rooting for me to seduce my husband.

Girl's girls.

In the aftermath of our confinement, Hades had been so kind, which was frustrating. If he was that mean, cruel man I'd met that first night, I probably could have walked away. At least, that's what I'd convinced myself. Instead, he brought me books and a record player. He'd cooked me dinner every night, always something exotic and intricate. He'd spent hours in the kitchen while I drew or wrote or read or played music. Never demanding on my time, always the gentleman. We talked about some of the ages he'd lived through, and he'd told me about the fall of Olympus. Day after day, little bits of my memory slipped through, and the pain was as little as it had ever been at their release.

It made it all the more frustrating that he wouldn't touch me.

I seemed to remember our sexual escapades the most ardently and I craved the taste of him. After that first night, Hades made sure to lock down the shadows tightly. They wouldn't listen to me, wouldn't obey or even speak to me once the sun went down, and we were in our respective rooms. They swirled and settled near the foot of the bed, but wouldn't touch. I'd gotten us all grounded, and it made me feel like a sex-crazed monster the way I lusted over him . . . but when he was so gentle and kind and looked the way he did?

Fuck, it was difficult to function with him standing so close. I felt worse about the monk-like existence Hades had lived for so long. This penthouse was minimalist to the extreme, with no soft touches or sentiments. A few paintings here and there but no photographs, no life. He just *existed* here.

"Why don't you have any photographs or anything personal here? Is this just a safe house?" I asked. Hades glanced up from the book he was reading, looking so casually fucking delicious it made my cheeks burn. "You promised," I reminded him. "Whatever I wanted to know."

He folded the book over in his hands, using his long fingers to mark his space without bending the corner of the page. I stared at them for a beat too long, and he cleared his throat, calling my attention back to his smirking face. "This is my house that I live in while I'm in New Orleans. I don't really take photos and most of the ones you'll find belong to the others. I have . . . my trinkets. I keep them safe."

I studied him closely, gathering up the courage to ask my next question. "Were you . . . Did you . . . You said you didn't take a lover after me. But did you ever love before me? I can't be angry, but I'm curious." My voice stayed steady, though fear gripped me.

I wasn't sure why I wanted to know so badly, but I *did*. I wanted to know everything.

Hades tilted his head to me thoughtfully and I watched a storm roll behind those blue eyes. "Before you . . . I had many lovers. None of them ever more than once. Save for one." He shifted his feet flat on the floor in front of him and bent forward, resting his forearms on his thighs, steepling his fingers together.

Sadness bloomed over me as I prepared myself for his next words.

"She was beautiful and, I *thought*, kind. She was a Naiad Nymph of the Cocytus. Her father was the River God Cocytus himself." He looked at me, face pained.

She meant something to him. I hated her already. I locked my jaw and threatened to pluck my own eyes out if one irrational tear fell.

"Seph, you don't need to know about this," he pleaded.

I crossed my arms over my chest, determined to hurt my own feelings. "Continue," I demanded.

Hades closed his eyes and took a breath. "We met on one of my patrols and we spoke for a few moments before I had to return to my duties. I never even got her name. I rarely ever left the Underworld except to attend Dionysus's gatherings. He insisted I attend at least two a year, not including his birthday, which was mandatory. She was there. And during the ritual, we . . . *found* each other." Hades looked like he might be sick, which did leave me with a little satisfaction. I knew I was being unreasonable, but I couldn't stop. I needed to know who she was, what had happened between them.

"And what was her name?" I sniffed.

"Minthe," he said, but the word held no reverence, no emotion at all. Not like how he said my name. I softened a little, as that low pressure pushed at me from the wall in my mind. I had heard this before, I just couldn't quite grasp it.

"Can you tell me what happened? I want it to be your choice, not because you promised." I *did* want this from him, but freely given. The initial jealousy had faded the moment I'd registered the coldness in his voice.

He gave me a small smile, then rolled his lip under his teeth. "With any lovers I ever took, I never let them know who I was, and I made sure there were no . . . lingering effects. Minthe knew who I was, but she didn't care. We danced, and we fucked, and I allowed myself to open up to someone for the first time in my existence. She didn't want anything from me, and she didn't care that I was the dark ruler of the Underworld. She lived in that darkness too. It was the first time I entertained the idea that something beautiful could love a cold, twisted thing.

"Her father was . . . not a good father, or god. He used her and her beauty to make deals with those who wished to cross his river. If the price was high enough, he would throw in an evening with her. I forbade the practice as soon as I found out and almost killed him when he didn't, but she stopped me. She *begged* me to spare him. He abused her, but he was her father, and she loved him. I cared about her—I thought, deeply. But in the end, I think I felt responsible for her and her fate. It was happening in my domain, but if she didn't object then I couldn't do anything to stop it." Hades moved onto the floor, kneeling before me as he reached for my hands. I opened my palms, and he sighed with relief as he ran his fingers over the lines there.

"She begged me not to turn her away, and Hells help me, I was weak. I knew she was being turned out to the highest bidder, but I thought I cared for her, so I stayed. I washed her shame away, I healed her bruises from when they were too rough. I fucked her in a way that she craved, a way that made her feel safe. It tore bits of me apart, but I did it because it was the love I thought I deserved." Hades sucked in a shaking breath.

"One day, a deal went bad with Zeus, and Cocytus ended up with a chest full of Poisoned Ambrosia. It corroded him from the inside out, breaking the most sacred of our laws. We don't kill other gods, but Zeus . . . He never gets caught with dirty hands, you know? Minthe witnessed the whole thing, and it destroyed what was left of her. She didn't speak for months. Zeus ordered her to resume her father's duties, and she had no choice but to oblige, but she was never the same after he died." Pity welled up in my chest for the woman.

"Long after, I returned from helping Thanatos reap a battlefield to find her bent over, fucking Zeus. He looked me in the eye as he slapped her, degraded her and she liked it. He knew I cared for her, and he wanted to hurt me, keep me in check, so he took it as an opportunity to put me in my place. They had been meeting that way since he'd had her father killed. When she finally saw me, she tried to stop me from leaving, even tried to get me to join, but I was done. I turned and left. When she begged to see me, the shades turned her away too. I mistook her attention for love. In the end, she had demons I couldn't fight."

I squeezed his hands in mine. Hades brushed my knuckles across his lips. They were soft as he kissed over my hands, something like an apology in every pass over my skin. I shuddered. This was the most he'd touched me since that first night, and my mind raced with memory and possibility. *Not the time*, I reminded myself, but it was difficult to reign in. I'd gone a year without feeling any sort of sexual attraction at all, and a week with him had me a walking puddle of lust. This moment wasn't about that, though. Hades was letting me in on real pain, and he deserved my focus.

I cleared my throat. "Did I ever meet her?" I asked. I hadn't had time to process the memory waiting for me, but something about that name was so familiar.

Hades let out a low chuckle and smirked. "Yeah, once. You, uh . . . You turned her into a plant."

My mouth dropped open. That didn't sound like something I'd do, did it?

"To be fair, she was, well, more than a bit intoxicated off of Dio's wine, and she made some inaccurate and disrespectful claims," he laughed. I dug deep for that waiting memory, too curious to wait. I wrapped around it, pulling it to me, then I closed my eyes and let my body melt into it.

A whimsical forest, Hades, Dionysus, and Hermes moved to intercept a screeching woman with wild black hair and slurred words. The snap of my fingers, their shock as her body transformed in less than a blink into a small, fuzzy, green plant . . . Hades's hands and mouth and tongue and teeth against my skin, pulling me beneath him, desperate to have me . . . The shadows parting around us just enough for me to see that little plant, the satisfaction in my bones as my husband thrust inside me, rocking my body reverently . . .

"I love you," he whispered, repeating the words against my skin, kissing the tops of my cheeks, the corners of my lips, swallowing my whimpers, and not once did his attention stray from my eyes.

Helios

CHAPTER 35

Hermes's house was filled with all of us, large and pristine. On the far wall multiple clocks kept time around the world, and we were spread out as best we could in the open concept living room. Everything had its place, not an ounce of clutter or disorder, a true reflection of the obsessive control the Messenger God exuded. His house was on the farthest end of town, out of the way, but for Hermes distance meant nothing. Hephaestus and Medusa were close by, she on a barstool and he leaned up against the marbled counter. Artemis stretched out over the extensive couch, Hermes on the other side in the same position, hands thrown behind his head. His winged feet sat crossed on his low table, but it was Hecate who commanded the room, standing just near his mantle.

"I've had a vision." Cate announced.

"Is that what the kids are calling getting your back blown out by Hermes these days?" Artemis quipped. Hephaestus snorted, and I had to bite back my own laughter as Medusa buried her face against his arm to stifle hers.

"Yeah, yeah, yuck it up, arseholes. It's called being a *consort*, not like any of you fuckers are mature enough to understand," Hermes sniffed, raising his nose into the air like he wasn't the least serious of us all. He liked order when it came to everyone else, but he was a mischievous little shit by nature.

"Yeah? How much for an hour of that 'consorting,' in case anyone asks?" Medusa teased on a choked wheeze, and I did break then, along with everyone else. Even Cate was cracking up, shoulders shaking with silent laughter as Hermes shot her a scandalized look.

"None of you could afford me," he snapped back haughtily. "Except you, darling. *Obviously*," he winked at Hecate, and she flipped him off, rolling her eyes. Their auras reached for one another across the space naturally, and though their arrangement was supposedly a means to an end, I could see it. The attraction between them. That spark.

She cleared her throat.

"No, I mean . . . I've had a vision. About the abomination. We used the necklace to help zero in on a faint signal. Thank Nick for that, by the way," she said, tipping her head to me. I reached down for Persephone's necklace, the one Nick had noticed she'd always worn, that he'd pulled from her neck just before the city had come under siege. A simple conversation had led to revelation.

"So, this is how they've been doing it," I asked, twirling the little pendant between my fingers, the unassuming little pomegranate necklace that Hades had bought on a whim.

"It's a tracker of some sort, but it seems to be specifically activated when Hades's power mixes with Persephone's," Hecate explained, voice tight. She looked healed after the shit that had gone down, which was good. She'd been considerably wounded during that attack.

Nick had too.

My palms itched, ready to get back to him. Any moment he wasn't in my sight had me crawling out of my fucking skin.

"They must have been tracking him, somehow," Medusa offered. Next to her, Hephaestus leaned back, arms crossed, looking less at ease than I'd seen him in a long time.

The room grew tense, the previous teasing and lightheartedness vanished with the seriousness of the situation. If they could get to Hades, the strongest of us, then none of us were safe. If his power hadn't detected the underlying dark magic, then how could we trust any of ours to hold against what was coming?

Nick.

"There's a chance I might know where they're creating the abominations from, and that would make sense if they're portaling them in, rather than housing them locally. We've scried; Hermes has worn tracks around the entire state of Louisiana. They aren't holding them here."

"Where?" I asked. Hecate exchanged a tense look with Hermes.

"The Underworld."

Artemis let out a low whistle, "Shit. *Shit*. So what's the plan then?"

Hermes spoke. "We need to get more information. We can't just go out, guns blazing. If this is the real spot, we could spook them and tip them off. Recon only. Intel. Then back with a plan. We're looking for volunteers."

"Is that really a question?" Artemis scoffed, standing, looking around at us. Hermes cocked his head, rubbed his fingers just under his lower lip as he considered her words.

"Yes," he replied seriously. "This is unlike anything we've ever faced. This magic is weird, it's almost . . ." He trailed off.

"Patchwork," Hecate finished for him. He nodded.

"Patchwork, right. There's no single discipline or power source we can latch onto. It's an amalgamation of dark arts and stolen tricks, and that smoke and mirrors is dangerous. The magic inside these abominations is necrotic and it affects us," he winced, his gaze flicking fast to Hecate's hands, resting over her chest. "So you need to understand the risks. Hades has made it clear he doesn't expect anyone to put themselves in harm's way over this. I told him to fuck off, but I am going to give anyone here the option to stay behind. No shame. No judgment."

Hephaestus stood, joining Artemis, then Medusa too, beside him. Her snakes rubbed against his bicep, but he just clicked his tongue at them good-naturedly.

"I'm in," he announced. "Me too," she agreed.

Hermes's eye caught mine. "Same."

I owed this to Persephone. To Hades too.

"Right then. Pack your shit, we're catching a portal in five hours," Hermes announced, and at that, I did blanch. If we were leaving the city, I didn't have anyone to keep an eye on Nick. Anxiety twisted low in my belly as pockets of conversations broke out around me, but all I could do was panic.

"What's wrong?" Cate asked, stepping into my space. Shrewd eyes missed nothing, and she'd clocked me immediately.

"Nick. He's barely recovered from that shit at Electric Delphi. If we're all going, that only leaves Hygieia and she's going to need to be here for Persephone. Dio and Thanatos are already running protections at the clubs. . ." The Goddess of Witchcraft pursed her lips, considering.

"Aphrodite is in town. I could see—" she offered, but I shook my head, eyes cutting to Hephaestus.

"The last thing I need is to involve her in this. Something happens and she gets hurt too? Ares will kill us all," I grumbled, wishing, for not the first time, that the God of War wasn't fighting somewhere off in the desert. He was one of the only people I knew who could take care of himself against shit like this.

"What about Hades?" she asked. I shook my head. "He's not letting *anyone* near Persephone. I don't think anyone has been there since . . . the attack? Heph went to let him know what was what. He's got that penthouse on lockdown now, though."

"Yes, but he knows what Nick means to you. He won't ask you to die for his Bondmate if he won't protect yours while you do it," she reasoned. My eyes snapped to hers, but she only smiled softly up at me.

"How did you—"

"*Everyone* knows. It's nearly as obvious as Hades and Persephone's Bond. *Nearly*," she teased.

"Oh yeah? And what about you, *hmm*?" I asked, giving her a pointed look. I watched her eyes touch on Hermes for the briefest moment before continuing their perusal around the room.

"It's for ritual purposes only!" she defended in a hushed whisper, but the red tinging her complexion several shades darker than normal said otherwise. I cocked an eyebrow at her, crossing my arms. "Oh, shut the fuck up," she grumbled, but even she couldn't fight the smile pulling at her lips.

"Talk to Hades," she urged, bumping her shoulder against mine. "And for what it's worth, we're all happy for you. Really."

The phone in my pocket rang, loud and shrill. I excused myself, pulling it from my jeans to see Hades's name calling. I stepped out onto Hermes's back porch.

"Hades, what's up?" I answered, bringing the phone to my ear, but it wasn't the God of the Dead's voice that came down the line.

"'Los?" a soft, feminine voice whispered. My brow furrowed.

"Persephone? What's going on, are you okay?"

"Yep, Helios, can you hear me? I need a favor, do you know where the penthouse is?" she asked, her voice muffled against her hand, maybe. She didn't sound panicked though, only a little breathless.

"I do. Seph, why are you whispering?" I asked, bewildered.

"Because I stole Hades's phone so I could call you and see if you'd bring me some things. There's a Record Store Day pickup

I've been waiting on, and I really could use some stuff from the house. Will you come?"

"Why didn't you just ask Hades to get your shit?"

"Because he's gonna say no, be all, *it's not worth the risk*," she replied, her voice lowering in a hilarious but surprisingly accurate impersonation of Hades's broody accent. "Fuck, 'Los, are you a cop? What's with all the questions?" she grumbled. I chuckled, the smile on my face stretched from ear to ear. He certainly had his hands full with her. No one dared to brat out at Hades the way she did.

"Helios? Can you do it? Pretty please?" she asked impatiently. Somewhere in the distance, I heard him calling out her name. I considered that maybe having the conversation about Nick face-to-face with him might go over better, and maybe with Seph there, I'd have an ally in case he went full caveman about it. I sighed.

"Yeah, sure. What do you need me to get, love?"

Persephone

CHAPTER 36

The penthouse was huge; it had a library and a pool with a jacuzzi, but I found that any room where I couldn't feel Hades near me was too large. This morning found me curled up on a small settee with a book and headphones, and Hades sitting on the floor, leaning back against the frame. The doorbell chimed, and he stiffened, flattening his own book. His muscles were immediately pulled taut as he stood, but I hopped up first, excited.

"It's Helios," I assured him. He looked at me with confusion.

"How do you know that?" he asked, but I was already gone, racing down the hall toward the door. I heard Hades grunt in frustration before he tore after me, his large body gaining on me by the second. I reached for the doorknob, feeling triumphant, before large hands closed around my middle and yanked me back into a hard chest, expelling my breath as we tumbled, landing with a smack on the floor.

Hades absorbed most of the impact, but his body was warm against mine. He landed with a grunt, but I didn't relent, launching myself forward to freedom. His hands closed around my waist, tickling and grabbing me as he reached over my head. His reach was considerable, a perk of his height, and I growled in frustration as the locks clicked with a flick of his hand. Warmth bloomed in my cheeks as he pinned me to him, still laughing.

I stared up at him in wonder as he let out a throaty roar that shook his chest. I squirmed a bit more, desperate to keep that sound coming, wanting to hear it again, unrestrained. I hadn't heard him laugh outside of the precious few memories of our past, but there was nothing that compared to Hades full of joy. Hearing it in person was a symphony.

He was the most beautiful creature when he was like this, unguarded and unreserved. His full lips parted, a soft twinkle in those icy eyes. Straddling my abdomen, he held my arms pinned above my head, both of us breathing hard as the air around us shifted. He stared down at me, the twitch of him hardening slightly against the softness of my belly, but I couldn't tear my eyes away from his for long enough to confirm it. I wanted him to hold me like this forever, a desperate need that built behind my ribs, one mirrored in his gaze. But the doorbell chimed again, and I saw the moment he faltered, tempering himself down. The sadness that reflected in his eyes shook through me.

Something shifted between us over the week, and though I knew it, I was scared to admit how much it affected me. Hades was more than just a key to my past, he'd become a living, breathing reminder that I had been loved and happy. My body had *always* called to him, but this was different. I had gotten to know him, to the darkness underneath, and I understood why our love was one worth fighting a rebellion over. He was everything. The darkness, the shadows. *Everything.*

I just needed him to understand that I wasn't going to let him just walk away from me.

Hades hopped up in a fluid motion full of grace, pulling me with him. I struggled to be less awkward as I stood, as he moved past me, pushing me behind him before opening the door. Helios stood in the doorway with two large brown bags in his hands, a bemused expression on his face as his eyes swept between us. Our hair was wild and tousled, cheeks pink and flushed. I ducked under his arm, beaming at Helios, who held up the bags in offering. With a sigh, Hades gripped me around the waist, dragging me back inside with a roll of his eyes. The titan followed, kicking the door closed with his boot as he looked around appreciatively. I took the bags from him and placed them on the long table, digging in to find what I'd called for.

"What are you doing here? Is everything okay?" Hades asked, weary as he peeked over my shoulder. I shooed him away. Helios leaned back, amused, at our easy banter, crossing his arms. "Yeah, it's fine. She called me. Needed some supplies." He gestured to me over Hades's shoulder, and I grinned.

"Did you get it?" I asked, excitedly still digging.

Helios nodded, pointing to the correct bag, and I clapped my hands together before diving in.

"Perfect," I whispered, pulling the new-to-me record from the bag. The cover read "Paul Weller," and I jumped up and down excitedly, clutching it to my chest.

I shifted so Hades could see it over my shoulder, holding up the record. "It's Record Store Day. They did a limited pressing of this album, and I've had it on order for months. Helios grabbed it for me." I turned, disappointed, insecurity rearing its ugly head as Hades backed up an inch so I wouldn't be pinned between him and the counter. I liked him in my space.

Helios smiled. "I'm glad I could help, love. But I've gotta get out of here. We're moving on that safe house Hecate found." The last was directed at Hades but my ears perked up.

"What safe house?" Hades had told me nothing of any new developments, and Helios's brown eyes went wide as he scrambled to come up with something to tell me. I narrowed my eyes. Hades leveled a warning look at Helios.

"Did you find something?" I pressed, rounding on the God of the Dead. Helios's gaze darted between us in disbelief and mine matched his incredulity. Hades was *still* keeping shit from me, even though he'd *promised*.

"It wasn't anything concrete. I didn't want to tell you in case it doesn't pan out," Hades gritted out, looking pointedly at Helios who raised his hands defensively.

"What's in this safe house?" I demanded. Helios turned to leave but I held up a finger and the shadows swarmed the door, blocking his path. "No, 'Los. Stay a moment." I quipped sweetly, low and deadly as anger flushed through my veins. "*What's* in the fucking safe house, Hades?" His jaw ticked, but I stared him down. I wasn't going to ask again.

"Potentially the witch or warlock responsible for your imprisonment. We won't know for sure, but Hermes caught a few of the abominations that weren't destroyed during the exorcism process. They remembered parts of conversations, things of that nature. There is a *potential* safe house to explore. It's nothing concrete and so far, none of the other leads have panned out. I just didn't want to get your hopes up."

"Or yours," I whispered. He nodded, that small, self-deprecating smile quirked on his lips. I stepped back, shaking my head in frustration. I hated that I understood his logic, hated that I knew he was trying to save himself from having too much hope. Helios cleared his throat.

"There's something else," he said as he pushed his hands into his pockets. We waited, but the titan seemed to be working himself up to something uncomfortable. I'd never seen him look so . . . nervous.

"While I'm gone, I'm just . . . I need to know that Nick will be okay. They're attacking Otherworlders connected to Persephone all over the city and I can't do my job if I think he's in danger. Would you . . . Do you think he could stay here? Or at least I could give him the location in case he *needs* to come here?" He looked to Hades. Stunned, I stared up at him. He was a proud man, but asking for protection for Nick, seeing the fear on his face hammered home how dangerous this all really was.

What they were all sacrificing for me. *For us.*

"Of course," I said at the same time Hades responded with a resolute, "No."

Helios and I both turned to stare at him.

"Of course, he can," I restated, looking at Hades like he'd lost his mind. Helios shifted uncomfortably and I crossed my arms over my chest, bolstering myself.

"The more people who know the location of this place, the less safe it is," Hades murmured, apologetically. I reared back in disbelief. "Excuse the rudeness of my husband, Helios, he seems to have lost his fucking mind."

I rounded on him with narrowed eyes. "Nick is my *friend*. He was wounded *because* of *us*. Nick is Helios's partner, and he is welcome anywhere we are. We cannot treat him like an outsider, not when he means so much to Helios."

He worried his fingers through his hair in frustration before resting his hands on his hips with a groan. "*Fine*. Yeah. Give him the location. If something happens, he can come here. I'm sorry, brother. I'm just . . ." He trailed off.

Helios gave him a tight smile. "I do understand, Hades. I feel the same way and that's why I had to ask." He walked forward with that golden aura of his, arms outstretched to me, and when his arms banded around my waist crushing me to his chest, Hades huffed. It was cute, the possessiveness. Smirking, Helios placed a soft kiss on the top of my temple. The temperature dropped a few noticeable degrees, and we broke apart to see Hades sulking against the counter, shadows swimming moodily around him.

"Please be safe? I won't forgive you if something happens to you." I sniffed, and Helios promised with a smile. Hades walked him to the front door, heads bent together in discussion I couldn't hear. They clasped forearms, shared a long look, and then Helios was gone, off to immeasurable danger because of us. Because of me.

Hades turned, his back pressed to the door, eyes locked on me. The heaviness sat in the air around us, the weight of their sacrifice and friendship, the magnitude of their loyalty. Slowly, I gathered up the bags from the counter as Hades watched me, stalking me like a wild animal. Terrified to let me out of his sight for even a moment. Longing, that sweet ache that lived somewhere beneath my chest reached for him, and he sighed, this one full of possession and need. I could see the war waging behind his eyes, knew that there was something different about this mission they were going on.

"Can we pretend to be normal? Just for tonight? Just in case . . ." My voice broke as I looked away, unable to keep the intensity of his stare. Gracefully, Hades closed the distance between us, placing two long, slender fingers under my chin. He lifted my gaze back to his. I was asking for something *more*, and he knew it, more than just dinner, more hope. I was so damn tired of not giving in to what we needed, and I knew he was barely hanging on as well. But there was hope in Helios's eyes when he'd spoken of that mission, and I saw the way Hades clung to it even if he denied doing so.

"I don't know how to tell you no," he admitted on a sigh. "I guess I never really did."

Persephone

CHAPTER 37

I ran a bath in the massive tub recessed into the floor of his master bathroom. The water was hot, almost painful, but I settled into it, letting it calm my nerves. The tub reminded me of the bathhouses in ancient Greece, from the brief glimpses in my fractured memory, and for a moment I could pretend we were in the Underworld, together at last, with no pressure or psychopaths trying to kill me.

After a soak that left me feeling invigorated, I took my time drying and styling my hair with the pins Helios had brought. With little thought, my hands delved deftly through my locks, twisting and braiding intricate designs I had no memory of learning. It seemed that muscle memory wasn't as affected by chaos-induced amnesia as the rest of my brain, and for that, I was grateful. I slipped into the fuchsia fabric of the chiton with ease, feeling at home in my own body like never before.

The gown I wore had hung in my closet since I'd arrived here, yet every time I'd gone to wear it, something stopped me. It was as if the dress whispered to me to wait, to hold out for the perfect moment. I knew now that it was waiting on *this*, waiting on *him*.

The fabric crossed over my chest in a low swoop that banded around my torso, both fitted and comfortable. Two slits rode up each side of my thighs, exposing my long legs beneath them. This fabric felt old, almost magical. I had worn this in my old life, I could tell by the way my hands expertly folded the fabric in perfect knots around my body. Tonight, I wanted to remember the old ways. I studied myself in the mirror, at all the small parts of my body that held secrets of their own. How much had these arms held, these lips tasted? I twirled, savoring the way the fabric lifted around me. The shadows that followed me like puppies nipped at my legs in approval.

"Think he'll like it?" I asked, and I swore they purred in response. Hades was letting us have a rare opportunity tonight. He could say he didn't think this raid was going to be important or pan out, but I could tell he didn't believe that, not truly. The others didn't either or else Helios wouldn't have come to us about Nick, and we hadn't heard a peep from the rest in days.

They were gearing up for a showdown and this could very well mean the nightmare was going to be over, or that we were all going to die. Mostly me, probably. I'd be the one to not make it, and if these were going to be my last few nights on Earth, I intended to savor every moment. I stepped into the hallway and the music of my special edition vinyl wafted from the record player in the living room. As I came around the corner, my breath caught in my throat.

The lights were dim, the floor littered with black, tall pillar candles encased in glass. The soft glow lit the place up with ambient light, one that celebrated the shadows, reveled in the way they danced. The large stone table was set with elegance, rose gold place settings and crystal tumblers. How had he done all of this, with no notice, in an hour? My mind raced, but I quelled my curiosity. Hades was a god, and there seemed to be few limits on what he could do.

And a god he was.

Hades sat at one of the two seats opposite each other at the large table. Blue irises looked up at me through the candlelight, shadows dancing on those striking cheekbones, pupils dilated as his jaw slackened. I could see the heat in his eyes as he raked his gaze down my body. "You Do Something to Me" cooed from the record player, and he stood, slowly, devouring the distance between us. He wore black trousers that tapered at the ankles and a fitted black tunic that split open in a deep V, exposing the hard planes of his chest. His pale skin was decorated with elaborate lines of ink that peeked out from underneath the impossibly black fabric. A single chain swung low around his neck, and I saw two baubles hanging there. Recognition gnawed at my mind, but I could only focus on *him*.

His hand extended out to me as he approached, and I took it, savoring in the way his breath hitched at our touch. He pulled me closer to him, and we swayed, the music cocooning us in a soft lullaby. Hades entwined our fingers together, rested them between our chests as we moved, his other hand splayed wide across the curve of my hip, up and over the small of my back, so large against my body. He bent his cheek low to rest on the side of my temple, and I was engulfed by his aura, his presence, the rumble of approval that fell from his lips and caressed my cheek.

I had never seen him so open to me, so at ease.

The muscles of his pecs and abdomen were eye level with me as he held me close, and I snuck a peek at the ink hiding there. Not all of it was just ink, there was scarification, runes that looked fuzzy and unfamiliar at first, but they clarified the longer I stared. Those runes bound him to the Underworld. Offered power and protection. The raised skin looked beautiful against his pale flesh, and I longed to trace the raised edges with my fingers, my tongue, but I made myself be patient. Savor this. Savor him.

My eyes traveled down his chest, settled on perhaps the oldest ink on his body. The lines light, too pale even for his skin. I gasped, bringing my hand up to it. Hades shuddered under my touch, casting his eyes low to capture mine.

"What is this? I have one too." I traced my fingers over the lines with soft, reverent touches.

Hades let out a breath that ruffled my hair as he bent low to me again. His lips pressed against my temple as the hand on my back slid up to my shoulder, resting over the exposed, marred skin that matched his. "It's our Bondmark," he whispered in that sweet accent that sent bolts of pleasure down my spine. "It's like a wedding ring, only more."

The song petered out and Hades pulled back, tugging me to the table. I frowned, annoyed by the space between us, but he just laughed and pulled my chair free. I gathered the bottom of my dress and sat as gracefully as I could, allowing him to scoot me closer to the table. His fingers danced over the side of my cheek, pulling my hair over my shoulder, and I preened as his lips found that tender spot at the crook of my neck, at the ghost of the kiss he left against my skin. I watched, a little lust drunk, as he walked to grab the bottle sitting in a bucket on the other side of the long table.

Hades popped the cork and poured blood-red liquid that darkened the wineglass in front of me. I watched him with rapt attention as he filled his own cup before sitting and raising his glass in my honor.

"Tonight, there are no prophecies, no gods, no monsters. Tonight, I am just a man who made dinner for his stunning wife. Tonight, and every night, you are the loveliest bloom to grace the Underworld, my Queen." My cheeks flushed under his words, but I smiled and raised my glass to him before sipping the dark liquid. I could taste a sweetness that carried a dry backbite, a familiar flavor that danced over my tongue.

A small smile rested on Hades's lips while he watched me over the top of his glass as he drank. "Pomegranate wine," he said with such intensity I blushed. The table was set so beautifully, the slate trays between us overflowing with cheeses and meats and fruits. I took one of the grapes and plopped it into my mouth as he bit into a piece of the cured meat near him. The grape was delicious, but it tasted somehow sweeter than any I'd tasted before.

I made a small noise of pleasure, and Hades's gaze darkened over the rim of his glass. He set it down gently, then splayed his fingers on the table in front of him, as though he were controlling himself. The intensity unraveled me, pressure building low in my belly as I shifted slightly.

His eyes were sharp, tracking all of my movements. I felt pinned, exposed to him in a way that disarmed me. Hades looked me up and down, and I could feel his stare as it traveled hungrily over my arms, across my chest that was rising and falling dramatically, but I made no effort to hide from him. I wanted him to know what he did to me, how my body, my soul responded to him. *Shades*, they called it. The tension hot and impossibly thick in the air, the shadows circling low between the candlelight.

"So . . ." I swallowed thickly, before reaching for another drink from my glass. "What are the rules tonight?"

Hades stared at me, amused, before leaning in to rest his elbows on the table. "Rules?"

I nodded my head. "With you, there's always a bargain. I get this if I do that. Deals and bargains, isn't that what we do with Death?" I asked, this time taking a bite of a chocolate-covered strawberry, the taste so divine on my tongue that it sent a ripple of pleasure through me as I tried to catch the falling crumbles before they could rain havoc down my dress.

Hades's jaw tightened. "I am not Death, Little Flower, I merely *rule* the dead. To answer your question, the only rule tonight is that if you continue to make those noises, I'll be obligated to lay you across this table and devour that sweet cunt until every noise you make belongs to me."

My heart stopped beating in my chest, eyes wide. The second heartbeat pulsing in my core throbbed and I wanted him to touch me. *I needed it*. More than oxygen, more than life.

My eyes scanned across the table, landed on a broken-in-half pomegranate in the middle of the medley of fruits. I brought my eyes back to his and gasped; the blue rings were almost completely gone, replaced with black pupils that homed in on me as I slowly slid my hand across the table. My fingers closed around the broken fruit, so simple and unassuming in my palm. I brought the pomegranate to rest on my plate, dug my fingertips into the flesh of it, peeled back the thin, pale membrane to expose the blood-red seeds below.

Hades's fingers flexed.

I grabbed a handful of the small seeds and watched in wonder as red juice stained my fingertips, my fingernails. I looked him in the eyes as I brought my hand to my lips and took a bite of a large bundle stuck together. The seeds burst under the pressure of my mouth, soaking my tongue, dripped down the corners of my lips.

I was already so on edge from his stare and words—the fruit tasted so heavenly, I closed my eyes with the moan that built in my throat. It was only when I heard the scraping of a chair that I realized what I'd done. Hades threw his chair back with such force that it skidded across the wood as he rounded the table toward me. He was the God of the Dead, an unholy darkness, and I wanted nothing more than for him to drag me to the Hells. His eyes pierced through me, pinned me, slid over my skin like ice, slow and deliberate, igniting every place it lingered.

I stood to meet him, but before I could turn, he was ripping me from my seat fully, hand wrapped around my throat in a possessive grip. His lips met mine in a punishing kiss that curled my toes as my arousal dripped out of me, slid down my thighs.

Hades reached behind me and swiped the contents of my side of the table away with impatient urgency. Plates and glasses crashed to the floor, sending fruit flying across the table as he walked me back, invading my space with his fingers still deftly circling my throat.

Hades brought both of his arms down to rest under my ass and lifted, depositing me on the stone table, but it was his stare, his need, raw and reverent, that rattled me from the inside out. His fingers traced the lines of my face like he was memorizing it. He peppered open-mouthed kisses down my neck as he pushed between my legs, laying me flat on my back as he nestled between my thighs. His hands were hot, and cold, fire and balm, as they trailed over my skin, as his tongue made me wild. Skilled fingers grabbed the knots holding the top of my dress up around my neck and slipped them free with no effort, and I gasped as the fabric slid off my chest, spilling my breast to the open air between us. Hades stiffened, zeroing in on them hungrily.

The God of the Dead was urgent with his movements, gone was the cool control he normally exuded. His hands came up to massage the swells of my breasts as he nipped and sucked my heated flesh into his mouth. He moaned, scraping his teeth just slightly over the sensitive peaks, and I bucked as I cried out, hands fisted in his hair. His hard cock pressed against my core, hot and steel and overwhelming. *This* was what I had been waiting for. The last few weeks had felt like one long edging session, and finally, I was getting Hades unrestrained.

He pulled back, straightening to stand between my thighs, and I whimpered as the cool air pricked at my exposed torso. He ran his hands under my hips and pulled me flush against him, the thin fabric of our clothing all that separated his cock from me. One hand slipped between us to unbutton the top of his pants and the other he laid palm down against my stomach, teasing me. Hades looked down at my exposed body hungrily, stroking himself as he pushed back the loose fabric of my dress.

My hands came down to my hips, gathering the material up and holding it for him obediently. Cold air hit the inferno that burned between my thighs, and I hissed with pleasure when his fingers slipped between my lips, slid right down to my weeping core. Hades's palm brushed against my clit, and I cried out, arching forward.

"You are everything." He praised. I burned.

I was nothing before the feeling of his hands on my body. Cheeks flushed, panting, Hades ground his palm with swift strokes over my clit, slipping those long, thin fingers inside me. The stretch. *Fates*, the stretch of him. I shook.

"That's my good girl. You're so ready for me, such a sweet little cunt. You want me to fill you up, my Queen?" His voice was smooth, playful, like he was enjoying this, and I didn't care as long as I had him. I whined, reaching a hand up to pull him closer, needing his weight on top of me. Hades pulled his hands away and I whimpered again, but he settled himself right against me and I could feel the tip of his considerable cock as it laid across my lips, slicked in the arousal he inspired. One tilt of his hips had the fat head catching on my entrance, and I gasped, struggled at the intrusion, but Hades didn't push. No, no, he made me wait, rocking in shallow thrusts to tease me.

"I don't know if I can go slow," he admitted, worry clear in his tone.

My eyes found him, dazed and glassy, and I brought my fingers up to entwine with his, still coated with my arousal. "I don't want slow. I want *you*, all of you, right now."

With a smile, Hades leaned over me, blanketing every inch of my body with his comfort as he pushed inside. I cried out and then his mouth was on me, swallowing those cries, the pain just on this side of pleasure as he worked me wide open for him. I felt so full, so sated, blissed out beyond recognition with him pressing deeper, feeding me inch after inch until there was nowhere left to go. Nothing could have prepared me for the sensation of having him, for the warm, weightless feeling I'd have when his words fell against my cheek, landing over my brows, my lips. Whispers of perfection, of Fate and rapture and redemption.

Declarations of love.

A tear slipped down my cheek at the awe of it, and he kissed that too, catching the salt on his lips, feeding it to me from his mouth. His tongue plunged deep in tandem with his thrusts, and I opened to him, offering my body, my shade, anything he wanted if he just kept worshipping me.

His eyes stayed locked on mine, only glancing down briefly to watch himself slide in over and over, slow and fast, rough and gentle all at once. I melted around him, watched him shudder, the sensations ripping through us both. Hades pulled out to the tip before pushing in again, this time over the second and third ring. The tip of him hit something sacred and deep in my sensitive core as he rocked in the last ridge to the hilt, his base flush against my clit. The stretch was intense, nearly unbearable, but I would have died without him inside my body.

I never wanted it to end.

"Incredible. I love you, see, a perfect fit, Little Flower. You and me," he soothed as I lost use of my limbs, my hands useless as they clung to the nape of his neck. I cried out, sobbing, arching my head back to expose my neck as I screwed my eyes shut. Shadows danced around us, playful in their blessing as their king and queen once more were one.

Hades stilled, breathing incredibly hard. I looked up into those eyes, pupils wide with desire, and I nodded, urging him on. He took a measured pull, separating us slightly, and I trembled at the loss of him. The vein in the side of his neck pulsed as he gripped my breasts, guiding me back down onto him.

A perfect fit.

Soft and strong. Light and dark.

The sounds that escaped his lips as he split me in half were barbaric, and I craved them, wanting more. I squeezed him so tightly from the inside that with every snap of his hips the recoil sent me farther across the hard stone. A hand braced near my head, and I turned to press my lips against his wrist, to nip at his skin as his pace became more brutal, erratic even. My legs shook from the ecstasy building between us. Hades propped himself up, still driving his cock into me, to grab a handful of pomegranate seeds. He nipped at my bottom lip, trapping it between his teeth, dragging it open. *Open*, his silent command, and my lips parted obediently, tongue flat for him, offering.

He smirked, shoving the handful of seeds into my mouth along with his fingers, crushing them against my tongue. Juice spilled down my lips and chin as he gave me everything he had, running his tongue along the sides of my mouth, the hollow of my throat to lick me clean.

"My good girl, you're so close. I love the way you suck me so deep inside you. Do you want to come?" he asked, sweetly. I mewled beneath him, desperate, frantic. My entire body a livewire of raw need, but he held on, driving me into a table that felt more like an altar.

Memories ripped through my mind in a whirlwind, compounding the pleasure with infrequent stabs of pain as Hades moved. I was lost to him, lost to the ownership, the worship. Hades's cock pulsed deep, sending me over the edge as indulgent, decadent pleasure ripped through my trembling body, taking everything that made me whole with it as I came. I clamped my legs around him, milking his cock, my walls clenching and flexing to keep him right where he was. Hades stilled, a pained expression on his face as he bit his bottom lip on a groan until he broke skin.

He panted, muscles constricting as he rubbed lazy circles on my clit. "I wanna come on that pretty chest, can I do that, hmm?" I wanted to give him anything, everything to satisfy the need building within him, the powerful longing that accentuated each thrust. I nodded and he frowned, leaning down to kiss my lips fiercely. "I need you to tell me, Persephone. Beg me for it." His words were rough and hollow, strained, and I would have told him anything, given him everything.

I loved seeing him fighting for his life buried inside me. "I want you to come on my chest, Hades. *Please*. Let me wear you. Mark me." I brought my hands to the outside of my breasts and pushed them together for him before obediently opening my mouth and extending my tongue in a muscle memory that felt both foreign and familiar.

The body remembers.

Hades let out a strangled roar, faltering as he ripped his cock from my core, causing us both to cry out at the loss of connection. Before I could move, his body was on top of mine, straddling my torso as he stroked his throbbing cock between my breasts, far too graceful for a god of his stature.

"*Fuckkkkkkk*," he panted, pushing my slick across my chest. His hips jerked wildly as he gripped his shaft with strangling force, close enough that my breath washed over the sensitive head on each labored groan. Thick ropes of his cum spilled over my breastbone, slid down my sternum, pooled at the hollow of my throat. He shuddered as I lay still, savoring the heat as it licked across my skin, the attention as his eyes drank me in. I felt light, almost dizzy, as I rode out the high coursing through my system.

Hades sat back on his heels, balancing his weight on his knees so as to not crush me. His cock lay, still hard, between my breasts and he made no motion to move it when he bent low and kissed my lips, smoothing the sweat-plastered hair from my face. He ran a finger through his cum around my throat and smiled. "I once gave you a very different type of pearl necklace. You look so lovely with either," he praised, and I melted, preening.

I brought my finger to my neck, swirling in his seed, intending to bring it to my lips, but Hades grabbed my wrist and pulled it back. He shook his head, reaching for my discarded cloth napkin, stealing my prize. I frowned as he gently cleaned my hands and torso before placing a reverent kiss on my temple.

I was boneless as he stood and lifted me, cradling my body to his chest as he walked us to the bedroom and into the en suite bathroom. The candles blew out with a single breath as we left the dining room, all pretense of dinner forgotten. The bathroom glowed with a subtle light, a touch of shadows swirling around us, turning on the taps to fill the giant pool with water.

Our clothes dropped, discarded and forgotten, onto the tile floor as he settled us down in the hot, soothing water that awaited in the recessed tub. I settled against Hades's chest, lulled by the warmth of him, and the steady beat of his heart.

His fingers traced over my skin, soothing and gentle as he held me to him. We lay together silently as Hades washed me, running his hands over my sore flesh and kneading out knotted, tight muscles. He massaged my scalp and took care to inspect every inch of me for any bruising or damage.

Time ceased to exist in the space we occupied here, and I found myself tracing the raised lines of his runes, committing every one to my inconsistent memory.

When he stood to carry us out, his naked form illuminated by the ambient moonlight through his skylight, I was struck again by his deadly beauty. A need so profound it shook me from my haze gripped me, and I moved forward, reaching for his cock. I wanted to taste him, to bring him all the pleasure he'd shown me, but he had other ideas.

Hades sat and gently pulled me against him, twisting me around so my back was to his chest as he lined up our bodies and slowly pushed inside me. It was intimate and intense just like we had been earlier, but he was softer now, hyperaware of how sore I was. I felt him everywhere, not just inside me, but in the fractured, distressed parts of myself, in every breath that filled my lungs. He knew me with such surety, every movement he made a memory of what I liked, of what he *knew* I craved. I ached with jealousy. I wanted to know his body the way he knew mine.

He coaxed two more orgasms from me, his lips pressed into the side of my neck while the water splashed lightly around us. When it was his turn to come, he gently slid out of me and came against my back. I drifted in and out as he cleaned us up and tucked me into bed as the exhaustion overwhelmed my body. His strong arms pulled me into his chest, cradling me against him, and I drifted off into a post-sex dreamless sleep as the God of the Underworld stroked my hair.

Helios

CHAPTER 38

I could hear him in the foyer, the jingle of his keys, the soft footsteps as he made his way down the hall toward me. I took a long drink of my sweet tea and sat the cup down in the sink as he came around the corner.

"Hey, Daddy," he purred, wrapping his arms around my waist, his cheek resting on my shoulder blade. I smiled as he hummed against me, content and comforted just being in my space. Not for the first time since this all had begun, I felt an odd sort of trepidation roiling through me as every molecule in my body raged against the very idea of leaving Nick alone.

Unprotected.

But this was important. Hecate was sure, and I had assurances from Hades that should shit go sideways, he would be looked after, and I trusted Hades to keep his word. He owed me that much. I spun, gathering Nick close to my body, inhaling that sweet scent from his shampoo as I pressed a kiss to his forehead, my palms stroking down the lean planes of his back, his shoulders.

"Hey baby boy. How was your day?" I asked, voice low as he smiled up at me with closed eyes, a dreamy expression overtaking his face. I dipped my head to drop a kiss on his nose, and rocked us together, swaying in the golden hues of the dying sun.

"It was fine. I wasn't expecting you to be home first," he mused, and the primal beast that lived inside my chest wherever Nick was concerned beamed with pride that he felt comfortable here, that he'd fallen so easily into accepting what we were to one another.

"Mmm-hmm," I breathed, because on the back of that pride was a nervous drip of anxiety, the one that had repeated this conversation over and over again on the walk home from Hades and Persephone's penthouse. Nick's body slowed our sway, his brown eyes fluttering open to look at me. I watched as a tightness overtook his brows, worry lines creased around his lips, muscles stiffened under my touch.

"Helios? What is it, what's wrong?"

I swallowed. Rolled the words around in my mouth, desperate to fulfill the oath to my friends, dreading being too far away from him.

"I have to go away . . ." I began, my thumb stroked over his spine, caressing, reinforcing with each touch how much I wished I didn't have to. He pulled back, and I cursed the distance between us.

"For how long?" he whispered.

"Few days. Maybe more. Listen, I don't want to go, but I have to, Hades—" I pleaded, ready to launch into some sort of practiced spiel, but his hand came up to silence me, like he did anytime I even tried to mention the two of them, but there was a pinch to his eyebrows, a wince of pain that had me crowding him back into my arms, but he wasn't having it.

"Baby boy, what's going on?" I asked, but Nick only shook his head, using his hands to brace against my chest and stop me from dragging him closer. The distance between us ached, and I couldn't take it. "I don't want to go, especially after what happened at Electric Delphi, but this is it. Just a little longer and this will be over, we've—"

"Helios, stop." he moaned, flinching back from my arms, hands cradling his temples. Concern overtook my need to explain what was happening, because these headaches had become more and more frequent the last few weeks, leaving him borderline debilitated.

"We need to get Hygieia to take a look at you," I insisted, not for the first time, but like he always did, he shook his head, blond locks swaying over his forehead as he pressed his palms against his eyes.

"I'll be fine. I j-just haven't eaten," he stammered. I frowned, crossing my arms.

"Why won't you let me care for you?" I asked on a low, desperate breath. His trembling hands lowered slowly as he took me in, a look of devastation on his face.

"It's not about that. I just . . . I need some time to figure things out. Maybe the next few days will be good. We can get some space and—" he gestured around the room with a pained expression, his voice hollow and bereft but I could only see red. It clouded my vision, tainted the taste of the air with his rejection.

"Are you telling me you don't want to be with me?" I nearly choked, the words acrid as they fell from my lips. His brown irises widened in a panic as he looked up at me, mouth opening and closing around words he just wouldn't fucking say. I stumbled away from him as my knees gave out, and I fell into the dining room chair just past the bar. The sting of him, the distance between us when he was so close my arms could reach out and touch him was too much. There was an ache behind my ribs, dull, resounding.

I hung my head between my knees, as my shocked lungs got the wind knocked out of them. He rushed forward, squatting between my legs, lithe fingers splayed over the tops of my thighs as he gazed up at me.

"Helios. I am *never* saying that. I love you. I've fallen *in* love with you, and nothing changes that," he grabbed at the bottom of his ribs, mirroring the same spot I could feel throbbing behind my own bones, and shook his head. "But I also have some things from my old life to work out, you told me you understood. You promised." His bottom lip quivered, and the sound of relief that cracked through my chest at his words shook me to my core. I blew out a hot breath as my chest rose and fell rapidly.

"While I'm away, you need to know where to go if things go bad. You, no listen!" I insisted, when his lips parted to protest, "I need you to hear this. I can't do what needs to be done without you being taken care of, and if I'm worried about you it may get all of us killed. Please," I begged as he scooted back, just a hair. "Hades has a safehouse, and I asked him today if you could be let in on it, in case of an emergency. He and Persephone both agreed, so if you hear anything, you need to go there, okay? It's—"

"No, no!" he shouted, *shouted* at me, standing in a flash worthy of Hermes. He paced, tugging at the loose strands of hair on the base of his neck. "I told you that I don't want to know anything about them. The more people that know about them, the less safe it is, and I won't be the reason they get hurt. That Persephone gets hurt. I can't, you can't tell me. I don't want to know." he seethed, eyes pleading with me, but I couldn't understand.

"It's honorable that you want to protect them, but they've given permission, they know you're my Bondmate, Nick." I stood too, running a hand through my hair exasperatedly. "I don't want to fight with you, or make you uncomfortable, but you took a knife for them. Helping them. It was you who got that necklace off her. They trust you, baby boy, you've earned it. I trust you." I grabbed him around the shoulder, tugging him gently against me, dropping my forehead against his.

"I trust you," I repeated.

Then waited.

I hated how much he took onto himself, hated that his proximity to me and this whole mess had put him in the crossfire, but

I couldn't give him up. Selfish, whatever the cosmos would call it, I don't care.

"Fine, but—" He sighed, eyes falling shut as I kissed his lips gently, "I don't want to know now. Write it down. Fold it up and seal it so if I need to use it, I can. But that way they know I haven't betrayed them. That I'd never betray them . . ." He trailed off, and I realized he was shaking in my arms. I picked him up, and he let me carry him to bed, undress him, and tuck him in tight. I laid with him in quiet contemplation, until my phone rang and we both knew it was time for me to go.

Nick rolled onto his side, facing away from the door as I packed up a few provisions. I crawled, as gently as I was able, across the bed and kissed him on the cheek, nuzzling my nose against the crook of his neck, breathing him in.

"I love you. Come home safe," he whispered as I promised I would.

I closed the door as we both pretended the air didn't taste like tears.

In the kitchen, I pulled a piece of notepaper to me and scribbled down the address before rummaging around in the junk drawer to grab an envelope to stuff it inside. Once sealed, I sat it on the table where he could find it and turned off the light.

Persephone

CHAPTER 39

The next few days passed in a blissful haze of mind-blowing sex, incredible food, and the unwavering image of Hades's face twisted in pleasure as he came. We had christened every inch of the penthouse, some places more than once. He was insatiable and I loved every second of it, loved the smell and taste of his body, the possessive reverence in his eyes. The only point of contention between us was his militant diligence to make sure his cum never made it anywhere inside me, an effort he explained, to keep me safe. It was a hard take that I couldn't truly understand, especially when in the throes of passion all he talked about was filling me up.

We were on borrowed time, but I couldn't let myself think about what would happen when the sands ran out of the hourglass. Reports were coming in from the mission daily and I knew they, too, really had hope that we could walk away from this together. The last intelligence Hades had received just had one word scribbled on a fire message: *tonight*.

I leaned over the board game we were playing, pulling the hem of his oversized T-shirt up as I reached for him. There were much better uses for his hands than rolling dice and a hunger in my body that only he could sate. I kissed Hades hard as he pulled me roughly across the board, sending paper money flying around us, but before he could pin me down, I lunged away from him, tearing off to the library. He was behind me in seconds, crowding my space as he pushed me onto the beautiful settee we normally read in together. His front pressed against my back, and I moaned as he captured my lips in a kiss.

I was hot and needy, and I wanted him inside me. I bent low, arching my back to him as he unbuttoned his jeans. He had taken to wearing minimal clothing since we kept tearing our clothes away in sex-fueled fury.

The tattoos that circled his chest and shoulder were magnificent. The tendrils of hair I'd seen inked under his shirt went with the image of me he had tattooed there. My eyes open and bright, with flowers in my hair, and an intricate pearl necklace—very different from the one I'd worn the other night—rested on my collarbone. I laid flat against the armrest of the settee, exposing my ass to him. He growled as I ran my hands over the side of my cheeks and gently spread them apart, teasing him with the one place he'd yet to go.

Hades stiffened behind me, and I shivered at the drop in temperature. His hand slipped around my neck as he cradled my face and brought my eyes up to look at him. "Are you sure?" he asked breathlessly, and I nodded. I wanted him to own me in every way, needed him branded on every inch of my body as I commanded his attention from all positions. A brilliant smile lit up his face as he let me go, kissed my temple and stood up. I turned, confused.

"Stay," he commanded, and heat flooded through me at the word. Something about the way he handled me with his soft tone made me burn for him. I turned back to the armrest and laid my head down obediently, clinging to the electricity thrumming through my body in anticipation of what was to come.

Hades returned with a small bottle of clear liquid in his hand, a small black object that looked like a ring, and a foil packet. It took me a moment to recognize the packet as a condom. I frowned and arched up to look at him; he had never used one of those with me. Maybe it was for the potential mess. It wasn't as though I'd exactly planned this, and I'd remembered a few things from observing mortals in ancient Greece: this *could* get messy.

He pushed up behind me again, running his hand over my spine, pressing me back down onto the armrest. "We need a word you feel comfortable with, Little Flower. If the pleasure gets to be too much, too intense, or too painful, I need you to be able to tell me to stop." His hands continued to roam over my back and my cunt ached in anticipation as wetness slicked down my thighs.

I nodded, spreading wider for him. "Pomegranate," I breathed, and he chuckled, ripping the foil packet open with his teeth and sliding the condom down his length. I watched him over my shoulder as he rolled it on, pinching the tip. It sucked to the four ridges of his cock and my mouth started salivating, desperate for him. I needed Hades inside me—like a compulsion, like my very own religion.

"Good girl, now bend for me a little more. I'm gonna open you up a little. Think you can handle that?" he asked, and I nodded, trying to relax.

Cool liquid splashed down the seam of my ass and his warm fingers slid through it, circling my hole, which pulsed on its own in anticipation. Hades dipped the tip of his finger in that tight ring and my hips bucked at the intrusion, but there was a familiarity to it, a thrill of electricity that shot through my nerves.

"We've done this before?" I asked, breathless. Hades groaned, nodding his head.

"Many times. Your mind has forgotten, but your body remembers, doesn't it, sweet girl?" he asked, adding more lube, then another finger. I moaned his name, pushing back on him, nodding through labored breaths.

Another hand wrapped around me over my hip, as something foreign settled over my clit. I looked down to see the pads of two of his fingers locked together, pressing a vibrating toy between my lips. The sensation was unlike anything I'd ever experienced before and I bolted forward, hands clawing at the upholstery. The concentration of the toy over my clit exclusively was almost too much and I cried out, shaking and running from the bliss shooting up my spine.

Hades kept his finger moving slowly inside me, and as I ran from the vibrations, I pushed farther into him until he was knuckle deep and I was a mess. He worked the toy over me more and more, still plunging his fingers—now two instead of one—as he scissored between my cheeks, stretching me, prepping me, praising me. The slight burn gave way to another sensation, this one a foreign fullness that had my toes curling.

"More," I begged.

Hades crowded over my back, kissing along my spine, tracing his tongue over my Bondmark. "Tell me how it feels." His words calm, almost curious as he pressed against me from the inside.

I whimpered. "It feels like I'm full, too full." I panted, rocking back into him.

He tucked his tongue behind his teeth and let out a tsk. "Should we stop, Little Flower? If it's too much for you to take, we can stop right now, just say the word." His fingers stilled. I cried out in frustration.

"No, please, more!" I whined, out of my mind. The vibrations on my clit amped up with the push of a button. I slammed back into him, his fingers as deep as my body could take him. "I want it. I want it, let me, *please*." My words were garbled gibberish on broken sobs, but he understood. Hades pressed the swollen tip of his cock inside my stretched hole, and I hissed at the intrusion, at the depravity of it. He added more lube and pressed deeper, stretching me, teasing me, mixing praise with strokes over my clit.

I wanted to be so fucking good for him. My legs faltered, knees buckling. I pressed an open-mouthed moan into the cushions as I trembled for him, his words almost my undoing as he worked.

"Baby, *oh Hells*, Persephone, this is too tight. So fucking tight. Is this all mine? Can I fill you up anytime I want? I can make it feel so good, baby, so good. *Shh, shh,* that's a good fucking girl, your body loves this doesn't it?"

Every word was the truth. He knew just how to spin me up, how to work me to the edge and draw me back, teasing my release until I was nothing and everything in his arms.

"I missed this so much," he murmured into my hair, resting his forehead against my spine as he drove into me. "I missed coming inside you. I wish I didn't have to use this fucking condom, I want to feel your flesh against mine, want to fill you up until I'm leaking out of you, but next time, baby." His voice was tight as he bottomed out.

"Take. Off. Take it off," I stammered as he worked my clit. I was so close to my orgasm that any moment I'd be writhing underneath him. I gasped, fire licking over my skin.

Hades pressed kisses to my shoulder and over my claiming mark, making us both groan. "Can't, Little Flower. It's not safe for you to have it inside you. You could get hurt." His thrusts became more erratic, both of us trembling as I crashed headfirst into a wave of pleasure, dragging him with me. Hades jerked once, twice, three times deep within me before he stilled, filling the condom to the brink.

My body quaked with release, electric and too sensitive as he ran his hands and lips over my skin. He pulled out of me slowly, and reluctantly, I relaxed to let him go. Each of his rings dragged against my walls in a final wave, as I tried to not suck him in deeper.

The condom peeled off with a wet smack, and Hades pulled my back against his chest before lying us on our sides on the settee.

He grabbed something from overhead to wipe off his cock before running it back through my lips, lifting my cheeks as he sought entrance. I shook with the pressure and cried out when he was fully seated inside me, his hands pulling my hips back into him. Hades rolled his hips lazily, sweetly, rocking into me with languid strokes. I called to the shadows, willed them to bind us together. I felt them as they slithered around and between us, crisscrossing over my sensitive flesh and his torso.

Hades wrapped his arm over my shoulder and across my chest so I could rest my chin on him while he fucked into me. The aftershocks of my previous orgasm still reverberated through my bones, and my eyes rolled back in pleasure.

So lost was Hades in the building ecstasy that he didn't seem to notice the way the shadows lassoed around him, binding us together. He pressed kisses to my cheek as he praised me, talking me through the orgasm that ripped through me too soon. I spasmed around him and he bucked as I clamped down on his cock, stealing his pleasure with mine. He wanted to be inside me, to fill me fully and by Fates I wanted that too. I needed to feel him, a primal urge to bear him anything, and everything tore through all my reasonings. I could give him what he denied himself, for my safety.

Hades pushed on my lower back to ease out of me, but I grabbed hold of the shadows and gripped him tight. "This is what you want," I panted, twisting to face him. He shook his head no, and I relented the shadows, freeing us but he made no move to back away. I smirked. "That's what I thought." I clamped down around his shaft. Hard.

"*Fuck, fuck, fuck*," he groaned, too slow to withdraw. He came explosively, still locked deep inside, and I grinned as warmth flooded me, fulfilling a divine impulse between us. Hades roared with fear and satisfaction as he filled me up, cock pulsing as the warmth kept washing through my body.

He shook out his head, pulling out of my body. Hades jumped over the settee to look over my face, panicked. “Persephone, baby, look at me. Are you okay?” His face was anguished, so worried. He looked *mortified*.

I frowned at him, swatting his hand away in the dewy afterglow of my orgasms. I felt fine, better than euphoric. A slow heat burned inside me, licking up my flesh from my core to my stomach and then higher to my torso. I felt so heavy, my arms and eyelids suddenly required Herculean strength to lift.

My body went slack in Hades’s arms as he frantically tried to get me to look at him. “Baby, please. Seph, please don’t do this, don’t leave me. Fuck, what have I done?” His words were a broken cry, and I reached for his face to wipe away the tears that fell, but my arm wouldn’t move.

More fire licked up my spine, shooting straight to my brain, scorching the walls of the scar tissue I’d worked so hard to befriend. My spine arched and someone was screaming, writhing, crying in agony. The pain had me bowed and bent like I was underwater, my lungs compressed and flayed alive, and those were my screams. *Oh*.

Hades curled me into his chest, cold tears splashing over my face, and then everything went black.

Hades

CHAPTER 40

Persephone was out for an hour before Hygieia made it to the penthouse, and I was completely out of my mind. I'd managed to get a shirt on her and get her into bed, but she was burning up and kept thrashing. A thin sheen of sweat blanketed her skin, and I hung my head in my hands as Hygieia worked. She'd kicked me out of the room not long after she'd arrived, and if I wasn't so worried she wouldn't treat her if I didn't listen, I'd have refused to leave Persephone's side.

I paced. Back and forth. Back and forth.

I racked my brain. *What the fuck had I done?*

More pacing. More prayers to the Fates. More silence broken by Persephone's screams.

It was like we'd been locked in a spell, dazed and drunk off one another. I hadn't been able to pull out of her fast enough and she'd wanted me, wanted my cum. How could I have been so fucking reckless?

More screams. They dug under my skin like grit in a wound, each one more persistent, and increasingly harder to bear.

I'd broken her.

Hygieia emerged hours later, dark circles tattooed under her eyes. I stopped pacing and rushed over, my body rife with fear and panic.

"She's stable."

The dam in my chest broke and I hit my knees with relief, head in my hands. Hygieia placed an awkward pat on my shaking shoulders and squeezed, but I was little more than a puddle on the floor.

"Is she going to wake up?" I asked through cracked sobs.

Hygieia studied me, before glancing over her shoulder at the now-closed door. "I honestly don't know. Right now, your power is rocking through her. If she survives this, she may have memories. Or she could be a basket case or catatonic. Hades, what were you *thinking*? *I warned you*." Her words were harsh but true. She *had* warned me.

"I was careful, I swear." I shook my head, frustrated. "But the last time, she just . . . We just . . . And I didn't realize I was so close." My words stuck in my throat. Hygieia's gaze softened. I should have known better. I should have been more observant.

She looked at me, pity etched on her face. "All we can do now is wait. Either she's going to come out of this, or she won't." Hygieia sat on the couch opposite me, brushing back the stray hairs that had escaped her bun. "Have you heard any word from Hermes and the others?"

I shook my head and checked my watch. "It's too soon. They are supposed to go in at midnight. We may not hear anything for a few hours. Let's hope it's good news because I have to tell ya, Doc, I don't know how much more bad I can stand to hear." I buried my head in my hands and waited. The minutes ticked by in torturous heaves, sand dropping in space. The knot in my chest never once relented.

After long hours in the silence, without warning, a hot branding pain shot through my chest as though I were being flayed alive. I was thrown on the ground, writhing and clawing at my shirt to see what had burrowed there, shredding the very flesh of my chest. Hygieia knelt over me to try and help, panic clear in her eyes. My fingernails dug into the fabric of my shirt, and with a tug it was gone, ripped to shreds beneath my nails. Hygieia's eyes went wide, as she scuttled back several paces. I looked down at my chest, horrified, to see my Bondmark pulsing red and angry like a fresh branding.

It had been a faded-out stamp against my skin for about fifteen hundred years. I'd watched it go in agonizing slowness, along with my hope that she'd ever return. Tears stained my eyes at the intense pressure, at the world-bending pull I had to go to her. It was as though the tether between us were suddenly revived and it demanded my skin be on hers, that we occupy the same air, the very same moment in space and time.

With a grunt, I flipped onto all fours and launched myself upward, bracing against the doorframe. I could hear her, crying out for me in the same way I needed her. The Bond was hungry, angry, and *needy*. It demanded payment for its years of neglect and had come to collect on the debt it was owed. I pushed forward again—this time almost taking the door off its hinges to get to her.

Persephone writhed on the bed, hands fisted in the sheets as she tried to clutch her shoulder. I looked at Hygieia, whose face showed pure terror, for guidance, but was met with nothing but her own confusion. She had no idea what was happening either, and I was moments away from being too far gone to be any help myself.

Persephone

CHAPTER 41

Every fucking nerve in my body blazed with a fire that burned from the Hells, and I couldn't move a muscle to stop it. It was like being paralyzed from my head to my toes, and my heart started to race with panic. Even in the coffin, my hands had been free, and I could scratch at the inside lid, an unpleasant detail I'd remembered of my previous life.

My head felt like it might split in two, but the worst was when the pain began in my back. My shoulder blade felt like someone was taking a white-hot branding knife to it, digging in my flesh, burrowing under my skin. I cried and silent tears streamed down my cheeks as my body lay perfectly still, unyielding to my waking mind. I needed Hades—needed him to make this go away. My mind burned and burned as rage tore down the fortress inside it, torching all of the work I'd spent so much time cultivating. It was all gone—all just embers.

Something snapped and my chest jerked, arching against the mattress. I cried out for him as anger and need and want tore through me like a backdraft. The door flew open, and he stood, ragged and clutching the frame for support. I sobbed as a fresh wave of pain seared through me.

Somewhere in the distance, I could hear Hygieia. "What's happening to you both? Is it the Bond? Is it broken?" Gone was the cool and calm tone of the Goddess of Healing. I could only hear panic.

I balked, crying out again. Hades was too far away, too much air separated us. Inside, the fire raged louder, more destructive. In no time it would be all-consuming and there would be nothing left of me. I had gotten too close to having it all; even though the memories were selective and fractured, I'd worked to build something of my life again and now it was all being razed to the ground and I was powerless to stop it.

Hades stumbled over to me and sat on the bed before pulling me up into his arms and kissing my sweat-dampened forehead. The moment our skin touched, the fire lessened, and I clawed at him, urging him to touch me more. His skin on mine acted as a balm, and I was desperate for it, willing to do anything and strike any bargain for the relief it promised. I grabbed his neck, winding my body against the cool planes of his shirtless torso while he ran his hands under his shirt and over my spine. I cried out in relief and a very different kind of heat flooded through me. I reached down between us, frantically trying to undo his pants. Hades stilled, grabbing my wrists and pulling back.

"Please," I begged, eyes wild, tears rolling down my cheeks. "I need this, it hurts. Make it stop, *please*. It *hurts*, Hades." My words breathless sobs. Another wave of pain rocked through my skull. I wouldn't survive this. I needed him to touch me.

"Do it," Hygieia said, still far away. "Perhaps the Bond is reforging. Give her what she needs and let's hope your essence can overwhelm the chaos."

Hades looked torn, wrenching his eyes from my shaking body to Hygieia. He nodded slightly and released his grip on my wrists.

I pressed into him, relief instantly flooding through both of us. It was burning him too.

We would burn together.

"Stay close," he croaked, and Hygieia nodded, slipping out the door with a click. Hades turned his gaze back to mine.

"Please," I cried out as my eyes rolled back from another lash of pain, this time at the base of my skull. Hades bent his head to mine, pressing our foreheads together as he brushed a sweaty curl back from my face. "I'll make it better, Little Flower. I'm so fucking sorry." I clawed at the fabric covering me, desperate for more of his skin on mine. "Shh, it's okay, I've got you, baby. I've got you. I love you."

Hades shifted on top of me, his pants slid down past his hips. I cried out in relief as he sank into me—raw and bare and obscenely full of pleasure. The tattoo on his chest glowed and pulsed in time with his thrusts and I felt the same rhythm settle in my back over my mark.

He held me close as he moved, slow and easy but enough to temper the flames inside us. I cried for him, whispered his name as he held me like the most precious thing to ever exist in the cosmos, speaking promises against my flesh.

"I love you, come back to me. Come back to me, my Persephone."

I lost count of how many times he brought me to climax or how many times he spilled inside me. Each time, I felt the fire falter, and each time, something blossomed within, an electric power that buzzed over my entire body. Sometime in the night, as he made love to me, Hades realized my Bondmark was tender, flayed too raw. He flipped me over to drive into me from below.

The sun rose as I rode him, slicked in sweat, pressed close. Hades's hands wrapped around my torso, foreheads pressed together as I wound my hips, riding his cock. Pleasure shot up my spine and the vein in Hades's neck flexed. I pressed a kiss to his lips as we both shuddered, losing ourselves in one another. Hades groaned, and the muscles of his stomach spasmed as he painted me from the inside. My own orgasm rolled through like an old friend, electric and beautiful and satiating the pain in my head. I snapped my head back as it snuffed the burning flames out with a final shove.

Weary and utterly spent, I passed out, exhausted, onto Hades's chest, wrapped in his arms, a sticky mess owned completely by him.

I awoke in the smoldering ashes of what was left of my mind. As I delved through the mind palace, the chaos burnt to char, I did all I could to assess the damage within. My mind was raw, flayed but intact. The wall of scar tissue surrounding the core of my memories was reduced to nothing—merely a dark stain burnt to cinders. I set to work, running my hands over the ruined tomes. I wondered if I would ever know what memories were lost.

I picked up the book labeled Artemis and brushed the thick char from its spine. The ash came off in my hand with ease and I cracked the pages open, steadying myself for heartbreak. Instead, where once I had a few chapters of memories filled, each page spilled with memory after memory, stretching back to the dawn of our existence. I grabbed another, Hephaestus this time. Again, pages and pages. Tears streaked down my cheeks as I realized that the ash and burn hadn't torn away my memories, it had implanted them back where I needed them to be. Whatever chaos that lived inside me was no more, burned away by the intensity of Hades's power—his love.

The power of us together.

The tome laid open on the pedestal to my right. I rushed to it, desperate to check the pages. I ran my hand across the exposed paper, brushing away the remaining ash and soot. I cried out as the sweetest relief rushed through me. The page open to a memory of Hades and me lying together in a grassy meadow. My body sprawled across his chest with my hand entwined with his as he stroked lazy patterns on my shoulder with those beautiful pianist's hands.

My knees gave out as tears of joy crashed over me, because I didn't need to touch the page to know that he was moments away from pressing a kiss to my temple and threatening to murder a bug for landing on me.

I remembered. *I remembered.*

Hades
CHAPTER 42

Persephone slept for a long while curled up on my chest. The Bondmark glowed happily and content on both of our skins, and I breathed deep as I buried my face in her hair. I didn't know if she was okay, but she wasn't writhing in pain anymore and that was at least something hopeful to hold on to.

Hygieia poked her head in while I was lost in thought, startling our peaceful stillness. She cleared her throat softly and I lifted my eyes to hers, still stroking Seph's back as she slept. "There's been news. You should come," she whispered, beckoning me out.

I reluctantly repositioned Persephone to lie on the bed without me, hating every inch of air that separated our skin. She curled into the pillow and whimpered softly as I placed a kiss on her forehead before forcing myself to follow Gia into the living room.

"I'll be right back," I promised, still unsure if she could even hear me. I stepped silently through the room, crossing the threshold with a last look back at Persephone's sleeping form. I found the Goddess of Mental Health looking far worse for wear as she paced, a charred piece of paper clutched in her hand, and the worry flowing from her set my teeth on edge. Fire messages were a mark of Hecate; flames were doorways and as the goddess of them, she could use fire to send warnings.

"What does it say?" I asked, unable to bring myself to look, but Hygieia couldn't look at me either. Her fingers trembled as she held out the paper and I reluctantly took it. My eyes scanned across the hasty scrawl. Dread clawed through me.

A trap. Betrayed. Don't come. The words were burned at the edge. Blood flecked the parchment. My world spun.

"When did this come in?" I asked, frantically.

"About ten minutes ago. They were supposed to go at midnight, I don't understand," she whispered, hand over her mouth.

Strategy poured through my mind, assessing the intel, and I did my best to think like Hermes. Persephone and I had been lost in the haze of feeding our Bond, and I hadn't even been able to think about what danger our friends were walking into. Guilt bloomed like poison in my chest.

Don't come.

But I had to. I couldn't leave them to whatever fate this was.

I turned on Hygieia. "Stay with Persephone," I commanded, calling my shadows to me. Power pulsed through my bones, a thrill I hadn't felt in a very, very long time.

Though the Gods of the Underworld and Death still retained more of our power than the others, we were still very diminished in what we could wield, compared to our former glory. Reforming my Bond with Persephone seemed to have strengthened me, and I flexed with the darkness that swirled around us, pulsing and pulling. With a wave, they dispersed, and I stood fully clad in the Armor of Hells. I flung my arm wide and my bident came sailing to me, crashing into my hand with enough force to send out a shock wave.

Hygieia stumbled back from the force, eyes wide.

"Hades."

I turned toward the bedroom to see Persephone leaning against the frame, staring at me in awe. I crossed the floor to her hastily, taking her into my arms, looking her over. She smiled softly as I turned her face back and forth with gentle fingers until I was satisfied she was unharmed. She pressed up on her tiptoes, her head tilted back as she waited for me to close the distance. I obliged, feeling her soft lips meld with mine. Fire shot up my spine again as I pulled her to me tightly, too tightly, as I devoured her mouth and fisted her curls in my hand. The Bond thrummed contentedly between us, and I feasted on the connection I'd missed so desperately. I had lived lifetimes touch-starved, and she was my life's blood.

She pulled back, those green eyes staring into mine with wonder. Her small hand cupped my cheek gently. "Am I yours?" she whispered softly. "And are you mine?"

Shock spasmed across my face and I clutched her, disbelieving. Our wedding vows. Those were the words she'd spoken when she'd asked me to bind myself to her forever. Tears pricked at her eyes, and I knew without her saying it that she was here.

She was mine.

She *remembered.*

"How?" I asked, pulling her into me. My chest ached with relief.

She shook her head. "I don't know, I just do. Everything was burned up in my mind palace, the chaos wall too. I'm back. I remember." Her words were precious, so precious to me. I kissed her again. "Why are you in battle armor?" she asked as she stroked over my shoulder pauldron.

"Something went wrong with the others. I need to go to them," I said, already knowing what was coming.

Persephone straightened, matter-of-factly. "Okay, I'm coming with you. Is my armor here?" she asked, looking around.

I grabbed her hands in mine and brought them to my lips. “No.”

She grimaced.

I let out a frustrated breath. “I cannot be effective if I know you aren’t safe. I promise to return to you. Please, do your part to keep me safe by keeping me sane,” I pleaded.

Anger rocked through her, but I knew she would do this for me. She hadn’t fought in two thousand years, and we weren’t even sure who it was I’d find when I got there. She nodded once, curtly. I kissed her lips again and stepped back, aching at the space between us. “I love you,” I whispered, and Hygieia moved to comfort her. The last thing I saw before the shadows enveloped me was the angry determination in those deep green eyes.

My shadows brought me to the beacon I focused on—the power signature I could wrap around and cling to—*Hermes*. My boots crunched hard on the dirt beneath them, snapping twigs as the beacon echoed through the early morning darkness. An unnatural power seeped over this land, but I knew without a doubt where I was—Greece. The land called to me, bolstered my divinity with the blood-soaked soil of our ancestry. My essence was tied to this piece of earth.

I raised my bident as I surveyed the damage around me. The plains were on fire, low burning embers glowing like dying stars in a sea of ruin. Ash drifted from the sky like snow, soft and gray, clinging to my armor, to scorched earth, to what was left. Blood was thick in the air. The stench was thicker. Burnt wood, singed flesh, blood gone copper cold. I saw the bodies of mangled mortals, eyes blackened from possession, hollow and destroyed as I made my way through the ravages of battle. A house stood in chunks of smoldering rubble, choking the air with smoke and decay.

Hermes.

The God of Thieves was impaled on a tree, weakly thrashing and grunting as he tried to rip himself free to get to Hecate.

She was lying at an impossible angle on the ground, blood pooling down the corners of her mouth. I rushed to grab Hermes as he slashed off the spear in his side, catching him as he fell. He grabbed my arms for support but kept moving toward Hecate, eyes wide with fear as his knees buckled.

"Hermes, what happened?" I asked, but he ignored me as he led me toward Hecate's body.

"Is she breathing?" he asked, frantic to get to her, but I held him upright. He surged away from me, crying out as he hit the ground, crawling the rest of the way to the Goddess of Witchcraft in the blood-soaked soil. His bruised fingers found her neck, checking for life against her ravaged flesh. My own heart stopped, waiting. He let out a sigh of relief, slumping back against the ground.

I bent low, checking his wound. It smelled like corroding flesh; I knew the only thing that could do that kind of damage to gods was Poisoned Ambrosia.

"Hermes!" I demanded, snapping my fingers in his face as his head lolled back. "Hermes, where is everyone? You've been poisoned. Tell me how to fix you," I pleaded, running my hand around the wound. The blood was caustic, blackened, and necrotic.

"Can't," he breathed. "Was a bomb." His breath was labored, shallow. "Can't get . . . poison out here. Need Hephaestus. He has . . . med bag." He slumped, unconscious. I put my hand to his nose to make sure I could feel him breathe. It was shallow, but there. I exhaled in relief.

My eyes swept the clearing and landed on Medusa's stony form in horror. Someone had used something reflective enough to bounce her Stare back at her, but I could see no other visible wounds. That effect wouldn't last long, but without any other means to check her flesh through the hard rock, I had to just hope she was otherwise unharmed.

Footfalls hit my ears, and I rounded, bident poised to strike. Hephaestus stopped dead, hands high, breathing hard. His chest was littered with cuts and bruises, his body battle worn in the firelight. A messenger bag was strapped across his torso, his leather kidney belt and bracers heavily ravaged with slices. I sighed in relief, glad that the skilled blacksmith and leatherworker he had been had kept him safe. He crashed into me, hugging me tightly.

"The bag?" I asked, and he reached for the satchel. "Cate," I pointed. Hephaestus went to Hecate, dropping down beside her. I rushed to Hermes, still unconscious on the wet ground.

I took his chin in my hands, giving him a few hard slaps to his cheek. "Open your eyes, you son of a bitch. You don't get to die on me," I growled, smacking harder.

His eyes fluttered, unfocused as he groaned. "Don't enjoy this so much, arsehole." He choked and sputtered as I grabbed the bag and wrenched it open. Inside were bottles and packets, some slicked wet with broken potions. "Grab the gold one," he grunted, voice tight.

I dove in, searching. My fingers found the sharp edges of a bottle, glistening with a golden sheen. I held it up between my fingers to show him and he groaned.

"*FUCK!*" I spit, tossing the bottle aside. Hermes threw his head back, sucking in a pained breath. "Hermes, tell me what to do," I demanded, urgently. Hecate was looking worse by the second and he kept floating in and out of consciousness.

"Syringe," he coughed, and again I was searching. A roll of syringes lay nestled in the side pocket, and I pulled it out gingerly, unfurling the soft leather. The material was wet with broken contents, but I managed to find one golden syringe unruptured. Hermes bit his lip and jerked once in frustration.

I uncapped the needle and made my way over to him, but he pushed my hand away, jerking his head toward Hecate. "No, *her*. Give it to her." My heart softened for him, but we needed *him*. Hermes was the only person who knew everything. He kept the rest of us compartmentalized, ensuring we could survive any loss. He was the only one of us who was indispensable.

I shook my head, reaching for him again. "Hermes, we need you fit. We can't save her if you're dead. You can get her back to civilization faster than me," I reasoned. He had about thirty seconds before I accosted him and plunged the syringe into his fucking neck, but again, he shook his head.

"You don't understand, she's the most important—" he started, but I cut him off.

"Hermes, listen to me! I know you love her, but we have to save *you* first. Everyone depends on you. Medusa has been stoned! Helios and Artemis are missing. I need you with me, brother. We will make sure she's okay."

Hermes spat up a deluge of blood as he tried to sit up, but I put a hand back on him. "You aren't fucking *listening* to me, Aidoneus! *She* is the fucking gateway. She's the Witch of Witches. We are fighting a very powerful witch. I'm already healing. It wasn't enough to kill me, but it *will* kill *her*. And then we're all fucked. If she dies, the protection on your safe house goes away too, exposing Persephone. *Now fucking give it to her!*" he growled, frustrated and in pain.

I acquiesced, and he dropped his head back in relief, chest still heaving.

Poisoned Ambrosia was one of the only things that could kill our kind outright, other than the River Styx. If one stayed too long in the river, it'd burn through our divinity, then our humanity, until only the shade was left. This held true for every divine being save for myself, Persephone, Styx, and Thanatos. Poisoned Ambrosia was extremely difficult to make and to procure, but it was deadly as could be. It could only be made with the extract of the essence harvested from the flowers that bloomed from the carcass of a dead god. There had only been a handful killed in our lifetime, so harvesting enough to create a bomb like this was concerning. Killing another of our kind was the greatest of sins because it left us all open and vulnerable. The flowers would grow where the last breath was taken and there was no way to destroy them before they could bloom.

There was a reason my father was locked in a crypt in Tartarus instead of enduring the True Death he deserved.

I was grateful that Hermes had spent so much time perfecting the serum that acted as the antidote. I stepped over him to Hecate, her dark skin unusually pale as I gently righted her body and laid her flat to the earth. There was blood down the sides of her face, a massive gash in her chest full of broken glass, the black ichor of the poison oozing from the wound. I pushed aside the stray braids that wrapped around her neck.

"Rip off her armor," Hermes instructed through a wheeze.

I ran my fingers over the metal breastplate, searching for a clasp I couldn't find. I gripped the rim on the top and bottom of her plate and wrenched with all my strength, shredding the metal with a sickening crunch. She lay exposed beneath me, covered in blood and muck and seeping rot, barely moving. My hands shook seeing her this way. Cate was family and the thought of losing her paralyzed me.

"Put your hand on her rib cage, Hades," Hermes said, pushing himself to sit while he clutched his side. "Left side. Feel her ribs? Bend her up a bit to arch her back, they're already pronounced but you need to be sure that this hits her heart."

I did as instructed, the syringe clutched lightly between my lips as I manuevered her. I felt for her rib cage, pressing through the flesh until I could feel the bone.

"Alright," he panted, "now I need you to feel for the space under the third rib. Got it?" I pushed my fingers into the soft flesh there, unobstructed by bone. "Okay, now Hades, listen, you're going to have to shove the needle through there, and make sure you feel the pressure. It will feel like you're hitting resistance, the heart. You're going to have to do it quickly because she's going to jerk at the intrusion. Heph, hold her down." Hermes inched forward to grab her hand, pressing it against his chapped lips. Hephaestus pushed his weight on both of her arms and legs, as I lined up the syringe. Hermes stilled. "I never told her, Hades. She doesn't know." His words were soft, an admission to himself more than us.

I understood. "You'll tell her, Hermes, you'll tell her."

He nodded, tears in his eyes, as I plunged the syringe deep into her side. I felt the force crack something inside her, breaking ribs. I pressed on the plunger as Hecate's eyes blew wide, the goddess bowing as she arched upward, thrashing. I ripped the needle from her as she continued to gasp and cough, naked from the waist up in the dirt. Hephaestus released her quickly, allowing her to curl in on herself. She clutched for Hermes, and he pulled her into him, wrapping his arms around her as black sludge seeped from her chest violently.

The antidote expelled the poison from her for several minutes and Hecate's breathing calmed as Hermes held her. The Messenger God sat, soothing her, pulled off his shirt, slid it over Hecate's head. She leaned into him, forehead on his, breathing each other's exhales for proof of life.

"Where are Helios and Artemis?" I asked.

Hecate shook her head. "They took them," she whispered, and my brows furrowed.

"Why would they take them and not you four?" I asked, looking around.

"One stoned Medusa with a pair of steel sunglasses. I've never seen liquid like that, except for Athena's armor. When I got to the door of the cottage, I opened it and there was a loud bang, and then the next thing I knew, I was on the ground with a hole in my chest. They trapped Artemis and Helios together with a net. I watched them fall. I've never seen Artemis bested in a fight. I should have seen this coming, I'm so sorry." Her voice cracked. Hermes held her tighter, stroking her face.

"This isn't your fault, darling." He soothed as she cried, but he locked eyes with me. "We can't stay here, Hades. We need to get back. This was . . . an ambush. Someone betrayed us, but I don't know who."

"Who all knew about the raid?" Hephaestus asked.

"Just us. Hygieia. Persephone." My mind raced ahead, working backward through all the information I'd gathered the last few months. Something was missing, a glaring piece of the puzzle. The others were speculating around me, but my mind pooled and pushed me toward the conclusion I should have seen coming ages ago. But no . . . surely not.

I'd cleared him. *Vetted him.*

"Nick," I said, voice flat. Silence followed. Hecate stared at me stricken.

"Helios wouldn't have told him. He knew how sensitive this was. And Nick loves Helios, he wouldn't put him in danger," she rationalized, but it was becoming clearer now.

"Hecate, when you sent that fire message that things had gone wrong, you said *betrayed,* but how did you know?" I asked.

Hecate looked at me confused; her head tilted to the side. "I didn't send a fire message. It takes too much effort, and I was on my back before I could get anything out," she said, terror taking over her features as she came to the same conclusion I did.

I kept my voice calm, but something like panic licked up my spine. *He knew how to get to the safe house.* "We have to go—get back to Persephone. He knows where the safe house is."

"*How?*" Hermes spit, grimacing as Heph and Hecate helped him to stand.

I ground my teeth together. "*Because I fucking told him.*" I pulled the shadows to me and willed them to take us back to my wife.

Persephone

CHAPTER 43

Hygieia took more time than was comfortable looking me over, checking my vitals, staring into my eyes with a very bright flashlight. The best either of us could figure was that the Bond being reforged had pushed me into my power.

I had practiced a little, pulling forth tiny buds on the table with fruit seeds from the bowl on the counter and dirt and fresh herbs from the yard that Hygieia had gathered. The stone table lay overrun with new blooms, and though I was worried about the others, having my power back made me feel just a tiny bit better. If something came for me, I could protect us. I hadn't been prepared when they'd taken me, knocked prone under the magic of that net; I was ready now.

A knock on the door pulled both of our attention to the foyer. "Stay here," Hygieia ordered, but I followed behind her anyway. She peered out the small peephole and stood back on her heels confused. "It's Nick," she said, backing away from the door warily, but I pushed forward.

"No, it's fine. Hades told Helios he could come here if things went sideways. I imagine Helios sent word to Nick to shelter here."

I reached up and flicked the lock, flinging the door wide. Nick looked horrible, beautiful honey eyes rimmed with red and hair tousled with worry. I put my arms around him, and he embraced me with a soft sob that wracked his chest. I pulled him into the penthouse as Hygieia moved to close the door, and pulled back to look at his handsome, tear-stained face.

"Hades has gone to find them. What do you know?" I asked, and a sob tore through him again. He sniffed and lifted the soft paper in his hands to me, matching the one Hades held when I'd found him earlier. I took it, running my fingers over the burned edges to examine the four words scrawled hastily.

Helios has been taken.

I gripped him tight and brought his thin frame to mine. Real fear, debilitating and overwhelming shook through him. I held him tight, using the weight of my body to calm him, until his sobs quieted. Only then did I pull back slightly, still running my hands over his shoulders. "Would you like a drink?" I asked, and he nodded.

In the kitchen I started pulling out glasses while he grabbed the wine off the counter. He filled each of the three glasses just under half and walked back to the table, hands still shaking, handing one to each of us. We sat as he downed his almost completely in one gulp. Hygieia and I sipped, trying to calm our nerves, but the silence sank all around us, the trepidation at what was happening to our family out there.

Nick looked at the flowers overtaking the table and a small smile ghosted his lips. "You learned how to grow?" he asked.

I nodded. "After a fashion. I actually . . . I got my memories back, and with it, my power."

A genuine smile cracked on Nick's lips, something flashing across his face that looked a lot like . . . hope? He poured himself another three fingers of wine. "I'm so happy to hear that, Persephone, you have no idea." The relief was clear in his tone, but I couldn't understand it. Hygieia looked at me, confused as well.

"Thank you, Nick . . . I know that's not the most important thing right now, but it makes me feel better to know we have some protection," I said, twirling my glass. Uneasiness pricked at me as I looked at him, a soft shimmer that surrounded him like an aura prickling in my vision. There was something about his voice . . .

"Yeah, no, I mean it. I'm so grateful that they've returned. It's going to make this next part so much easier," he said, downing the last of his glass with a rueful look. Nick brought his watch up to his face and studied the ticks. My shadows spun in the corners, hushed whisperings, as something familiar scratched at the edges of my memory. Suddenly, and without warning, Hygieia coughed, then slumped unceremoniously from her chair with a thud.

I jumped up but Nick did too. Gone were the sobs but I could still see the tremble in his hands as he put them up in front of himself. I twirled my fists, and my shadows shot to me, but he held his hands high in surrender.

"She's fine, just knocked out. I promise to tell you everything along the way, but we have no time for me to tell you a very, very long story now. If you don't come with me, Helios and Artemis are going to die." He spoke urgently and nothing about it felt rehearsed. "I'm not going to make you come with me. I'm asking. But those are the stakes." He was breathing hard, studying me, a plea etched on his face.

"Where are they?" I demanded, command lacing my tone. I watched his knees buckle a bit under pressure of my power. *Good.*

Nick checked his watch, voice frantic. "They're with *her.* I promise I will tell you but they're coming back, and we don't have the time to do this here. This is our one shot, Persephone, please," he pleaded.

I studied him, calculating. "Who has them, Nick? I won't ask again."

Nick ran a frustrated hand through his hair, looked back at me with anguish. "Not Nick," he replied, glancing at me sideways, "Narcissus. And Minthe has them."

Several things happened inside my brain all at once. For one, I recognized it then, his voice. Thousands of years I'd heard it, in my ear, in that box. Secondly, the rage I felt for him and what he had done, had put us all through, ripped through me like an aftershock, and I curled my shadows tighter around me, suppressing the urge to rip him in half. But if I killed him now, I'd never know where Helios and Artemis were. And lastly, *Minthe*.

That fucking cunt. No part of me doubted that she was responsible for all this wreckage. Broken people, hurt people, and that bitch had lived her life in pieces. Another wave of fear whipped through me—if she had Artemis and Helios, she most *definitely* would kill them to prove a point.

I called my shadows to me. I didn't know where my armor was, but I knew I needed to protect myself. *Bind to me, be my shield*, I commanded them. They molded my body, solidifying in a black so dark it rivalled the emptiness of the cosmos. Skulls adorned the corset rib cage armor on my torso, and large swaths of shadows settled like a cape over one of my black, spiked shoulder pauldrons. My boots were tall, coming together in a spiked heel that laced up to my thighs. A bone circlet materialized on my head as my shadows twisted my hair up into a battle braid with loose tendrils.

I was ready for war.

I turned to Nic-*Narcissus*, gesturing for him to lead the way. He stared in awe, a mixture of rapture and guilt, the self-loathing clear on his face. I bristled. "If you step one toe out of line, or they die because of this, I'll rip you apart. Slowly. Painfully. Where are we going?" I demanded, walking forward.

Nick nodded, fiddling with his hands. "The Underworld," he replied. I snapped my fingers wilting all the fresh flora growing wildly from the table. All except the pomegranate bush and sprigs of mint.

Hades would know and he would come.

Nick

CHAPTER 44

APRIL 21, 1996

THE DAY PERSEPHONE AWOKE IN NEW ORLEANS

It began with breath.

Sudden. Violent. These lungs, new lungs drowning in reverse as I choked. Air flooded foreign passageways inside me that hadn't existed a moment before. I gasped, not for oxygen, but for existence, the sheer weight of being pressed against the fragile seams of a body still stitching itself around me. I curled forward, twitching, every nerve flaring with borrowed memory and not one of them mine. My mind was a chaos of echoed screams, the endless drag of time across my shredded sense of self.

Thousands of years in the dark. Thousands more after that.

Persephone.

I winced, groaning through the pressure and sting, the thunderclap of synapses refiring in my mind. Where was the goddess? Where was she? I couldn't leave her alone, not again, no. Not again.

The hard surface beneath my body was cold and cracked, stone slick with moss, and blood. I opened my eyes. This place was rotting, but not silent. It breathed, groaned in its bones, whispered through ancient, tattered tapestries that clung to the walls like dead skin. The whole of it swam in my unfocused vision, the recognition prying at my mind. I'd been here before, a different time, long before magic sunk into the walls and festered.

The air reeked of old, sharp, too sharp to these senses, too harsh against these lungs. I raised up slowly, bones weary and weak, the muscles slow to respond to my thoughts. Every inch of this body ached, not from use, but from arrival. My shade hadn't settled yet, instead it clung to the flesh, testing it.

Two thousand years of torment couldn't be shaken off like dust.

The memory of Persephone's screams lingered in this throat, in this chest. Fates, where was she? I pushed to these knees, crawled across the filthy floor, searching for reason. I found nothing but a grime-streaked, cracked looking glass against the wall. Brown eyes staring in the reflection, lips, a face, hands that mirrored each touch against flesh.

Too strange. Too new.

"Do you like it?"

I found her gaze in the reflection, a wild, serpentine smile on her face. She looked different, her clothing unfamiliar but her eyes were the same. Fury sparked inside this chest, and I turned, lunging toward her, fueled by betrayal. She made no move to retreat or recoil as I closed the distance, and when these feet stepped into her space, I found out why.

Pain twisted through this body, spasming the muscles from toe to head, the agony unrelenting as this body fell back to the ground, a scream erupting from this throat. These eyes rolled back, unseeing as this body convulsed, skin scraping and scratching against the rough stone.

Somewhere above, Minthe's tongue clicked disapprovingly.

"Is that the thanks I get for getting you a body, a nearly perfect one, at that, and helping your shade back to life?" A snap of her fingers had the pain relenting, had this face dropping against a disgusting floor as muscles twitched.

"G-getting me a body?" I gasped, coughing as lungs seized and shook.

"Yes. This body is yours now. Your shade is returned to it," she announced. Nausea roiled through this stomach, my stomach, as her words sank in.

"Whose body did you take, Minthe?" I groaned, disgusted. What other life had she stolen?

"It doesn't matter. He wasn't using it to its full potential anyway," she waved it all away, like she hadn't stolen a life. My life. Persephone's. Whoever's body this was.

"Hello? You're welcome." She sneered impatiently as I struggled to sit up, drawing breath into lungs that had belonged to someone else, once.

"Where is Persephone?" I insisted, maneuvering over to rest against a stack of books with covers half-eaten by mold and the ravages of time.

"Why do you give a fuck about where she is?" she asked, eyes narrowing. "I'm the one who saved you, Narcissus. I kept all my promises. You're here, in a body that isn't horrifically disfigured. You're not acting very grateful."

"You lied," I panted, "to me. About everything." She stilled, then threw her arms up in an exasperated huff.

"That is ridiculous. I only ever told you truth, Narcissus," she insisted, but I shook this head, my head, doing my best to stave off the dizzying spin.

"Persephone didn't bewitch Helios. Or Hades." I countered. She looked at me as though I'd lost my mind.

Nearly.

"Of course she did. You saw it yourself, firsthand—"

"No," I snapped, voice flayed and strained and thick. "I saw firsthand that goddess succumb to madness in her mind. Thousands of years, you left us down there. If she had the power you claimed, enough to overcome a titan and a god as powerful as Hades, surely she would have broken free."

Flashes of the unthinkable torture she endured echoed in my ears, in my mind. Fates, what had I done?

"I was simply stronger than she," Minthe assured, her voice sweet and placating but I could see her now, for what she was. See the rot and evil. The manipulation.

"She cried out for Hades until her throat bled. For Artemis. For her mother, even. But she never once said Helios's name. If she coveted him, why didn't she cry out for him?" I shook the thoughts of my naivety, my blind faith, and my participation that allowed her to make me a martyr. "You used me. You used me to torture that girl. Where is she?" I demanded, as firm as my hoarse voice could muster. Minthe's smile dropped instantly, her posture shifting from warm and open to venomous in less than a thought.

"Protective of the spring cunt, are we? That will make this most interesting. I imagine that she's being excavated from a hole in the dirt about now. I imagine her mind isn't as sound as yours, is it Narcissus? That chaos probably did a number on her. Pits," she sighed, smiling to herself menacingly, "I wish I could have seen it firsthand. The dissolution of her mind."

The glee in her voice was sickening.

I wretched. Bile and the contents of this stomach spilled onto the ground next to me, muscles in my abdomen bunching painfully to expel it all. There were flecks of objects I didn't recognize, tiny oblong capsules with unknown writing.

Pills, my mind whispered. Those are pills.

"Ahh, unfortunate side effect. He swallowed a bottle of sleep medication, so I'm afraid there will be more of that, while your

new body gets it all out. Now, on to your role in the rest of this . . ."

I wiped a shaky hand over my mouth, clearing the rancid liquid from my lips. "I'm not going to be a part of this. Ever again. Ever again. You may as well kill me now."

Minthe tilted her head to the side, studying me. "Narcissus . . . I went through a great deal of trouble to find you this vessel, and the magic it took to root you out of that box? Expensive. You agreed to help me see this through a long time ago, and now you think you can just what, walk away? Die?" She laughed, cruel and shrill. My head rolled.

"No. I don't fucking think so. You still have a part to play in this, and this body is spelled to obey me, Narcissus. If I tell it to not harm itself, you won't be able to lift a finger to inflict danger on yourself. Do you understand?"

"I'll tell them. I'll tell them everything," I warned. She squatted down in front of me, elbows resting on her thighs.

"Go ahead. Try," she snapped. "I had a lot of time with this body before I pulled your shade back. It's hardwired to obey me. I'll be able to hear everything that's said around you, and everything you say. I forbid you to speak, talk, sing, write, paint, sketch, or communicate your true origins, my involvement, or anything that would alert anyone to what's to come. You'll give information strategically, as I tell you to, exactly how I tell you to, and if you disobey me?" She shook her head as tears pricked at the back of my eyes, "I'll kill that flower cunt, and your lover boy sun titan too. Now be a good dog, and obey."

"Why not just kill her?" I asked, unable to understand this level of destruction. Her eyes narrowed.

"The cruelty is the point. Suffering is the point. It isn't her time to die, yet, but soon. Soon."

Hades

CHAPTER 45

My shadows dropped us in a heap, and I had to dart forward to catch the stone form of Medusa before she crashed to the ground. Hephaestus grabbed her gently from me, laid her on the floor with a pillow under her head. I tore through the house, stopping short at the dining room. Hygieia lay unconscious on the floor, still as death. Hecate pushed past me and ran to check her as Hermes hobbled around, looking for Persephone. But I knew, staring at the three wineglasses on the table and the dead flora that lay sprawled across it, that she wouldn't be here.

I was too late. *Again.*

"Where are they?" Hephaestus asked, checking rooms.

I studied the table while Hygieia was coming around groggily. Hecate worked over her. Persephone had obviously been testing her powers, judging by the small, dead garden suddenly rooted on our table. She had seeds bloomed into flowers all over, herbs and fruits alike.

All dead.

All except the sprawling pomegranate bush and an herb that sent a chill down my spine. I grasped the tiny green leaf between my fingers and gave a small yank, freeing it from the root. It smelled cold and bittersweet.

Minthe.

"Hades!" Hecate yelled from the living room. I hadn't noticed her leaving with Hygieia, but she must have taken her to the couch.

Hermes wobbled into the dining room, face pale. "You need to see this, I think we know where they are."

I crushed the mint between my fingers. "So do I."

He led me through to the others. Hecate had her hands splayed wide, running over the runes now drawn on the inside of my door.

"What does it mean?" Heph asked as he approached from behind to look over her shoulder.

Hecate turned and looked at me, the tension and rage in hers mirroring my own. "Minthe," we both said.

Hermes looked like he'd been slapped. "What the fuck?" he demanded, but I shook my head.

"There's no time. Hecate, where does it go?" Though I already knew.

"The Underworld. Cocytus River." Her face was tense. She turned to Hermes, her hand on her hip. "You're staying," she instructed, but he laughed at her.

The God of Thieves matched her stance, gearing up for a battle of wills. "If you think for one *fucking* second I'm letting you go down there with that unhinged psychopath—" but Hecate cut him off.

"You're hurt, you can barely walk. And you'll be slightly weakened down there. She'll smell the weakness, and she'll go for you first. You don't understand what she's become. Minthe's learned witchcraft from other cultures after I forbade her. I'm not arguing with you, and if I need to break your fucking kneecap to make you stay, I will."

Hermes looked at me, but I wasn't going to be any help. I agreed with Hecate fully. I also knew how much he couldn't stand that Minthe had outsmarted him, but she had outmaneuvered all of us. None of us even considered her a real threat, and that gave her the impunity to do as she wished unobserved.

I had no patience to listen to this conversation. My wife was missing. *Again.*

"You have more antidote stashed away somewhere, I'm sure. Go get it. Heal yourself and then come find us." He nodded his acquiescence. Logic always won out with him. "We've wasted too much time already. Open the doorway, Hecate."

Pushing Hermes away from her, she concentrated on the runes etched there. We could have just portaled in, but that would have cost me greatly in energy and power, and the Underworld was vast. Minthe would have all entrances watched, probably even this one. She'd been one step ahead this entire time, and there was no reason to suspect any differently now.

The door swung wide, revealing the dark cavern entrance to The Lost Road—Hecate knew it well. Hermes grabbed her by the wrist as Heph and I went across the threshold, giving them a moment.

The cavern was dark, but I could smell the trace scent of spring and the bite of winter, that heady combination of Persephone in full power. *She had come through here.*

Hecate joined us, closing the door with a final snap. We followed her as she led, deftly navigating the tough terrain. The feeling of being home settled in my bones, and I reveled in the chaos that wrapped around me like an embrace. Being topside was an existence that I punished myself with for losing Persephone, but with her alive, and hopefully in my arms again soon, I felt the pull to return.

It felt like a cruel joke that just as quickly as I'd started to picture showing her the new world, she may be ripped from me yet again.

My mind raced, pulling puzzle pieces together. I still didn't know where Nick fit in. Was he just a lackey? Did he have a personal stake? Did he even really give a fuck about Helios?

He did. I was sure of at least that much.

Persephone must have known what was happening. She had time to leave me the clue with the pomegranates and the mint, had trusted me to understand. The path wound on, over and under crevices, and all around was the thrum of rebirth, a thread of excitement that manifested in every bloom and shadow.

The Queen had returned, and the Asphodels rejoiced.

Nick

CHAPTER 46

"Why is this happening, Narcissus?" she asked, voice tight. Persephone seethed behind me, but I couldn't think about that now. Helios and Artemis were with *her*, and if we kept Minthe waiting, she'd kill them for the inconvenience. I tested the limits of my magical constraints, formed words on my lips and waited for them to freeze before I could get a sound out. But they didn't. With the totem removed, I could speak freely once more.

On a tight breath I bared my shade to my once greatest adversary, and now possibly, greatest ally.

"I've loved him for thousands of years. It's not an excuse for what comes next, it's just the truth." Persephone dipped her chin, but didn't interrupt me as we walked through the dark cavern together, moving nimbly over the stones.

"I had never loved anyone but myself before him. I think I haven't since, not in that same way. It's always been him, which was fucking terrifying for me. Helios owned me so completely that when he chose you, to fight for you on Olympus, to go to war for your hand—it broke me. The rejection." I sucked in a deep breath, knowing no explanation could ever be enough.

"I'm not proud of this, but that day on Olympus when Hades marked me, I lost myself. I was an ugly, scarred thing, and I justified that Helios didn't choose me over you because I was no longer perfect. I wanted to die. But then I met Minthe, and she . . . She understood. She was my friend. *I thought she was my friend.*"

My chest tightened, the phantom pains heavy as I dug into my wounds, deeper and deeper, until I hit bone. "But she lied, and took my pain and twisted it up into this wretched thing and Persephone, please," I stifled back a sob, "I was drinking a lot at the time, so a lot of it is still a blur, but I . . ." I stopped, turning to face her, "she'd completely convinced me that you were some formidable witch who destroyed lives on a quest for power."

I glanced over, but Persephone's face was a mask of stone. She didn't spare me a glance as she listened, but she didn't look disgusted or enraged, either. I couldn't read her.

"She had a plan, and looking back, knowing what I know now, it was insane. But I couldn't see it then. When you ended up in that box . . . she hadn't told me what would happen to you. To your mind. I was there. For all of it. She betrayed me, put me in there like a trinket that she could take out when she needed again, but I was there, in that darkness with you, and I swear, I didn't look away. As soon as I realized that she had lied, that you were just a victim of all of this, I stayed awake and tried to talk you through the worst of it. There was so much fucking screaming."

"Why tell me all of this now?" she asked.

"I underestimated Minthe's capacity for crazy." My voice broke and I turned away, ashamed. "Can I . . . Can I just show you?"

More silence. I rubbed my hands against the fabric inside my jeans, wiping the sweat from my palms, then offered it out to her. I thought for a moment she would deny me, knew she'd be well within her rights, but the Goddess of Spring placed her hand in mine slowly, soft and gentle.

I let the memories flow, showing her everything inside me.

I showed her my awakening, every humiliating minute of it. The nymph whose body she'd stolen because she'd thought him beautiful, because he was alone in this world, easy to manipulate into taking his life. I showed her the hours I spent opening and closing my mouth in frustration, crushing pens in my hands whenever I tried to spill my truth . . .

Memory of the spelled, a necklace, and the acolyte she had sell it to Hades in Jackson Square . . .

Persephone brought her hand up to the hollow of her throat, where the pendant used to rest.

"He imbued it with his power, so he could always find you. He didn't realize it meant she had a leash on you both. I thought that I might hate you, but you were so kind, Persephone. That night at the club I took the necklace, I exploited a loophole, and she punished me for it. *Brutally.*" I lifted the hem of my shirt to show the long, jagged scar on my side. "But it gave you and Hades some time. Some distance."

The next memories were freshest.

I showed her everything, guiding my mind to share the events that had led me to her door, willing her to see that I had tried with everything in me to protect her. Anger rose within the goddess as she watched, her fury a low thrum between us as she *saw*.

It wasn't just pain, burrowing down into the marrow of my skull, it was presence. Her presence, so deep inside this body, a second heartbeat in my skull, sharp. Deliberate.

Fucking debilitating.

"Narcisusssss . . ." she whispered in the darkness, boring down impossible depths until her voice twisted up my shade, or whatever was left of it. "Get up. Obey me, or else. I'll kill him, I swear by the Fates . . . Don't make me do this, Narcissus . . . Give me

what I want." Her demands scraped against the inside of my mind, unrelenting as she tried to claw her way out of this prison of flesh she'd leashed me to. For hours, every throb came with a whisper, not just in words, but in urges. Urges that this traitorous body longed to fulfill, impulses dark and foreign that were not my own. Intrusive thoughts twisted like smoke, working hard to turn my own convictions against me, and behind it all was her and the ever-gnawing pressure of her magic working to bend my shape into her will. Her voice didn't even scream, just taunted, patient and cruel as though she knew I was weak, and it wouldn't be much longer until I broke.

But I wouldn't. I couldn't.

Never again would she use me to hurt them. I fisted the sheets, crying out against the onslaught. How long had I been here? Hours? Days? Weeks?

The voice never rested, never gave me a moment of reprieve from the tears that stung my cheeks raw, the blistering ache in my throat from crying out, but it offered sanctuary, if I only just obeyed.

I thought of Persephone, of the agony she endured for countless centuries as the chaos consumed her. I thought of Hades, and the pain of losing the person closest to him. And when all else failed, I thought of Helios.

I thought of this new world, of the guilt of what we were building together, and I knew that no matter the outcome, as soon as I was able, I had to tell him everything. Fates, how many times had I tried, only for blinding pain to render me incapacitated? For the lips on this body to stall, the breath trapped in my lungs?

When the pain finally ebbed away, days had passed. No word from Helios, or any of the others. I peeled myself up off the soiled linens of the bed, soaked with sweat and blood from where I'd torn pieces of my own hair out in my anguish. On wobbling legs, I made my way into the kitchen, in desperate need of water.

My fingers fumbled over the glass as I filled up from the tap and chugged it down, not stopping until the dryness of my throat abated enough for me to draw a deep breath. My eyes fell to the now dead clippings of flowers in the window, on the table.

And between them, the envelope Helios had left for me.

I pressed my eyes together, quickly looking around, praying that Minthe was too preoccupied with whatever Helios and the others were doing that she wasn't paying me attention. Maybe they'd killed her.

"Not quite," her voice rumbled through my brain, and I jumped back, startled to find her face staring back at me through the reflection of the chrome of the sink. Her laugh echoed around me, inside my own mind as I spun, catching glimpses of her in every reflective surface.

"What did you do?" I spat, tears burning the corners of my raw eyes. The one saving grace to this was that Minthe couldn't be here, in the Upper Realm, and keep her thumb on the abominations she created, but this . . .

"Open the envelope, Narcissus." She rolled her eyes, bored. "I've got them. Their little ambush was pathetically predictable, and I've grown bored of these games. Open the envelope and let's be done with this, or I'll chop up Mr. Tall, Gold, and Titan right now. Feed him to the River." She laughed, cruel, hard. I knew she had him, knew there was no way she would have been able to break through the wards that protected his house without his blood. I was the only access she had to see anything, but here she was, projecting on every inch of this place.

My fingers trembled as the glass fell from my hand, exploding in a spray all over the floor.

"Chop, chop!" she clapped, and the shrill tones of her voice stood the hair on the back of my neck on end as her voice echoed inside my mind. My feet moved, traitorous, helplessly keeping me trapped inside.

A marionette. A puppet. I watched in horror as my hands reached for the envelope, fingers slipped between the sealed paper to tear it open. I cried as tears obstructed the vision of Helios's hasty handwriting, and while she devoured the location of Hades and Persephone, I forced my mind's eye to only focus on Helios's final words: "yours, forever."

"Right then, see? All the dramatics, and I got what I wanted anyway. Now, go there. Bring the flower whore to me. Tell her everything you wish, but be sure to include that I have her Artemis too, if Helios isn't enough to persuade her to leave the protections of that home."

I shook my head, but I knew it was no use arguing. A fire message, burnt and singed appeared on the table, along with a small baggie of a white substance.

"She won't be alone. I've already drawn Hades to me, so you need to go and convince her that she has no choice but to appear before the true Queen of the Asphodels, and face punishment for her crimes against me. And, Narcissus? If you don't produce her, I will tear him apart, peel all that pretty flesh from his bones. You know I will." She vanished then, and for the first time since I'd woken up, I felt her presence lift like a weight from my mind. The relief rocked me, and I swayed, then vomited all over the floor. I left it there, along with the glass and blood from the shards sliced into my feet as I bolted for the door because she had meant what she said.

I knew all too well, what she was capable of.

"My fire message came the same time yours did, I'm sure. The second part of mine had Artemis penned as well, but the message was clear: come or else. She took Helios to make sure I'd deliver you, and Artemis to make sure you came if Helios wasn't enough to make you move. I'm sorry, Persephone. *I'm so fucking sorry.*"

Persephone's hand clamped down on my shoulder and I flinched, half expecting to be run through with a sword. Instead, her small hands pulled me into a grip that crushed me into her shadow armor. She only came up to my chin, but she held me so fiercely.

"I forgive you," she whispered.

I pushed away from her embrace, unable to accept the forgiveness she was laying at my feet. "What? How can you even say that? I don't deserve salvation. Just please help me save Helios."

Something wet and warm splashed over my cheeks, and I realized that I was crying.

Persephone pulled me back into her embrace, wiping the tears from my face. "You have suffered for what you've done, and the part you played, but this was Minthe. We will get Helios and Artemis back and we'll find a way to be well. I heard you, in the box. I thought you were just my consciousness, but you woke me up. You kept me together when you could, in the darkness. Ending this is what matters now."

"She's crazy, Persephone. I've never seen anything like it. That little conscience with so much unchecked power . . ."

"I know. I saw. *I saw everything*, and I get it now. I do, but Artemis and Helios are waiting for us, and I'm not afraid. I'm fucking *pissed*."

The conviction in her voice roused something inside me, as I worked to regulate my breathing. Persephone grabbed my hand, and turned us back to the path, dark power licking at the air around us. I couldn't help the release of tears, the ease on my shade I felt as the weight I'd been carrying lifted from my shoulders. The unburdening was a tangible relief.

She kept her grip firmly in mine as we rounded the last corner of the cavern before the path deposited us at the Cocytus River.

Persephone

CHAPTER 47

As the blueish-green glow of the Cocytus came into view, Nick put out a protective hand to hold me back.

I shook my head, trudging forward. "She knows we're coming. There's no need for pretense." He tightened his grip in mine, but straightened, walking on with his head held high.

I could understand his fear, but I didn't share it. Seeing what she'd done directly in his memories had eviscerated any anger I'd had toward him. I knew too well what someone with unchecked power and a master key into a mind could do, had only narrowly escaped that mental prison before I'd been thrown into a physical one. Minthe's manipulation made Demeter's look tame.

I felt alive here, more powerful. Minthe thought she held a home advantage on the river, but she forgot one thing—*this was my domain*. Every nook and cranny of the Underworld opened to me, and I could feel the earth beneath our feet tremble in welcome, feel the bend and flex of my shadows and power as every creature under my rule was alerted to my return. I stretched them wide, calling for the calvary I needed. He was coming for me.

And she would pay for her crimes, but it would be my judgment that swung the scythe. Something akin to a lock sliding into place washed over me the moment Hades crossed into the Underworld. A calm certainty that bolstered my resolve.

Minthe stood on an island bridge separating the Styx and the Cocytus. Behind her, Helios and Artemis were tied together with the golden knots of a net I remembered all too well—it had snagged me in the field on the day I was taken. Nick's gaze fell on Helios, and he let out a strangled cry. I squeezed his hand, calming the tremble there, lending strength.

The River Guardian smiled, her once beautiful features contorted into an ugly sneer. She twirled an athame in her pale hands, dripping with a black substance I recognized immediately as Poisoned Ambrosia, the stench overwhelming, even from the distance. Her blue-black hair fell in sheets around her, a crown of mint on her head. I smirked a little at it.

"Minthe, my, my . . . How long has it been? I see you're reclaiming the look. Good for you." I smiled. Her eyes bugged wildly, maniacally. Nick squeezed my hand tighter. He looked so young and vulnerable. He'd once been a god, but he possessed so little of those powers now. Hells, I didn't even know what powers *I* still possessed or their extent after the fall, but I knew that nothing more was going to happen to the people I loved by her hands. I'd bury her ass first.

"You have a lot of nerve speaking to me like that, flower whore." Minthe snapped her fingers and the ropes of the golden net constricted, dragging Artemis and Helios closer to her. They thrashed inside, but the net held.

I kept my face as neutral as possible as I searched the shadows, feeling for the tether that vibrated with every inch of ground my calvary covered. *Just a little longer, c'mon.*

"Do we really need to resort to name-calling? Is all of this because I turned you into a plant?" I baited, and for all her amassed power, she still rose to it. Perhaps she felt bolstered, and entitled, an ownership to this realm . . . Rage and fury burned in a vortex inside my chest, the chaos and shadows within begging to be released.

She looked at Nick with distaste, but his eyes were only on Helios.

"*Pathetic.*" She spat. "You truly are my biggest disappointment. She really got to you too? After all of the plans we made, after your sacrifice? You're standing with *her*? I shouldn't be surprised. All you men do is take, take, take. You pillage and you fuck and when you're done, you leave the land spoiled, and the conquests broken." She looked down at him, her gash of a mouth thinned as she snapped her long fingers.

Out from the shadows, possessed, undead abominations appeared, closing in, flexing their might, their caustic aura killing everything in their wake.

"So, *you've* been dragging up shades and putting them in bodies? Minthe, that upsets the balance. It's not good for any of us, even you. Let them go," I chided like I was speaking with a child. I could hear the faint sounds coming from across the riverbed, but I kept talking, kept stalling. I put my hands up and took a step forward.

Minthe swiped her own arms high and the golden net uprooted, banging Helios and Artemis together. Her arm arced wide, an invisible tether on the net mirroring her movements. In moments it was suspended over the Styx. I lunged forward but she held the athame aloft, gesturing a no-no as she waved it. Helios and Artemis were helpless, and less than thirty seconds in that river would strip them of their divinity.

A minute in and they'd be dead as any mortal.

"Where did you get that Poisoned Ambrosia, Minthe? Hmm?" I asked.

"Ask your mother. Oops . . . wait." She smirked, tilting her head toward the tip of the blade innocently.

"My mother took her own life," I corrected, ignoring the lance of complicated pain that ripped through me at the thought. Minthe lifted an eyebrow, tapping at the air once with the athame.

"Did she, now? Or did they only *find* her washed up on the banks?"

"Just let them go and you can have me," I offered through clenched teeth, inching forward. My attention was half split between the Guardian in front of me, half on that net, but the subtle vibrations of the earth were like a thundering train coming our way.

Minthe shot me her most pleasant smile and clasped her hands together. "Oh, my dear little virgin queen, I'm going to have you anyway. And then I'm going to kill them. When I'm done, Hades will finally see that we are meant to be together, a consort worthy of his power, his realm. I don't need your permission."

The shock that dropped my jaw was genuine. "Minthe, I don't control Hades." Nick had been right. There was something more wrong with her than there had been the last time I saw her, when she'd been loose off the sauce. No, there was madness behind her eyes, genuine delusion.

I felt a shadow tendril up my leg but didn't dare look down. *Hades*. He was here. Close by. A little more time. I just needed to keep her talking.

Persephone
CHAPTER 48

"LIAR!" Minthe yelled, brandishing the athame. "He was *mine* and then you stole him from me. When you're gone, he'll love me again. He will." She looked rabid, deranged. How had none of us noticed this acceleration?

Minthe looked over my shoulder, smoothing her black, skin-tight dress down as she did so. "You can come out now. I know you're here, Aidoneus." She smiled sweetly as Hades rounded the corner, Hecate and Hephaestus hot on his trail. "I didn't know you were going to bring friends." Her voice was cloyingly sweet, like artificial candy.

He approached her slowly. "Min." His voice was soft, and I hated it, though I knew he was just trying to regain her trust. "Min, put the knife down. Let them go." A step toward her. Then another.

Minthe smirked at me, daring me to say anything. "Have you missed me, Hades? You never come home anymore. Always up there." She rolled her eyes toward the ceiling in a pout. I seethed.

He gave her a small smile, shy, even. "I have responsibilities, Min. It's not my time to rule the Death Realms, you know that.

But I have other obligations. Do you want me to come see you more?" Hades purred, and I flexed my fists by my side, nails slicing against my palm. His voice had taken on a bedroom tone, and it sent my blood boiling to know anyone else got to hear it, that even in an act she got to think it was for her.

Mine.

The shadows on my leg twined higher, caressing me as my jealousy ran rampant. *It's an act,* they whispered.

Minthe nodded her head as her eyes followed him, like a cat stalking its prey, caressing the side of her breasts seductively. Hephaestus made a noise of disgust and Minthe's eyes snapped to him, as though she had forgotten anyone else was here. With a snarl, she flicked her wrist, and several abominations lunged for Hecate and Hephaestus, wrestling them to the ground. They struggled behind us, the outcome of the tussle still unclear as Hades continued his trajectory.

"I want you to come home, Aidoneus. It's been long enough. We could be so good together again." She ran her hands down the planes of her stomach, trailing the athame. "Do you miss fucking me? I miss that cock terribly."

My brain glitched. *Fuck waiting.* There was no realm in this or any other in which that bitch spoke about my husband's cock like that. I lunged, but Minthe snapped her fingers again, almost lazily. The golden net dropped another foot, dangerously close to the water. I froze, fuming.

"Let them go, Min. Let's go home and talk about this," Hades reasoned.

Minthe cocked her head to the side, thoughtfully, giving him a flirty smile. "Okay, Aidoneus, I'll let them go. But first, I need you to kill her." She motioned toward me expectantly.

Hades hesitated.

Minthe erupted in a fit of hysterics. "I *knew* it!" she hissed, "You're still under her spell, snap the fuck *out of it*!" Minthe grunted in frustration, pacing back and forth on the small island, clutching at her hair. "This is what she does! Look at poor Helios! She led him on for *centuries*, and the fool neglected his *true partner.* Literally *threw* Narcissus away like he meant *nothing.* The only reason Helios is in a stable relationship now and has a second chance with the person he was *supposed* to be with, is because she's been locked away from him!" She turned to Helios then to Nick and smirked. "You're welcome, by the way."

Helios looked stunned, eyes connecting with Nick's. ". . . Nick?" he asked, voice faltering.

Minthe laughed an ugly, taunting sound. "No, no, no, not *Nick*, my dear golden boy, *Narcissus,*" she crowed before rounding on Nick who looked like he was about to be sick. "What's wrong, titan? Don't recognize the shade of your beloved in another's eyes? I watched you mourn him for centuries . . . Tell him!" she demanded, gesturing to a morose Nick.

He looked at Helios, pleadingly. "I'm so sorry, Helios . . ." But his expression was dead, one look at the pain and betrayal on Helios's face had shattered him.

Minthe rounded on me, leveling the knife. "You see, this is what she *does*. She sows discord, and she uses and takes what doesn't belong to her. It would just be better for all of us if she were gone. So, I'm going to do what none of you could and you'll thank me later." She raised her hand and snapped again, dropping the golden net.

"Cerberus, *FETCH*!" I screamed, as a pair of thundering paws *finally* made their way to the bank's edge, his three heads snapping wildly. He lunged, snatching the net as it fell, and with a mighty shake of his head, flung it safely on the opposite shore. Helios and Artemis sprang to their feet, disentangling themselves just as a group of abominations posted Hephaestus up onto a barbed fallen tree, impaling him through the chest. Hecate screamed, her whip slicing through the air as she cut the horde down one by one.

Three arrows sailed past me in quick succession, shining like moonbeams. They struck Minthe's chest, and she let out a blood-curdling scream as she dropped to the ground. I turned to see Artemis notching her bow as Helios jumped into the fray, the light from his flaming sword illuminating the banks in glowing embers.

Hades reached for me, but I yelled at him to go to Hephaestus. Again, he hesitated, but something in my power must have warned him off, because in a moment, he was gone, and I turned to start toward the fight. My fight.

"You fucking cunt! I'll kill you!" Rang out from behind me, and I turned to see a very mangled Minthe hurl the poisoned athame at me with lightning speed.

A blur of pale hair obscured my vision before I could call my shadows, and I saw Nick's eyes blow wide as the athame found purchase in his back. The shock wave passed through him and into me, and I watched in horror as the blade tip burst through his sternum, splattering me with thick, warm blood.

A blood-curdling roar from Helios tore through the cavern as I lowered a sputtering and shaking Nick to the ground. The poison took root quickly, traveling up his spine. Black tendrils leaked from the wound in his chest as he choked, gasped for air that wouldn't come. Helios crashed into us, dragging Nick's body close. Tears fell from his anguished face as he watched, for the second time, the man he loved die in his arms.

Minthe rose to run but I flung myself into action before her steps fell. Not now. *Not ever.*

The Underworld around me fell silent as my eyes narrowed. Adrenaline thrummed through my body, the power from the depths of the Asphodels surging into me through the bedrock at my feet. I stood, crowned in bone and obsidian, clad in fabrics of smoke and rage that danced together in a hollow rush of air pulling inward. Heavier, the power beat against me, seeking and searching for purchase in my skin.

In my chest, the power condensed, building and writhing like a living weapon. *A bomb*. Gravity lifted my hair, my chiton, shadows whipping around my hands and outstretched arms in terrifying spirals, sucking all the air from the space around me.

The pressure intensified as I thought on the pain she'd caused, to me, to Nick and Hades, and if she were to be believed, my mother, in her greed and madness. I stalked toward her as she ran, her legs unsteady as mine shook the earth they treaded upon. Power built low in my belly, swirling, swarming.

I expected a scream when the coil snapped, but my fury didn't need a voice. Devastation pulsed from the center mass of my chest, shadows tearing free from my skin, detonating a shock wave of darkness through the plains of the Asphodels. The eruption shook the ground, rattled the gates of the hells, sunk the Pit of Tartarus a little deeper. Every shadow was a sharp, living, snarling thing that loosed from my hands with deadly precision.

The hounds of the hells, come to do their ruler's will.

The air went cold, thick, choked with smoke and screams that didn't belong to any living throat as the abominations were torn apart in my righteous rage. The ground beneath us cracked, sucking them back into the Pits from whence they came, until all that was left was her. My shadows descended, wrapping her tight, dragging her back to me, kicking and clawing at the dirt. The silence was deafening, save for Minthe's screams.

"This *ends*," I spat, drawing her back to the land bridge, the sliver that separated the Styx and Cocytus. Her claws dug divots into the banks, but I wrenched her back to me with a heave. With a wave, the shadows binding her relented as cold fury consumed me. I could have killed her with the shadows, sent her to the Pits with her monstrosities, but I wanted to feel the life leave her body.

I demanded my retribution.

We stared at each other in mutual hatred as she lunged at me, teeth snapping together, clawing and kicking. I absorbed the impact of her body with a grunt, losing my footing. We crashed into the river, the splash of cool water smacking us both in the face as we tussled. She fought to top me, pushing my head under the water, triumphant as she laughed. I sent my palm upward with all the force I could muster, snapping her jaw, making her cry out. This river gave her power, a Guardian in her waters, but she was nothing more than a custodian.

I wrapped a hand around a hefty chunk of Minthe's hair, dragging her up the banks as she kicked and screamed and squirmed. In her fit, she lunged again, knocking us both back into the water, but she miscalculated the angle.

We landed in the Styx.

I wrapped my hands around her throat, already feeling the power leaving her bones as she struggled. I squeezed. Her eyes went wide, a crazy smile on her lips as I saw my own gaze, completely obscured by the shadows in the reflection of hers.

"You may kill me, but I'll take you with me. None can survive the River Styx," she gasped, thrashing in the slice of frigid water. My grip tightened as power flowed through me, squeezing, breaking, snapping bone through skin and flesh. Her dark blood coated the water around us, as I brought her halfway out of the depths, our noses nearly touching as she clutched at my hands. "I'm the Queen of the Underworld, and I have returned to walk the dark. You fucked up when you brought this to my home, *bitch*. You'll die for that mistake today." I snarled.

My shadows sliced into the water, shackling her, calling to wayward shades to claim their own. Ghastly hands pulled her deeper, and I watched as her eyes filled with terror and realization. She never had time to beg, if she were even capable of it.

Her body went limp in my arms as the Styx took her divinity and then her mortal life, but it wasn't enough. I could still hear Helios's sobs, his cries for help, the tremble in his voice as he begged and bargained. I plunged my fist deep into her rotted chest, rooting around until my fingertips clasped around the withered shade she bore. I ripped it from her, shredding it to pieces in my hands.

There would be no afterlife for her, if there ever was one for our kind. Not after what she'd done.

I willed my shadows to take her body away from mine, to bury it deep into the banks until the bones cracked to dust. Hades waded through the water gracefully, towering above me. We stared at one another for only a moment, and then he was pulling me into him, crushing my mouth with his. He looked me over, kissing my hands and knuckles, my cheeks and eyelids, hands shaking.

"You're okay," I soothed, pulling his body to mine.

On the shore, Helios yelled and pleaded for Nick to wake up as broken sobs wracked his body.

"Nick . . ." I began, pulling back, but Hades growled, his grip stopping me. He looked murderous.

"It's a better death than he deserves."

I cupped his cheek, understanding his pain. "There is more to his story than you know, and even if there weren't, he's paid his penance. If he weren't here, I'd be dead, Hades. And whatever you think of Nick, we owe Helios."

I grabbed his large hand in mine, and he let me lead him back to the banks. The water evaporated from us as soon as we left the River. I knelt to take Nick's other hand. He was pale, so pale, with black poison climbing up his face like vines.

Hermes had arrived and he was digging through his messenger bag. He turned to Helios, pain and regret etched there. "I only had one left. I'm sorry, I used it. I'm so sorry, Helios." Helios coughed, sputtering as snot and spit leaked from him.

Nick's breathing slowed, brown eyes dulled as he looked for Helios, a smile on his face. "I love you," he choked between shallow breaths. "I g-got a chance for you to love me b-back. It's okay, this is o-okay. Tell Persephone I'm s-sorry." I squeezed his hand, but he couldn't see me. I could tell by the way he searched for Helios in the light. The poison had done its work, and there was nothing left to save.

Hades stepped behind Helios, bending low, whispering something even I couldn't hear. The titan looked up at him in anguish then back down at Nick's too-pale face. He nodded. The Titan of the Sun gave me a wry smile and lifted Nick's body as he stood. He tucked his lover's head to his chest, cradled it with soft assurances as the nymph went still. Composing himself, Helios stepped off the banks, plunging knee deep into the destructive waters of the Styx. I lunged forward as panic seared through me, reaching for him, but Hades's arms tightened around my body, locking me in place.

"Let me go!" I demanded, but he only pulled me closer. Helios walked until the glowing blue hues washed over Nick's body, still cradled against his chest.

"What's he doing?" I cried frantically. "We can't let him kill himself, do something!" I screamed, but Hades just held me tight.

"It's his choice," he soothed, pressing a kiss to my temple as tears streamed down my face. I watched in horror as the divinity stripped out of Helios and what was left of Nick.

"That's enough," Hades commanded. Helios rose, water falling in a deluge from the two of them as he exited the River on weak, unsteady legs. I ran, let free of Hades's hold, with the God of the Dead following behind. On the banks, I dropped to my knees next to the lovers, frantically checking them both. I pressed a hand to Nick's wound left by the athame but there was only blood, no ichor.

"Poisoned Ambrosia is only deadly to the divine," Hades reminded, "The knife wound was deep, but in the Underworld, he can survive until it's healed."

Helios ran his hands over Nick's face, begging him to wake up. The blue of his lips lightened, brown eyes peeking out through fluttering eyelids. Helios let out a cry of relief, pressing kisses to his cheeks, all across his mouth and nose. I felt my lungs deflate with relief. Hades pulled me back and away, giving the two their space as Nick lifted a weak hand to Helios's jaw.

"Does this mean they're mortal?" I asked.

Hades nodded. "Helios made that choice for them both. I hope it was worth it."

Helios

CHAPTER 49

There was no sun in the Asphodels.

Well, that wasn't entirely true, there *was* a part of New Elysium that saw sunshine, but was far, far from the palace. When we were in our prime, ruling the realms, I never wondered what it would be like down below in the Underworld. This room, suite really, seemed too big and too confining, all at once. Nick's shallow breaths and painful cries had been the only noise in these four walls for days, but yesterday, his breathing had slowed.

He didn't wake up, but I would take the good where I could.

I hadn't slept . . . much. When I was a titan, there had been unmarkable stretches of time that I'd stayed awake, but now, in a mortal form, things that had always been second nature, or a luxury, were downright necessity. I sighed, leaning back in the chair, stretching out stiff legs. The muscles in my back ached from sitting for so long, but I was too tired to pace.

I just wanted him to wake up.

I rested folded hands over my torso, let my chin fall forward into too long scruff. The nail on my index finger picked at the torn skin of my thumb, raw and pink. He looked too frail in that big bed.

I needed him to wake up.

Food piled up by the door. My body needed to eat, but I didn't have an appetite for it. I kept them all out, even Persephone. I felt it, Hades's rage, even from here. Unwelcome guests to the King, given sanctuary by the Queen. Hephaestus was somewhere in this wing. I should have checked on him, but I had to be here when Nick woke up.

He had to wake up, right?

I'd gambled with our divinity for this. I'd do it again in a heartbeat, for even a chance, but I needed him to meet me halfway and wake the fuck up. Fabric rustled. A whimper sounded.

My eyes flew open, body bolting upright. I was on my feet in seconds, crossing the space between us as his eyelids twitched, then opened. A lump lodged itself in my throat as he blinked slowly a few times, adjusting. Through his haze, he smiled at first when he saw my face, when I took his fingers in my hand, kissed the tips on choked exhales. He looked around, orienting himself, and I saw with stunning clarity the moment he remembered.

Pain. Remorse. Guilt.

They flashed across his face as he recoiled from my touch, shrinking in on himself. He whimpered as he forced his body to turn, curling in on his side, hiding from me, the white blond of his tangled curls flattened and matted against the back of his head. Slowly, I walked around to the other side of the bed, knelt on the plush carpet. My knees groaned, but I rested my elbow on the comforter, laid my head on top. I reached out to touch his face, to wipe away the silent tears that slid over the curve of his cheek with the pad of my thumb.

"Hey, baby boy," I whispered. My throat throbbed, rough from the drain on my divinity, all the yelling and crying I'd done the last few days. He squeezed his eyes shut as painful hiccups jolted his shoulders. He wept. I stroked his face.

"What did you do?" he cried softly, knowing already, *remembering*.

"What I needed to do to keep you alive," I replied, caressing his cheek. He nuzzled against my palm even as red-rimmed brown eyes leered at me, as a strangled wail left his chapped lips.

"You s-should have let me die. I-I—" He coughed then, spiraled into an uncontrollable fit. I patted his back gently, reached for the bottle of water the shades had brought me, and uncorked it. I helped him take a sip and he sighed, resigned, eyes full of torment.

"I couldn't do that. I could never do that." I shook my head as he processed, as he grieved.

"After e-everything, how c-can you s-say that? You d-don't even k-know me." He panted, every breath a labor. I stroked his hair back, carded my fingers through his locks, leaned in to press a kiss over his eyebrows, his forehead.

"I know your heart, Narcissus." He flinched. "Nick?" I tried again. "I know that you got that necklace off of Persephone and you nearly died for it. I know you stayed conscious in that box with her, so she wouldn't be alone. I know you took an athame to the chest for someone I love. And I know that I love you. That's enough for me."

"H-how—" he worked around the sentence, lungs straining. I shushed him with another kiss, leaned back to look him in the eyes.

"Persephone showed me everything you showed her. All of it." The little color left in his face drained as he curled in tighter, until the stitches in his chest forced him still.

"Does everyone know?"

"Yes," I answered, honestly. There was no point in denying it.

"They're going to hate me. I can't s-stay here." He sniffed. I pursed my lips, considering.

"We'll move. We can go anywhere," I offered, and he rolled his eyes at me. It was so inherently *Nick* that I couldn't help the smile that pulled at my lips.

"They're your family; you can't just act like what they think doesn't m-matter," he deadpanned.

"They are my family, but so are you. If they can't work out their shit, that's on them and them alone. They know as much as I do, as much as Persephone does. I know that Minthe was dosing you, in the wine. Did you know that?" I asked, and he shook his head with a grimace.

"Henbane. Enough to knock a horse on its ass, and baby boy, you aren't that big. She made your mind susceptible, but she never would have been able to get her claws in you if I hadn't been so fucking stupid. All of us played a part in what happened all those years ago. Everyone but Persephone. I like to think I've learned, and I told you before, I've got no intention of letting you go. Where you go, I follow."

He looked miserable as he winced, rocking his shoulders to turn more onto his side.

"It matters what they think," he repeated, closing off. It scared me shitless, the way he retreated.

"I've spent thousands of lifetimes with them. I intend to spend my last one with you." I caged his face in my hands, stroking my thumb across his cheek, inching forward. "Do you want me to beg? Because I'll beg. I'll stay on my fucking knees for the rest of my life, I'll call you Nick or Narcissus or any other name you want. I don't care about your name, or your body, or what you look like, I just want *you*. Please," I did beg then, kneeling, at his mercy.

His silence was oppressive. Debilitating nearly.

"*Nick*." He sniffed.

"Hm?"

"My name. I'd like to go by Nick, I think." He chewed at his lip. I pressed my forehead against his, sharing his air, breathing the scent of him deep.

"Hi, Nick. I'm Helios, and I can't go a single second more without kissing you, so tell me you love me and let me take care of you, dammit."

He smiled, arched into my space as I kissed him. Spoke his words against my lips, through tears and sloppy pants and tangled tongues.

"Hello, Helios. I love you."

Persephone

CHAPTER 50

"So . . . only one Death God needs to be in residence in the Underworld at a time? And it holds all the other Underworlds together, no matter what pantheon they're from?" I asked. Hades turned my hand over in his, studying the lines on my palm like a scholar from beneath me. The throne room was empty, quiet, and calm as I sat on his lap and he told me about the changes in the rules, the lessening of ties that bound us to the Lower Realm.

"That is correct, Little Flower, gold star," he teased, leaning in to nip at the tender spot under my ear. I squirmed away, but his arms held me closer, gentle and rough all at once.

"Hey, listen, I'm trying to do my royal duties here, no distractions," I chastised. Hades groaned, rolling his eyes before turning my head up, tasting my lips.

"When it comes to the Affairs of State, you've always been an exceptionally good student." His eyes danced to the throne that sat next to his, and I smirked, remembering all the things he'd done to me on that chair.

"What else?" I asked as he smiled, a low, hungry hum emanating from his chest with every drag of his lips across the column of my throat.

"Much of the same . . ." *Kiss*. "Coins for Charon . . ." *Bite*. "And no extended stays for mortals . . ." He kept moving, until I stilled, back straightening at his words, at the reminder that though my immediate threat had passed, we were far from out of the woods. Hephaestus had been severely wounded at the Cocytus and had yet to wake up at all. Hygieia and Hermes had been working diligently with Hecate on antidotes and cures, but the necrosis had spread from the cavity of his torso outward, and they were lucky to even try and keep up.

And then there was the whole Nick and Helios of it all. Freshly made mortals, one half dead, crashing in the far south wing of the palace. While the others and I understood that what had happened to Nick wasn't entirely his fault, Hades struggled with having him here, under our roof. In our realm. I suspected it was only his fondness for Helios that kept him tempered, but the Lord of the Underworld was stretched thin over that particular resident in the Asphodels.

"We need to talk about it," I said softly. Hades let out an exasperated groan against my neck, then buried his face against me.

"But we were having such a lovely, non–blood pressure straining conversation," he sighed sarcastically. I turned, pulling back, and he leaned against his throne, resting his head against the plush cushion.

"I'm serious." I frowned.

"I am too. I've done all that I'm willing to do at this moment for that situation. I gave them my blessing to step into the Styx. They're convalescing in our home . . . What else would you ask of me, Persephone?" His lips tightened as he spoke, and it wasn't quite anger that laced his tone, but perhaps a weariness? Before I could answer him, the large doors at the back of the room creaked open, effectively pausing the conversation.

Thanatos, the God of Death, strode in, so different from how I'd always known him that it momentarily stunned me. His dark hair was dyed and styled in a bright green mohawk, pointed spikes that added another foot to his already too-tall stature. He was a tapestry of piercings, and tattoos. They wrapped his arms, his neck, up the shaved sides of his head. His black cloak had been replaced by a leather jacket, but his bright white wings still protruded from his back, a stark contrast to his punk look. From his fitted, ripped black jeans to his heavy-duty combat boots, the God of Death looked like an anarchist's dream.

His handsome face cracked into a wide, warm smile as he crossed the floor, arms open. I squealed, jumping off Hades's lap, and ran across the room at full speed to slam against him. Thanatos lifted me gingerly, swinging me around in gentle lifts, peppering my cheek with a chaste kiss before setting me down.

"Ah, my dearest Lady of the Underworld, how we have missed your light." He bowed low and I swatted at him for the unnecessary formalities. His voice had a cockney accent to it, and suddenly the underground punk look made sense—he'd embraced British punk.

"Did every Death God decide to lean into the British Invasion, or . . . ?" I teased.

"Oi. Welsh, thank ye" Hades defended, letting the full weight of his accent loose.

"I bloody missed you too," Thanatos chuckled.

"Missed you. The new look is rad," I praised, and he smiled wider.

"Make sure you tell Hypnos when you see 'em, luv. He thinks it's *unprofessional* to reap mortals in anything but the traditional garb. Snob." He lifted his hands in air quotes as he said "unprofessional," and I cracked up.

Hades gave him the side eye, before reaching over and pulling me back against him.

"Why are you here, Tos?" Hades asked.

"Well, yeah, I just came to let you know I reaped the mortals on the banks, so they're all tidied up on our end." Thanatos rubbed the back of his neck and glanced up at Hades, almost shyly.

"Is something wrong?" I asked, concerned.

"Well, that's the thing. I dunno what your husband's told you about the rotation of the Underworlds, but whenever there's a new shade, the list has to be amended. It helps keep everyone equally engaged in topside activities without showing any favoritism. I've come to update the list."

"Well, Persephone would be added to my rotation, of course. We rule together. We're what? Three rotations out?" he asked. Of course, we would rule together.

The tips of Thanatos's ears turned bright pink as his boots shuffled back and forth over the throne room floor. "Well, 'ting is, boss, Seph's *always* been on the list. She was MIA, but her position was accounted for. That's not the shade I'm talking about . . ." His eyebrows went high, then low, as his gaze dropped pointedly to me.

Oh? Oh. *Oh*.

All the blood rushed from my face as my hands dropped to my abdomen. *Oh*. Hades looked like Medusa had stoned him as realization barreled into the God of the Dead.

Thanatos pursed his lips, tapping his finger against them a few times. "Ah, so I see we're understanding. Well, yeah . . . so I'll be going, maybe we can pop around for dinner soon. Umm, but yeah, congratulations, mum and dad. Well, if you want to be that is, not to assume. Uh, I'm gonna—" He clicked his tongue against the inside of his teeth and gestured his thumbs over his shoulder.

I was too stunned to speak, too stunned to register he was already gone.

Hades hadn't moved. Hadn't breathed. I was beginning to think he really was stoned. Could a god go into shock?

"Hades? Are you okay?" I asked. He jerked, his face blank, nodding his head a quick few times before standing and moving past me to pace. His hands were stiff, and he wrung them as he walked, sucking in great gulps of air. I sat on the throne and watched him have his freakout, pushing down one of my own.

A new shade.

He turned to me, panicked. I kept my breathing as even as I could while I processed too.

Hades turned suddenly, skipped up the steps to tower over me. With trembling hands he grabbed my face, looking me in the eyes. "How?" was all he asked. I shouldn't have laughed, but the bewilderment was borderline comical.

"*Welllllll*, we spent a week locked in a penthouse together."

"Yeah." He sank to his knees in front of me, so tall that he was in my eyeline.

"And we weren't playing Monopoly . . ." I raised my eyebrows.

"Not the whole time." He shook out his head. Hades looked like he was unravelling, and it made me feel insane because I . . . wasn't?

"If you want me to get rid of it, I can. It's your choice." he blurted, looking stricken.

"*What?*" I snapped, rearing back as a protective instinct flared to life in my chest.

"No, I mean— Are you hurting? Are you okay?" Hades swallowed hard, having a full-on meltdown. The panic in his voice kept the hurt that washed over me at bay.

"Hades," I said softly, bringing his face to mine. "Do you *want* me to get rid of them?"

He swallowed, unsure, fingers twitching as his eyes trailed down to my abdomen. "My father was not good to me or my siblings. Demeter wasn't good to you either. Maybe gods aren't built to be good parents. What if something is defective within us?" he whispered, and in his words, I heard his fears, his insecurities. For all his power, the prospect of parenthood sent Hades spiraling.

I smoothed the hair from his face, ignoring the fresh wave of grief washing over me at the mention of my mother. I had been told of her passing before my memories returned, but then she had always felt so far away, a ghost of a memory I couldn't know. Just another forgotten bauble.

Now, with the bridge between my past and future securely in place, I *could* recognize the pain welling up inside me.

Now that there was no one left to fight and all was still and quiet in our lives, I could ache for the relationship we would never have, because of the goddess she was.

Now that new life grew inside me, and I would be a mother myself, the grief of what I'd never have swelled over me. She had let me down in every way, in all ways, really, but I had survived and grown. I'd built a love that stretched through time, strong enough to withstand distance and madness in all the messier parts of the cosmos.

I built that with Hades, and though he looked downright terrified, I didn't hold those same fears. Because I had him. He would protect us, would make sure our child grew fair and strong. I knew it, down deep in my bones.

"You are *not* him, Hades. And I am *not* her," I said firmly.

His jaw tightened. "Of course you aren't, that's not what I meant. *Fuck*, I don't know what I mean."

"Hades, do you want me to get rid of our child?" I asked, locking his gaze.

So many emotions flashed across his face, but when he brought his forehead to mine and let out a low breath, I saw the spark in his blue eyes ignite. "No," he conceded, his voice a rasp. "It's half you. I could never want to destroy that which you created. But I would do it if you wanted me to." He looked so vulnerable, so open.

I loved him. I wanted this.

I smiled, kissing his lips, nipping at the bottom one with a gentle tug. He relaxed in my arms. "*Of course,* I want our child, Hades."

His eyes lit up and a shaky smile broke over his face. "We're gonna have a baby?" he asked, his tone reverent, eyes misty, like saying the words gave them more weight, like hearing me confirm what I'd only just found out myself set it in stone.

I smiled as tears welled up, and I didn't even try to stop them as they fell, an unimaginable joy that I couldn't begin to describe. In the stolen moments and darkest embraces during the war, we'd spoken of starting a family, maybe. One day. After the war, we'd said. We have time, we'd thought. But that time had been stolen from us.

Here and now, we had a chance to forge the future we wanted.

"Yeah, I think so." Hades grabbed my face, kissed me deep, groaned into my mouth as he pulled me down to the floor on top of him. Greedy hands, hushed *I love you*s, the warmth of his palms as they pushed my dress up over my thighs, caressed my belly. The rapture on his face as I sank down on top of him, our fingers intertwined . . . These were our moments, hard won. *Cherished.* The problems outside those doors meant nothing as we cried out our joy, as Hades made promises with his body and mouth and shade.

Rebuilding our life was the next hard thing. For now, I was content to let my dark prince ravish me on the throne room floor.

Acknowledgments

First, I want to thank Waffle House, for allowing me to sit like a bat in the booth; order my sausage, egg, and grit bowl; and furiously type away at three a.m. when Hades and Persephone were screaming at me (along with hundreds of readers) to write part two.

To all my readers who were left on that brutal cliffy in *Prophecies*, I hope this gave you closure. I hope you healed up nicely, because I assure you, I will break your heart again. Love you though.

To Janessa. You know there's no me without you. Ever.

And the entire Krewe du Kraven. We are truly a unit—we live this life together. I hope the expanded *Prophecies* and *Desires* was worth the wait, because it made me cry to write. I love y'all to the moon, you feral raccoons. <3

To Jess, Brittany, Anna, Dakota, Kenna, Brandy, and Dana. You know why. There will never be enough words, but you know.

To Snow, for your incredible talent in bringing the Dark Fates to life. Truly, my Goddess of the Arts.

To Amy, my amazing agent, for sticking with me through breakdowns and a thousand deleted emails that never saw the light of day because you'd yell at me. Love you big big.

To Toni, and the rest of Diversion for giving the Dark Fates a home.

And lastly to my city. This series is my love letter to the house that built me, to the culture and flaws and food and laughter. The Dark Fates is for you.

Of FORGES *& Fury*

A DARK FATES NOVEL

Hephaestus

My chest ached as a soft pressure settled over my body. Hands, two hands, perfect and delicate pressed against me. Coaxing, giving. I felt the tingles course up my body where our skin connected, and lungs relaxed, breathing deep with ease for the first time in decades—*Aphrodite*.

I struggled to open my eyes, the desperate need to see that beautiful face a gnawing ache that chewed at me from the inside.

I was hurt. She had come.

Affection in my chest split past the pain and I cursed the darkness that paralyzed me, pinning me under as my divinity tried and failed to heal what had been ravaged by poison and rot. Where it had failed, she wouldn't.

Aphrodite shifted, panting as she pulled the damage from me, using our Bond as it was intended. The power share, the accelerated healing, all perks of the sacred Bond. If only ours didn't come with so much pain. I hadn't felt her body on mine in so long and she felt so fucking *good*. She panted, knitting me back together, giving and giving and . . .

Something felt . . . *off*.

Definitely off. There was a bite to the pull, a starving, insidious leeching of life. I grew stronger every second as the Bond worked on healing my wounds, but it was taking from her, far more than it should have been able to. My eyes flew open, only to watch in rapt horror as Aphrodite's beautiful face contorted into a grimace above me. Fingernails dug into my skin, my chest, as she pushed, drawing blood from the effort to remove herself.

But the Bond had been neglected for so, so long. It was ravenous, as it drew on her power. I put my hands on her shoulders, shoving with all my strength, but the magic held her locked around me.

"*Help!*" I rasped as her eyes rolled back, jaw slack on a mangled scream that set the hairs on the back of my neck on edge. Panic built in my chest as I fought to break the hold, as she convulsed and seized.

Black streaks of corruption crawled up her arms and chest, tracing her veins. The wound in my chest was almost healed, but the Bond took and plundered, unrelenting.

Hygieia and Hades burst through the door in alarm. Hades's shadows wrapped around Aphrodite's body as it sagged against mine, as wave after wave of pain tore through her. He pulled his hand back, wrenching his shadows and, with them, the Goddess of Love, breaking our connection. She let out a blood-curdling scream, arched back in midair, reaching for me. Begging through broken sobs and tears.

Hygieia held me back as I lunged for her, the Bond in my chest snapping tight. It was unnatural to let her be in pain. I could take it, could fix it, but the Goddess of Mental Health pinned me with her full weight and power. My mind fogged.

Hades kept a light touch on Aphrodite, only allowing her to be physically in contact with the shadows. She floated, suspended in midair, soft tendrils of her long blonde hair lifting and swirling around her.

"What's happening to her?" I demanded, frantically. Hygieia instructed Hades to lay her on the opposite bed, and he complied, setting her gently between the sheets. Aphrodite's hands sought my touch, a clear instruction. *Stay.*

"Where is her Bondmark?" he asked. I gestured to her torso, and he instructed the shadows silently to lift her shirt, to expose no more than necessary. I balked at the sight. Our Bondmark was bruised and oozing, the lines puffed out like an infected tattoo, the skin around it red and angry. I reached over my shoulder to mine but found it fine, smooth and not painful to the touch at all.

Hygieia grabbed a pair of gloves to slip her hands into before taking her place next to Aphrodite. She pushed her hair back, ran a small touch across the mark. Aphrodite cried out, the sound slicing through me to the bone.

Hygiea and I both winced.

"How long has it been since you've been together?" she asked. I ran my fingers through my hair.

"About eighty years," I answered.

Hygiea let out a hiss and turned back to Aphrodite, shaking her head with an impatient tsk. "None of you have *any* damned sense. I should never have let her in here," she scolded, working deftly. Magic flowed from her hands, now stripped of gloves and moving fast over Aphrodite's flesh.

"You can't neglect the Bond and then *demand* from it. It's not how it works." She was frustrated, too preoccupied concentrating on soothing the Bondmark to notice Hades shifted uncomfortably, but I caught it.

I pushed myself out of the bed and made my way over to him.

"I should tell you, Ares has passed into my realm. I expect whatever she's feeling he is, too, considering he shares a mark as well, and he's on a trajectory to come straight here."

I nodded quickly, eyeing Aphrodite's frail form. It was good that he was coming, right? She might need him. Something in our Bond was corrupted. Perhaps he could take her pain away and I could see enough reason to know this was about more than ego or infidelities.

The door to the room nearly blew off its hinges, and it was as though the pep talk I'd given myself about this being a *good* thing flew right out the damned window. Ares pushed through the door, massive, eyes wide and searching until they fell on Aphrodite. He charged forward, every inch of his six-foot-three frame radiating rage and energy. Blood boiled in my veins as those dark brown eyes pierced through me, full of rage.

He stopped short of her bed, muscles bulging as he barely restrained the fury tearing through him.

"What did you do to her?" he snarled, and I felt my anger amp, rising to the bait.

It was always a fucking fight with him.

"I didn't do anything to her. I didn't even know she was here until I woke up and she was on top of me," I snapped back.

Ares's nostrils flared at the innuendo and an immature, sadistic lick of satisfaction bloomed over my chest. There was a time when I'd felt badly for the situation we were all trapped in. I'd *empathized*. But that was before I learned what a truly unsanctimonious prick he could be.

The God of War's longing for her was violent, a flame that only seemed to burn hotter the more he tried to smother it. It usually ended with her heartbroken, and I hated him for it, hated myself for not having had the strength to walk away all those years ago.

He bowed up into my space, just a few hairs shorter than I, but I reveled that he had to look up at me. His lip curled in disgust, in challenge, and all I wanted to do was punch him in that stupidly chiseled jaw of his. We were so close that I inhaled his exhales, he mine, but neither of us were willing to back down. There was something about the God of War that chipped away at my calm, the way he burrowed under my fucking skin. It set me on edge.

"Don't . . . Don't fight." The words, broken and exhausted, rose between us and like magic, the tension instantly deflated as we both looked at *her*.

The reason for the war we'd waged for thousands of years.

The reason the air filled my lungs every day.

The most stunning goddess to walk this realm or any other.

Aphrodite.

Don't miss the next installments in the epic Dark Fates series

APRIL 7, 2026

JULY 7, 2026

Available wherever books are sold.

But wait, there's more . . .

BLOOD & BEDLAM, a brand-new title by T.C. Kraven and the first in the NOLA After Dark series, publishes Fall 2026

DIVERSION BOOKS